Also by Yahrah St. John

The Stewart Heirs
At the CEO's Pleasure
His Marriage Demand
Red Carpet Redemption

Locketts of Tuxedo Park
Consequences of Passion
Blind Date with the Spare Heir
Holiday Playbook
A Game Between Friends

Also by Shannon McKenna

Their Marriage Bargain
His Perfect Fake Engagement
Corner Office Secrets
Tall, Dark and Off Limits

Discover more at millsandboon.co.uk

VACATION CRUSH

YAHRAH ST. JOHN

THE MARRIAGE MANDATE

SHANNON McKENNA

MILLS & BOON

First Published in Great Britain 2022
by Mills & Boon, an imprint of HarperCollins*Publishers* Ltd
1 London Bridge Street, London, SE1 9GF

www.harpercollins.co.uk

HarperCollins*Publishers*
1st Floor, Watermarque Building,
Ringsend Road, Dublin 4, Ireland

Vacation Crush © 2022 Harlequin Enterprises ULC
The Marriage Mandate © 2022 Shannon McKenna

Special thanks and acknowledgement are given to Yahrah St. John for her contribution to the *Texas Cattleman's Club: Ranchers and Rivals* series.

ISBN: 978-0-263-30385-8

Prin

VACATION CRUSH

YAHRAH ST. JOHN

To my friend Kiara Ashanti, who pushes me to keep
writing even when I hit a wall.

One

Never let 'em see you sweat. That's what Natalie Hastings reminded herself when she walked into the Royal Diner and all eyes trained on her. She kept her head high, letting her jet-black microbraids swing in the wind as she sat down in a booth in the corner of the diner. Natalie had maintained a low profile since the infamous Texas Cattleman's summer bash last month. She had made a horrible fool of herself in front of the entire club by confessing her secret crush on Jonathan Lattimore to her best friend, Chelsea Grandin, while on Facebook Live.

Her feelings for the sexy rancher had been on display for the entire crowd. She had no idea they had switched from the prerecorded videos to going live. Luckily, only her voice was heard on the jumbotron as she talked to Chelsea while Aubrey Collins set up Facebook Live. But to make matters worse, she was certain Jonathan had heard every word. Once she came from the filming tent, she'd been stunned to see everyone pointing and snickering at her.

Her grandmother Claudette Hastings pulled her aside and to her horror filled Natalie in on the details. She wanted to talk to Jonathan and explain, but he was nowhere to be found. And since then, he had actively avoided her. Although they weren't close, they did run in the same social circles. She was hurt that Jonathan wouldn't at least talk to her. If nothing else, she thought they were friends, but it sure didn't feel that way now.

When is this going to blow over? Natalie thought. Wasn't there some other gossip the citizens of Royal could talk about? Like Chelsea getting engaged to Nolan Thurston, the hunky twin of Heath Thurston who was making a claim against Chelsea's family's ranch. No...instead, they were gossiping about why Natalie was crushing on a man who never paid her one ounce of attention.

"Natalie, so great to see you," Gloria Brown, the diner's waitress, said when she came to her table. "Where have you been hiding yourself, darling?"

"Hiding?" Natalie played dumb but Gloria knew how much she loved the diner's peach pie. She treated herself to the delicious confection at least once a month.

The older woman smiled and patted her shoulder. "Don't go being a stranger because some tongues in this town are wagging. You have nothing to be ashamed of. That Lattimore boy would make a fine match for any woman, especially a woman as smart as you."

"Mrs. Brown," Natalie whispered to make sure no one else heard her. "Can we please change the subject?"

"Sure thing. What can I get you?"

"I'll have the buffalo chicken salad and a Coke Zero," Natalie responded.

"Coming right up." Blessedly, Mrs. Brown left without another word about Jonathan.

After the Texas Cattleman's party, Natalie had been afraid to show her face in town, so she did what she always did when she was stressed: she comfort-ate ice cream and ordered Chinese and pizza and kept to herself the last two weeks. She even ignored Chelsea's calls. Consequently, she gained five pounds.

After Natalie saw the scale ticking in the wrong direction, she knew she had to shake off this depression and get on with life. So what if she lived out her worst embarrassment in front of the town? She would take it on the chin and move forward.

It wasn't, however, easy to forget her infatuation with Jonathan Lattimore. Why? Because when she was thirteen, Jonathan saved her from a band of bullies who relentlessly teased her about being overweight. Although he'd been a few years older than Natalie, he'd been kind and it had meant the world to a young girl with poor self-esteem. Natalie quietly tracked him over the years, which was made easier since Chelsea's family and the Lattimores were neighbors and close friends.

As the years went by, her admiration led to a healthy dose of lust, especially when at sixteen she began working at the diner. Jonathan would come in with the ranch hands and he looked so darn sexy in his jeans and plaid shirt that Natalie's heart went pitter-pat. If she was on shift, she always made sure he got an extra-large piece of pie. Peach was his favorite, too. And she knew he liked gravy over his french fries and didn't like onions but loved pickles on his cheeseburgers.

God, what's wrong with me? Natalie thought.

She was embarrassed that everyone learned during the livestream that she had a crush on Jonathan. She'd told Chelsea that "Jonathan is the most amazing man I've ever met. I can see myself with him because he would make a great husband and father." Chelsea had been shocked by her confession. She hadn't realized the depth of Natalie's feelings.

Chelsea and Jonathan grew up together because their ranches bordered each other. Both families were powerful and wealthy, the Royal elite. Natalie often saw Jonathan at social engagements she went to with Chelsea, but he'd never shown any interest in her. When Natalie came home after her freshman year in college twenty pounds lighter, she had been ready to go after what she wanted. Instead, she discovered Jonathan had married. She felt like the rug had been pulled out from under her, but surprisingly his marriage hadn't lasted long. Natalie thought she might be the woman to help heal his broken heart, or so she'd hoped, but in the years since his divorce, Jonathan had become a workaholic and rarely dated. And so her feelings remained unrequited and hidden—until last month.

The glass doors of the diner swung open moments later and to her dismay, Jonathan walked in *alone*. A convulsive shiver ran down her spine as she stared at him. He looked like a double scoop of Ben & Jerry's chocolate ice cream in faded jeans, a crisp white shirt, a Stetson and his famous well-worn cowboy boots.

What was it about this man that spoke to her every female mating instinct and made her want to have his babies? Perhaps it was his height. At six foot two, Jonathan towered over her own five foot seven inches. Or was it his taut, sexy butt outlined in those jeans? Jonathan was no stranger to physical labor, having worked on his family's ranch his entire life. Or maybe it was his sinfully sexy lips and hella fine smile surrounded by a scruffy beard that did the trick? Or was it the sexy Ford F-450 Platinum truck he drove or the opulent ranch-style home that she'd heard from Chelsea was an architectural dream? She'd never been invited, but she would love to see it. Whatever it was, she was drawn to him like catnip.

Quickly, she pulled out her phone and tried to appear engrossed in the device. Would he come over and finally talk to her so they could quash this like two adults? Or would he turn tail and run? Dying to know the answer, she looked up and her nerves leaped in shock when she found his gaze on her. His dark brown eyes were sharp and probing, and panic plunged through Natalie.

Was he going to make a scene? No, that wasn't in Jonathan's character. So why was he staring at her intently as if she knew the secrets of the universe, which she absolutely did not? She needed to do something. She had to take control of her own fate and when she was about to get up, Mrs. Brown came strolling back with her buffalo chicken salad.

"Here you go, darling." Mrs. Brown laid the delicious-looking salad in front of Natalie with a flourish. "Hope you enjoy it."

"Thank you." Natalie slid out from the booth, but when she did, Jonathan was already gone. She glanced around the diner, but he wasn't there. Just then, she heard the slow rumble of a truck outside and rushed out the door to see Jonathan pull away from the curb.

So he was taking the "turn tail and run" approach. Just great! Natalie huffed and walked back to her seat. This standoff between them had to come to a stop, but if Jonathan refused to talk to her, she would respect his wishes. She would focus on work instead and clearing her plate before her upcoming vacation. Picking up her phone, she glanced at the calendar. One week until her trip to Galveston. And it couldn't come fast enough.

Damn. Why had he done that? Jonathan Lattimore thought as he pulled out of the Royal Diner's parking lot and edged onto Main Street. Because he couldn't bear to see the hopeful look in Natalie Hastings's eyes. As soon as he walked in and saw her, he'd been unable to look away. Natalie was every man's wet dream. She had a voluptuous figure with a behind and full breasts. Her face was angelic and encompassed by big brown eyes, a pert nose and kissable lips. He'd always thought she was attractive, but dating someone so close to home was a no-no for him. After his divorce from Anne, he'd kept his relationships casual, but Natalie? She was the type of woman you got serious about. And he was done with commitment. Marriage to Anne had been one of the worst mistakes of his life and their split was acrimonious. The entire fiasco had done a real number on his head. Made him doubt himself and not trust members of the opposite sex. Consequently, he refused to ever marry again.

He'd always known Natalie had a crush on him, but he'd kept her at arm's length even though they had a lot of the same friends in town. She was friends with Chelsea Grandin, whom he'd known since childhood. But last month, everything came to a head when he heard her voice through the speakers at the Texas Cattleman's party. Her sweet declaration of how she thought he was amazing and could see herself with him because he would make a great husband and was father material had been disconcerting because Natalie had no idea who he really was. He wasn't deserving of her—or anyone's—admiration.

If Natalie really knew him, she'd run in the opposite direction and never look back, just like his former wife, Anne, had done. Anne told him he was a workaholic with no time for a spouse. Said he loved the land more than her. When all he was trying to do was expand his family's legacy. Anne hadn't understood. She'd told him he was cold, unfeeling, and incapable of loving and caring for another human being. Maybe she was right. They'd both been unhappy in the marriage and were thankful when it ended so they could go their separate ways.

Jonathan wasn't interested in dipping his feet into those muddy waters again. The divorce weighed heavily on him, and he'd been unable to let go of the pain. He felt responsible that he couldn't make it work and that his ex-wife had been forced to do the unthinkable without even telling him. The guilt ate at Jonathan. He must be a horrible human being if she felt she had to do that to them. So when he saw Natalie at the diner moments ago, he did the only thing he could—he ran as fast as his long legs could carry him. He didn't want to give her false hope there could ever be more between them.

Out of his rearview mirror, he saw her exit the diner and watch him flee. He knew he was being a coward by not facing her, but he wasn't altogether certain he could do the gentlemanly thing if the situation ever presented itself for them to get to know each other. Hearing her spoken declaration of her desire for more between them was tempting. It made him want to throw caution to the wind and take her up on the unspoken offer in her eyes and lose himself between her thighs.

Jesus, he had to get his mind out of the gutter. He was due to meet his parents this evening. He'd gone to the diner so he could bring dessert. Instead, he would come empty-handed because he'd been afraid to face a beautiful, sexy woman in a figure-hugging maxi dress. He was hoping the dinner wouldn't be about Heath Thurston's claim that the oil rights on the Lattimore and Grandin ranches belonged to him. Both families had devoted a lot of time and energy to uncovering the truth. Jonathan didn't believe it for a second. There was no way his grandfather would give up rights to their land to an outsider. Jonathan wasn't about to let Heath come in and take what was theirs. He would fight for his legacy.

When he pulled his Ford F-450 into the Lattimore family ranch a half hour later, it was nearly sunset. It was one of his favorite times of day. He loved to sit on his parents' wraparound porch and watch the sunset across the vast horizon that was the Lattimore ranch. The ranch comprised hundreds of acres that had been in his family for generations, and was now at risk because of Thurston's claim against them.

Turning off the ignition, he headed inside. He found his parents in the living room of the sprawling five-bedroom, two-story home. They were seated on the sofa. His father, Ben Lattimore, was in his usual button-down shirt and dark-washed jeans. His hair was short and trimmed with bits of salt and pepper. His mother Barbara Lattimore's jet-black hair was styled in a chic bob, and she had on a tunic and palazzo pants. Jonathan favored her with his rich honey-brown complexion.

"Hey, Mom." Jonathan walked forward and leaned down to plant a kiss on her cheek. "Dad." He gave him a quick one-armed hug.

"Jonathan, I'm so glad you could make it," his mother replied, putting down the book she'd been reading. "Please have a seat."

Jonathan's mouth curled into a frown as he sat across from them in an adjacent chair. "Have I done something wrong? I feel like I've been called to the principal's office."

Both of his parents looked very serious and Jonathan wondered if they were worried about him. He knew he had been putting in a lot of hours for a long time now. He'd used the divorce as an excuse, but then the oil claim came up. There always seemed to be a need for a little extra man power.

His father let out a big belly laugh. "Nothing so dire, son, but it has come to our attention how many hours you've been working at the ranch."

"There's a lot to be done." There was a dizzying array of activities to keep their horse and cattle ranch in operation. Their father was general manager. Jonathan handled the office administration as well as sharing operational duties with his younger brother, Jayden. His sister Alexa was an attorney and was handling the oil case for the Grandins and Lattimores.

There wasn't any friction between the Lattimores like there was with their friends. The Grandins were in disagreement over who would take over the ranch one day. Although he was eldest, Jonathan was happy to have someone to split the workload with.

"True, there's a lot to do," his mother said, "but you don't know when to stop and smell the roses. That's where we—" she glanced at her husband "—come in."

Jonathan leaned back and regarded them. "I get the feeling I'm not going to like what you have to say."

"We've paid for a week's vacation for you in Galveston," his mother responded. She stood up and handed him an envelope.

"Vacation?" Jonathan said as if it were a dirty four-letter word.

"Yes, *vacation*," his father reiterated with a smirk. "You need one. You've been working much too many hours and it's time you took it easy and let someone else do the heavy lifting."

"That's not necessary, Dad," Jonathan said, sitting forward. "I've got things handled."

"We know you do," his mother said softly. "And this isn't some sort of punishment, Jonathan, but ever since you divorced Anne, you've become a workaholic, never taking time for yourself."

"I take time when I need to."

His father folded his arms across his chest and asked, "When was the last time you took a day off?" When Jonathan began to speak, he added, "And not because you were sick, which you rarely are."

Jonathan paused and had to think about the question. He couldn't recall the last time he had any sort of *real* vacation. Since the oil claim, he'd been busier researching the case with Alexa, all the while keeping himself busy so he could forget about Natalie's confession and not be tempted to take their relationship to a more personal level. "All right, fine. I admit I've been a bit busy."

"Then you'll admit you need some time off to recharge the batteries," his mother responded.

"And before you say anything, you should know that this isn't a request," his father stated, looking him dead in the eye. "We are ordering you to go on vacation. Your mother has already taken the liberty of paying for a full week at the resort."

"But, Dad…"

"It's a done deal, Jonathan," his father replied. "Now how about we eat one of your mother's delicious meals."

"Sure, but where's everyone else?" Jonathan inquired.

"Caitlin and Alexa are having a double date with their fiancés, Dev and Jackson. I think they are talking wedding shop. And as for Jayden, you know your brother likes the ladies," their father responded.

Jonathan laughed. He would have loved some reinforcements to help convince their parents to change their mind, but he was on his own.

Reluctantly, Jonathan left his parents' home a couple of hours later. He wasn't happy about the forced vacation. There was a lot on his plate, but he couldn't deny his parents had a point. When was the last time he'd taken some real time away from the ranch?

Too long.

Maybe while he was away, he would find a beautiful lady to spend some time with. In bed later that night, Jonathan dreamed of a curvaceous woman twining her legs around him as he thrust deep into her body. The passionate entanglement sent fireworks exploding through Jonathan's chest and he wanted more. As she came into focus, he realized who it was he craved.

Dammit.

Natalie Hastings.

Two

Ohmigod, it can't be him, Natalie thought, rolling her luggage behind the tall column of the beachfront Galveston resort. Peeking around the column, she had another look.

Crap! It is.

Of all the places in Texas, Jonathan Lattimore had to show up at her vacation spot?

He stood at the reception desk casually dressed in black jeans and a white T-shirt that perfectly accentuated his tall, athletic frame. Even in profile from where she stood, there was no doubt how handsome he was and strongly male. Damn her heart for beating so madly because he was a few feet away.

Natalie wanted him—had always wanted him, but how could she feel this way for a man who didn't want to talk to her so much, he'd done an about-face at the diner? She was trying to get away from the embarrassment and the humiliation of everyone knowing about her unrequited feelings. She constantly wondered if they were judging her again as they had in her youth. Why would a man as handsome, educated and powerful as Jonathan Lattimore ever want her? Natalie was ashamed of her behavior and desperately wanted a do-over, but in life you didn't get one. So she'd come to Galveston for a change of scenery and to stop thinking about Jonathan Lattimore. Natalie slapped her hand against her forehead.

What am I going to do? There was nowhere for her to run without Jonathan seeing her. She had to stay hidden. Glancing nervously around, she saw the concierge walking in her direction and quickly motioned the bespectacled man over.

"Ma'am? Is there something I can help you with? Do you need a bellboy for your luggage?" the older man inquired, inclining his head to her Louis Vuitton luggage behind the column. The luggage had been a special treat Natalie purchased after her company, H & W Marketing, took off.

"No, no." Natalie shook her head. "I need to change hotels. Do you have a sister hotel perhaps where I can rebook my stay?"

"I'm not sure if there's availability, ma'am, but I can certainly inquire for you," he responded. "Why don't you have a drink at the pool bar while I try to sort this out for you?"

A drink was exactly what she could use right now, Natalie thought. "That sounds lovely, thank you."

The concierge reached for the handle of her luggage. "I'll take your bag and put it in storage while you wait."

Natalie nodded, releasing the handle she had a death grip on. She hazarded another glance from behind the column and saw Jonathan walking toward the elevator. If he was headed to his room, it would give her plenty of time to figure out her next move, because there was no way in hell she was staying in the same resort as Jonathan Lattimore.

After the concierge took her bag and the coast was clear,

Natalie shuffled down the hall toward the sign pointing to the pool. She would drown her sorrows in a very strong margarita and pray the hotel gods would shine down and offer her a get-out-of-jail card.

Jonathan didn't want to be here. If he had his druthers, he would be back on the Lattimore family ranch in Royal. He was a country boy through and through. He had no idea what he was supposed to do in a sleepy beach town for a week, but his parents had given him no option.

They paid for an all-expenses vacation, and he was damn well going to take it because he'd need to be strong to fight Heath Thurston's claim. His family ranch was at stake. The ranch meant everything to him. It was his birthright. His grandfather Augustus Lattimore handed the reins to his son Ben, and his father would do the same to Jonathan one day. He wasn't about to let an interloper come in and take what was his. Jonathan had sacrificed a lot, including his marriage, to ensure the ranch would continue for generations.

He dropped his luggage in the lavishly furnished suite complete with a king-size bed, large living room and dining area, fully stocked wet bar, and luxurious bathroom. Then he walked over to one of two balconies that overlooked the Gulf of Mexico. This was more like it. He wasn't used to being indoors. He was an outdoors kind of guy, and he was in desperate need of a beer.

Jonathan wondered if this bourgeois hotel even offered a good beer or whether they were all about expertly crafted cocktails. He intended to find out. Although he hadn't been primed for a vacation, Jonathan had to admit getting away from prying eyes in Royal wasn't a bad idea. Ever since the TCC party last month, folks had been gossiping about him and he didn't like it.

Even Alexa had gotten into the mix, asking him if he'd

spoken to Natalie and pushing him to call her. *To say what?* A conversation would be awkward for them both. It was better to just let the whole thing blow over. Eventually, everyone would find something or *someone else* to talk about. He, however, couldn't stop thinking about Natalie and how earnest she'd been about her feelings. Like most men, he wasn't one for laying his feelings bare; he kept things close to the vest. But Natalie, she had him tied up in knots.

Right now, he was going to go find that beer.

Natalie had to admit she'd chosen well. She was in marketing, after all, and research was her middle name. The resort's pool lived up to the hype. It was adorned in soothing shades of white and coral and was exactly the chic coastal hideaway she'd envisioned when she thought about lounging poolside on a sun lounger in one of the many bathing suits she bought. She'd even let Chelsea talk her into purchasing not one but *two* bikinis. Was her best friend the reason Jonathan was in Galveston? No, Chelsea wouldn't do something like that without discussing it with her first.

As a curvy woman with large breasts and wide hips, Natalie didn't do two-piece swimwear. But Chelsea, who was tall as she was willowy, told her, "If you've got it, flaunt it." So Natalie decided to go for it. Would she even get the chance to wear the bikini? Or enjoy the outdoor firepit and watch the sun set in the Gulf? Not if Jonathan Lattimore was here.

Why, oh why was this happening to her? She was a good person. She helped the elderly, volunteered at an orphanage and liked puppies. Why had fate conspired against her to reveal her deepest darkest secret?

She was so nervous about his presence at the hotel, she was drinking her second margarita. It had taken the edge off after discovering Jonathan at the same resort. After calling the concierge every fifteen minutes, he just informed her he was unable to locate another room at one of their sister hotels. Instead, he'd come to the pool bar, given Natalie her key card and asked if she would like her luggage taken to her room. She had no choice but to say yes; she wasn't going to forgo her stay. Damn! She would stay and take the risk; somehow, she would weather the embarrassment if she ran into Jonathan.

"Can I get a beer?" Natalie heard Jonathan's voice seconds before her eyes landed on him two stools away at the bar. The bar was nearly empty because the happy hour crowd had gone in for dinner. With the exception of the bartender, it was the two of them. *Alone.*

No, no, no. She hadn't had enough margaritas yet.

Plastering a fake smile on her face, she spun around on her stool to face Jonathan and like always her heart lurched at his sexy features. Perhaps she should act as if she didn't know him? No, he would see the ploy a mile away. She decided on the direct approach. "Jonathan? What are *you* doing here?"

"Natalie?" The surprise in Jonathan's voice was evident because he stumbled off the bar stool but righted himself before he fell.

Natalie couldn't help chuckling. "Umm… Are you okay?"

"I was hoping you didn't notice that," Jonathan said, attempting a smile.

She chuckled nervously. "Sorry, but I did. Anyway, I'm here on vacation. How about you?" She tried not to look at his thick lips, which she was certain he knew how to use to make a woman want to drop her panties.

"Same."

One-word answers. *That* wasn't good. She felt as awkward as he did. If he'd just cleared the air after the TCC event, they'd be on better footing.

"I should get going." She rose with her margarita in hand and was shocked when Jonathan placed one of his large hands on her arm. "Stay. Have a drink with me."

Her brow furrowed. "Are you sure?" Wasn't she the last person he wanted to spend time with? He'd done a good job of avoiding her the last month since the party and let's not mention the diner when he rushed *away* from her. Natalie got the hint, loud and clear.

"Of course." He inclined his head.

"Very well." Natalie plopped herself back down on the bar stool she'd been about to vacate and peered into her drink. She was going to need another one of these if she had to sit next to her not-so-secret crush. She motioned to the bartender for another margarita.

"So..." Jonathan moved closer onto the empty bar stool beside her. "Will your friend or—" his voice trailed off for a moment "—or someone else mind us having a drink together?"

Was that his coy way of asking if she came to Galveston alone? If so, he wasn't very good at it. "I'm here alone if that's what you're asking," Natalie responded evenly.

He nodded and gave a small smile. "I was. Do you normally vacation alone?"

"Not usually, but in this instance, I needed to get away from Royal."

He was silent for several moments, as if he didn't know why she had to get out of Dodge, but then to her astonishment he said, "It'll all die down in a few weeks. No one will even remember what you said."

It was the first time Jonathan acknowledged he heard the live recording. Natalie didn't know how to react to his casual reference to the single most embarrassing moment of her life. She was surprised he didn't think she was a stalker being at the same resort as him.

Instead of responding to Jonathan's statement, Natalie ignored it. Wasn't that why she was here? She was attempting to put the past behind her and move forward, but that was hard to do when the object of your affection was sitting right next to you. In her wildest dreams, she never imagined they would be sitting side by side sharing a drink after the humiliation she suffered a month ago. The pitiful looks she received since then from everyone in town had been bad enough, but to have Jonathan actively avoid her had been the worst.

"I doubt that. Tongues have a tendency to wag in Royal."

"Listen, I appreciate all the nice things you said about me, but if it's all the same to you, I'd like to forget it. Put in the past. Can you do that?"

She nodded.

"Good, because I'm interested in some R & R and discovering Galveston. How about you?"

"Same."

"So let's toast." Jonathan held up his beer bottle. "To taking it easy."

They clinked beverages. "To taking it easy."

Jonathan couldn't believe Natalie Hastings was in Galveston. When he had thought about how this week would go, he would never have predicted this fine-ass woman would be sitting next to him. Natalie was sexy as hell in a floral halter jumpsuit with a deep V-neck showing off the swell of her full cleavage. An electric charge hit his groin.

He'd always known Natalie had a crush on him, but until he heard the audio, he didn't realize it was more than a silly crush. She wasn't staring at him, although he wished she would, so he could drown in her dark brown orbs. Her hair was an intricate updo of braids and showed off her face. After the erotic dream he'd had about her, Jonathan shifted uncomfortably in his seat. Having Natalie up close and personal would test even the holiest man's resolve. Every inch of his body throbbed with awareness. Which was the exact opposite of forgetting about her. Maybe in order to move on, he would have to burn out this attraction between them? That sounded like fun. And wasn't that what a vacation was all about?

"How long are you staying?" Jonathan inquired.

"A week."

"Me, too. Not by choice. My parents forced this vacation on me. Told me I'm a workaholic and to take time to smell the roses."

"Are they right?"

Jonathan shrugged. "I don't think so." He was fine with his life. He lived and worked on the multimillion-dollar ranch he loved that had been in his family for generations. He turned to look at Natalie and she looked as if she didn't believe him. "Sounds like you think they're right."

"I only know what I see," Natalie replied.

"Which is?"

"Every time I see you in town, you're on ranch business. Do you ever take time for yourself? To do something for fun?"

He had some fun ideas for this week. All of them included Natalie in his bed.

"Don't you ever get lonely?"

Jonathan was silent. He was comfortable with his solitary existence. If he did want company, he went for long rides on his favorite horse, or he called one of his lady friends for hot sex. It worked, but his family seemed to think he was stuck in a rut. Maybe he was. He hadn't always been this way. Before Anne, he'd been more social and enjoyed spending time with family and friends. After the divorce, he'd become closed-off and guarded.

"Everyone needs somebody, Jonathan."

Jonathan leaned away from Natalie. Her comment

made him think of his ex-wife, Anne, who thought he was a workaholic, an unfeeling and cold bastard, but it wasn't true. Even though he regretted the decision afterward, when they'd married, he'd fancied himself in love, but she wasn't the woman for him. She was needy and clingy, wanting Jonathan all to herself. Anne wanted the status of being married to a Lattimore and when she realized that equated to some lonely days while he worked, she cut her losses. Jonathan wondered if she ever really loved him at all.

He blinked rapidly, focusing back on the current conversation with Natalie, but she was pulling several bills from her purse and throwing them on the bar. "If you'll excuse me," she said, and quickly exited.

"Natalie, wait!" Had he done something to offend her? But she was already several yards away. He slipped a twenty from his billfold and slid it onto the bar. Then he was rushing after Natalie. He didn't want their evening to end like this. Although he hadn't planned it, he didn't want to let this feeling of anticipation go and he wasn't about to let her go, either.

Three

Natalie couldn't believe she'd been foolish enough to think she could sit beside Jonathan Lattimore and have a drink like they were two normal strangers meeting on a holiday. This wasn't *Roman Holiday. I'm such an idiot. He probably thinks my comment about everyone needing someone was some sort of come-on attempt. That I want to be the* somebody *he needs.*

As much as she might wish that were true, it wasn't. She had to face the facts. Jonathan Lattimore would *never* be interested in her other than as a passing acquaintance. The sooner she got over the romantic notions that they would make a great couple, the better.

Once she reached the hotel lobby, she glanced around for the elevators and furiously pressed the up button. She heard Jonathan calling out after her, but she didn't stop walking. She wasn't interested in anything he had to say. She wanted to get to her room, have a hot shower and figure out how she would stay out of his path for the rest of the week. Because why should she leave? She paid for this trip and had as much a right to be here as him. She wasn't about to let him run her off.

The elevator arrived several seconds later, but it wasn't fast enough.

"Natalie!" Jonathan called her name and within seconds, he'd caught up to her.

She glared at him before entering the cab. Natalie thought her withering look would be enough to deter him, but he joined her anyway. The silence inside the short climb to the third floor was deafening. She certainly wasn't about to apologize for attempting to care about him, but he wasn't easy to ignore, either. With his commanding stature and presence, he seemed to take up all the oxygen in the cab.

When the elevator dinged on her floor, Natalie quickly exited and rushed down the hall, but Jonathan's sure steps followed. Reaching her door, she swiped the key card and was about to open it when she found Jonathan behind her. She turned and faced him. "What do you want?"

"If you'll give me the chance, I'd like to apologize," Jonathan replied.

Natalie was shocked. She hadn't expected that response and felt like someone had let the wind out of her sails. So much for righteous indignation.

"Can I come in?" Jonathan asked, peering at her intently.

Natalie didn't know why, but she held open the door. As Jonathan walked past her, she caught a tantalizing whiff of his sexy scent that was male and earthy with a hint of spice. Everything about him assailed her senses, and it made her think of all sorts of naughty things she'd like to do with him. She shook her head to erase the image and shut the door.

Walking inside, she was impressed with the corner suite

the concierge had given her. A big bed stood center stage and there was a small, nicely appointed seating area with a desk. The curtains were open, and she could see a balcony. But nothing was more impressive than the six-foot-plus man standing in the middle of the room dominating the space.

Although he was broad-shouldered and slim-hipped, there was an inherent strength in his gait and Natalie found herself unable to look away. Jonathan fit the mold for tall, dark and handsome.

"I'm sorry, Natalie," Jonathan began. "I guess I don't know to act around a lady anymore. I'm sorry if I appeared standoffish because that wasn't my intent. I got caught up in some past memories."

Natalie shrugged as she slipped her purse off her shoulder and placed it on the cocktail table. "It happens sometimes."

He cocked his head to one side as if he didn't believe her. "Are you being real with me? Or telling me what I want to hear, so I'll get out of your room?"

"I'm being straight up. I accept your apology." She took a seat on the sofa.

"Good. Because I enjoyed talking to you downstairs and I don't want that to be our last conversation."

"You don't?" She didn't understand what was happening. Jonathan always treated her as if she were a friend and nothing more. Did he see this vacation as a way to deepen their relationship? She'd always wanted that, but she didn't want to be used, either. He knew how she felt about him. It would be easy for him to lay on the charm. She had to be on her guard.

He shook his head. "No, I want to get to know you better. Can we start over?"

"I suppose," Natalie said uneasily. Her mouth was dry, and her knees were weak, so she kicked off her sandals.

She didn't know what to do next; there was a palpable energy pulsating back and forth between them. "Umm… would you like a drink?"

"I'd like that very much." Jonathan's eyes met her gaze with a directness that stole her breath.

Natalie blinked, snapping her out of the spiderlike web she felt he had her in. "I have no idea what's in the fridge."

"Why don't we find out?" His voice was like dark chocolate and red wine, rich and full-bodied, full of flavor. She watched him walk over and bend his tall frame to peer into the mini fridge. From her viewpoint, Natalie saw some water, Coke, mini spirits, and small orange and cranberry juices, but she would much rather focus on his bum in his jeans.

Jonathan pulled out several beverages and made a screwdriver for her and a rum and Coke for him. Afterward, he came down and sat beside her on the sofa. She was surprised when he asked, "Have you heard anything about Aubrey Collins?" She doubted he was here for conversation. Or was that the excuse he was going to use for his being in her room?

Nonetheless, she answered his question. "Last I heard, she's suffered some memory loss," Natalie replied, "though the doctors are hopeful it's temporary."

Aubrey was a mutual friend who'd been injured at the Texas Cattleman's Club party a month ago when the podium she was standing on collapsed. When she fell, she'd hit her head and was knocked unconscious.

"I'm sorry to hear that," Jonathan said, sipping his drink. "I hope she recovers."

"So do I," Natalie responded. She also prayed they moved on from this topic of conversation, but her prayers weren't answered.

"Are we ever going to talk about the elephant in the

room?" Jonathan inquired, turning to his side. His eyes narrowed and he raked her face with his gaze.

"Why?" Natalie's pulse leaped and she found herself ensnared by the look he was giving her. "I want to forget that day ever happened. Plus we agreed to start over. Why dwell in the past?"

"Because it's necessary to move forward," Jonathan responded. "Listen." One of his large hands grasped one of her thighs and Natalie sucked in a deep breath at the unexpected contact. A jolt hit her like an electrical charge reverberating lower, and her core tightened in response. "I was flattered when I heard how you felt about me even though your feelings might be misguided."

She frowned. "You were flattered? Then why did you avoid me?"

Jonathan shrugged. "Because I didn't know what to say. I'm really not all that great."

Natalie burst out laughing and suddenly the ice was broken between them. All this time, she'd been so worried to face him, but she could forget her humiliation when he was self-deprecating. "Thanks for that," she said. "I think I've been taking this way too seriously and I guess we could both learn to lighten up."

"Yeah, we could."

Natalie looked up and found Jonathan's caramel-colored eyes, rimmed with thick, curling lashes, looking at her intently in a way she'd never seen before. They stared at each other for several long, compelling seconds. It set her pulse racing and Natalie had to remind herself that Jonathan wasn't interested in her. In the past, she might have thrown herself at him, but this time he would have to make the first move. And…there was something dangerous in his stare.

Jonathan should have never come to her room. After being shocked to see Natalie at the pool bar, he should have walked in the other direction, but there was something about her. About the way she looked at him so sweetly that made a flare of desire run through him. His gaze swept her face, and he knew she registered his interest.

Did it surprise her? It shouldn't. Her body was perfect in every way to him. It's why he hadn't removed his hand from her thigh. He'd given in to the impulse to touch her and if given the slightest indication she wanted more, he would touch her all over from her generous breasts all the way down to her petite feet.

Her eyes were fastened on his and Jonathan felt the throb of sexual energy pulsating between them, dimming out anything but the two of them. He reached out his hand and slowly trailed a path down the curve of her cheek. She was as entranced as he was, so when he curved his hand around the nape of her neck and brought her toward him, she came willingly. Seconds later, his mouth closed over hers and an urgency he'd never felt before rushed to the surface. When he coaxed her lips apart, to deepen the kiss, she obliged. So Jonathan held Natalie in place and plundered her mouth, but even that wasn't enough.

He pulled her closer and only then did he give in to temptation to shape her breasts. He splayed his hands over them, and they ripened at his touch. When her nipple crested against his palm, Jonathan wanted to feast on it, but this was Natalie. She had feelings for him. He didn't want to hurt her or have her confused by what this was. Lust pure and simple.

Reluctantly, he pulled away and tried to regain his composure. "That was a revelation." His voice sounded low and husky even to him. Because if he was honest, he wanted to stay the night with Natalie and lose himself in all her delicious curves, but it wouldn't be fair.

It wasn't a surprise to her, Natalie thought. Although she was taken off guard, her lips had parted when he moved his ferociously over them and she greedily wanted more. Because deep down she'd always known it could be good between them, but she never had the opportunity to explore the attraction she sensed might be there. Now, she knew, it hadn't been completely one-sided. At the very least, he desired her.

"Are you about to apologize for kissing me?" Natalie asked. She wasn't sure she could bear it because she had been lost in his drugging kisses.

He shook his head. "No, I've been wanting to do that for a long time."

A slow smile crept across her face. If she wasn't careful, Jonathan could break down all her layers of defense. But there was no way she was going to turn back from the one chance she had to have her heart's desire. So she said, "What happens in Galveston, stays in Galveston."

That seemed to be all the encouragement Jonathan needed because they came toward each other once again. They kissed, their mouths fusing, and he pulled her into him. Natalie was breathless, but she didn't care. Jonathan ignited a furnace inside her and she was engulfed in the heat, in the heat of him. When she felt his hand behind her neck unclipping the snap of her jumpsuit, she welcomed it, especially when it slid slowly down her trembling body.

It seemed she'd waited a lifetime for this moment, and she didn't want to miss a single minute. She raised her hands behind her and unclasped her bra, letting it fall to the floor.

"God, you're beautiful." Jonathan's voice was raspy as his eyes devoured her naked bosom. "I can't wait to see all of you." He took her by the hand and pulled her off the sofa so the rest of the garment could fall to the floor.

Although there was a niggling worry in the back of her mind that he could be using her for sex, this felt right and she refused to talk herself out of it. It was a dream come true to be in Jonathan's arms, and she wanted him. Jonathan wanted her, too, because he was feasting his eyes on her, and she let him right before she lifted her hands to loosen the topknot of her intricate updo. Her braids fell in a cloud around her shoulders. Jonathan wasn't motionless any longer and pulled her firmly to him. Natalie felt his hard length against her middle as he claimed her mouth and kissed her once more with the same rabid hunger he had before.

Natalie went up in flames in his arms and rational thought evaporated in a groan of craving. Desire surged and she couldn't wait to help divest Jonathan of his clothes, which were an impediment to her feeling all of him. She wanted his naked flesh against her skin. Once his clothes were flung aside, Jonathan half carried her to the bed, yanking back the covers to lay her feverish body against the cool sheets.

"Natalie." He gazed down at her, and she knew she had to look crazed with desire. She lifted her arms, welcoming him, and he came down on top of her. His kiss was hot, hungry and urgent, drugging her and pulling her deeper into a carnal spell where her very existence was reduced to this moment with him.

And she gave as good as she got, pulling and tugging Jonathan's tongue into her mouth again and again. But then he broke the kiss to trail hot kisses down her nape, shoulder and lower until he came to her breasts. He worshipped the full mounds, sweeping his tongue over the cresting brown peaks. Natalie cried out at the hot, sucking heat of his mouth and clasped his head to her bosom. She wished she could keep him there forever, but instead he went questing further, down over her abdomen until he came to her panties.

Hooking his thumb, he pulled the silky material past her thighs and lower until he could fling it away. Then he sat back on his haunches and looked at her. Usually this was when Natalie was self-conscious about her figure, but not with Jonathan. There was a naked hunger in his eyes that she'd never seen with another man. She could only watch as he lowered himself to the bed and pushed her thighs apart to nuzzle at the dark vee of her arousal.

She sucked in a breath when he pressed open-mouthed kisses to her thick thighs. And as she felt his breath get closer and closer to the center of her, she squirmed, but he put a hand on her belly, holding her still.

"I've got you," he rasped. Then he was reaching underneath her to grasp her bottom and pull her forward to his waiting mouth. Natalie bucked at the feel of having his tongue on the secret folds of her damp flesh, but he didn't stop there. He used his fingers to thoroughly explore every inch of her, eliciting more and more pleasure. It was bliss beyond her wildest dreams. Tension began spiraling deep inside as Jonathan took her to new heights that had her legs shaking. When he delved deep and flicked his tongue on the right spot, Natalie's world exploded, and she saw stars.

She was vaguely aware of Jonathan coming back to pay homage to her breasts before moving away for long moments to reach for something. She heard foil rip and then he was back, moving over her and nudging her legs apart. Then in one sure movement, he thrust deep, joining their bodies as one. He took a moment for Natalie to catch her breath. He gave her that time to adjust to his size because he was rather large. As if sensing her discomfort, he pulled out and then slowly eased back in again.

Natalie breathed out.

She felt full. Full of Jonathan. It was amazing, but she wanted more and moved beneath him, letting him know he could go faster. He took the hint and lifted her leg so he could go deeper. Natalie gave a helpless moan of pleasure as he stroked again and again.

She wound her other leg tightly around him and his movements became faster, more urgent. Her skin was growing damp with the need for a release, and she clutched him tightly, clenching her muscles around him. His head was thrown back, and she felt each mind-blowing stroke. He made every cell of her body throb, which told her she was coming near the crest. It didn't take long for another wave of bliss to strike her.

"Oh, yes!" She gave a rapturous exhalation when she toppled over. "Oh yes!" Her orgasm thundered through, shocking her with its intensity. Jonathan reached for her then, giving her the silken thrust of his tongue, teasing and cajoling it with hers until the waves finally eased.

But it wasn't over for Jonathan. His thrust became harder and more urgent until eventually he tensed and gave a shuddering groan as his climax hit. Natalie held him through the storm.

Did he feel as completely undone as she felt?

It had been so potent. So passionate. So necessary.

She moved her hands down his back, listening to his breathing quiet until eventually he moved away from her to lie on his back. She lay beside him utterly exhausted but feeling totally sublime. Her eyes sank shut and she breathed in the male scent of his body as sleep overtook her.

Four

Natalie awoke hours later, or so it seemed. As she eased into consciousness, her mind started remembering the night before. She couldn't believe this was happening. Felt like it was dream. And if it was, it was one she didn't want to wake from. She and Jonathan had made love not once, but twice. After the first time, they made love again hungrily as if they hadn't just had sex. Jonathan had been ravenous and had taken her from the side and behind.

In answer to her memory, there was a dull ache between her legs. She was by no means a virgin, but it had been a couple of years since she'd been intimate with a man. None of them, however, had known how to play her body quite like Jonathan. But then again, she'd never felt about them the way she did him. Speaking of…

She hauled herself upright, clutching the sheet to her bare bosom, and blinked. The bed beside her was empty. She was worrying he may have escaped for the hills, but to her surprise and delight, he emerged from the balcony, clad only in a pair of jeans and carrying a mug that she presumed held coffee. His bare torso was on display and Natalie fought the urge to lick her lips.

In the early-morning hours, she'd run her tongue down every inch of his hairless chest and he loved every minute of it, especially when she went lower and took him into her warm, waiting mouth.

"Good morning, sleepyhead," Jonathan said.

Natalie bent her head and blushed. She didn't usually sleep in. Her eyes momentarily flickered to his. "Why didn't you wake me?"

"You were tired, so I let you sleep." His eyes gleamed softly. He had worn her out the night before with their extracurricular activities. "So, about last night…"

Oh God, here it comes, the morning-after speech. She supposed she should have expected he would have second thoughts, but she hoped not. "As I said last night, what happens here, stays here." She knew he was gun-shy about getting involved.

"Yes, I know, but I rather enjoyed last night," Jonathan replied.

"So did I." She'd never had so many orgasms in one night. It was a heady feeling knowing he knew exactly how to please her without her saying a thing. She'd soared with the butterflies all night long. She would store this night away as a precious memory, an unbelievable dream, so that if it never happened again, she could keep it with her.

"I'm glad." He placed his coffee mug on the nightstand. "It wasn't my intention when I followed you to…"

"Take me to bed?" Natalie offered, gazing up at him with a grin. She needed to do something to ease the uncomfortable look on Jonathan's face. What did he think she was going to do, ask him to marry her or something? She was a twenty-first-century woman and knew how to handle herself, but that didn't mean she wasn't as flummoxed as he was by the unexpected attraction that flared between them.

Jonathan smiled. "That's right." He walked toward her and Natalie couldn't breathe. Everything stopped—her breathing, her heartbeat. She felt like she was suspended in time with Jonathan looking down at her with the strangest expression in his dark eyes.

When he brought his hand up and brushed the tips of his fingers against her lips, a soft sigh escaped her. "You're so lovely…"

Then his head was lowering to hers and Natalie's eyes fluttered shut as he covered her mouth with his. She relished his confident and hungry kiss and wanted it to go on forever. The shape of his lips fit hers and when the tip of his tongue parted her lips, she melted into him. She couldn't help it. It was too good between them, and her body knew it. She released a throaty groan.

Jonathan intuitively understood and leaned her backward onto the bed until she collided with his body. She *felt* everything. His hot, hard chest, the flat muscles of his abdomen and the proud shape of his erection. Her hand spread over his behind, bringing him exactly where she needed him. His breath hissed and he plundered her mouth, consuming her with his kiss.

His hand rode up her thigh to snatch away the sheet separating them, and Natalie arched her breasts into his chest. When his hand went south and his fingertips unerringly found her plump, aching center and drew the slick folds apart, her breath hitched. When he added another thick finger, her muscles clenched around him. It was pure torture and she moved restlessly against him, desperate to have him fill her.

"Please…" she cried.

He reared back onto his knees and with a primal growl, wrenched off his jeans. He returned to the bed but not before putting on protection over his erection. Then he was back, settling his weight between her parted legs. She hitched her ankles around his waist as he guided himself home in one delicious plunge.

Pure pleasure coursed through her veins. It felt so good having him inside her, filling up every available space. Their mouths locked together as he eased in and out in a delicious rhythm that made her taut with tension. Natalie tried to fight it, but she couldn't, not when his strokes became harder, deeper. He seemed as lost as she to this clawing need for satisfaction. After one final thrust, they reached the pinnacle together and released a long sigh of joy and contentment as they came tumbling back down to earth.

Jonathan felt a kick in his stomach. He hardly recognized the man he'd become. He'd done it again. Lost his mind in Natalie's arms. When it came to sex, he'd never been insatiable before, but he was inexplicably drawn to Natalie. To the beautiful glow about her and her infectious spirit. So he'd given in to desire and slid his hands beneath the fall of her braids and brought his mouth down on hers. This woman spoke to him and filled every sexual need his libido had and then some. She was his match in every way.

And that was a problem. She had stars in her eyes when it came to him. She didn't know him, not the *real* him. According to his ex, he was a cold and unfeeling bastard and only cared about the ranch. Jonathan was damaged goods and didn't have his whole heart to give to a woman of Natalie's caliber, warm and compassionate.

Emotions warred within him. He had never meant to make love to her, but now that he had, there was no way they could go back to being friends or casual acquaintances. Now he knew she was a real flesh-and-blood female with breasts and a behind that went on for days. She was a woman he could no longer gloss over. It was as if she'd suddenly snapped into existence before his very eyes.

But if she was looking for *more*, he couldn't offer her that. Since Anne, he kiboshed serious relationships. Anne had burned him and Jonathan wasn't altogether sure he'd ever recover from her betrayal. Or that he wanted to. Before *this* went any further, he needed to be sure Natalie understood that.

"Well, that was unexpected," Natalie said, glancing in his direction.

"Yes, my intention was for us to talk and clear the air, so there are no misunderstandings in the future." Jonathan glanced up at the ceiling.

"I understand perfectly," Natalie said, and to his shock, slid away from him, wrapping a sheet around her bosom and standing to face him. "This was a onetime thing." She paused as if considering her words carefully and said, "I mean, it was a one-off. Nothing more."

He frowned. "Is that what you want?"

Natalie cocked her head to one side and regarded him. "You like your solitary life, Jonathan. I get it. I won't disrupt it, not now or in Royal."

Jonathan sat upright, pushing several pillows behind him. "I appreciate that…" His voice trailed off. He hadn't been anticipating her easy reception. He thought she would want more from him than he was willing or capable of giving.

"Is there a 'but' in there somewhere?" Natalie asked.

"We're both here for the week…"

Natalie nodded and understanding crossed her features. She somehow knew what he was asking without him having to say it. "I'm open to a no-strings-attached vacation fling if you are."

"Really?"

"You sound surprised."

"You're just…"

"The kind of girl you marry?" Natalie inquired. "Us nice girls know how to have fun, too. We're not all waiting for a man to put a ring on it."

Jonathan chuckled. "I suppose that was presumptuous of me."

"Yeah, it was. So what's it going to be?" She put her hands on her wide hips.

"It's going to be a hell yes!" Jonathan roared. "Now get back in this bed and let's pick up where we left off." He held the duvet open and to his surprise and delight, Natalie tossed the sheet and slid in beside him so he could gorge himself yet again.

As she sat across from Jonathan at one of the famous seafood houses on Galveston's pier, Natalie's mind was reeling. Reeling from the whirlwind of emotions she'd experienced the last twenty-four hours. The shock and disbelief that Jonathan Lattimore, the beautiful, sexy rancher she'd crushed on for as long as she could remember, was her lover—and not for one night as she'd thought when she woke up this morning, but for the entire week! Although she was ready for more, she was willing to accept this time with Jonathan because she'd always wanted him and this week allowed her the opportunity to live out her fantasies.

Natalie felt as if someone had truly sprinkled fairy dust over her and brought her in full Technicolor to Jonathan. She'd been nervous dressing for the evening, but eventually she settled on a blush off-the-shoulder cap-sleeve dress with a ruffle detail from the waist to the knee. Why was she nervous? Because he was looking at her. Truly looking at her for the first time. Hell, he hadn't just looked, either. He'd kissed, licked, touched, tasted every inch of her until she was putty in his hands. When he mentioned they were going to be here the week, she realized he wanted a fling while they were in Galveston. She had enjoyed their night and morning together. Was it wrong to want it to last for a little bit longer? It was risky because of her long-held feelings, but it was worth it.

"What would you like to eat?" Jonathan asked, disturbing her wayward thoughts.

Natalie swallowed. "Umm, I don't know." Her eyes glossed over the menu. She quickly rattled off something and while Jonathan ordered, she simply drank him in. He'd showered and changed into black pants and a black silk button-down shirt. He looked scrumptious! When he ordered appetizers and a bottle of Dom Pérignon, she raised a brow.

"I'm hungry, woman, you wore me out." Jonathan gave her a smile. The way it altered the planes of his face made a whole flock of butterflies swarm in her belly. "I need sustenance so I'll be ready for night two."

Natalie blushed. She wasn't used to the intense physical intimacy they shared. At first their conversation was a bit stilted. She felt awkward and could only respond with short phrases. When he asked her about her job and if she enjoyed it that's when Natalie blossomed. She shared how she and her partner, Brent White, got started, opening the firm with a small investment from both of their families. Her grandparents believed in Natalie's dream and wanted to help in any way they could. Once she and Brent found a space in town, they were on their way.

She was thankful when the waiter returned with the champagne because it gave her something to do other than stare at Jonathan. As her flute gradually emptied, Natalie found she could relax and enjoy the evening.

Jonathan loved talking about the ranch and the latest innovations they were making to help the cattle operation run smoother. They also bred horses, which they sold to private owners and polo players.

"You're very passionate about ranching."

"It's in my blood," Jonathan said, sipping his champagne, "and it's what we Lattimores have been doing for generations."

"You're lucky to have a close family," Natalie replied. "I'm envious."

He leaned back and looked at her. "Why is that?"

Natalie shrugged. "Because it's always been me and my grandparents. My mother wasn't interested in being a parent, at least not in the long-term. She dropped me off with them when I was six years old."

"I'm sorry, Natalie. I had no idea." He reached across the table and placed his large palm over her hand.

"It's okay. It is what it is."

"That may be so, but it has to hurt not feeling wanted," Jonathan responded.

"It does, but I made my peace with the situation a long time ago. It doesn't affect me like it did when I was growing up being motherless—hell, fatherless, too. But then my grandma and grandpa stepped in and took care of me. For that, I will be forever grateful."

"Sounds like you love them a lot."

"I do," Natalie said with a warm smile. "They're the only parents I've ever known."

"That's how I feel about my grandpa," Jonathan said. "He's ninety-six now and still physically fit, though sometimes he's forgetful of people and places."

"The era he lived through and the stories he tells must be amazing." She loved hearing her grandparents talk about how they first met in the sixties, participating in the Civil Rights Movement and getting married.

"It is. My fondest memories are of riding side by side on our horses as he regaled me with the history of the Lattimore family in the 1900s and our long friendship with the Grandins. But then again, you know about that. You and Chelsea are pretty tight."

"Yes, when we met, we became instant best friends," Natalie said as the waiter arrived with their mouthwatering appetizers. They dug into the meal all while enjoying panoramic views of the Gulf of Mexico.

"Chelsea is good people," Jonathan said, responding to her earlier statement as he munched on calamari. "The whole family is the salt of the earth and have been entwined with mine for years. It's why we were so surprised by the allegations from Heath Thurston. Did you hear?"

"Chelsea mentioned it, but didn't go into detail," Natalie said.

"I appreciate her discretion. Anyway, Heath is claiming he was given oil rights that just so happen to be beneath both the Lattimore and Grandin ranches. Sounds absurd, right?"

Natalie's brow furrowed. "Is there any truth to it?"

"That's what we're trying to find out," Jonathan responded. "We've hired a private investigator to look into the matter and my sister Alexa is representing both families."

"Sounds like you have it under control."

"We do, but needless to say, it has us all up in arms," Jonathan responded. "For me, the ranch is my whole life. I have so much sweat equity in the place, not to mention it's our family legacy. We won't let some outsiders come in and take what's ours, what we've all worked so hard to build."

"Of course not. You're a fair man, Jonathan. It's who I've always known you to be," Natalie replied.

"How can you say that? You hardly know me."

"I know that you'll step in when teenagers are bullying a young girl because she's a few sizes bigger than everyone else." His brow furrowed, so Natalie spilled the story. "You don't remember, do you?"

He shook his head.

"I was thirteen and some boys were making fun of me in the diner. You stepped in and told them they should pick on someone their own size. And if they didn't, they'd have you to deal with."

Jonathan laughed. "Did I really say that? I had mad swag."

Natalie couldn't resist smiling, too. "Oh, don't get full of yourself. I'm merely saying you have integrity, and I haven't met a lot of men like you, Jonathan Lattimore. It takes a special person to step in and help someone else."

"Now you're going to make me blush." When the waiter came back to their table and asked if they wanted dessert, Jonathan looked at her. "What do you say we share the blueberry cheesecake?"

"I'm absolutely on board."

Jonathan was surprised at how easy Natalie was to talk to, but that didn't mean he was ready for anything more after this fling was over. Thus far, she had proven to be an amazing lover and conversationalist, but he liked his life as it was. He only did casual relationships because there was no chance of anyone getting hurt. Rather than talking about the past, he moved to work and shared with Natalie his mother's plan to branch out her culinary business.

"My mother is an amazing cook. We've been telling her for years that she needed to share her recipes with the world, and she did. She got a book deal for a cookbook."

"That's fantastic," Natalie said, beaming across the table at him. "Is she going to do more than cookbooks? I mean, if you look at the celebrity chef market, she can have her own line of cookware, dishes, spices and so much more."

"I know. Alexa told her the same thing, but it wasn't

until her agent mentioned it that she's finally listening. Anyway, she's going to be entertaining proposals soon for marketing firms to help with her products."

"If there's anything she needs, let me know. I'd be happy to help."

"Thank you, I appreciate that," Jonathan replied, and he meant it. "If you're ready, how about a walk?" He patted his stomach. "To walk off some of this meal."

"Sounds lovely."

They took a stroll along the pier past half a dozen restaurants. The pier was alive with nightlife and people milling around. Without consciously thinking about it, Jonathan reached for her hand and laced their fingers together. He heard her suck in a deep breath as she fell in step beside him.

Natalie looked up at him and smiled but didn't say a word. He wondered what she must be thinking with his hot and cold responses. He never envisioned this scenario in his mind when he thought about visiting Galveston. He considered he might meet someone, which is why he bought a pack of condoms. But he and Natalie had already finished the pack.

He'd quickly remedied that situation when he'd gone back to his room. He made a pit stop at the small sundry shop within the resort. Now he couldn't wait to get her back to the room so he could indulge himself in her luscious curves.

Natalie was a surprising but not unwelcome distraction. His life had become rather mundane of late. Work and more work. If he wasn't at the ranch, he was spending time with his family and the Grandins, but lately given the commotion Heath Thurston caused even those gatherings had become rather unpleasant.

And a love life, well, that was nonexistent. It had been

years since his divorce from Anne, and Jonathan still had trust issues.

He kept his relationships casual, and it suited him. There were no misunderstandings or hurt feelings because Jonathan explained from the get-go exactly where he stood on a long-term scenario. He didn't show emotions, so he was better off alone and indulging with a partner when time allowed. This way he'd never let anyone down as he had Anne in their marriage.

He knew everyone in Royal probably thought him some sort of playboy, when that couldn't be further from the truth. He was discriminating about who he went to bed with and often preferred spending time with women outside of Royal, but this thing with Natalie was in his own backyard. Would she be able to handle the end of their fling when it was over?

"What's on your mind?" Natalie asked when they suddenly stopped. Those big brown eyes of hers were staring up at him questioningly.

"I'm wondering if this going to be enough for you," Jonathan answered honestly.

"I thought we agreed to what happens in Galveston, stays here."

"We did."

"But?" Natalie's brow rose a fraction. "You don't believe me?"

"I believe you have feelings for me that you haven't fully sorted out. You don't know me as well as you think you do, and I don't want to lead you on, Natalie. I wouldn't want to hurt you."

Natalie spun away from him to face the dark waters of the Gulf. Anne really had done a number on him. He blamed himself for the demise of his marriage. Jonathan wondered if he could have done things differently. Been more open, been more caring. But he wasn't built that way and he wasn't about to change. He didn't want Natalie to have any illusions that she could change him. He was who he was, and all they would ever have was this vacation fling.

Five

Jonathan hurt Natalie with his lack of faith in her. Natalie was angry that she allowed herself to believe they could have a week together, no strings attached. Swiftly, she began walking away from him back to the resort.

"Natalie, wait!" Jonathan said, catching up to her in a few quick strides.

"Why?" she asked, twirling around to face him. "When you think everything coming out of my mouth is a lie. I can't go back in time, Jonathan, and take back what I said a month ago. I said it. I own it. I've been my authentic self and if you can't trust that, then you're right. This isn't going to work."

She started to move away, but Jonathan caught her arm. "Please don't go."

"Why? You don't trust me." She folded her arms across her chest.

Jonathan sighed audibly. "It's not you, Natalie. I don't

trust many people, especially women, but that's about me. Not you."

"Then tell me about it," Natalie asked. "Help me understand."

Jonathan shook his head. "I don't want to talk about it. All I can say is my ex-wife lied to me and did something unforgivable and it's made me leery."

"You don't have to be that way with me."

"I don't want to be," Jonathan responded hotly. "You're a great woman and in case you can't tell, I like you a lot." His fingers drifted into her braids. "And I want to spend this week with you." His bent his head and brought his mouth closer to hers.

Anticipation zinged through Natalie, and she tried to put the worrisome thought out of her mind that Jonathan might not ever be able to trust her or express his feelings, because her entire body craved his kiss. Kisses that were as exciting as each one he bestowed last night. Was that because she had such strong feelings for him? Feelings she was putting on the back burner so she could have this amazing week with him.

Perhaps he was right to be wary of her, but was it so wrong to want a moment in time she would always remember?

His lips brushed hers lightly at first. The initial pressure was soft, but then his lips changed direction as they slid sensuously over hers. He parted her lips so his tongue could delicately probe the inside of her mouth. Pleasure of the purest kind shot through her in every direction and Natalie couldn't help it—she curled her arms around his neck.

He was hot and hard. She felt his unmistakable desire pressing against her and she surged closer, sizzling with need for him. Jonathan broke the kiss long enough to rasp, "We should get back to the hotel."

Even though she had her doubts about whether she

could trust Jonathan with her emotions, she nodded in agreement.

The walk from the pier back to the resort was shorter than Natalie remembered. Could that be because she couldn't wait to get naked with Jonathan again? The disagreement they had was suddenly gone and in its place was a demanding and urgent need for fulfillment.

When she'd been young, being around Jonathan had caused joy to flood through her bloodstream, but now that she was a woman, his impact was more powerful. To know he found her desirable and couldn't wait to get back to the sexual intimacy they shared was disarming. Her mind told her to let the fantasy go and keep a clear head when it came to this man, but her heart said it needed everything Jonathan was offering.

"You feel so good," Jonathan said once they made it back to his room. He slid his arm around her waist and scooped her into full contact with his body. And then his mouth was crashing down on hers, hot and wild. He plundered her mouth, smashing away any barrier Natalie might put between them. He'd fumbled earlier with his words. He wouldn't with his actions now.

Natalie didn't hold back. Her mouth exploded into his again and again and he took it, wanting to taste the very essence of her. His hand burrowed underneath her braids to find the zip at the back of her dress. She was greedy for him as well because her hands dropped between them to tear at the buttons on his shirt. Their clothes soon hit the floor, followed by their shoes. He lifted her off her feet and tossed her onto the bed.

She held her arms open and he joined her, taking her mouth until she was clawing at his back. He lifted his head and saw the gleam of passion in her gaze. He moved his head so he could dip down to her breasts and give them his attention. He lashed them with hot strokes of his tongue and then sucked on her engorged brown nipples until she was grasping his head and moving him exactly where she needed him most.

He eluded her will and tore himself away so he could trail kisses down her stomach and move lower. When his hands came to the moist folds between her legs, his fingers stroked the seam until she purred and opened wider for him. That's when he used his mouth to anoint her with licks and flicks of his tongue until the sweet flood of sensation flowed from her body.

"Jonathan!" A cry ripped from her throat as he lapped her generously. "Please... I need you now."

He surged upward, stopping long enough to rip a foil packet open and sheath himself. Then he was making the entry they both craved. His penetration was deep, and her inner muscles squeezed tightly around him.

Sweet heavens, she made him delirious. He pulled back momentarily and then drove forward again. He repeated the withdrawal and resurgence until she quivered in anticipation; only then did he come in again.

"How does it feel?" he demanded hotly. He wanted to hear, to know she felt as intensely as he did.

"So good..." she moaned underneath him. "So good."

He closed his eyes, expelling a long breath, and then he got caught in the rhythmic union of their bodies. She climaxed first and it seemed to go on and on, but Jonathan didn't stop, not even when he felt her nails on his back. Instead, she urged him toward his own completion and when he finally came, it was so explosive, he let out a roar and she held him against her.

Natalie knew this feeling of bliss couldn't last forever. She and Jonathan had already spent the last couple of days on the beach, in the pool or exploring Galveston. Known for its antique shops, they meandered through them picking up pieces that Natalie wanted for Chelsea's wedding gift. Jonathan discovered she liked taking old pieces and making them fresh again with a little elbow grease or a new coat of paint.

What was most surprising, however, was when she learned Jonathan knew how to play the piano. One night after a four-course meal in one of the resort's high-end restaurants, they went to the piano bar. A pianist was singing and playing a melody of big band classics and pop songs. Natalie couldn't remember how long they stayed, talking and sipping martinis; certainly well past midnight. Eventually, they shut the place down and it was Jonathan and Natalie.

That's when he surprised her by going up to the podium and sitting on the bench to play Beethoven's "Moonlight Sonata." She had no idea he knew how to play or was so gifted. The way his fingers stroked the keyboard and brought her melodic sounds was beautiful. Natalie felt privileged Jonathan allowed her to see another side to him, a softer side. He was always so hard and tough with everyone else, but not with her. He was soft and gentle and tender, but he could be passionate and aggressive when the moment struck.

She joined him on the podium, sitting beside him on the bench. "When did you learn how to play?" she inquired.

"When I was seven years old. My mom was determined that her children learn something cultural and refined other than ranching. She made me learn the piano. My sister Alexa played the violin, while my brother, Jayden, played the saxophone. Eventually, when we adopted Caitlyn, she learned how to play the clarinet."

"Sounds like the Lattimores had quite the band."

"Oh yes," Jonathan laughed. "My dad was amazing on the drums so when the whole family got together, we would make quite the ruckus. I think my mother regretted her decision afterward."

"That's wonderful. I would have loved being part of a big family like yours."

"Was it lonely being the only child?"

Natalie nodded. "My mother was my grandparents' only child, too, so I didn't have any cousins so, yes, it could be lonely at times. Eventually, I learned to embrace the solitude, but tell that to a six-year-old who wants someone to play with."

"Give me your hand," Jonathan ordered.

"Why?"

He didn't wait for her response. Instead, he took Natalie's small hand in his and showed her where to place it on the keyboard, then he walked her through a song, letting his fingers guide hers along the way.

The tune sounded familiar to Natalie. "That's 'Twinkle, Twinkle Little Star.'"

He smirked and tweaked her nose. "How bright you are, Natalie Hastings." Then he leaned over, and his hot, demanding mouth slanted over hers, fusing her with pleasure and firing up all her senses. When the need to breathe forced them apart, he growled, "We should go upstairs."

It didn't take them long to make it back to her suite this time. They quickly divested each other of their clothes and climbed onto her bed, reaching for each other simultaneously. Jonathan cupped her breasts, his thumbs mercilessly teasing the peaks that were desperate for his mouth on them. When he finally sucked one into his mouth, Natalie moaned, her mind fracturing as he grazed his teeth on one nipple. It felt so good to have his mouth on her, but she wanted to do something for him.

She pushed him backward against the pillows and, feeling adventurous, tightened her fist around his virile girth. Heated words spilled from his lips as her hands encircled him, stroking and squeezing until he swelled to life. Then she took his erect length into her mouth and seduced him until he couldn't contain himself and cried out her name.

But Jonathan wasn't a one-sided lover; he hauled her up and she watched him as he slid on a condom with one hand. Then he was setting her astride him until he was buried to the hilt inside her. Then he commanded her, "Ride me."

She did, slowly swaying and gliding on top of him. He grunted and thrust upward to meet her every move. Natalie wasn't sure how many times she called out his name as their bodies became slick with sweat. She only knew that they were on this glorious pleasure ride together hurtling toward a bottomless vortex. When it struck, Natalie cried out her release and Jonathan was right behind her, jerking inside her as they both met the inevitable conclusion.

Natalie knew then that this experience would be one she would remember forever.

Today was going to be one of her favorite memories, Natalie thought two days later. Jonathan had chartered a private yacht for a romantic day getaway for the two of them. She hadn't known what to expect when Jonathan told her to pack her swim gear, lounge attire and something to wear in the evening. She'd been trying not to lick her lips at seeing Jonathan in a tank top that showed off his broad shoulders and the drawstring shorts that revealed his muscular thighs and toned legs.

"Eyes up here." Jonathan jokingly smirked, making Natalie blush because she for sure had been thinking about what she'd like to do later with him.

As each day passed, she was becoming more and more infatuated with Jonathan. He made it clear to her that this week would be all they had. She was terribly disappointed that he couldn't see how great they were together, but she always did her best to curb her feelings so he couldn't see how she wished for more between them. It had been risky for her to move forward with a vacation fling knowing how deep her feelings ran, but at the time it seemed like the only way she could get to know him without an audience. She didn't know how she would be able to walk away when the week was up. Instead, she kept her emotions buried deep. She would analyze them once she was back in Royal.

A limousine picked them up at the resort and whisked them away to Galveston Harbor. A quick ten-minute ride later and they arrived a few yards away from the most beautiful hundred-foot yacht Natalie had ever seen. It was a sprawling two-story masterpiece with an upper balcony.

"Welcome aboard," a white-haired gentleman said, helping her onto the back deck where there was a large outdoor seating area.

"Thank you." Natalie could only imagine he was the captain of the vessel, because he wore an officer's hat with a gold embroidered anchor and wreath, crisp white button-down shirt with an epaulet showing an anchor insignia and four stripes, and black trousers.

"And you must be Mr. Lattimore," he said, lending a hand to Jonathan, who climbed on board with her.

"Yes, sir. Please call me Jonathan."

"The name is Jeff, and I'll be your captain today."

"Pleasure to meet you." Natalie and Jonathan spoke in unison.

"Allow me to show you around the vessel." Jeff walked them through the large open-concept salon and kitchen, which boasted a huge island that currently had a vase filled with roses while rose petals adorned the counter. A bucket of champagne and two flutes stood beside it.

"Jonathan…" Natalie turned to him wistfully, but he shrugged.

"It came with the package," he responded.

So much for letting her get her hopes too high that he held any romantic feelings toward her. She needed to be careful because he was right—she really didn't know him. "I appreciate the effort," she replied as Jeff led them past the powder room downstairs to reveal a spacious bedroom and bathroom at the rear. Eventually, they climbed the stairs to the second floor, which held the balcony. From there, she could see large beanbag chairs on the bow at the front of the yacht.

"This is great. Thank you, Jonathan," Natalie said once the captain left them to their own devices in the salon.

"You're welcome." Jonathan headed to the champagne chilling in an ice bucket and began removing the foil. "Our time is ending soon, and I wanted to make this trip memorable."

He's already thinking about when our affair is ending.

Natalie supposed she shouldn't be surprised. Jonathan was very cut-and-dried about how he felt about continuing a relationship after Galveston. But Natalie wondered how their interactions would be once they were back in Royal. How were they supposed to treat each other? Were they supposed to act indifferent toward each other as if she hadn't known what it was like to have him buried deep inside her?

Natalie wasn't sure she could do that, but if Jonathan didn't want to continue this fling beyond tomorrow, she wouldn't want him to. She wanted a man who *wanted* to be with her. She knew what it was like to feel unloved and unwanted. Her own mother hadn't wanted to keep her.

"Natalie!"

"Hmm…" She realized Jonathan was speaking to her, but she'd zoned out.

"I asked if you would like a glass of champagne."

"I would love some, thanks."

He poured them each a flute. Once she'd sipped hers,

Jonathan came from around the bar and wrapped his big strong arms around her waist. She loved it when he did that. It made her feel safe and secure. Too bad it wouldn't last much longer.

"Is there something troubling you?" Jonathan inquired, peering down at her. "You seem distracted."

"Am I?" Natalie feigned a smile. She couldn't very well tell him what she was thinking; he'd run for the hills.

"You are. Did I do something wrong? Is this too much?"

She heard the doubt in his voice. "No, it's just right." She understood their time together had an expiration date, but that didn't mean it didn't hurt that Jonathan wasn't willing to give more than this moment. She couldn't forget that when they were in Royal, he'd avoided her. She would be a fool if she allowed herself to get too attached.

"Good, I wanted you to know how much I've enjoyed spending time with you," Jonathan said. "You've been the greatest surprise, or shall I say revelation, of this forced sabbatical by my parents."

"That's because all work and no play is not very fun, Jonathan." Natalie forced a smile even though her stomach was churning about the end of their fling. "You have to learn to have some sort of work-life balance."

He stared down at her and the sizzle in his eyes made her blood heat and her senses stir. "You're all the balance I need."

Then his mouth covered hers. His warm lips grazed hers seductively and his tongue tantalized with the promise of the all-consuming passion that always surged between them. His kiss was powerful and persuasive as he penetrated her mouth and cleared her mind of negative thoughts.

All she could feel was need. Jonathan understood and hauled her to him, pressing her into his hard arousal. Natalie reveled in the fact that she, a curvy woman, could turn

Jonathan's head. He'd steadfastly ignored any of her previous attempts to get him to notice her. Until now. Now she had his undivided attention.

Eventually, it was Jonathan who pulled away first. "Jesus, woman, what are you doing to me?"

"Little ole me?" Natalie asked, touching her chest. "Whatever do you mean?"

"Let's get changed and go swimming," Jonathan suggested. "I think we could both afford to cool off."

"That's probably not a bad idea." Natalie followed Jonathan down the steps to the master bedroom, where he'd placed their bags. While she slipped off her sundress, he used the powder room.

Natalie pulled out a cream-and-black-striped high-waisted bikini she'd been holding out on wearing. She never wore two-pieces because she felt self-conscious about her weight. But she was alone with her lover and there would be no prying eyes except his. So she took the plunge and slipped it on. She put a black crocheted cover-up over it. Grabbing her sunglasses, she exited the bedroom and headed upstairs.

The captain had already pulled away from the harbor and they were now cruising the Gulf. She could see Galveston Island in the distance, but all around them was the ocean.

She found Jonathan lounging on deck bare-chested, wearing swim shorts and sunglasses. His body was breathtaking and Natalie was glad her shades hid her reaction to the electrifying stimulus of seeing him half-naked. He watched her as she approached. Even with his sunglasses she could see his gleaming eyes raking over every inch of her figure until she crossed to the lounger beside his. Suddenly self-conscious, Natalie hesitated to take off the cover-up.

When she glanced at Jonathan he was waiting expectantly. "C'mon, don't be a tease," he murmured. "Take it off."

Sucking in a deep breath, Natalie lifted the cover-up over her head. The hiss that escaped Jonathan's throat made her breath catch, especially when he jerked upright and turned to fully face her.

"You're sexy as hell!"

"You don't have to keep saying that, Jonathan." Especially when she knew it wasn't true. She'd struggled with her weight her whole life and although she was comfortable now in the skin she was in, it was a constant battle.

"Why do you always do that?" Jonathan frowned.

"Do what?"

"Put yourself down. It's not the first time you've done it."

"C'mon, Jonathan." Natalie's sharp burst of laughter surprised Jonathan. "I'm not blind. I know how everyone else sees me."

"And how's that?"

"As the big girl?" Natalie answered. "And I know the in thing right now is about loving yourself no matter your body type, but I've lived with this my whole life. You have no idea what it's like to walk in my shoes and have people snicker behind your back or have boys or men want to date you because they think you're easy."

"Is that what happened to you?"

Natalie shook her head and rose to her feet. She walked over to the rail and looked out over the water. "I don't want to talk about this."

Seconds later, she felt Jonathan behind her. He wrapped his arms around her middle and Natalie leaned back against him, allowing herself a second to imagine that they were more than just lovers and that they were two people in love enjoying a romantic day cruise, but in her gut, she knew it wasn't true. She was on borrowed time.

"I'm sorry you were made to feel that way, Natalie." Jonathan slid his palm around her neck and turned her to face him. "But that doesn't mean that *I* don't find you attractive. You're sexy. Can't you tell? If you leave here with nothing from our fling, know this—you're a beautiful and desirable woman."

"Thank you."

"I didn't say it to you for the accolades. I want you to *believe* it."

"That's easier said than done, Jonathan."

"Then before I leave, I have to some convincing to do and show you exactly what I mean."

That's what Natalie was afraid of: that Jonathan would burrow so deep inside her heart, she would never be able to look at another man, let alone fall in love—and she was already halfway there.

Six

From his chair on the lounge deck, Jonathan watched Natalie on her phone searching Pinterest for ideas on how to modernize the two mid-century modern furniture pieces she found in the antique stores earlier that week. He didn't understand how Natalie couldn't see what he saw. A gorgeous woman who loved seafood, had a penchant for making old things new again and was passionate in bed. He was still trying to figure out how he ended up on a yacht in the middle of the Gulf with a woman he'd tried to steer clear of for years.

But he'd been unable let her leave the bar without him. He'd been eager to test out those full, sensuous lips of hers. She was everything he hadn't known he wanted. He thought the occasional hookup was good enough, but he'd been dead wrong. Natalie awakened his libido like no other woman. He was already thinking of all the places on the yacht where he wanted to make love to her today.

When he told the captain they would need complete

privacy, Jeff understood, no questions asked. Maybe he would finally satiate the incorrigible hunger he had for Natalie, because once they got back to Royal, things would change. They had to.

Jonathan refused to have the entire town gossiping about them, especially when he had no intention of putting a ring on her finger. And that's exactly what everyone would expect for a fantastic lady like Natalie. It's what Jonathan wished he could give her, but he'd deadened that side of himself long ago. Marriage, family, children—those were goals and aspirations other people could look forward to, but not him.

He considered his divorce one of his greatest failures. He should never have married so young. He hadn't really known Anne. They'd had a great physical relationship, she came from a good family and he'd thought he was in love, but it had been infatuation. They'd married without his parents' blessing. They'd been sidelined when he and Anne showed up married by a justice of the peace. His mother felt slighted because she hadn't been able to give him a big fat Texas-sized wedding and reception. At least she would get her opportunity with Caitlyn and Alexa, because Jonathan never intended to walk down anyone's aisle. He was done with marriage and relationships altogether, so he couldn't offer Natalie any more than this week. A fling was all he was willing to give.

"Captain Jeff has stopped. Ready for that dip in the ocean?" Jonathan asked, eager to take his mind off the end of their affair and his divorce.

Natalie looked up her phone. "Sure." As she rose to her feet, Jonathan couldn't keep his eyes off her. She was alluring and although she may not like flaunting her curves, she drove him mad. Once they got back to Royal, she would cover her curves in elegant loose-fitting suits.

"Don't you need more sunscreen?" he inquired. He would love to run his hands all over her body.

"Oh yeah." Natalie reached inside the beach bag she had brought upstairs and handed him the bottle. He poured a small amount in his palms and Natalie spun around and pushed her braids forward. The first glide of his hands onto Natalie's silky skin had Jonathan rethinking this scenario, but he couldn't stop now. He applied sunscreen on her shoulders, back and lower until he came to her butt. A peek of her cheeks could be seen in the audacious bikini and Jonathan allowed his hands to roam over them.

"Jonathan..." Natalie damn near purred out his name.

"Hmm...?"

"Are you putting on lotion? Or are you doing something else?"

His body wanted something else, but Jonathan lifted his hands up in surrender. "I was merely making sure you were properly protected."

"Why don't I finish?" Natalie asked and took the bottle from him to apply lotion to her legs. When she was done, she stepped closer to him and slid her hands up his chest. Her eyes flickered up to his. They were both silent. He reached down and traced his finger over her lower lip. She breathed in sharply as he continued moving his finger. She parted her lips and began sucking it into her mouth.

The woman was bewitching him. Suddenly, he pulled away his finger and Natalie had a bereft look on her face, but she didn't say anything. She spun on her heel and to his immense surprise dived off the back of the boat and into the ocean.

He glanced over in time to see her surface in the water. "How is it?"

"Refreshing. You should get in."

Jonathan did because it was exactly what he needed. Otherwise, he would start making love to Natalie and never stop. She made him lose control and it made his head spin. If he wasn't careful, she could strip away all his defenses and make him want to reconsider and extend this fling once they returned to Royal.

As she lay on one of the floats the captain threw out to them, Natalie wished Jonathan could give her his heart as much as he gave her his body. Sometimes she wondered if he was still hung up on his ex-wife. Was that why he refused to commit to another woman? She wanted to find a love like that someday. Find a man who would love her and no other. She supposed that's why it hurt knowing Jonathan would never feel the same way about her.

Natalie wouldn't beg him to reconsider. She had more pride and self-respect than that. So she had to ride this wave until it ended. Once they tired of the ocean, they returned to the boat for the light lunch the captain had catered in for them. Sandwiches, pasta salad and fresh fruit were laid out on the back deck.

"Looks great," Natalie said, patting herself dry with one of the fluffy towels that came with the yacht. Then she sat down and began making a plate. Jonathan did the same and sat across from her. They tucked into the food and crisp white wine in silence. Natalie liked that neither of them felt the need to fill up the quiet moments. With other men, she would be trying to think of something witty to say to keep the conversation going, but with Jonathan she didn't.

Once their bellies were full, Natalie resumed her location on one of the lounge chairs, but not before putting on her large brimmed hat. She was prepared to get deep into a book on her tablet, but Jonathan must have had other ideas because before she could protest, he was pulling her onto his lounger.

"Jonathan, what is—" Those were all the words she got out because he was the aggressor, reaching out to run both his hands through her braids and pull her head down to meet his hungry mouth. He licked and tasted her. Vaguely, she heard herself moan as he put his hands on her hips and pulled her firmly against him. Their lips, teeth and tongues swirled in a delicious mating dance and Natalie barely recognized he'd flipped them over so he was on top.

He reached behind her and untied the knot at the base of her neck, freeing her breasts from their confinement. His hands sought them out, stroking and caressing the tight nipples. Then he lowered his head and feasted on the nearest bud. He alternated between licks, flicks and suction; Natalie closed her eyes as the most exquisite sensations took over her.

His fingers trailed down her leg until he hit the top of her thigh. When he removed her bikini bottom, she parted her legs, allowing his hand into the warm cocoon. "Please…" Natalie would beg for this and only this because that's all Jonathan would give her.

He obeyed her order and slowly began stroking her. Her gasps became louder, so Jonathan accelerated the pace, rotating his thumb around her sensitive nub. She stirred against him, and he increased the pressure until all Natalie could hear was her soft moans and all she could feel was the moisture between her legs.

"That's right, baby. Come for me," he muttered.

Natalie's hips began to buck, and she rotated her pelvis as his fingers drove her wild.

"Jonathan!" When the shudder ripped through her, her inner muscles clamped around his fingers. Her mind blanked completely as sensation after sensation catapulted her into ecstasy. She was still in a haze when she felt the weight of his body settle onto her. He'd already protected them, and her excitement skyrocketed because he thrust inside her in one fell swoop.

When Jonathan began moving in slow, sure strokes,

Natalie knew then he would break through any barrier she had put up to prevent herself from falling for him. With each movement, he filled her, becoming one with her, becoming a *part* of her. "Oh yes…"

She arched to meet him, running her nails down the taut muscles of his back. She kissed his neck, lightly nipping as he liked to do to her, but he still kept the pace. The intensity of his movements as he began pounding into her made Natalie's mind blank. Spasms rocked through her very core, sending her hurtling over the edge, and Jonathan roared as his release crashed around him.

Sometime later, they left the deck to head downstairs to shower together only for Jonathan to wrap her naked body around him once again and press her against the cold tile of the bathroom shower. He departed long enough to roll on a condom before returning so Natalie could tighten her legs around his rock-hard buttocks as he pushed inside her. A groan escaped him as he thrust into her again and again, causing her breasts to push upward. He nipped at their fullness. She screamed, but Jonathan was right there with her exploding all around him.

She fell forward against him like a limp noodle, and he lifted her into his arms and carried her back to the bed. She heard him quietly murmuring her name as she drifted off to sleep.

It took Natalie several minutes to open her eyes and realize she was alone in the bedroom downstairs. She was spent. Natalie knew she should be concerned where this intense lovemaking was leading, but the compulsion to feel everything with Jonathan went beyond sexual gratification. When they were together, they were *making love* and Natalie had to remind herself not to imbue the moment with feelings because Jonathan would never return them. How could she not when he knew her intimately as no other man had? She was in danger of being seriously in love with this man. She knew he didn't want to hear her feelings and refused to have any of his own. So she kept them to herself, buried along with all the other words she wanted to say, but knew would go unsaid.

Jonathan emerged at the doorway several moments later. "Hello, sleepyhead." His dark eyes were fierce as they regarded her.

"I'm exhausted."

"Too tired for a sunset and dinner?" Jonathan asked. "Captain Jeff called down to tell me the sun is about to set in another fifteen minutes so if we want to catch it, we'd better head up."

"Oh yes, that would be lovely." Naked, Natalie threw back the duvet and rose from the bed. With other lovers, she would have reached for the nearest sheet because she wanted to hide her body, but Jonathan loved every inch of her.

As she walked past him to the bathroom, he smacked her on the rear. "Jonathan!" She spun around.

"What?" He shrugged. "I couldn't resist."

Natalie dressed quickly in a paisley maxi dress with a lightly smocked waist that accentuated her bust. Minutes later, they were climbing upstairs to the balcony where the captain was already looking out over the horizon. He glanced behind him when he heard their footsteps. "C'mon up. You don't want to miss this."

Natalie scurried forward to the railing just as the sun was setting. Jonathan came up behind her, planting his arms on either side of her, cocooning her in his embrace. Closing her eyes, Natalie wished she could stay here forever with Jonathan.

"Do you always watch the sunset with your eyes closed?" Jonathan asked, glancing down at her closed lids.

Natalie's eyes popped open, and she looked straight

ahead, embarrassed at having been caught daydreaming. "Not usually. I was just soaking it all in."

A rumble of laughter escaped from behind her. "It's all right, Natalie," he whispered in her ear. "I'm enjoying the moment, too."

"Do you think Captain Jeff heard us earlier when we were…" Her voice trailed off.

"Making love?" Jonathan offered. "I hope not, but even if he did, I'm sure he knows how to be discreet."

As the minutes ticked by, the vibrant yellow and orange hues of the sun turned to dusky pink and purple. But just as quickly, it was over, as their relationship soon would be.

"I guess that's it, folks," Jeff said. "I've got the makings of your dinner and will go set up, so give me a few minutes and enjoy the view."

"Sounds good, Captain," Jonathan replied as the older man left the balcony. "You're quiet."

"Merely introspective," Natalie responded when she finally hazarded a glance behind her.

"Stay in the moment with me," Jonathan said, sweeping her braids behind her back. "Can you do that?"

"I can try."

"Good." They stayed together like that until the sky turned purple; only then did Jonathan grab her hand. "Let's go eat."

Natalie took his proffered hand, but knew she'd lied to him, because she wouldn't be able to keep her word. She was already thinking about tomorrow and all that it would bring.

Seven

Jonathan awoke the following morning later than normal and instantly knew something was different. Rolling to his side, he glanced to the empty spot where Natalie had lain with him the night before. All that remained was her indentation as well as a note.

He bolted upright as he picked up the slip of paper folded in half. Opening it up, he read:

Jonathan, You have no idea how much I've enjoyed the time we've spent in Galveston. Unfortunately, work beckons. Take care, Natalie.

Take care.

That's it? That's how she was going to leave what could only be described as the best six days of his life? Did she not feel the same? Why hadn't she woken him up so he could have properly told her goodbye? They'd shared an amazing day on the yacht yesterday. Because if she had, he most certainly would have tried to talk her out of going home. Work be damned! She'd done the right thing, but he had to admit he felt an odd sensation—something like regret because he wouldn't get to enjoy the last day of his trip with her.

Perhaps it was for the best. They had been joined at the hip since they arrived. In and out of each other's beds. And if he had his way, it would have continued until they were due to leave the island. But oh, how he would miss her sweet demeanor, and that gorgeous, sexy of body of hers. They fit together so perfectly. It was like she was *made for him!*

Jonathan had never had a partner who was compatible with him in the bedroom. Natalie left him satisfied and fulfilled each and every time. Whenever they were together, he felt like he couldn't get enough of her. After dinner on the yacht last night, he'd pushed away the plates and had *her* as his dessert.

He smiled at the memory. He'd sat her on the table, hiked up her dress until it bunched at her waist and worked his way lower until he was between her legs. Then he'd spread her wide so he could taste the very heart of her. He used his full tongue to lap her until she was quivering and gripping his head with her hands and crying out his name. Only then did he pull himself up long enough to drop his trousers, slide on a condom and bury himself to the hilt in her. She had felt incredible. Amazing. Glorious.

Throwing back the covers, Jonathan went to the bathroom and turned on the tap as cold as he could take it. He stepped in and hoped it would relieve him of the ache of not having Natalie here to fulfill his fantasies. But worse, he wondered if that wasn't all he craved.

He craved Natalie, the woman who in a short span of time had crept up to fill a void he hadn't known he had. Now what was he supposed to do? He had no room in his life for emotional entanglements because those led to heartache. He made that clear to her, but had he made it clear to himself?

His heart was telling him Natalie was a great girl and perhaps he was doing them an injustice leaving their relationship here in Galveston. But that's what they had agreed to do because he couldn't offer her a commitment or marriage. And if she truly knew him, Natalie would know he was the cold and unfeeling bastard Anne said he was. So he would go back to Royal, and they would go back to the way things were—two people passing in the night.

"Natalie, I appreciate you cutting short your vacation to come back and deal with this. When I texted you an update, I didn't expect you to immediately hop on a plane, but I'm relieved you did," Brent White, her partner, said while he and Natalie looked over the current marketing strategy they had for one of their largest clients, a boutique hotel chain in Houston. The hotel had undergone a multimillion-dollar renovation and was seeking to reinvent itself. H & W Marketing was going to help achieve it.

She and Brent had decided to go into business together after they both worked in corporate America and realized it wasn't for them. It had been an effort of love, but after five years, they were finally making a profit, which allowed Natalie to treat herself to a vacation. It's why this campaign was so important to her and worth cutting her trip to Galveston short.

"Of course. This is my baby," Natalie replied. "We've been working on this marketing campaign for months. I wouldn't want anything to go astray."

"Did you at least enjoy your vacation?" Brent inquired, glancing up at her.

Natalie thought back to yesterday and the way Jonathan had reduced her to moans and gasps on the dinner table, then again on the salon bar and later in bed before they'd eventually made it back to shore. "Yes, I did." She couldn't help the smile that spread across her lips.

"Sounds like someone might not have been alone," Brent stated.

Natalie shook her head. "A girl never kisses and tells."

Brent chuckled. "Your answer told me all I need to know. Let's get back to work."

They worked steadily over the next hours, calling in lunch and dinner while they figured out how they could adjust the campaign now that news had leaked with images of the reno before they were ready.

Marketing had changed dramatically since Natalie first went to school. With social media becoming more and more relevant, she had to stay on the cusp of trends and the best approaches to marketing her clients. She'd even gone back to school and taken a night course on social media to make sure she was on top of her game. In an elite community like Royal, competition was fierce; it's why their firm had gone to neighboring cities like Houston and Dallas to ensure they could stay afloat. She was proud of the progress they'd made.

By the time she drove to her cottage at the end of the night and pulled her oversize Louis Vuitton luggage inside, Natalie was dog-tired. She left her suitcase at the door and kicked off her shoes. Heading to the kitchen, she went to the cabinet and pulled out a wineglass and an opener. When she opened her fridge, she was thankful to see the pinot grigio she kept on hand for such occasions was stocked. After pouring herself a glass, she padded to the living room and plopped down on the sofa.

She'd been so busy for much of the day, she hardly had a chance to check her phone. The one time she had, there had been a text from Chelsea asking her when she was due home so they could catch up.

Little did she know, Natalie thought. She had much to

tell her about the week and who she spent it with, but who there wasn't a message from was Jonathan. They had exchanged phone numbers in Galveston so they could reach other, especially when Natalie treated herself to a few hours in the day spa while he went fishing. It came as a surprise to see her phone displayed no notifications that she'd missed a call or text from him.

Really?

Natalie stared down at the phone in her hand. Although they agreed that what happened in Galveston, stayed in Galveston, she expected *something.* Anything. An acknowledgment he received her note. A goodbye. *Hi, how are you? Did you make it back safe to Royal?* But there was nothing. Nada. Apparently, she was under the delusion that she meant more than a warm, willing body next to him. She was wrong.

At least the text from Brent about their marketing campaign gave her an excuse to leave with her dignity. While Jonathan was in a deep, peaceful slumber, she'd written a quick note and placed it on the bed next to him, so he would see it when he woke up. Then she'd sneaked out of his room. She had to. Not just for her business, because Brent probably could have solved this crisis without her.

Deep down, Natalie had run for her own self-preservation. If she hadn't, she would have fallen harder for Jonathan when she was already in too deep. She might have spilled her feelings for him. But not Jonathan. He didn't have any. For him, their fling was finito, over and done with, and she had to think the same. So why did it cut to the quick knowing she meant so little, he couldn't even bother to text or call her? Natalie sighed and sipped her wine.

The last week had changed things between them. Jonathan was no longer an enigma and the hero she crushed on. He was a strong, kind, talented and passionate man who loved to play the piano but also could make her laugh and forget her hang-ups. And when they'd been intimate the passion and connection she and Jonathan shared wasn't like anything else she'd ever experienced. Natalie wished it could have lasted a little bit longer than six days. She would have to put up a brave front the next time she saw him and act like theirs was a meaningless affair. When she knew it was so much more.

Eight

Jonathan was up before dawn. Instead of going into the office to look at figures or research ways to assist Alexa with the oil claim case, he was helping his ranch hands feed and groom the horses and cleaning their hooves while checking for nicks and scratches. Once the horses were tended to, he thought about going up to the main house for breakfast because the smell of his mother's frying bacon always lured him in as well as homemade pancakes, but not today. He'd already eaten at home, fixing himself a quick sausage-and-egg sandwich before filling up his canteen and heading out the door.

He saddled a beautiful Arabian horse named Beauty and after making sure the cinches were tight, stepped into the saddle. Jonathan was going to help his ranch hands find some scattered cows that were on hundreds of miles of open terrain. The fresh air and open fields would give him time to clear his head and get back on track after the week in Galveston. Sometimes cows were like wild animals and began scattering as soon as they saw humans, so he took off galloping so he could herd them back in.

Jonathan desperately needed to get back on track because he'd slept fitfully the night before. Ever since he got back from Galveston two days ago, he felt off. Something was different and he couldn't put his finger on what it was, but everything looked and felt different. The joy he usually got out of being on the ranch was gone and he felt sullen. The exact opposite of how he usually felt. Ranching was in his blood, but not even a hard ride through the acres of Lattimore land could get him out of his slump.

The more he thought about it, the more it occurred to him that he missed Natalie. A sudden memory of her in his bed, looking thoroughly tousled, popped into his head. Then another—of Natalie giving him one of those sweet seductive smiles. Of Natalie looking up at him with her large, trusting brown eyes. Jonathan shook the images from his mind. They had laid out the ground rules of their affair—it would last as long as their vacation, and when it was over, they would go their separate ways. But something about it felt unfinished, as if there was still more to the book and he needed to keep turning the page.

But the truth of the matter was he wasn't looking for a long-term relationship. Ever since his marriage to Anne ended, Jonathan hadn't wanted another foray into the world of heartbreak. He'd learned his lesson and seen what loving someone did. It made you weak and helpless. Made you believe things that weren't true. He had gotten so caught up in the idea of being in love, he never stopped to figure out if Anne truly was the right woman for him.

She checked all the right boxes. Beautiful, smart, came from a well-respected family in the community, but she couldn't be trusted, and he didn't find that out until it was too late. Until she'd done the unthinkable—something they could never recover from. Anne blamed him for causing her to do it, and he resented her for doing it. Divorce papers quickly followed. And so, he retired himself from relationships. It was easier that way.

But… Natalie.

No, he didn't want that for Natalie. She was a good, decent woman. She was so sweet. Trusting. He refused to be the person who hurt her. He would rather remember her lovely face as she slept with her body pressed against his, with warmth and contentment radiating from her every pore. She believed in happy endings, but they weren't for a man like him who couldn't even be bothered to know how unhappy his wife had been. He was too selfish and work-obsessed to see what was happening in his own household. And Jonathan couldn't give her the emotion and vulnerability she craved. He wasn't made that way.

Natalie deserved a man who would love her. Instead of a broken man.

Natalie was happy for a day off. The last few days had been stressful getting the launch of the hotel back on track, but now that it was, she could take some time for herself doing one of her favorite hobbies on Sunday.

After her hour-long Pilates class, followed by a smoothie and shower, she was on her way to Priceless. The antique store owned by Raina Patterson. The store also served as a studio for people interested in classes like candle making and mosaic design, but Natalie was on the hunt for another piece to go along with the two spectacular finds she'd discovered in Galveston and had shipped home. The entire set would be her wedding gift to Chelsea.

Parking her vehicle, Natalie climbed out and headed toward the large red barn with the white trim. She was perusing an assortment of old tables and bookcases when she stumbled on a beautiful maple slanted-front desk. She was leaning over it and thinking about what she could do to transform it when she heard him.

"See something that catches your eye?" Natalie didn't need to turn around to know the owner of that voice, because he'd been the star of her dreams as well as in person when she'd been in Galveston.

Inhaling deeply, Natalie rose to her feet. "Jonathan." Why did he have to look so damn good in those jeans, a crisp white button-down shirt and his Stetson? She knew the rippled muscular body that lay underneath and her mouth watered.

"Natalie." His eyes were smiling at her, but she wasn't returning the sentiment. He hadn't bothered to call or text her. "Fancy meeting you here."

"I could say the same. Though I don't recall you mentioning antiquing as a hobby." She made sure her voice was calm, so it belied her inner turmoil at seeing the man she'd become intimately acquainted with in the flesh. After being in each other's company day in and day out, being without him felt like acute torture. And now they were acting as if they were complete strangers. It was frustrating.

"Perhaps it might have grown on me after my time away," he responded with a grin.

After his silence since their return to Royal, Natalie wasn't taking the bait. "Raina has some good pieces. You might find something you like."

"Natalie... I'm not here to purchase anything. I was dropping off a piece of furniture my mother no longer wants."

"Oh, okay then. Well, nice to see you." Natalie started toward the door.

"What about your purchase?"

It could wait for another time as far as Natalie was concerned. She needed to get out of Priceless. Anger and hurt were all rolled into one and she refused to allow him to see how deep her feelings went.

"Natalie, wait!" Jonathan strode behind her and caught up with her outside. "Why does it always feel like I'm chasing after you? Can you just wait a damn second?"

"Why should I, Jonathan?" Natalie hissed, and glanced around to make sure no one was listening. "We are not in Galveston anymore."

His eyes narrowed. "I know that."

Natalie cocked her head to one side. "I suppose you do."

His brows bunched into a frown. "What's that supposed to mean?"

"You know exactly what it means, Jonathan Lattimore. And I have received your message loud and clear." Natalie clicked the remote on her Lexus. "Have a good day." She quickly hopped into the vehicle and turned on the engine.

She wouldn't dare let him see how upset she was—that she felt like rubbish on the bottom of his shoe after he carelessly disregarded what happened between them. She was better off without him.

What the hell just happened? Jonathan stared at Natalie's car revving down the road and away from him. When he'd seen her in Priceless, bending over the desk with her gorgeous ass up in the air, he breathed a sigh of relief. Seeing Natalie again made him want to reignite their affair, see if they could still burn up the sheets.

He could have imagined how intense the attraction was between them in Galveston because of the illicit nature of their temporary arrangement. But on the other hand, his mind was telling him to steer clear of Natalie. She didn't know him well enough to know he rarely showed his emotions or told people how he felt. If she knew, she might rethink the crush she'd had.

Instead, he'd gone for flirtatious, but he must have said something to offend her because she emitted angry vibes. What had he done wrong but honor their arrangement?

They hadn't exactly laid the foundation of how they would act toward each other when they were back home in Royal. Maybe if she hadn't rushed away so quickly, they could have figured it out.

But they hadn't.

Instead, he was left with Natalie being mad *at him*.

What had she expected? That he would call and text her like some besotted schoolboy? They were two grown people who *chose* to have a vacation fling. She wasn't about to make him feel guilty as if he'd done something wrong. They had discussed this in Galveston. She said what happened there, stayed there.

She was now acting as if they were an item and he *owed* her something. He only owed her courtesy and respect, which is exactly what he gave her, but he couldn't say the same for Natalie. Had the week in Galveston made her want more from him than he was ready to give?

Given her previous feelings, which the entire town had been able to hear, should he be surprised? Becoming lovers had probably made Natalie hope for more, even though he told her he wasn't looking for a long-term commitment. She must have gotten it in her head that she could change his mind. She couldn't. He was haunted by his disastrous marriage. He blamed himself for not being a better husband. It made him feel unworthy of love.

That didn't mean he didn't want to take Natalie back to his bed. He needed to exorcise her from his mind *and* his body. Only then could Jonathan go back to the solitary life that had become the bedrock of his existence. But as he stared down at the empty road, Jonathan wondered if he and Natalie could really go back to the way they were *before* Galveston.

Natalie called Chelsea on her way home in the car, but her bestie didn't pick up, which meant she was on her own.

She wanted to rail at the sky, but she had no one but herself to blame for the predicament in which she found herself in. She'd painted herself into a corner with Jonathan when she agreed their tryst would be limited to their vacation.

At the time, it seemed like the best avenue given how wary Jonathan had been after the first time they made love. Secretly, she'd been thrilled to know that the man she crushed on for ages found her attractive. She suggested a vacation fling knowing it was the *only* way she could keep Jonathan in her bed, but it backfired. Because although she may not have been expecting a Hollywood movie ending where Jonathan suddenly realized she was the woman he'd been waiting his whole life for, she certainly thought he'd at least call or text her.

When neither of those things happened, Natalie realized how delusional she'd been. Jonathan was only with her for sex and companionship and now that the vacation was over, so were they. It hurt so much seeing him today and knowing how good they were together and having him want nothing more to do with her. No, correction, she'd seen the hungry look in his eye when she'd spun around to face him, so she could only imagine he wanted another roll in the hay for old times' sake.

Well, she wasn't going to do that again. She had to at least demand a relationship. Sex for sex's sake was no longer on the table. She was done doing things his way. She wasn't going to apologize for wanting more.

Nine

Jonathan and his younger siblings, Jayden, Alexa and Caitlyn, gathered at their family home later that afternoon. It wasn't unusual for the entire family to be in one place. There was nothing his mother loved more than having all her children present so she could be in full mother hen mode.

One of the big reasons she was thrilled was because Alexa had come home *permanently*. Originally, his sister had visited for Victor Grandin Sr.'s funeral, but after Layla Grandin asked Alexa to stay on and help with Heath Thurston's claim, she had remained in town. That's when she met and fell in love with her former school rival, Jackson Strom. Now she and the CEO of the PR firm were head over heels in love and engaged to be married. Jonathan couldn't believe that *both* his sisters had been struck by Cupid's arrow. He refused to go down that road again. He would be happy with his casual affairs.

I wonder what Natalie is doing?

Dammit, he had to stop obsessing about Natalie and instead focus on enjoying family time.

After everyone dispersed, Jonathan stayed behind because he wanted to talk to his mother. He'd been mulling this over in his mind since his return and he was certain he was doing the right thing.

"Jonathan, I thought you'd gone," his mother said when she came into the kitchen and found him raiding the cookie jar. Like him, she liked an evening treat and he'd banked on the fact that she would grab a snack before she and his father headed upstairs to bed.

"You know I can't resist your oatmeal chocolate chip cookies."

She beamed with pride. "No one knows the secret to making chocolate chip cookies taste amazing is the extra bit of oatmeal." She went to the commercial-sized fridge and pulled out a jug of milk. She poured herself and Jonathan a glass.

"But something tells me that's not the only reason you're here," she said, handing him his glass.

"Thanks." He took a large gulp of milk, uncaring he had a milk mustache. "And no, it's not."

"What's on your mind?" She reached over and with her thumb wiped away the milk.

"I wanted to know if you've selected a marketing firm to help take your culinary products to the public." Despite the chilly reception Natalie gave him earlier, he still believed in her talent.

His mother shook his head. "No, not yet. I'm still entertaining offers."

"Could I be bold and make a suggestion?"

"I'm all ears."

"Natalie Hastings. She and her business partner own a marketing firm here in Royal," Jonathan said. He glanced in his mother's direction, but her expression remained neutral. "If you're looking for a local firm, I don't think you can do any better than Natalie's company."

His mother tilted her head to one side and her dark brown eyes pierced his. "Is that so?"

"You sound doubtful."

"Not of Natalie's firm. I've heard of them, and I'd be happy to entertain a proposal. I'm more curious about why you're making the recommendation."

"I don't follow."

"C'mon, Jonathan," his mother said, chuckling, and he could see he wasn't fooling her for a second. She was on to him. "Don't act dense. If you recall, the entire family was there last month at the Texas Cattleman's party. We heard Natalie's declaration and know you're the object of her affection. And suddenly you think she's the best thing since sliced bread. What gives?"

Damn. His mother wasn't going to let him off the hook easily. He had to give her something. Throw her a bone. "I recently got to know her and found her to be a charming and talented woman."

His mother smiled at that statement. "That's high praise coming from you, considering you haven't brought a woman home to meet the family since Anne."

Jonathan rolled his eyes upward. That name was persona non grata in this house. "Please don't bring up my ex."

"With pleasure. She's one of my least favorite people," his mother replied. "And I'll give your Natalie an audience, but she'd better bring it. I don't give out handouts."

He doubted she was "his Natalie" anymore. The lady was mighty upset with him. "Thanks, Mom." Jonathan strolled over to her and, grasping her by the shoulders, kissed both her cheeks. "I appreciate it."

Jonathan quickly exited the kitchen before his mother could pepper him with more questions about how and *when* he'd gotten to know Natalie. Because he knew he hadn't fooled her for a second. She knew something was afoot and she would use her powers of persuasion and the rumor mill of Royal to find out the truth. Lucky for him no one knew he and Natalie had become lovers and that's exactly the way he intended to keep it.

"Natalie, baby girl, it's so good to see you," her grandmother said when Natalie stopped by her childhood home to check on her grandparents that evening. They'd raised Natalie after she was dropped off *unwanted* by her biological mother.

"Hey, Mimi," Natalie said, using the affectionate name she'd given her at two years old. She kissed her cheek as she stepped inside the three-bedroom home located in the center of Royal. "I brought you over a caramel cake from the diner."

"Thank you, sweetie. You didn't need to do that."

"It's no bother. I thought it would go great with whatever you were cooking up for Sunday dinner."

"I made the usual, some baked chicken, fried cabbage and some corn bread. You hungry?"

"If that's what's for dinner, then that's an absolute yes. Where's Granddaddy?" Natalie dropped her purse and glanced around the room.

"Oh, he went over to help give the neighbor a jump. He'll be along shortly. Come on in and sit for a spell. We can catch up about your trip to Galveston. Was it the getaway you needed after the hoopla of the last month?"

Natalie chuckled inwardly. How could she forget professing her adoration for Jonathan live in front of the entire town? It all seemed like a moot point now, given they'd become lovers. He may not have been into her before, but he hadn't been able to get enough of her during their vacation.

"Yes, Mimi, it was exactly what I needed to put the past

behind me," Natalie responded. Maybe that would be all the closure she would get. For a brief moment, she got to have her heart's desire, and now she knew Jonathan was bad for her.

"That's good. Because I wouldn't want you to get hurt and think the Lattimore boy would be interested in you when he's never approached you."

Ouch. Is that how everyone saw her? As some desperate female?

"It's over now. I'm moving on."

"So, you're willing to date someone else?" her grandmother asked. "If so, I know a great young man from church who's been dying to go out on a date with you."

"No, thanks, Mimi. Really, if you don't mind, I'd like to focus on my business."

"You're not getting any younger, my sweet. If you want a family someday, you can't wait around. It's not so easy for women to get pregnant these days. You have to take the bull by the horns if you want to meet a good man."

Natalie chuckled. "I do want a family and kids, but it doesn't have to be right now. H & W Marketing is doing so well now. We can't lose momentum."

"All right. Well, you can't blame a mother for trying, can you?"

Natalie grinned broadly from ear to ear. He grandmother didn't often refer to herself as Natalie's mother, so it was great to hear because Natalie felt the same way. Claudette and Carlton Hastings were her parents, and she loved them.

Seconds later, the back door opened and her grandfather walked in. "Baby girl!" He swept Natalie into his arms and any negative thoughts she had instantly melted away in the safety of his arms. He'd always had that effect on her. Even when she was a little girl, there was nothing her daddy couldn't do.

"Hey Pop-pop," Natalie said when he finally placed her back on her feet.

"I didn't know you were stopping by."

"Spur-of-the-moment thing," Natalie replied.

"She brought one of the diner's famous caramel cakes."

Her grandfather rubbed his belly. "It's going to taste great after the meal you prepared, sweetheart." He rushed over to give his wife a quick peck on the lips. "Are you staying for dinner, Nat?"

"Yes, sir."

Natalie wouldn't miss this for the world. A chance to be with her family, with people who truly cared for her. Her mimi was right. She had to stop wishing things might be different with Jonathan, because they weren't. He made his intentions clear when he didn't contact her. Whatever they might have shared was over. She was moving forward with her life and if that didn't include Jonathan Lattimore, so be it. She refused to be his booty call.

Ten

"You won't believe this," Brent said when Natalie came into H & W Marketing the next morning and he stopped by her office. "Guess who is publishing a cookbook and looking for a marketing firm to help with the launch of a corresponding product line?"

"Who?"

"Barbara Lattimore."

"Really?" Natalie fiddled with papers on her desk and tried to act like she had no idea, but Jonathan had mentioned his mother was branching out into culinary products.

"She asked to meet with us," Brent replied enthusiastically. "She's sent out a request for proposal, but apparently she's already found a publisher for her new cookbook and her agent indicated she wants to get into spices and homemade baking mixes. I'm told eventually this could lead to cookware and bakeware."

It was fantastic news and normally Natalie would be

excited, but it could potentially put her in Jonathan's orbit and after their last foray at Priceless, she wasn't keen on a repeat performance.

Brent frowned. "Why aren't you more excited?"

"You do remember I was outed in front of the entire town for having a crush on her son?" Natalie replied. "Or did you forget?" She had never revealed to Brent *who* she had a tryst with while on vacation.

"Of course I haven't. But this is business. We can't let emotions get involved. Snagging a campaign like this in its infancy stages could put us on the map."

Natalie took a deep breath and tried to be more excited. "I'm sorry if I'm being a Debbie Downer. I don't mean to be. This is great! And yes, we will absolutely put together a proposal for Mrs. Lattimore—one that will knock her socks off."

Brent touched her nose. "There's my girl. I need your fighting spirit on this one. And who knows, this could be exactly what the older Lattimore son needs to finally get off his horse and ask you out."

If he only knew, Natalie thought as he left her office. She and Jonathan shared a connection in Galveston, but did she really know him? A relationship took time, and they'd only been together less than a week. There was probably a lot about him she didn't know. At times, her heart wanted to know what secrets and hurts lay hidden beneath the real reason Jonathan preferred casual hook-ups, but her mind warned her to protect herself. And instead find a man ready for love.

Later, after they worked on the RFP, Natalie left the office for the Texas Cattleman's Club. She was meeting Chelsea there for lunch. While she drove, she tried not to think about what having Barbara Lattimore as a client would mean.

Surely, if she was at the main house working with

Jonathan's mother, she would hardly see her son? If she recalled, Jonathan handled the ranch's administrative functions as well as operational duties with his brother, Jayden, which kept him plenty busy.

Natalie had only met Barbara Lattimore a few times in passing. She was warm, bubbly and never met a stranger; she easily conversed with everyone.

When Natalie arrived at the club, she stopped at the valet and handed him her keys while she went in to meet her best friend.

She was waiting at the hostess station when she saw Jonathan exiting the restaurant with another man. They shook hands and the other gentleman departed. At first, she was considering not speaking because he seemed deep in thought, but then again, she would have to get used to facing Jonathan in public situations even though her heart rate ratcheted up a notch when they were in close proximity. "Jonathan."

He glanced up when he saw her and blinked several times. "Natalie?" He looked surprised to see her. It was as if she was suddenly invisible to him again as she'd once been. How was that possible after everything they shared?

"Is everything okay?" she asked instead. She hadn't seen him since Priceless, but she'd cooled down since then. Natalie refused to be one of those women who couldn't take a hint after a hookup was over. She understood the rules of their fling, but that didn't mean it didn't hurt. She wasn't made of stone.

"Everything is fine. Just a lot going on right now." He lowered his head and instead of looking at her, his eyes shifted restlessly back and forth.

"Anything I can do to help? I'm a pretty good listener."

He shook his head. "No, but thank you. It's a family matter."

Natalie nodded curtly. "Of course. Didn't mean to overstep. If you'll excuse me." She headed straight for the exit. If she stayed another minute and watched Jonathan act as if nothing ever happened between them, she was going to scream.

Every time they saw each other, the situation was becoming more and more awkward. She wanted to tell Jonathan he had nothing to fear from her, but the keep-away vibes he gave resonated. And she would do just that. Natalie was done wishing and hoping the situation would get better between them.

"Hey, where are you?" Natalie asked after dialing Chelsea's number once she was in her vehicle.

"Sorry! I'm just leaving now. I'm running late. I was preoccupied with Nolan."

"It's okay. You're newly engaged. How about I come there instead after work?"

"That would be perfect. Come on over. I miss you. We are overdue for some girl talk, and it's easier to talk here than at the TCC anyway."

"I hope you have some liquor, because I might need the hard stuff."

"Only beer. Can you pick up some on your way over?"

"I'll buy a big bottle and see you this evening."

Natalie ended the call. She had been holding this inside for far too long. She hoped that by finally sharing her feelings with Chelsea, she could figure out how to get past making the biggest mistake of her life by becoming intimate with Jonathan.

Damn.

He'd blown it again, Jonathan thought, watching Natalie drive off. He hadn't been able to get the risk his family was facing out of his head. Despite his grandfather's failing memory, Jonathan suspected he knew more than he was letting on. It's why he arranged to meet with the private investigator Jonas Shaw himself and go over the details. It wasn't that he didn't trust Alexa, but every rock had to be overturned to ensure their family legacy would be preserved. Jonathan had worked too hard, given up too much of himself to the land, to let an outsider come in and take his inheritance.

But he hadn't meant to be dismissive with Natalie. He was distracted by what was going on with his family. Was he using it as an excuse not to think about Natalie and all they shared? Hell yes! He hadn't been able to get the curvy vixen out of his mind. Usually, after he was physically intimate with a woman, he turned his focus back to work, to the ranch he loved, but with Natalie, she made him *feel* things—happiness at seeing her face each morning when he woke up, relaxed when he was with her and excited at sharing a bed with her each night.

And he didn't like it. Jonathan preferred not feeling anything because he knew how to handle that existence, but these emotions were too much. He didn't know how to deal with them. And he certainly couldn't give Natalie the relationship he knew she wanted.

It's why Jonathan asked his brother, Jayden, over to his house later that evening. Maybe talking things out would help bring him some clarity.

"Bro!" Jayden slapped his back when he came into Jonathan's. "Not that I don't appreciate the invite, but what's going on? You sounded stressed on the phone."

"I've got a bit of female trouble." As they passed by the foyer, Jonathan glanced at his piano. Usually playing helped, but it had done little to alleviate the insomnia he'd been dealing with since returning from his vacation.

"That's what brothers are for," Jayden responded, following him into his oversize living room.

"Thanks, Jayden. I appreciate it. I've had a lot on my mind lately. I was hoping I could bounce it off you." Jonathan flopped onto the sofa in front of the ninety-inch high-definition flat-screen television.

"Sure, but I admit I'm surprised," Jayden replied, sitting in the armchair across from him. "You've always kept your feelings to yourself. You're a hard shell to crack for your family. I can only imagine how someone else might receive you."

"Thanks a lot." Jonathan frowned.

"Listen, don't be mad, but I speak the truth. You can be a little bit of a brick wall."

Jonathan snorted. "Tell me how you really feel."

Jayden laughed. "That's exactly what I'm doing. Listen, we can go back and forth like this for hours. Why don't you take it from the top and tell me what happened?"

"I slept with Natalie."

"Whoa!" Jayden sat forward in the chair. "I wasn't prepared for that confession, but just so I'm clear, is this the same Natalie who announced to all of Royal she had a huge crush on you and thought you were—" he put his hand up in air quotations "—the most amazing man she'd ever met? You mean that Natalie?"

"Yes."

His brother was silent for several minutes and rubbed his chin. "When did this happen? I don't recall seeing the two of you around town recently. Otherwise, the gossip mills would be on fire right now and Mom would be hearing wedding bells."

Jonathan shook his head adamantly. "No, I'm not ever getting married again." He wasn't cut out for relationships or commitment. He didn't deserve a happy ending.

"You say that now, Jonathan, but you may not mean that a couple of years from now," Jayden replied. "You got married young before you really knew each other. You didn't do your due diligence."

"You don't need to tell me that," Jonathan replied.

"And is that how you feel about sleeping with Natalie?" Jayden asked. "Because you shouldn't beat yourself up. We've all had one-night stands, though you've yet to tell me any details including how you were able to keep this quiet without it getting back to the family."

"Because it wasn't one night, and it didn't happen in Royal."

Jayden used his fingers to reach up and scratch his head. "Excuse me? You told me you slept with Natalie."

"Yeah, but I never said it was just once, you made an assumption."

"Which you didn't correct," Jayden replied. "What's going on, Jonathan?"

"It's exactly as I've said. Natalie and I hooked up. It happened more than once. Hell, it happened often while I was in Galveston. And I have to tell you, Jayden, it's the best sex I've ever had in my life."

"Get out!"

"She blew my mind, bro. Maybe because the chemistry between us was so unexpected. I didn't go there looking for anything. I was annoyed because Dad and Mom made me go on vacation, but then on the first night, I saw Natalie and…well, we became lovers. And it was so damn good."

"So you had a vacation fling with Natalie?"

"Bingo. Give this cowboy a cowboy hat." Jonathan smirked. "We had an incredibly hot and passionate fling. It's like she's got me punch-drunk and I can't seem to clear my head of her, of her gorgeous body and everything she can do with it."

Jayden put a hand up in the air. "Enough with the visuals, please. We know each other and I don't want to think about Natalie getting busy with my brother."

"I'm sorry, but it's how I feel," Jonathan replied, jumping up and starting to pace his hardwood floors. "She's in my head and I can't get her out."

"Have you ever thought that maybe she shouldn't come out?" Jayden responded. "You've been living like a monk for years. Maybe it's time you let the *player* come out to play."

"That's crude, Jayden."

"But true. All this has done is show you that you can't cut yourself off from the world. You have to let someone in at some point, Jonathan. You have needs."

Jayden's words sounded familiar. Natalie had told him that everybody needed someone, but he chose not to focus on that. He said instead, "Yes, I have needs."

"But since Anne, you've been closed off. Afraid to take a chance."

Jayden was right, but Jonathan refused to tell him so; he wouldn't give his baby brother that much vindication.

"I'm happy Natalie took a chance on you. How did you guys meet up?"

Jonathan filled Jayden in on their first encounter at the resort and how after that night Jonathan considered walking away, but once Natalie indicated she was open to a vacation fling, they carried on a passionate affair.

"The whole time?" Jayden inquired.

"Yeah. A little under a week, but she was called back to work unexpectedly."

"Do you feel shortchanged because you two didn't have the full week to explore each other?"

"No, not per se."

"Then what? Spit it out, Jonathan, I'm getting older by the minute."

Jonathan chuckled. "I miss her and not just in bed. I miss her smile. Her warmth. She's all heart, ya know? And so much more than I bargained for."

"Then maybe you should see where things go between you?"

Jonathan shook his head. "Nah, man. *We* are not going

anywhere. I told you, I've been down that road before and if you don't remember, it ended in disaster."

"That may be so, but not every woman is like Anne. You can't generalize. You already said Natalie is special, and she must be because it's the first time in nearly a decade I've heard you talk like this about a woman."

Jonathan refused to give anyone that kind of power over him. Anne had him in knots. She might have been beautiful but she was utterly needy and no matter what he did to try to show her he cared, it produced the opposite result. Jonathan aspired to do things well—he supposed that was the curse of being born the eldest—and failure hadn't been an option.

He'd been devastated by the demise of his marriage and felt to blame because Anne complained he wasn't there for her or was always working on the ranch. Jonathan wanted a woman who was independent who didn't need him like Anne did.

Natalie was definitely the antithesis of Anne. She was not only beautiful, but she was strong and independent. He loved listening to her ideas for H & W Marketing, the firm she started with her best friend. In fact, even though he sensed she was angry with him, she didn't stay and cry or pout like Anne would have done. Instead, she kept it moving. He appreciated that. Respected it.

"I think you're doing yourself a disservice," Jayden replied. "If Natalie is all that, you should be trying to snatch her up before another fella comes along and realizes what a prize she is. Then you'll be the one with regrets."

"I don't know, Jayden." He wasn't sure he could reciprocate her feelings.

"You would rather stay single?" Jayden inquired. "Because who knows, you could be rejecting your future wife."

Jonathan shook his head. "I'd rather stay single forever than experience the highs and lows I had with Anne. I can't do that again."

"You're willing to forgo all you and Natalie could be because you're afraid?"

"I'm not afraid. I'm practical. Trust me, I've thought about this long and hard. There may be some residual attraction left between me and Natalie, but in time it will fade. Just like her feelings if she ever got the chance to really know me."

Jayden shrugged. "All right. I don't know why I'm here if you've already made up your mind. But don't say I didn't warn you."

"I'm so mad at myself," Natalie said to Chelsea. After work, Natalie had shown up at Chelsea's with a bottle of Jose Cuervo and margarita mix and a bag of limes. And once she got all the ingredients into Chelsea's Ninja and pulsed, the drinks were flowing, and Natalie was spilling her guts.

"I can't believe you kept this juicy news to yourself this entire time." Chelsea shook her head with disbelief. "You're usually not good at keeping secrets, and about Jonathan of all people?"

Natalie took a huge gulp of her margarita. "I wanted to tell you, but you've been so busy with Nolan being happy in love. I didn't want to bring my misery to you."

"We're besties," Chelsea said. "You can call me anytime. My door is always open. Even once Nolan and I are married, that won't change."

Natalie glanced down at the beautiful diamond ring Chelsea was sporting. "You're so lucky to have found someone who loves and wants to be with you. I want that someday."

"And you will find it, too," Chelsea replied, reaching

across the sofa to squeeze her hand. "I truly believe there's someone for everyone."

"I thought that someone was Jonathan."

"You've always had a soft spot for him," Chelsea responded, sipping her drink. "I'm not surprised that when the opportunity presented itself you went for it."

"It was so passionate. So intense." Natalie's eyes grew large with excitement at remembering how hot the sex was. "I didn't know I could feel that way."

"With the right person, sex can be transformative. Who brought up the idea of having an affair?" Chelsea inquired.

Natalie raised her hand. "That was my bright idea, but you have to understand the circumstances. We had just slept together and the next morning, the attraction was still simmering on the surface. I wanted to act on it, but I could tell Jonathan was afraid and ready to run, so I clutched on to the first life vest I could find and said what happened in Galveston, stayed in Galveston."

"You were giving him an out at the end?"

Natalie nodded and hung her head low. "I didn't want it to end, and I feared he would walk away, but maybe I should have let him. It would have been a one-night stand that we remembered fondly. Instead, I let myself get in too deep. We became lovers and I stayed in his bed night after night."

"And you fell harder for him, didn't you?" Chelsea asked over the rim of her margarita glass.

"I did, so when Brent texted about issues with the hotel campaign, I used it as a way out to save face so Jonathan wouldn't see how hard it was for me to walk away. But I… I never imagined he wouldn't at least call or text me when I got back. If nothing else than to know I made it back safely, but nothing. It was like I was out of sight, out of mind. This isn't some crush anymore. I got to know him, share our common interests, become lovers. I have feelings for him, and it hurts to feel rejected."

"Of course it does, because you want him to share your feelings."

"But he doesn't."

"You don't know that. He stayed with you for six days in Galveston," Chelsea responded. "It tells me you meant something to him."

"Then why has he been silent?"

"Because he doesn't know how to proceed from here. He's trying to respect your wishes. Despite his protests to the contrary, Jonathan likes you. You should capitalize on that. Pursue him. You might be surprised on how things turn out."

Natalie shook her head. "No, I couldn't do that." She couldn't put herself out there like that. What if he rejected her?

"I've known Jonathan my whole life. He's a good man who went through some hardships in his first marriage, but it's possible he could change. I mean, look at me and Nolan. The odds were against us from being together with his brother going after my family, but we thrived despite the odds against us. I think you can, too. You have to be willing to take a risk to try to break through the walls Jonathan has erected."

Chelsea had a point. She had given herself a pep talk that she was going to take control of her life. The best way to do that was to go after what she wanted. And Jonathan was *who* she wanted. Who she'd always wanted, not just for a weeklong fling, but for a lifetime. "Okay, I'm going to do it."

"You are?"

"You sound surprised."

Chelsea shrugged. "I shouldn't be. I've never seen you talk this way about another man because none of them have ever measured up against Jonathan, the man you've used as the yardstick for all the others."

"You're right," Natalie acknowledged. Her schoolgirl crush for Jonathan was over. In its place were the feelings of a grown woman who knew what it was like to be in the arms of her lover. A lover she would have to pursue until he could see the potential she'd always known—which is that they were meant to be.

Eleven

The next couple of days went by slowly for Natalie. She couldn't get Chelsea's advice out of her head. Natalie was trying to figure out the best approach. Or maybe honesty was the right one. She should come out and tell Jonathan that she wanted him, but not to be friends with benefits. She had to make it clear that she wanted a relationship that led to a long-term commitment. But what would he say? It was risky and went against her self-protective instinct to walk away.

Jonathan had ample time to come to her and let her know he wanted to rekindle their affair, but he hadn't. Instead, he'd given her mixed signals, being flirty at Priceless and distant at the Texas Cattleman's Club. It was hard to read him or know what he wanted.

Rather than a full-on pursuit, she chose instead to go to the Lattimore ranch after receiving an invitation from Barbara Lattimore. Mrs. Lattimore had reviewed H & W Marketing's proposal and wanted to speak with them.

However, this morning Brent had come down with a stom-ach bug, so Natalie was going solo to the meeting. Natalie didn't know if she would seek Jonathan out afterward. She would decide once she made it there. Just in case she ran into him, Natalie wore her favorite dress. A geometric-and-chain-print dress with a trumpet sleeve. The belt around her waist helped show off her curvy figure.

An hour later, she pulled her Lexus through the gates of the Lattimore ranch. She'd never been here before. She'd been to the Grandins' ranch many times with Chelsea. It had been Chelsea's father who convinced Natalie to try horseback riding. She'd been wary of entrusting her safety to the large animals and certainly hadn't thought with her weight she could get on one, but Mr. Grandin assured her she was in good hands. And now Natalie considered her-self a competent rider. She wouldn't win any competitions, but she knew how to handle a horse.

She parked her car outside the beautiful two-story home with a brick facade and made her way up the steps to ring the doorbell. Several seconds later, a woman who had Jon-athan's honey-brown complexion and warm smile opened the door to greet her. Barbara had on jeans, a stylish tunic with beading around the V-neck and cowboy boots.

"You must be Natalie," Barbara Lattimore said.

"I am, and you're Mrs. Lattimore?"

"The one and only. Please come in." She motioned Nat-alie toward a sitting room right off the foyer. "Would you like some sweet tea or lemonade?"

"I would love both if you don't mind," Natalie replied. "I love a good Arnold Palmer."

"Coming right up, and please call me Barbara."

"Thank you, Barbara." While Barbara left to fetch the drinks, Natalie moved over to the sitting room's wood mantel that held several images of the family.

Natalie easily found Jonathan in the family photos. She

was admiring them when Barbara returned with a tray carrying a pitcher of iced tea and lemonade and placed it on the coffee table.

"You have a beautiful family, Barbara."

Barbara smiled and poured equal amounts of each pitcher into a glass for Natalie and handed it to her. "Hopefully that's to your liking."

Natalie took a sip. "It's delicious. Thank you. Though I have to admit I was surprised to receive the invitation to meet with you."

Barbara angled her head to one side. "Really? Jonathan spoke very highly of you and your firm."

"He did?" Natalie chucked nervously and sipped her drink. She hadn't expected he would do anything for her given they weren't on speaking terms. "I mean, he mentioned your cookbook and new products but didn't give me any indication he recommended me."

Barbara shrugged. "That's Jonathan for you. Of all my children, he's always been the hardest to decipher his feelings. He keeps them close to the chest, but not you, my dear."

"What?" Natalie nearly spit out her drink and began coughing instead.

"My apologies for being blunt." Barbara handed Natalie a napkin from the tray, which Natalie used to quickly wipe her mouth. "It's one of my many flaws. Unlike my son, I don't like to beat around the bush."

"Ma'am?"

"At the Texas Cattleman's party, I believe you gushed about how amazing my son was."

Ohmigod, Natalie was mortified. If she could, she would wrinkle her nose or snap her fingers to transport herself out of the room, but instead there was no way out. She glanced up and met Barbara's gaze head-on. "Uh, yes, yes, I did."

"It was nice to hear someone was so fond of him given his rather solitary lifestyle these past years. It gave me hope that maybe he would get out of the rut he's been in and meet a nice young lady like yourself who so clearly adored him, but then weeks went by and nothing. I thought all was lost."

Natalie didn't know where Mrs. Lattimore was going with this line of conversation, so she remained mum and Jonathan's mother continued.

"Imagine my surprise when he spoke so highly of you. Indicated you'd spent some time together. That's when my mom radar went off and I couldn't resist picking up the phone to contact you. Lucky for me your partner, Brent, answered. A wonderful young man."

"I think so."

"Indeed." Barbara smiled conspiratorially at Natalie, and she wondered what his mother knew that she didn't. She soon found out. "Brent told me about your business, how you were thriving and making a profit, so much so, you had just gotten back from a vacation in Galveston."

Natalie swallowed the lump in her throat.

"Did you know my husband and I sent Jonathan to that very city for a weeklong getaway?"

"That was very generous of you." Natalie's throat felt as dry as sandpaper.

"Yes, it was. Small world, isn't it? That you and my son would be in the same city, at the same resort, at the exact same time?"

"Did you arrange for Jonathan to be there?" Natalie inquired.

His mother shrugged. "I may have overheard Chelsea Lattimore saying you were going to a fantastic resort in Galveston and seeing as how you adored my son, I thought he might need a kick in the right direction."

"Barbara..." Natalie couldn't believe her ears. His mother was playing matchmaker.

"Jonathan has been so lonesome all these years. He needs a fine woman to spend time with."

"Things didn't quite go as you envisioned. We aren't together."

"Not yet." She responded with a smile and Natalie wondered what else Mrs. Lattimore had in store. It appeared nothing, because Barbara began discussing her next goals for her culinary empire and soon, they were talking marketing strategies.

They were so engrossed nearly an hour later that Natalie didn't hear the front door open until she glanced up to see Jonathan's towering figure standing in the sitting room doorway. He looked sexy in a designer navy suit with a gray tie that looked like it cost more than she made in a month. Natalie didn't recall ever seeing him in business attire. He definitely wore the suit well, as it was molded to his chiseled frame. "Natalie? What are you doing here?"

"Jonathan Lattimore! Is that any way to treat a guest in our home?" his mother admonished.

Properly chastened, Jonathan lowered his head. "I'm sorry, Mom. I was just surprised."

"*I* invited Natalie over to discuss my expansion plans for my culinary business. You did recommend her firm," his mother stated.

At the comment, Jonathan's dark brown eyes pierced Natalie's waiting for her reaction, but she didn't have one. She was thoroughly disconcerted by the entire meeting. First, learning Jonathan recommended her and his mother's matchmaking by sending Jonathan to her Galveston resort.

"Well, I should be going." Natalie rose to her feet and began shuffling papers back into her shoulder briefcase. "It was lovely to have met you, Barbara. I truly hope I've shown you that H & W Marketing is the right firm to represent you on this journey."

"Of that, I have no doubt," Barbara responded, and walked over to shake Natalie's hand. "You're hired."

"I am!" Natalie couldn't contain the glee from her voice. She never expected Mrs. Lattimore would actually hire her firm.

Barbara nodded. "Send over your contract and I'll have my attorney look it over."

"Yes, ma'am!"

"Jonathan, do be a dear and walk Natalie out," his mother said. "I have to attend to dinner."

"Of course." His eyes never left Natalie's. "It would be my pleasure."

Once his mother left the room, Natalie didn't know what to do. She wanted to take Chelsea's advice and let Jonathan know what she wanted, but they were in his parents' home and now wasn't the right time.

Natalie reached for her briefcase, but she was too slow because Jonathan stepped into the room and grabbed it from her. "I've got it."

"Uh, thank you." She followed him outside and down the steps to her Lexus. He stopped in front of the driver's side and Natalie clicked the open button on her remote, but Jonathan didn't move out of her path.

She hiked up her chin, and heat and confusion spiked anew through her when she met his wolf's gaze. She knew what she saw. Desire. He wanted her, but that wasn't new. She was certain he would be happy to have her back in his bed, but what then? Natalie wasn't prepared to give all of herself and get nothing back in return.

"Don't go," Jonathan whispered.

Natalie shook her head. "I appreciate you giving my company a recommendation to your mother. That was kind of you, but if you think I owe you some sort of payback…"

He frowned. "Of course not. I would never think that, Natalie. I just want to talk to you." He paused several beats and added, "I miss you."

Those words were her undoing.

Jonathan hadn't meant to say that aloud, to let Natalie know how he truly felt, but now that the words were out there, he couldn't, wouldn't take them back. Because they were true. Seeing her sitting in his mother's sitting room made all those feelings come rushing to the surface. It hadn't helped that Natalie wore a deliciously short dress that showed off her legs while the V-neck of the print dress gave him an ample view of her cleavage. She looked amazing and the desire that always seemed to burn brightly between them was waiting to be unleashed again. However, he needed to take care not to hurt her. He was already on thin ice after his two previous fumbles.

"Can we talk?" he asked.

"Where?" She glanced back toward the main house.

He shook his head. "Not here. My house is up the road. Will you come with me?"

"Yes." She didn't hesitate. She was ready to share her feelings, too. It was time *she* pursued him.

He opened her car door, and she took her briefcase from him before sliding inside. "I'll be ahead of you in the Bentley." She glanced around and saw instead of driving his Ford F-450, he had the expensive supercar nearby.

Jonathan didn't realize he'd been holding his breath until a sigh of relief escaped his lips. He noticed his mother peering out the window at them, but didn't care. He took several long strides to his Bentley and within seconds was climbing in and turning on the ignition. He pulled out of the driveway with Natalie following behind him.

His four-bedroom ranch-style home was several miles from his parents'. His parents had gifted him the land on his twenty-fifth birthday. At the time, Jonathan thought he wanted a family of his own. He even hired an architect to design his dream home, which he'd thought he and his ex-wife would share, but by the time the first shovel went into the ground, their marriage was over.

And this was the first time he was bringing a woman to his domain. Usually when he took a woman home, they went to her place, and after their mutual pleasure, he usually drove himself home *alone*. He never stayed over because he wanted to be in his own room at the end of each night. But with Natalie, they'd spent every night together and he hadn't wanted separate rooms. Most nights they'd stayed in his palatial suite. Having Natalie in his home was monumental, but somehow it didn't feel wrong.

He was frustrated as hell and maybe having her here would bring back his sanity. He pictured her warm and naked in his bed with plenty of time to explore and taste every inch of her. Oh yes, this was a good idea.

When he exited the Bentley, Natalie was already out of her car, looking up at the house with oversize double wood doors.

Natalie turned to him. "It's beautiful."

"Thank you," Jonathan said, and walked to the front door. He didn't get to unlock it because his housekeeper was there opening the door.

"Thank you, Josie."

"Natalie, this is Josie, my housekeeper. She's been with our family for years."

"Pleasure to meet you," Natalie said.

"It's nice to meet you, too. I was just leaving to head up to the main house," Josie stated, grabbing her purse from the nearby console table. "Jonathan, I've left some steaks and asparagus for you to grill, potatoes are in the oven."

"Thank you," Jonathan said. Once Josie had gone, he turned to Natalie. Her awe was audible, and he watched her glance at the piano in the foyer and move inward to the formal living room with a floor-to-ceiling stone fireplace and morning area. Sunshine filtered through the kitchen windows and from the wall of glass doors, which showed a covered patio.

"Wow! You have a lovely home." A smile lit up her whole face and made him want to step closer to feel the warmth of it against his skin. "Who designed this place?"

Jonathan was bemused. "You don't think I had anything to do with it?" He removed his business jacket and tossed it over the leather sofa.

"Did you?"

He laughed. "Sort of. I hired an architect to design it, a general contractor to build it and, as for decorating, my mother helped me hire an interior designer."

"She did good," Natalie stated, and then her expression turned somber. "So, why did you want to talk to me?"

Jonathan took off his Stetson and placed it on the console table. When he moved toward her, Natalie took several paces backward, *away* from him. He didn't want that. "What's wrong?"

"I'm here because we need to talk. *I* need to talk."

"All right." Jonathan stayed where he was. "I'm all ears."

She was silent for several beats. Jonathan sensed that whatever it was, it wasn't easy for her to say. "I've always had a crush on you, Jonathan."

"Natalie…"

She held up her hand. "Please let me finish. I need to say this."

He inclined his head for her to continue.

"It was a schoolgirl crush because you were my hero saving me from bullies, but I don't feel that way anymore."

Jonathan didn't know why, but hearing those words made his stomach plunge and he felt like he might be sick.

"What I meant to say is that my crush developed into feelings that a woman has for a man," Natalie continued. "Feelings that were enhanced when we became lovers in Galveston. I want to see where we can go beyond the bedroom."

Jonathan was stunned. This talk wasn't going how he envisioned. He was usually in control of most situations, but with Natalie he never was. He, too, had feelings for her, but they were all jumbled, and he couldn't make sense of them. He also knew that if he let her walk out the door without at least trying, he would regret it. "I want to spend more time with you, Natalie."

"You do?"

"I do." He stalked to her and when he was within striking distance, he tangled his fingers in her braids and drew her close for a kiss.

It was impossible for Natalie to look away from Jonathan because his gaze imprisoned hers. Memories of the incredible week they spent together came flooding back. Oh God, she couldn't run away now and she wasn't sure she wanted to. He must have read her mind because his fingers tightened at her nape and prevented her escape. "Tell me you don't want this."

Natalie did want him, but he wasn't offering her commitment, either. He wanted to spend more time with her *in bed*. She desperately wished she was brave enough to tell him how she really felt—that she wanted marriage and babies and the white picket fence—but she wasn't. She didn't want to lose him, so she was willing to stay with him even though he wasn't offering her marriage or kids. When Jonathan bent his head and brushed his lips over hers, she let him. It was the softest of kisses and she hadn't expected it. She thought he was going to be all hunger and fire, but then another caress of his lips on hers came. And then another. She couldn't help her slight gasp and the parting of her lips, which allowed him to deepen the kiss. Slowly and thoroughly, he explored her mouth, and Natalie couldn't stop from kissing him back because it felt so good to be pressed against him. Soon they were lip to lip, breast to chest, hip to hip.

Of their own volition, her hips circled against him until they were grinding, and she could feel his hard arousal in his pants. They were teetering on the brink of him tumbling her to the sofa and taking her. She had to think. Natalie pulled back from him and to her relief he let her go.

"Is this why you brought me here?" Natalie asked. "For sex?"

"We're good together," Jonathan responded. "We should stop ignoring the obvious."

He was right. The man packed a serious sexual punch, but she wasn't going to make it easy for him, not after the last week of keeping her at arm's length. Everything couldn't be Jonathan's way, all the time.

"I ask you again, what do you want from me?"

Jonathan stared. "I want you in my bed, Natalie, for however long that is, but I'd like to keep this between us."

Natalie nodded. "I see. So you want to be bed buddies."

"Don't you?" When she began to speak, he interrupted her. "Before you say no, I want you to know I'm not trying to keep you a secret, but after the livestream everyone in town knew our business. I don't want that again. I'd like to keep this private. Can't we just see where this goes without putting a label on it? We tried to categorize it in Galveston and clearly that didn't work because we're both miserable. Let's put all our cards on the table. I like you. You like me."

"Are you sure about that?" she asked with a smirk.

He grinned. "I am."

She refused to be a foregone conclusion. "You think I'm easy."

"Absolutely not," he said, moving closer to her, "but I think you're hiding behind anger rather than admitting you want to be with me, too."

She hated that he was right.

His hands framed her face, and he was kissing her again. Plundering her mouth with his tongue. It seemed he couldn't get enough of kissing her, and the feeling was mutual. She *ached* to be with him, and when he pushed one thigh between her legs so he could press his hard length against her, *right there*, it felt so good, she began rocking uncontrollably against him to ease the need inside. Her nipples felt tight in her dress and begged for his mouth. She cried out when he took her jutting nipple into his mouth through the fabric and all.

"I want you," he muttered savagely, flicking the tight bud.

His hands dropped to the hem of her dress and hiked it high enough that he could push her panties aside. Then he slid a finger between her moist folds. She gripped his hand. Natalie wasn't sure whether it was to make him stop or make him go faster. Her hunger for this man was spiraling out of control. His thumb teased her sensitive nub while his fingers plunged in and out of her core.

Natalie released a sob of pleasure and Jonathan's mouth caught it. While his fingers worked her mercilessly, driving deeper inside her, Natalie arched to meet his hand.

"Oh, yes," she cried, trembling as an orgasm began to ravish her body.

"That's it," Jonathan rasped hoarsely. "Let go."

Natalie didn't have any other choice, especially when Jonathan's mouth crashed down on her in a hot, wet and carnal kiss that sent her over the edge. Her mouth broke free as cries of delight were torn from her. Jonathan held her body through the quakes until eventually she began to quiet. Only then did he straighten her panties and set her upright.

"I need a minute." Natalie rushed away from him and in the direction of what she hoped was the bathroom. She found it down the hall and immediately slammed the door, locking herself in. Gripping the sides of the sink, Natalie closed her eyes. She had climaxed on Jonathan's thigh in the middle of his living room like some randy teenager. What was wrong with her? She seemed to have no shame when it came to him. He could make her do anything, *feel* anything.

The schoolgirl crush she'd had morphed into feelings for a funny, sexy man she'd gotten to know in Galveston. She couldn't deny she wanted him, but she also wanted a future and Jonathan wasn't making her any promises that the fiery chemistry between them would lead to a commitment. She would be putting aside her dreams of a future to be with him, but the other option, to be without him, was something she couldn't fathom.

Several seconds later, she heard a soft knock on the door. "Natalie?"

She was afraid of getting her heart broken.

"Natalie, please open up."

"Go away."

He laughed. "I can't very well do that, it's my house."

She snorted. She would have to face him if she wanted to get out the door and back to the safety of her car. Slowly, Natalie stood upright and looked at herself in the mirror. Her eyes were glazed with passion. Passion that the man on the other side of the door seemed to bring out in her.

"Natalie," he called out to her again, and this time she opened the door.

He released a sigh of relief and to her surprise, held open his arms and Natalie rushed into them. He lowered his head, resting it against hers. "Please don't be embarrassed by what we shared. We enjoy each other. There's no shame in that." He lifted her chin so she was looking up at him. "Okay?"

She nodded. He assumed her turmoil was about their sexual encounter, but she was more worried about where they were going. Jonathan didn't want to put labels on them, and they only agreed to see each other and see where it went, which inevitably would lead to the bedroom, but could there be more? Or was she fooling herself into another sexual relationship with Jonathan? When would she finally get the courage to stand up and ask for what she wanted? Natalie didn't know. She only knew she was terrified of turning her back on the chance that she and Jonathan might become more than just lovers.

Twelve

"What do we do now?" Natalie asked Jonathan as she stared up at him with those beautiful deep brown eyes of hers. Her smile was unsure, but sexy even if she didn't know it. Jonathan would like nothing better than to take Natalie to his bedroom and make love to her all night long, but it was still early. His stomach was grumbling and reminded him he hadn't eaten since lunch.

"How about some dinner?" Jonathan inquired. "Josie left steaks for me to grill."

"You're going to cook for me?" She raised a skeptical eyebrow.

He laughed. "I'm no gourmet chef, but I can cook the basics including a mean steak."

"All right, then, yes. Dinner sounds good."

He smiled and headed for the spacious kitchen he had designed. He went to the double-door Sub-Zero side-by-side refrigerator and found the two nicely marbled rib eyes Josie had seasoned. While he occupied himself heating up the grill, he noticed Natalie put her purse on the granite counter and slide her luscious bottom onto one of the high-backed bar stools at the large granite island.

"Would you like something to drink? I'm afraid I don't entertain much so I have some Perrier and beer."

"I'll have a beer."

He grinned. He was pleased she wasn't too pretentious to drink a beer with him. He went to the fridge and pulled out two Heinekens. After screwing off the top, he handed her an ice-cold one and kept the other for himself. He watched as she tipped the bottle back and took a generous swig. The way her lips cupped the rim had Jonathan thinking about how good Natalie was with her mouth.

He blinked and took a pull of beer and returned to his task of cooking their dinner. "So how do you feel about taking on the marketing for my mother's products?" Jonathan asked when his back was turned to Natalie. Although he hadn't asked his mother to give Natalie's firm the job, he strongly advocated for her to use the local company.

"I'm excited," Natalie replied. "It's going to be exactly the shot in the arm we need to help catapult us in the market. Having a Lattimore use our firm is huge, and I have you to thank for it."

He shook his head. "No, you don't. I might have recommended you, but my mother is a businesswoman. She did her research and if she's decided she wants to use you, it's because it's the right thing for her brand."

Natalie grinned. "Thank you."

"For what?"

"You didn't have to put in a good word for me, not when you had no idea where we were going."

"I didn't do it as a quid pro quo and certainly not to get you back in my bed," Jonathan responded "You were passionate when you spoke about your company when we were in Galveston. I listened."

"I don't know what to make of you, Jonathan," Natalie replied. "One minute you're the distant and remote guy I slept with who can't be bothered to call or text me. And in the next breath, you're the man who's speaking on my behalf to his mother."

"I'm not that complicated," Jonathan responded as he checked on the potatoes baking in the convection oven. "I didn't text you because I was trying to honor our agreement. You have no idea, Natalie, how hard it was for me to stay away from you. When I saw you in Priceless, I realized that Galveston wasn't going to be enough. I wanted more, but I had already screwed up and you were angry with me."

Natalie drank more of her beer as she pondered her answer. "I was hurt and confused by your lack of communication."

Jonathan stopped making the dinner and moved toward Natalie at the counter. She didn't move away when he stepped between her legs and grasped her cheeks with his palms, forcing her to look at him. "I'm sorry." He didn't apologize often, but he needed to. Not communicating with Natalie made it easier to treat her as a casual hookup. He kept women at arm's length and he definitely didn't invite them into his home, his personal haven, but Natalie was different. He never wanted any woman as intensely as he did her—because he never wanted to feel the way he had after the failure of his marriage.

Desolate.

Broken.

Unworthy.

Realizing he wanted Natalie more than one week was a complication he hadn't foreseen; he didn't regret it, but he would have to be careful. Natalie wasn't someone who went from affair to affair.

She glanced up at him. "Thank you. I needed that."

He caressed her cheek. "Are we good now?"

She nodded.

"I'm going to finish up dinner." As hard as it was to slide from between her legs, Jonathan removed the asparagus from the fridge.

Soon, the steaks were sizzling on the grill. That's when Jonathan opened the glass doors so he could show Natalie the covered flagstone patio. His property faced the woods and led to a ravine in his own backyard.

The patio was his favorite place. It came with a wet bar, television and built-in stereo system facing a large infinity pool. Steps away was an outdoor stone-clad bar facing a wood-burning firepit with Adirondack chairs surrounding it. His favorite part of the fall season was sitting around the firepit with his brother or some of the ranch hands. He wondered if he would get the chance with Natalie.

They returned several minutes later so Jonathan could take the steaks off the grill and let them rest and put the asparagus in the broiler.

"The more I see the more impressed I am with your home."

"I designed it a long time ago." Jonathan's voice trailed off.

"When you were married?"

He nodded and began preparing their plates. "When I believed in happily-ever-after."

"And you don't believe in it now?"

"No." His answer was definite, and he noticed the smile fade on Natalie's face. But he had to be honest; he didn't want her to get any delusions that what was going on between them would lead to something more serious. He said he would try, but it wasn't a guarantee. "I will never marry again."

"I'm sorry to hear that. You could be missing out on something wonderful."

"That's because you have a fairy-tale version in your mind of what marriage is like," Jonathan responded. "But I know it's not all sunshine and roses."

He learned the hard way that marriage wasn't for him. It was committing to another person; he'd failed it. It was expressing his emotions that had been the hardest thing. It's not like his father or his grandfather showed any. They were men's men who didn't cry and got on with life. Jonathan was raised that way and he didn't know how to change. No matter how great Natalie was, he had no intention of making that mistake twice. He didn't do long-term commitment.

Jonathan's definitive response on marriage was certainly a buzzkill. Natalie finished off her beer and did her best not to show how disheartened she was to hear him say he would *never* marry again. If she continued down this path with him, it was quite possible she would be settling for the right now. The incredible sex and passion they shared was undeniable. The situation, however, was problematic because it went against her long-term goals and what she wanted for her future. She wanted a family of her own someday, but Jonathan was saying it wasn't on the table for him.

Yet she couldn't find the strength to walk out the door and away from him, a man she had wanted and lusted after since she was a teenager.

"Dinner's ready." Jonathan's words broke into her thoughts.

She smiled and slid off the bar stool, joining him at the table he'd set in the morning area between the living room and kitchen. He found some bottled water and poured them both glasses. Jonathan helped Natalie into her chair, and she couldn't help the awareness that rippled down her spine. Instead, she focused on the delicious meal in front of her. She cut into a bite of the steak and moaned at how buttery and succulent the meat was.

"This is amazing," she cooed.

Jonathan's chest puffed out. "I'm glad you like it. Steak is one of the few things as a ranch hand you learn how to cook over an open fire."

"I'm afraid grilling isn't my thing," Natalie replied. "I leave that to my grandpa."

"Do you ever hear from your mother?" Jonathan asked, cutting into a piece of rib eye.

At his question, Natalie placed her fork and knife on the plate. Where had that come from?

She must have had a sour expression because Jonathan was apologizing seconds later. "I'm sorry. You don't have to answer that. I was curious."

Natalie took a deep breath and let the air out slowly. She knew he didn't mean any harm. It was a touchy subject she didn't often speak about.

"When I was younger, years went by, and we never heard from her. Eventually, when I was about twelve and going through puberty and finding where I fit in the world, my mother came back, said she was ready to be a mother again." Natalie picked up her fork and knife and resumed eating.

"And?"

"Six years had gone by." Natalie took a sip of water. "My grandparents had legally become my guardians and were in the process of officially adopting me. She put up a big stink and put me in a very awkward position of choosing between her and my grandparents. The only stable parents I'd ever known."

"I assume you chose your grandparents?" Jonathan asked.

Natalie nodded. "And my mother was angry. We didn't speak for many years and when I turned eighteen, she showed up again asking for forgiveness and hoping we could have some sort of relationship, but by then it was too late."

"What's your relationship with her now?"

"I get the odd birthday or Christmas card from her," Natalie responded, "but we're not close, if that's what you're asking."

Jonathan's hand clamped over hers and he squeezed it. "I'm sure it's been difficult for you."

"Yes, it has, but I've learned to accept who Phyllis is and that she will never be the mother I need her to be. But trust me, growing up that wasn't easy to accept."

"Thank you for sharing that with me."

Natalie lifted her head to meet his eyes and found her mouth dry because there was something else there. And it wasn't pity or compassion. Her heart raced. Sitting here with Jonathan in his home felt natural, like they were a couple. She had to scramble to remind herself that this attraction could burn out, but instead she got lost in his brown eyes.

Her body felt engulfed in flames. With effort, she smiled and reached for her glass of water. She was crazy to consider getting on this roller-coaster ride with him *again*.

"We should take these plates to the kitchen," Natalie said once she'd put her glass down.

She was about to rise when he said, "Leave it." His response was more of a command than a request and Natalie was about to sit down again, but Jonathan was already up and out of his chair, coming toward her.

When he reached her, his hand cupped her chin, and he gently traced her lip with the tip of his finger. Once and then twice. On the second go-round, she couldn't resist flicking out her tongue and gliding it across his finger. She heard his swift indrawn breath.

Then he kissed her gently. She sank into the kiss, relishing every part of him she could touch with her lips and with her tongue. She ached to feel his skin against hers once more. He groaned and reached out quickly to lift her off her feet and before Natalie knew it, her legs were wrapped around his waist and he was carrying her down the hall.

Seconds later, he released her onto a sprawling king-size bed. "Are you okay with this?" Jonathan asked. "And what I can offer?"

Natalie knew she could walk away and that would be it, but she couldn't do it. Instead, she pulled him toward her and their mouths collided. She moaned when Jonathan's hands explored her body and he uncinched the belt holding her dress together. He lifted her up long enough to push the fabric aside and unclasp her bra, releasing her full breasts, which were achy for him.

He was everything she wanted. She cried out when he sucked one of her painfully tight nipples into his warm mouth. A low flame ignited in her belly, especially when he slipped off her shoes and ran his hands up her legs to her panties. He slid them down and off until she was naked, hot and ready for him.

"I've missed seeing you," he murmured.

"I want to see you, too." She reached for his button-down shirt to start unbuttoning, but he pushed her hands away.

"Later," he said, sliding down her body. "It's been too long. I need to taste you."

Natalie felt his warm hands on her thighs as he kissed his way lower. She splayed her legs wide to make room for him and before she knew it, he was licking her core and holding her to his mouth in the most carnal position imaginable. Sobs of pleasure escaped her lips as his tongue caressed her with swirls and licks until she started to tremble.

"Jonathan, *please*… I need you."

He broke free to come up and brace above her, she felt his hard length in his pants and immediately began attacking the buttons on his shirt. Once they were undone, he shrugged it off and allowed Natalie to slide her hands over the damp heat of his broad chest. Then she was unbuckling the belt, unzipping his pants and roughly pulling them over his slender hips.

She wanted him *now*.

He left for a moment to reach for the box of condoms in his nightstand. When he returned, he was already sheathed. He grabbed her hips firmly to him and she gasped. The look of raw lust in his eyes made her spellbound. She thought she was going to die if he didn't make love to her. And then he thrusted. *Hard.*

"Jonathan." Her body instantly locked on his and she clutched him closer, her legs parting so he could fill her completely.

"Hell, Natalie!" he ground out, and frantically began moving inside her.

"Yes," she cried, twisting beneath him. He felt so good. And when he drove deeper still and pumped faster, she rose to meet every fierce thrust. Her hands were greedy for him, grasping his taut bottom. "Oh yes!"

She didn't want him to stop. She wished they could go on and on, pounding together as one. She felt completely free, but soon her orgasm came crashing toward her. When she reached the peak, ecstasy coursed through her, and she shattered.

Jonathan growled and kept thrusting harder and deeper. His eyes were wild as he stared at her. And his skin glistened from the effort as he strained to fight the rising tide, but it was too much. A guttural shout escaped his lips, and he broke. Natalie rode the wave with him as aftershocks rocked his body.

It felt good to be here in Jonathan's home where she belonged.

Thirteen

"Look who is finally free to spend time with the boys," Jonathan's brother, Jayden, said when he met him and some of the ranch hands for drinks on Friday evening. It had been a long day. Several bulls had gotten loose and crossed over into Grandin land and it had taken a lot of wrangling to corral them back to the Lattimore ranch. Jonathan told his crew he would treat them all to some beers for their hard work at the local bar in town. His men had been appreciative, and Jayden decided to join.

"What's that supposed to mean?" Jonathan asked, taking a pull of his beer.

"This week, whenever anyone suggested going out after work, you always had plans," Jayden replied.

"And?"

"You're a bachelor, same as me," Jayden said. "Or maybe you're not." He lowered his voice and pulled Jonathan away from the group so they could talk privately. "Have you been getting busy with Natalie Hastings again?"

Jonathan glanced around him to make sure no one heard him. "You need to keep your voice down. I don't want anyone to hear your speculations."

"They aren't speculation if they're true," Jayden returned, "and your refusal to answer is revealing."

"Fine." Jonathan sighed. "I'll admit Natalie and I have rekindled what we had in Galveston."

"Meaning what? You're hooking up?"

"Something like that."

Jayden snorted. "Do you have any idea what you're doing, Jonathan? Natalie is not the kind of girl you mess around with."

"I know that," Jonathan stated. He thought about it all the time. He never wanted to hurt her. "I have been upfront with Natalie about my feelings on commitment and marriage, for that matter. She's under no illusions."

"Are you sure about that?" Jayden inquired. "Because sometimes women think they can change you."

"Natalie is not like that."

"So, you trust her?"

Jonathan paused before answering because he'd never really thought about it until now, but he did. Natalie was honest and truthful, unlike Anne, who was manipulative and deceitful. "Yes, I do."

Jayden shrugged. "Well, that's saying something because you haven't trusted a woman in a long time. Maybe you should consider whether hooking up is all you want from Natalie."

"Don't go reading more into this than what I've said. Matrimony is not for me." Jonathan was adamant that marriage, a family, the whole bit was no longer in the cards for him. Those dreams died when he stroked the pen on his divorce papers.

"If you say so, but methinks you doth protest too much," Jayden replied.

On his drive home back to the ranch, Jonathan wondered if Jayden was right. Was he leading Natalie on? It certainly wasn't his intention. He'd been as plain as he could be about what he was willing to offer, and he wouldn't promise her a ring. But maybe he should end things and allow Natalie to find a nice guy who'd give her a house with a white picket fence and two point five children?

The thought rang hollow. He ran his hand over his head. He was in quite the dilemma. Let Natalie go so she could find someone worthy of her or allow the flame between them to burn out of its own accord. When his phone rang and he glanced down and saw Natalie's name, he knew it was the latter.

Natalie couldn't believe she was seeing Jonathan. Since the day she went to the Lattimore ranch to meet his mother, they had been together nearly every day. That's when she and Brent weren't working on their plans for how to help Barbara Lattimore market her new line of culinary products.

No one knew about their relationship. Jonathan had made his feelings known that he had no intention of getting married again. *Ever.* They'd fallen into a routine of hanging out either at her cottage in town or as they'd done this past weekend, she stayed at his ranch from Friday night until early Monday morning. They cooked or watched television, or she listened to Jonathan play the piano. Eventually, Natalie would return home for a change of clothes and to get herself ready for the workweek.

She was addicted to the sexy rancher, and although they were acting like a couple, she knew Jonathan didn't want anything more from her. As for the explosive passion they shared, it hadn't diminished. In her opinion, it had become stronger the more time they spent together.

Why couldn't he see what a great life they could have if he only gave marriage a chance?

It didn't help that she was on her way to meet up with Chelsea at Natalie Valentine's bridal shop on Saturday. Chelsea's wedding was in several months and her best friend was looking for the most amazing dress. Chelsea wanted to get a general idea of the dress she wanted before bringing her mother and sisters.

"I want to listen to my own voice and select what I like for my big day," Chelsea had said, and now Natalie was at the shop to be Chelsea's wingwoman.

When she arrived, her best friend was already there talking with one of the shopgirls. She glanced around the brightly lit room with racks of white, ivory and blush wedding dresses of all shapes and styles. Stylish high-backed chairs and tufted benches were in abundance around the store. It had been Natalie's dream to be a bride one day; she just wouldn't be married to her groom of choice.

"Chelsea!" Natalie put on her best smile because she was indeed happy for her friend.

"Natalie! I'm so glad you're here," Chelsea said, rushing toward her and enveloping her in a hug. She looked gorgeous in a simple shift dress, but classic Chelsea because she was wearing cowboy boots.

"So am I. I can't wait to get this party started," Natalie gushed.

"Natalie, this is Miriam. She's going to be my stylist today," Chelsea said of the sleek blonde in a simple black shift dress.

"Pleasure to meet you," Natalie replied.

"Same," Miriam replied, and handed Natalie a glass of champagne as well.

"I was already telling Miriam that I'm getting married in December and it'll be cool out," Chelsea started, "I'm thinking a long-sleeved dress might be in order."

"I love a long sleeve," Natalie replied. "It's classic."

"Have you decided what type of silhouette you would like?" Miriam inquired. "Fit and flare, mermaid, ball gown or sheath?"

"As slim as I am, I'd get lost in a ball gown," Chelsea responded with a laugh.

"I couldn't agree more," Miriam responded. "I honestly think a sheath would be amazing. And if you like, there are dresses with a detachable overskirt. You can have the skirt on for the ceremony to give you the sense of occasion and the sheath as your reception dress so you can move around, have fun and dance."

"I'm definitely open to seeing them," Chelsea said, and went over to a mannequin with a gorgeous sheath dress made with handmade lace. "I definitely want to try on this one."

"Certainly. Come with me and I'll get you set up in a fitting room and then we'll get you in the first dress."

While Chelsea slipped into the confection, Natalie perused the store. She couldn't help imagining the dress she might choose someday if she were walking down the aisle. God, she wished it was to Jonathan. Natalie knew a ball gown wouldn't suit her curvy figure. She would definitely need straps to keep up her full bosom, but figured a fit and flare or mermaid gown would work best. Then Chelsea came out of the dressing room and Natalie was speechless.

Her best friend looked like a princess in a long-sleeved lace sheath dress with an illusion V-neck and corset bodice.

"You look stunning, Chelsea."

"Do I?" Chelsea asked, her pale cheeks turning rosy at the compliment.

"Absolutely."

"Come." Miriam led Chelsea to a dais and her friend stepped on and stared at her reflection in the three-way mirror. Chelsea spun around and looked at the dress from all angles.

"Wow!" Chelsea's chocolate-brown eyes grew large. "Do you see how great this dress makes my butt look?"

Natalie laughed. Chelsea always spoke her mind. It's why they were besties. "You would blow Nolan's mind in that dress."

"I would, wouldn't I? But I can't pick the first dress I've ever tried on," Chelsea admonished. She looked down at the stylist. "Let's try on a few more."

An hour later, Chelsea had changed back into her sheath dress and cowboy boots. Of all the dresses she tried on, her heart was set on the first. She planned on bringing her mom and sisters in to see it. "How about a cocktail? After all that girlie stuff, I could use a real drink."

"Sounds fabulous." Natalie was dying to talk to her about what transpired between her and Jonathan the last few days anyway.

They ended up in the bar area sitting at high tops at Sheen. The new restaurant made entirely of glass had become a favorite among the locals since it opened.

Natalie ordered a martini, while Chelsea opted for a whiskey. She was a cowgirl through and through.

"So." Chelsea leaned back in the chair to look at Natalie. "I loved my hour of being the center of attention, but you know girlie things aren't my thing. What I'm dying to know is, how has it been going between you and Jonathan?"

"Cutting to the chase, huh?" Natalie asked, raising a brow.

"You know it." Chelsea leaned forward on her forearms with a wide grin. "Now stop stalling and dish. Did you or didn't you put the moves on the oldest Lattimore son?"

Natalie laughed. "I didn't need to. He did."

"Really?" Chelsea tipped back her whiskey. "Do tell."

"He recommended me to Barbara to help with the marketing of the new products for her culinary line. She asked me to the ranch and when I was there, who should show up?"

"Jonathan," Chelsea finished.

Natalie nodded. "After our meeting, he asked me to talk. And let's just say talking led to more and then some."

Chelsea rubbed her hands together. "Sounds sinful."

"But…there's more."

"Go on."

"He told me he doesn't want to get married again."

"Urgh!" Chelsea threw her head back in annoyance. "People say that all the time, but that doesn't mean you can't try to change his mind. Hell, you're already halfway there."

"How do you figure that?"

"You got him off his game," Chelsea replied. "Didn't you tell me he usually has casual relationships with women?"

Natalie nodded.

"You're more than that, Nat. He spent the entire week with you in Galveston. And guess what? He couldn't stop thinking about you. And now that you're both back in Royal, he's become fixated with you. I'm telling you— you got that man by the…"

"Don't say it," Natalie said, wagging her finger at Chelsea's bold tongue.

Chelsea shrugged. "I'm merely stating the facts. Jonathan says he only wants to hook up, but is that all you two do when you're together?"

"No," Natalie said. "We talk, we laugh, we cook, watch television."

"Sounds like dating to me. Jonathan just doesn't know it yet."

"I suppose, but he hasn't taken me out on the town, either."

"How do you feel about that?"

Natalie shrugged. "He told me he didn't want the tongues wagging about us like they did after the livestream."

Natalie peered at Chelsea. "But you could be right." Her best friend might be onto something. Jonathan talked a good game and said he wasn't interested in a serious or committed relationship, but his *actions* showed her that they were having one. The million-dollar question was, where would it lead?

Fourteen

"Thank you for inviting me out for a ride," Natalie said on Saturday as she sat astride a beautiful palomino horse. The Lattimores owned a plethora of beautiful prize-winning horses. She was fortunate to be able to ride one of them.

"You're welcome," Jonathan replied. He looked sexy and dangerous in his rugged jeans, plaid shirt, Stetson and cowboy boots.

Jonathan often talked about his love of the open range, but this was the first time he was allowing Natalie to explore his world. Last night she'd been surprised when he hadn't come over to her cottage. Sure, she and Brent had a long night wining and dining a client, but usually Natalie and Jonathan spent their evenings together in bed.

Natalie had tried not to feel abandoned or unwanted. He had no clue that she had issues of abandonment because her mother left her. Even though her grandparents adopted Natalie and Phyllis eventually returned, the stain was still there and Natalie had never been able to blot it out no matter how hard she tried.

And so, when she'd come home to an empty house, she resigned herself to the notion of sleeping in her bed alone, but then Jonathan called, and they stayed up talking on the phone for hours like she had when she was a teenager. That's when he'd asked her to meet him this afternoon at the ranch.

"It really is majestic," Natalie said when, after an hour, they stopped so the horses could rest, get water and a treat. She needed it, too. She was no horsewoman and only rode upon occasion. She would definitely be sore tomorrow.

"I'm glad you think so," Jonathan said. "This is one of my favorite spots. It's why we've stopped. I brought a picnic for us." He untied a picnic basket from his horse Beauty's back and brought it along with a pillow and blanket to a patch of grass.

"You did?" Natalie tried to keep her tone calm, even though joy surged through her at Jonathan's romanticism. It was definitely a date, though she doubted he thought of it that way. And who cares if it wasn't in town; Natalie would soak up spending time with Jonathan while she could.

She watched as he laid out the blanket on the grass underneath a large oak tree and opened the basket. Inside was a delicious charcuterie board of meats from salami to prosciutto, soft and hard cheeses, fig jam, pepper jelly, nuts and fruit.

"Come, sit down and eat," Jonathan said when she stared down at him in bemusement because there was no way he'd made the picnic himself. He had to have help. Surely that meant he cared to go through all the trouble?

She slid to her knees and joined him on the blanket. "I'm impressed with your efforts, Mr. Lattimore."

He turned to her laugh. "You don't think these hardworking hands—" he lifted his large hands roughened from fieldwork in the air "—put this meal together?"

"Absolutely not." Natalie laughed. "But I'm enjoying it all the same." She put some brie and fig jam on a cracker and plopped it in her mouth.

"How about some champagne to wash that down?" Jonathan asked, reaching for the bottle of Veuve and popping the cork.

"I think I can go for that."

He poured them each two plastic champagne flutes and handed her one. "Cheers."

She tapped her flute with his and easily finished the glass in one swig.

"More?" Jonathan inquired.

"Are you trying to get me drunk so you can have your way with me?"

He grinned and his eyes were alight with mischief. "Yeah, is it working?"

"I'll need a few more of these," she said, holding up her flute.

He filled up her glass and they continued their charcuterie feast until the board was damn near empty, along with the bottle of champagne. "Ah, that was amazing." Natalie sighed in contentment and laid her head back on the pillow.

"I concur." Jonathan slid beside her on the pillow. He curled his arm around her waist and hugged her closer against him. She felt so content being held by him. She would take whatever stolen moments she could get, because she didn't want to pressure him into a commitment. On the other hand, she was afraid that moments like this might make her stay with him whether he chose to never marry or have kids. It was all too much; she closed her eyes and drifted off to sleep in the safety and comfort of his arms.

Natalie stretched as she woke from her nap and when she did, she realized someone was against her back. Jonathan.

And he was *hard*.

"Oh," she gasped, and began to move away, but his arm was around clutching her back to his front. Natalie felt the unmistakable shape of him against her bottom.

Natalie tried to wiggle away, but a grumble of dissatisfaction rumbled in his chest. "You're only making it worse."

"Well, what do you suggest we do about it?" Natalie asked. They were in the wide open where anyone could see them if they passed by.

As if reading her thoughts, Jonathan whispered, "No one comes out here, Natalie. Not my family at least. It's kind of like, my spot, you know. And as for my men, they're working hundreds of miles away."

She turned sideways and faced him. "What are you saying exactly?"

He grinned like the Cheshire cat. "That if you wanted to help relieve me of this condition…we're *alone*."

Natalie sat upright. She'd never had sex in public where anyone might see them. It was dangerous. Risky. But when she was with Jonathan, he made her unafraid to live out her wildest fantasies, and making love to her man out in the open would definitely qualify. Jonathan was the man she'd crushed on and had now fallen for; there wasn't anything she wouldn't do for him.

Jonathan watched the indecision on Natalie's round face. He sensed she wanted to live dangerously but was afraid. He would never want her to do anything she wasn't completely comfortable with, so it surprised him when she began unbuttoning her shirt. He was transfixed watching her as she unhurriedly undid each button. When she was free, she pulled the shirt free from the jeans he'd been dying to get her out of since she first arrived at his house. The damn things looked as if they'd been sprayed on and showed off her fabulous *ass*ets.

He sat still only as long as she unclipped her bra and shrugged out of it, sliding the straps off her arms until she threw it on the blanket. Then he rose on his haunches to whip off his shirt and stood to remove his jeans. He helped Natalie to her feet and when she looked down, he cupped her chin.

"You don't have to do this, Nat." He used a nickname he'd only recently started using.

Her eyelashes fluttered open, and she pierced him with her gaze. "I want to." She unzipped her jeans and with one fell swoop took them and her panties off until she was standing naked in front of him.

Jonathan nearly fell backward at being faced with her beauty in the daylight with the sun and flowers all around her; she looked like a goddess. He took her hand in his and laid her back down against the pillow and blanket and looked his fill. He wondered when he would ever tire of her delectable body.

"I can't wait to put my mouth on you," he said, using his fingertips to brush across her abdomen.

"Good, because I can't wait to claim every inch of you." She slid her hand up the back of his neck and, exerting pressure, pulled his head down to hers. Their kiss was wild, raw and incendiary. It spoke of greed and a need between them that had yet to be quenched.

Jonathan's lips left hers long enough for him to take an erotic bite at her nape. Natalie shivered underneath him, but she was claiming him like she wanted, too. She slid her mouth across one of his nipples and then treated the other to the same attention. He gathered her braids behind her neck and exposed her throat so he could take gentle nips of the soft flesh. She arched her body in surrender, mashing her mound against the firm ridge of his erection.

Jesus, if she kept that up, he'd be taking her swiftly, and he wanted to savor her because the longer this went on the wilder she was becoming. Jonathan didn't know how long he would be able to keep this up without wanting to make her *his* permanently. And that was not to be borne.

And so he did the only thing he could: he feasted on her.

Jonathan made her crazy. The way he'd taken her outdoors on the blanket had been nothing short of epic. Natalie was still thinking about it on Monday in her office.

She'd welcomed every moment of his thick intrusion as he stretched her. The way they fit, the delicious friction of his skin on hers. The suck of his lips on her neck, his fingers at her core. Even now, sitting in her office, Natalie still felt the way he ground himself into her, hip to hip, until a wave of orgasm threatened to take her under. There was no way she could have been as open and fearless making love outdoors if she hadn't been with Jonathan, the man she loved.

"Earth to Natalie!"

Natalie blinked out of her erotic daydream to find Brent standing in her doorway.

"Must have been some hot weekend," Brent stated.

Natalie fanned herself. "You have no idea." She reached for the water bottle on her desk and drank generously.

"I was hoping we could go over the best companies we should present to Barbara Lattimore for her brand."

"Yes, of course, come on in," Natalie said. "I was thinking how we could team up with some of the big-box retailers to get her products in their stores."

"I think positioning her as the next Pioneer Woman or something of that sort is the way to go. There's always room for one more at the top."

"I agree with you. Barbara has the down-home Southern feel that will resonate with the public. However, I was looking at her website and I feel like it needs an overhaul to make it fresh and more inviting and user-friendly for the home cook to find recipes. But even more, we need her to have an online shop where readers can buy her products, including those signed by Barbara herself."

"All fantastic ideas, Natalie. I don't know if your tryst with Jonathan had anything to do with us getting this contract, but I'm so thankful."

"I'm glad I could help," Natalie replied, and watched her partner leave her office.

She'd recently confided in Brent about her and Jonathan's vacation fling. She felt it was only the right thing to do, especially since they'd begun seeing each other since returning to Royal. She suspected Brent might worry about the effect this could have on their business, but Natalie wasn't.

The contract with Barbara Lattimore would be ironclad; their lawyers were putting the finishing touches on the document now. Business was business. She had only met Jonathan's mother once, but she struck her as someone of the highest integrity and no way would she fire H & W Marketing because Natalie and Jonathan ended their affair.

Was she nervous about when that day came? Absolutely. But until that day came, she would take this precious time with Jonathan and enjoy it while she could. She loved him and if he gave them a chance, they could have the fairy-tale ending deep down in her gut she knew they were destined for.

Fifteen

"Thank you all for coming," Alexa said when all of the Grandins—Victor Jr., his wife, Bethany, and their four children, Vic, Chelsea, Layla and Morgan—filtered into the Lattimore family room on Friday evening.

His sister had summoned both families to a meeting to give them an update on where they stood with Heath Thurston's claim.

"Have you discovered more information about my dad?" Victor Jr. inquired.

"I'll let Jonas speak on this matter," Alexa replied and turned to Jonas Shaw, the PI they hired to unearth the truth.

Jonas was an older gentleman with salt-and-pepper hair and had a perpetual five-o'clock shadow. He was tall and slim and was more comfortable in jeans than a suit.

"As you know, I had a lead on your grandfather Augustus's former secretary, a Sylvia Stewart. Unfortunately, she's a travel junkie and is off on some wilderness trek. I was finally able to make contact with her briefly, but she was in a remote area with bad cell service. She's agreed to talk to me when she returns."

"That's promising," Layla commented. As the middle daughter in the Grandin family, with long blond hair and blue eyes, she had always been the stunner. Jonathan knew both their families hoped he would have married any of the Grandins, but he'd fallen hook, line and sinker for Anne's schemes.

"As you all know, I have confirmed, after extensive research, that the deed promising Heath and Thurston's mother, Cynthia, the oil rights is legitimate," Alexa stated.

"I still don't believe it," her father responded.

"I'm afraid so, Daddy," Alexa stated. "We can no longer put our heads in the sand and act like this isn't happening."

Jonas stood and spoke. "I've also confirmed Augustus and Victor Sr. had both properties surveyed for oil a year before the rights were signed over to Cynthia."

"What has Augustus said about all of this, Alexa?" Victor Jr. inquired.

"Not much," Alexa answered. "When I asked him about the survey, he denied knowing anything about it."

"He may not be lying," Ben Lattimore stated. "His memory is failing." Jonathan looked at his dad. His dad and grandfather had always shared a close bond, and Ben refused to think ill of Augustus.

"Are you sure about that, Ben?" Victor Jr. asked.

"Of course I am. You've seen him."

"Here's where we are," Jonas said, getting everyone back on track. "The surveys were inconclusive."

"See, there's no oil underneath our lands," Vic, the only son in the Grandin clan, stated. "So there's nothing to deal with."

"I'm with Vic on this one," Jayden replied.

Jonathan wasn't surprised. Jayden and Vic had been

inseparable growing up. If you saw one, the other wasn't far behind.

"Inconclusive doesn't mean no oil," Jonathan's father said, sadly. "We need to talk to Sylvia and see if she can shed any light on this mess."

"I agree with Mr. Lattimore. We need more info from Sylvia and I'm working on that as fast as I can," Jonas stated.

There was a lot of conversation back and forth between the families. Eventually, they decided to have Jonas look into finding if there were any other surveys. He promised to get back with them on next steps. Jonathan was happy when the Grandin family filed out and it was just the Lattimore clan.

"Maybe I should talk to Dad again," his father said, looking around the room. "See if he can remember anything."

"Why upset Grandfather any further?" Jonathan asked, folding his arms across his chest. "It's like you said, his memory is deteriorating. He's ninety-six years old, for Christ's sake."

His father sighed and plopped down on the sofa. "I just hate that we're all in this mess because of something out of any of our control."

Alexa walked over and crouched down in front of him. "We'll figure it out, Daddy. No matter the outcome. I'll help the families navigate it."

He caressed her cheek. "Thanks, baby girl."

Jonathan glanced down at his watch and frowned. He wanted to go over to Natalie's, but it was much later than he'd imagined; the family meeting had taken longer than expected. He had an early morning tomorrow, so he would see her another day.

"Problem?" his mother asked, coming to his side.

Jonathan shook his head. "Not at all. It's later than I thought."

"Did you have plans?"

Her question sounded innocent, but it seemed like she was fishing. Jonathan knew she suspected something was going on between him and Natalie, but she hadn't pressed. "No. Early morning is all. I'll see everyone later." He waved good-night to the family and after kissing his mother on the cheek made a quick exit before she could start the Spanish Inquisition.

Once outside, he exhaled; he'd escaped the firing squad. Reaching in his back pocket, he pulled out his cell and dialed Natalie's number. She answered several seconds later with a breathy "Hello."

"Hey, babe."

"Are you on your way?"

"Afraid not. It's late and I have to get up early for a ranch meeting."

"Oh, all right." He heard the disappointment in her voice, and he felt the same. He liked falling asleep with Natalie in his arms and even more waking up and making love to her in the wee hours of the morning.

"I promise I'll make it up to you."

"I'm holding you to it."

He ended the call and walked to his truck with a smile. He and Natalie had only been seeing each other for a couple of weeks but she'd quickly become important to him. For nearly a decade, he'd kept his relationships casual because there had never been a woman he wanted to try to make a go of it with, but Natalie was chipping away at his resistance to commitment. Jonathan said he'd never marry again, but if anyone made him want to be wrong, it was Natalie.

"I'm so happy you could come out with me, sweetheart," Natalie's grandmother said when they met to go to the farmers' market on Saturday morning.

Every week, farmers and vendors from Royal and the

surrounding counties came to sell fresh produce, delight-ful treats, handmade items, plants, jewelry and sometimes even artwork underneath the shaded tree canopy of the town square.

"Sorry I've been MIA the last couple of weeks, Mimi," Natalie replied.

"It's fine. You're an adult now. I know you have your own life," her grandmother said.

"But I always have time for you," Natalie said, circling her arm into her grandmother's. "What do you want to pick up today?"

"Oh, a little bit of this and a little bit of that." Her grand-mother loved stopping at different vendors and seeing which vegetables or fruits looked good before deciding what to buy.

Natalie was much more decisive, going with a list of exactly what she wanted.

They stopped at a vendor selling fresh peaches and plums. Natalie was testing the fruit out for firmness when she heard someone calling her name. She was surprised to turn around and see Barbara Lattimore with Jonathan not far from her side.

"Natalie." Barbara came toward her and kissed both of her cheeks. "What a surprise running into you here. Isn't it, Jonathan?" She looked up at her son.

Natalie was thinking the same thing. Jonathan told her he was working this morning, which is why he hadn't come over to her cottage last night. Instead, he was shopping with his mother. Did he not want to spend time with her? If not, he only had to say so. They had been spending an awful lot of time together. She understood if he wanted some breathing room.

Natalie plastered on her best smile. "Barbara, have you met my mother, Claudette Hastings?"

"Oh yes, we know each other," her grandmother replied,

patting Natalie's arm. "Barbara and I sit on the same auxiliary committee for the church."

"I had no idea," Natalie replied.

"That's because you need to come to church more often," her grandmother chastised. "Then you could meet that fine young man I told you about," her grandmother said, giving Jonathan the once-over. She had told her mimi she was moving on from her crush, but that was far from the case.

"I declare." Barbara touched her chest and her eyes narrowed in on Natalie. "I had no idea you were dating someone."

Natalie could only imagine what was running through Jonathan's mother's head, that Natalie was doing double duty and dipping out on her son, which wasn't true. "Oh, I'm not dating anyone at the moment, Barbara," Natalie said, and prayed her nose didn't extend like Pinocchio's. "I've just been focusing on my business."

"Is that right?" Barbara hazarded a sideways glance at her son, who remained quiet and stalwart at her side. Natalie wondered what he was thinking. Was he jealous that her grandmother was trying to fix her up? When Jonathan didn't speak, she said, "These fruits look amazing, Claudette. Did you see the other peaches Mrs. Mabelle has two tents away?"

"No, I hadn't," her grandmother stated.

"Allow me to show you." Barbara led her grandmother away, but not before giving Natalie and Jonathan a conspiratorial wink. Did she know they had been seeing each other since she'd revealed her matchmaking scheme?

"What are you doing here?" Natalie whispered underneath her breath as several townspeople were milling around the square. She wanted to appear casual at their chance meeting and not portray any emotion or feeling at being this close to Jonathan. "I thought you had to work?"

Jonathan smiled as he glanced around him and murmured, "I did, but my mother asked me to come with her when I was done because she needed my brawn because she was buying cases of fruit for the annual Bake-Off coming up next week."

Natalie nodded as several people she knew passed by them.

"Am I going to see you later?"

"That depends," Jonathan whispered. "Do you have a date tonight with someone I should know about?"

Natalie chuckled. "Are you jealous?"

"Why would I be?" Jonathan said. "You're mine. I own your orgasms."

Natalie blushed at his incendiary words. For someone who wasn't interested in a relationship, he certainly sounded possessive. "Jonathan!"

"I missed you last night."

Underneath her lashes, Natalie glanced up at him. "You did?"

"You know I did. Let me finish up with my mother and stuff at the ranch, then I'll come by tonight. I'm all yours until Monday morning."

"I like the sound of it."

"Good. And you better steer clear of your grandmother's matchmaking. Otherwise, I might have to spank you later."

"Promises. Promises," Natalie whispered, and Jonathan laughed as he sauntered away. She was beginning to suspect Jonathan might be equally invested in their relationship despite his denials to the contrary.

It was hot as blazes in Natalie's garage by the time she dropped off her grandmother and got to her favorite Saturday afternoon activity. But she wasn't going to let it deter her from taking the old maple slant-front desk she had eventually gone back to purchase at Priceless and turning it into a wedding present for Chelsea. It was going to take some elbow grease, which is why she'd put on cutoff jean shorts and a tank top.

A lot had to be done. She removed the old hardware and then cleaned the desk with some mineral spirts using a microfiber cloth so she could fix any blemishes.

Going with the grain, she used sandpaper to take off the topcoat with her sander. Then she used a sanding sponge and hand-sanded the corners and edges. When she was done, she went over it one more time with her sander and another cleaning with mineral spirits. The desk was already looking better.

She was in the middle of priming the desk when she heard the roar of a truck engine come up her driveway. Natalie stood upright and saw Jonathan come swaggering toward her.

She grinned. "What are you doing here so early?"

"I finished my work, but you didn't answer your phone, so I thought I'd come by and see what you were up to." Jonathan pulled her toward him and into a long searing kiss. When he released her, he glanced around the garage. "What are you working on?"

"Remember that piece I was admiring at Priceless? Well, I'm refinishing it."

"Need any help?"

"Sure. You can help me prime it," Natalie said. "But we need to tape it off first."

"All right."

Natalie watched with glee as Jonathan unbuttoned the plaid shirt he'd been wearing and placed it over a chair, leaving him in one of his muscle T-shirts. She loved when he wore them because they showed off his broad chest and chiseled abs. Working on the ranch ensured there wasn't an inch of flab on Jonathan's abdomen. Natalie handed him some blue tape.

"So how did the meeting go with you and the Grandins last night?" Natalie inquired as they worked in tandem to place tape around the edges of the desk.

"Not much has changed," Jonathan replied as he filled her in on what happened.

"That sounds positive," Natalie said. She passed him one of the bottles of primer along with a face mask. "We're going to use this to spray the desk and then we'll sand it again."

"Sounds like a lot of steps," Jonathan said, putting the mask on, but he did as she instructed.

They sprayed the desk, and it was time to sand again. She wiped the sweat from her forehead with a rag tucked in her back pocket. Jonathan's T-shirt was soaked as well, but he'd never looked hotter. If she had her druthers, she'd strip him naked, and they'd make love on the floor of her garage. That's how oversexed Natalie felt when Jonathan was around.

She used a sanding sponge to clean the desk one more time before applying another coat of primer.

"Okay, I think this thing is ready for paint. We need to put a cloth down to protect the garage floor." She walked over and grabbed a few paint-splattered cloths sitting in a nearby bin.

"I have to tell you, Nat, this is an awful lot of work to go through. You call this fun?" Jonathan said as he lifted the desk so Natalie could place a drop cloth underneath it.

Natalie lifted her head up and smiled at him. "The reward at the end is so worth it because you have a beautiful new piece." She wished Jonathan could see that their relationship could be made new again exactly like the desk. With time and a little care, love could be their reward. She walked over to grab the gallon of blue paint she was using to paint the desk along with two paintbrushes. "One for you—" she gave Jonathan a brush "—and one for me.

"You'll see." Natalie squatted to the floor and commenced to lightly stroke the paint onto the legs of the desk. Jonathan imitated her actions on the opposite side. Along the way, Natalie used her sanding sponge to go over each coat of paint. In the end, when the legs and front of the desk were complete, Natalie cleaned the top and then stained it with an oil-based wood finish and finished it with a polyurethane seal coat. Jonathan was a godsend and helped her install the new gold hardware pulls.

Hours later, Natalie stood back to admire the finished product. "So." She gave a sideways glance to Jonathan. "What do you think?"

Jonathan nodded. "I have to tell you, Nat. When I got here, I thought you were out of your mind to take on a project like this but seeing the result, I'm impressed with your work."

Natalie beamed with pride. "You are?"

"Oh, absolutely," Jonathan said. "Your attention to detail is top-notch. I think Chelsea is going to be really happy with the desk and those other two pieces from Galveston."

"I hope so," Natalie said. She wanted to give her best friend something from the heart because Chelsea had always been there for Natalie and never abandoned her. "How about a beer? I think you deserve one."

"A beer and then a shower," Jonathan said.

"In that order?" Natalie asked.

He laughed. "Oh yeah. Because after the shower, I think we're going to need a nap."

Natalie smiled, knowing that the last thing they were about to do was sleep.

Natalie was feeling good. Better than she'd ever felt. Life was going splendid. H & W Marketing was going better than ever. The signed contracts had been couriered back to Barbara Lattimore's attorney and to her surprise, Jonathan offered to take her to RCW Steakhouse to celebrate. It was the first time he suggested taking her out in public. She'd understood he didn't want town gossips knowing their business, but it did sting a little that he didn't want to show her off.

Tonight was different, so she decided to treat herself to a new outfit at the Rancher's Daughter. Natalie didn't often visit the upscale fashion boutique owned by Chelsea's sister Morgan in the heart of downtown Royal, but a dinner out with Jonathan fit the occasion.

Morgan greeted her almost instantly upon her arrival with air kisses. "Natalie, it's so good to see you. Welcome to the Rancher's Daughter." Morgan was a vision in a green jumpsuit. It set off her long red hair and fair complexion perfectly.

Natalie smiled. "Thanks for the warm welcome." She glanced around and saw several other patrons milling about the store. "I've been dying to have a look around." She'd only been once with Chelsea for the grand opening.

"I have a slew of new items in the store. Walk around and have a look. Let me know if you need anything," Morgan replied. "I'm here to help."

"Definitely." Natalie walked over to the racks carrying several evening dresses. She was perusing the hangers when a pair of tawny brown legs came into her line of sight. She glanced up and saw a statuesque woman standing in front of her. She was taller than Natalie's five foot seven inches, slender with long dark brown hair and wearing what looked like designer clothes.

"Natalie Hastings?" the woman asked.

Natalie's brow crunched in confusion. "I'm sorry. Do we know each other?"

"No." The woman shook her head. "We've never met,

but I have some insight on Jonathan Lattimore you might want to know."

Instantly, Natalie's radar went into high alert. When she glanced back at the woman, her eyes narrowed sharply and that's when recognition dawned. She was standing in front of *her*.

Anne Lattimore, Jonathan's ex-wife.

"Ah, so you realize who I am," Anne stated, folding her arms across her small breasts. Natalie hated that she felt inferior to Anne in her frumpy pantsuit. She'd come from a business meeting and hadn't thought about changing when she decided to pop into the store spur of the moment.

"I do, but I'm not sure what you and I would possibly have to discuss." Natalie sidestepped Anne to continue looking through the array of clothes Morgan had on display.

"Oh, I think we do," Anne stated, moving back into Natalie's path. "Especially when you tell the entire town you've got a thing for my husband."

Natalie turned to face her and her eyes flashed fire. "Ex-husband."

Anne shrugged. "Semantics."

"If you'll excuse me." Natalie kept searching the next rack, flinging back hanger after hanger. She wasn't even looking at the clothes anymore. She just wanted out, but she refused to make a scene. She glanced up and saw Morgan stepping forward to intervene, but Natalie shook her head. She could stand up to the likes of Anne. This woman hurt Jonathan and *she* was the reason he wasn't willing to commit or marry again. She wasn't interested in anything Anne had to say.

"I will *not* be excused," Anne said. "Because you're wasting your time if you think Jonathan is some prize catch."

Natalie's head snapped up. "What are you talking about?"

"You think I can't tell you're sprung on him." Anne's voice rose several octaves and Natalie hated that several patrons were listening, or should she say eavesdropping, on their conversation. "The whole town can see it. You're not fooling anyone. But let me tell you something." She pointed her index finger in Natalie's face. "Jonathan is not husband material. If he can't commit to me—" she ran her fingers down her side "—he sure as hell won't commit to someone like you."

"You're really hateful, you know that?" Natalie had been faced with women like Anne her entire life and she refused to be put down again. "No wonder Jonathan didn't want to stay married to you."

"I divorced him!" Anne's face turned red. "Because he doesn't have it in him to commit to anyone. If I were you, I'd walk away now before he breaks your poor pathetic heart."

The dig hit the mark. Natalie wanted to recoil and hide away in a shell like a tortoise, but she refused to show Anne she'd hurt her, especially with everyone in the store openly staring at them. Instead, she lifted her chin and was about to give Anne a piece of her mind, but she didn't have to because Morgan intervened.

"Anne, I'm going to have to ask you to leave," Morgan said, moving between them.

"Why?" Anne huffed. "I didn't do anything but tell her—" she inclined her head in Natalie's direction "—the truth."

"You're harassing my customers and I will not have it," Morgan added. "Leave. *Now.* And you're no longer welcome in my store."

"Fine." Anne tossed her hair back and hazarded a glance at Natalie. "But don't say I didn't warn you. Jonathan will never love you or anyone because he's never gotten over me." And with that stinging comment, Anne left the store.

"Ohmigod!" Morgan rushed over and touched Natalie's arm. "Are you okay? That woman has always been a bitch. I should've banned her years ago."

Natalie shook her head. She was far from okay. The things Anne said resonated because Natalie wondered them herself. Would Jonathan ever get over Anne and his divorce? Was Natalie spinning her wheels waiting for him to realize she was what he'd been looking for his whole life?

"You can't believe a thing that woman said. She was being spiteful and vindictive because she's jealous of you."

Natalie heard the words coming out of Morgan's mouth, but she was in too much of a daze. She felt like the walls were closing in and she couldn't breathe. All she could do was thank Morgan for the help and rush out of the store. Once outside, she leaned against the window and took in big gulps of air.

Was Anne telling the truth? She knew her "advice" was fueled by anger and jealousy, but her words made sense. She and Jonathan had been dating for two weeks and nothing had changed. Natalie thought she could accept loving him without the things she held dear like marriage and children, but she'd been wrong. She couldn't do this anymore. She had to face facts: she was in love with a man who refused to commit to her and was quite possibly still hung up on his ex-wife.

Sixteen

"Someone is pretty chipper," Jayden said when he stopped by Jonathan's office at the ranch to get him to sign some papers.

Jonathan grinned. "Yeah, I am." He was happy. If he was honest, it had been much too long since he'd felt this way. But ever since he'd begun seeing Natalie in Royal, he felt like his entire outlook on life had changed. She was a positive influence and he mostly never thought about all the bad stuff that happened to him. Instead, he focused on the good things, and Natalie was one of them.

It's why he'd finally decided they needed to go out for a real date. The last couple of weeks they'd been holed up at either his house or her cottage. Enough was enough; he needed to treat Natalie like the lady she was and not some random hookup he casually had sex with. He'd invited her to dinner tonight at the RCW Steakhouse. When dinner was over, he intended to take Natalie back to his place and make love to her until the sun rose.

"And is there a cause for such elation? Or shall I say who is the cause?" Jayden asked, sitting in the chair opposite Jonathan's desk.

Jonathan leaned back in his chair. "Yes, and you know who."

A wide smile curved Jayden's mouth. "I'm so glad to see you are letting someone in. Natalie is a spectacular lady. I can't wait to get to know her better."

Jonathan wasn't making any family introductions anytime soon. They were taking baby steps. The first being a dinner out on the town. "She is, and I'm taking her out to RCW tonight to show her how much I appreciate her."

"Grand gestures," Jayden said. "I approve. Though I wouldn't know about all that. I'm quite happy with my bachelorhood status."

Jonathan chuckled. "Enjoy, my friend, because you never know when Cupid's arrow is going to strike."

After Jayden left and Jonathan was closing up shop for the day, he received a call from Morgan Grandin. She didn't usually call him out of the blue. "Hey, Morgan, is everything okay?"

Morgan sighed. "I'm afraid not. An altercation took place at the Rancher's Daughter."

Jonathan sat upright in his chair. "Are you okay?"

Morgan let out a low laugh. "Nothing like that, but I did want to make you aware that Anne made a visit to the store."

Now there was a name he didn't want to hear, especially not now when he was in a good headspace. "She did?"

"Yes. And it wasn't to buy clothes," Morgan replied. "She accosted Natalie at the store."

"What happened?" His voice was terse, but his body was already surging forward, ready for an attack.

"I couldn't hear the entire conversation. I only saw

Anne getting in Natalie's face and the expression Natalie wore. Whatever Anne said, her words were upsetting."

"Thank you for letting me know. I'll take care of things from here."

"Of course," Morgan replied, "but if you don't mind my asking, why would Anne be getting into it with Natalie? Is something going on between you two?"

Although Jonathan was taking Natalie on a public date, he wasn't ready to reveal his love life to all his family and friends just yet. "I'll talk to you later, Morgan." He quickly ended the call before she could ask any more questions.

Steepling his fingers, Jonathan wondered what Anne and Natalie spoke about. What had she said that could have upset Natalie? He hoped Natalie wouldn't take anything his ex-wife said at face value, but there was only one way to find out. He had to talk to Natalie.

Natalie stared at her reflection in the mirror. As much as she wanted to get ready for her date with Jonathan, she couldn't. Outwardly, she looked fine, but inside she was a hot mess. Anne's angry words kept running through her mind like they were on some kind of interminable loop. All Natalie could hear was that Jonathan was never going to love her because he was still hung up on Anne.

That cut because no matter how often she told herself she could wait and see if Jonathan fell in love with her, deep down she knew better. She'd been holding out hope that the more time they spent together, he would rescind his no-marriage proclamation, but she was fooling herself.

When they came back to Royal, it had been easy to put those feelings on the shelf because Jonathan behaved like a total jerk by not reaching out to her. But then he recommended her company to Barbara and that's when Natalie realized she wasn't the only one infatuated. But was that all she was to him? A convenient sexual partner who was compatible in the bedroom?

She had to accept the reality of her situation and give up the dream that Jonathan would ever feel differently. Natalie couldn't regret the few weeks she'd spent with him. She lived out her fantasy. However, she told Jonathan she wanted the white picket fence, and she had to hold out until she got it.

The doorbell rang, interrupting her musings. When she glanced through the peephole, she saw it was Jonathan. He was early and she wasn't ready. She flung open the door.

"What are you doing here?" she asked. "I thought you said six thirty." It was only five thirty, but then looking at him, Natalie realized he wasn't dressed for dinner, either. Instead, he wore a serious expression. "Jonathan? Is everything okay?"

"I could ask you that," he said, stepping inside without waiting for an invitation.

"I don't follow."

He looked down at her and Natalie understood. He knew. Knew about Anne and what occurred at Morgan's store. "You heard?"

"Morgan called and told me my ex-wife accosted you. She said you were visibly shaken. What did she say to you, Natalie?"

Natalie spun away from him. "I don't want to talk about it, plus it doesn't matter anyway. I can't believe anything she says."

Jonathan touched her shoulder and spun her around to look at him. "Don't do that, Nat. Don't act as if you're not hurting. I can see that you are."

Darn. She thought she was doing a good job of not showing what was brewing inside. "I'm fine."

"Don't lie to me. I thought you said you would never do that."

He had her again. Natalie lowered her head. She thought about what edited version she could give Jonathan of what Anne told her, but she knew she couldn't do that because she deserved to hear what Jonathan had to say in response to Anne's words.

Natalie looked up into Jonathan's sincere brown eyes. "She accused me of being sprung on you, told me the whole town could see I was making a fool of myself over you, a man that wasn't husband material and would never commit to me."

"Natalie. I'm sorry. You have to know that she was lying," Jonathan stated.

"About which statement?"

"That you're making a fool out of yourself. You're not," Jonathan said. "You know how I feel about you."

Natalie's eyes narrowed. "Do I?"

He stepped backward as if he was flummoxed about why she would think otherwise. He never told her how he felt. "Yes, you do. Natalie. C'mon, don't let Anne get into your head."

"I'm not," Natalie responded. "After Anne confronted me, I realized that you would never commit because nothing has changed between us and that doesn't work for me, Jonathan. I want a commitment, marriage and babies, and if I stay with you, I would be settling for less than what I deserve and giving up my dreams for the future."

Jonathan huffed. "Why are you letting her do this? Anne said those things to hurt you. If I didn't want to be with you, I wouldn't be here."

"Anne didn't do anything but say what I already knew. You told me yourself that you would never marry. Has that changed?"

"We're getting off track. We've had an amazing couple of weeks together. In case you hadn't noticed, I can't seem to keep my hands off you."

He moved toward Natalie and tried to wrap his arms around her waist, but she pushed him away. She couldn't, *wouldn't* confuse the conversation by putting sex into the equation. She'd done that enough with Jonathan and right now she needed answers.

"Jonathan, stop it!" Natalie yelled.

"What?" he asked, moving away from her. "I'm trying to show you how much I enjoy being with you, Natalie."

"And that's the problem. Our relationship is physical, but I want more."

"I've been trying!" Jonathan exclaimed. "All our time isn't in the bedroom. We've done other activities."

"And afterward, we ended up having sex. And I can't do this anymore…" She was finding the courage to speak her truth. She had to be brave even though it hurt.

"You can't what? Believe in me?" Jonathan inquired. "Because I've never lied to you."

Tears slid down Natalie's cheeks because they were finally getting to the heart of the matter. Down to brass tacks and what she'd known but had tried to hide from. "I want a commitment, Jonathan. I deserve it. Can you give me that?"

"Natalie, don't do this," Jonathan pleaded.

"Call you out?" Natalie asked, raising her voice and wiping the tears on her cheeks with the back of her hand. For too long she had been covering up the truth because they shared a phenomenal physical connection, but no more.

"Just say it, Jonathan. Because right now, I need to hear it again. Maybe then it will finally sink in."

Jonathan stared back at Natalie's tearstained face. He hated seeing her crying and so upset and knowing he was the reason behind it. He wanted to be able to give her the commitment she deserved, but he wasn't able to.

It was unfair of him to take advantage of her infatuation with him and her inherent kindness and goodness any longer. He hadn't realized how much he needed some joy and happiness in his life until Natalie. She was like a breath of fresh air. But she was also a woman who wanted marriage and babies. He couldn't give her that, and the best thing he could do right now was set her free so she could find someone worthy of her—because he wasn't that man. He didn't deserve her.

"I'm sorry, Natalie," Jonathan said. "You'll never know how much, but I will never commit to you or anyone else."

Jonathan saw the moment his words reached her because a light went out in her eyes. He'd crushed her hopes and dreams. Natalie clutched her stomach as if she was going to be physically ill and bent over. Jonathan wanted to go to her. Hold her in his arms. Kiss her. Make love to her and tell her everything was going to be all right.

But it wasn't.

They couldn't continue like this because it wasn't what Natalie wanted and he would never want her to settle for less than what she deserved.

When she finally righted herself, she asked, "Because you'll never love anyone else because you've never gotten over Anne?"

The easiest thing to do would be to lie to Natalie saying he was still hung up on his ex-wife, but Jonathan was no coward. He had to be honest with her, even if it hurt.

"I'm not in love with Anne," Jonathan responded. "I'm not cut out for the long-term."

Natalie stood, nodding furiously and swiping away tears off her cheeks. "You told me that. I should've listened."

"I wish I could be the man you need me to be."

This time when she looked at him, her eyes connected with his and they glittered with anger. "You can be, Jonathan, but you choose not to be. You've kept everything between us about sex so you can't be hurt. I'm here to tell you that people are going to let you down. That's life, but it doesn't make love and marriage wrong. You have to quit judging me and every other woman based on your past experience with Anne because she let you down. It's not fair to us and most of all, it's not fair to you."

"You don't understand." There was so much more to the story that he'd never shared with another soul. No one knew the heartache and pain he endured.

"And apparently I never will," Natalie said quietly. "I think it's best if you leave now."

Jonathan agreed. He picked up his Stetson and started toward the door, but then he couldn't resist going to Natalie one final time. He grasped her waist and at first, he thought she was going to resist, but she came to him like some limp rag doll.

He leaned and brushed his lips across her forehead and whispered, "You deserve the very best, Natalie Hastings. Thank you for sharing a few weeks with me. It's been the happiest I've been in a long time." Then he released her and walked out of her life.

Seventeen

"He didn't fight for me, Chelsea, for us, for what we could be," Natalie told her best friend later that evening when she sent out an emergency SOS. Chelsea left Nolan's and immediately rushed over to Natalie's cottage. "Instead, he gave me a forehead kiss and left. He left." Natalie snapped her fingers. "As if we meant nothing."

It's why she hadn't told him she loved him; she refused to give him those precious words knowing he didn't feel the same way, so she kept them to herself.

"I'm so sorry, Natalie," Chelsea said, consoling her. "I should never have advised you to chase after Jonathan. Not when I knew how strongly you felt about him."

"I don't blame you, Chelsea." Natalie sniffed into her Kleenex. "I blame Jonathan for being too cowardly to try again. So, what, Anne hurt him and did a number on him? No matter how many times you get on the horse and fall off, you're supposed to get back on. Instead, he's wallowing in his self-despair and carrying it around like some coat of armor."

Chelsea nodded. "I thought the more time you spent together, Jonathan would see what a great catch you are and that he didn't want to let you get away."

Natalie snorted. "He was more than willing to throw this fish back in the sea."

"Nat, I hope this doesn't deter you from trying again. You deserve a man who loves and wants you. Who's willing to fight for you."

"It won't deter me." Natalie shook her head. "If nothing else I think this experience taught me what I deserve and what I am and am not willing to accept. I think because it was Jonathan, I gave him way more latitude than I would any other man. Because for me, he's always been *the one*."

Chelsea nodded.

Natalie's head fell in her hands, and she began crying again in earnest. She couldn't stop herself. Once Jonathan walked out her door, she crumbled on the floor. It's where Chelsea found her after using the spare key—exactly where Jonathan left her.

"He broke my heart, Chelsea, and I let him. I didn't fight for what I wanted. All we were doing was hooking up."

"That's hogwash and you know it," Chelsea said. "You guys may have gotten busy quite a bit, but there was more to you than just a physical relationship. You told me so yourself."

"I was delusional. Like I was about everything where Jonathan was concerned."

"Hey." Chelsea lifted Natalie's chin. "I'm not going to let you get down on yourself. You misjudged him. We all make mistakes, but you were open and willing to give him your heart and if he can't see what a precious gift that is and grab it with both hands, he's a fool."

A smile formed on Natalie's lips. "Thank you, Chelsea. I don't know what I'd do without you."

Yeah, she did—she would drown herself in her despair by eating an entire peach pie.

Jonathan shrugged off his work jacket. He had been up with the sun because he needed physical labor to keep him busy and take his mind off Natalie and the look in her eyes when he once again confirmed he would never commit to her, love her like she wanted. He'd hurt her.

It had been two days since he left her Friday night and he was still reliving the moment, reliving the memories of their short time together. The way she laughed with him. The way she looked at him. The way she held him. When they were together, she felt so good, he never wanted to let her go. It made him want to become the man she needed him to be, but he couldn't. He couldn't take that risk. He was doing the right thing for both of them. She would get over him, over the possibility of them. She was better off without him and all his hang-ups.

"Whoa! What's with you this morning? You're attacking these chores like hay is your archenemy," Jayden said when he found Jonathan in the barn, hot and sweaty, helping the ranch hands with the horses and cleaning out stalls.

The devastation lurking in the brown depths of Natalie's eyes gutted Jonathan, and he'd been unable to sleep. "Couldn't sleep." Jonathan said, tossing a bale of hay across the stable, ignoring Jayden's attempt at humor.

"Oh Lord!" Jayden sighed audibly. "What the hell happened to make the old, sullen Jonathan return?"

"I'm not in the mood for your antics today, Jayden." Jonathan went to the next stall and began cleaning.

"I want to know how you can go from giddy happy one day to cold and mean the next."

Jonathan didn't want to listen to Jayden, so he grabbed

his brother by the arm and pulled him toward his office down the hall. Once the door was closed, he pulled off his gloves one by one. "Natalie and I broke up."

Jayden frowned. "Why? What did you do?"

"Why do you assume I did something?" Jonathan said, plunking down in the executive chair behind his wood desk.

"Because Natalie is a great girl who adores you. The way she gushed about you at the TCC party was nothing short of romantic."

"Fine, then it was me. Natalie realized she was never going to change me into the commitment kind of man she wanted, the kind of man she deserved."

Jonathan was upset with himself for not expressing his feelings more clearly, so Natalie didn't see a ring on her finger. "It's for the best."

"What is?"

"That Natalie called things off. We were never going to work."

"That's a lie and you damn well know it," Jayden responded. "I haven't seen you this happy in, hell, I don't remember when. Natalie lit up your world and you're an idiot for letting a woman that fine get away."

"You're wrong."

"Wrong that you're afraid to admit you have feelings for Natalie? Oh no, I'm right about that. Don't tell me it won't burn you to see Natalie with another man."

Jonathan closed his eyes and thinking about Natalie with another man made his blood boil.

"What are you so afraid of, bro?" Jayden asked. "You have a good woman who is ready to devote her life to you and have a bunch of your babies. You should be snatching her up in a heartbeat because I promise you, your loss will be another's man gain."

Jayden's words remained with Jonathan long after he'd

gone. He didn't know if he could change. The wounds Anne inflicted on his heart had scarred him. The past few weeks were the first time in nearly a decade he'd allowed himself to feel anything. And he had. He cared for Natalie a great deal.

No, it was more than that, but he refused to acknowledge those feelings. Instead, he pushed them down as far as they could go, because then he wouldn't have to put his heart on the line.

"Mrs. Lattimore, I'm so pleased to have you stop by," Natalie said when Jonathan's mother came to H & W Marketing's offices for an impromptu visit. The older woman was dressed in slacks, a silk shirt with a bow at the collar and pumps.

"I thought it was high time I meet your business partner, Brent. Is he here?" Barbara inquired.

Natalie was having a hard time believing Jonathan's mother was in her office because it made her think about Jonathan, and she'd tried her best to push him to the back of her mind. It was hard because time stagnated and after Chelsea left, the weekend dragged on. Natalie had paced, unable to sleep. She missed him. *Loved him.*

She was glad when Monday came. It hadn't taken much effort to get out of her pajamas she'd stayed in over the entire weekend. Now she could focus on work rather than how she'd foolishly allowed herself to get caught up in a sexual affair with a man afraid of commitment.

"Uh…no, I'm sorry. Brent is at a meeting," Natalie responded. "If we had known you were coming in, we would have made sure he was here."

"Oh, it's nothing." Barbara patted Natalie's hand. "It was spur of the moment." She glanced around the open office.

"Can I get you anything?" Natalie asked. "Coffee, tea, juice?"

"Coffee would be lovely, thank you."

"Coming right up." Natalie walked to the kitchen and was busying herself with the Keurig machine and selecting one of the delicious brews when she turned and found Barbara in the doorway staring at her.

"Why did you break up with my son?" Barbara inquired.

Natalie dropped the Keurig pod in her hand. "Ma'am?"

Barbara laughed and picked the pod up off the floor and handed it to Natalie. "Did you think I didn't figure out you and my son had become—" she paused as if searching for the right word "—better acquainted since Galveston?"

"Uh, no," Natalie said. "I hadn't realized."

"Well, I did. And since then, I've noticed how taken my son is with you. I see how he looks at you when no one is watching."

"I'm sorry, you're quite mistaken."

"Oh, I didn't say he knew it yet," Barbara replied with a wide smile, "but he will. Give him time."

"I'm sorry, Barbara, but I'm afraid I can't talk about Jonathan with you. I hope he's not the reason you gave me your business."

Barbara laughed. "My darling, I don't make business decisions based on who my son is sleeping with."

Natalie blushed furiously and lowered her head.

"Please don't be embarrassed. I only meant that I hired you based on your skill set and what you and your company bring to the table. I like having a local firm I can come to."

"I'm so pleased."

Barbara nodded. "Good." She stepped toward Natalie and lightly placed her hand on her shoulder. "Anne was not the right fit for Jonathan. I knew that from the start, but you have to let young people make their own mistakes. I'm asking that you keep an open mind where Jonathan is concerned. I heard how much you care for him on that live audio. It's why I sent him to Galveston. And I've seen how being with you the last month has changed him."

When Natalie tried to interrupt her, Barbara shook her head. "Don't try to deny it. I know you've been seeing each other since Galveston and I've been so happy, but last night when I saw my son, he'd reverted to the sullen man he was before he left. I can only imagine he's pushed you away somehow because that's what Lattimore men do, but he'll come around."

"You don't know that."

Barbara smiled. "I know my son. Promise me that you will give him the chance to redeem himself, because I believe he cares more for you than he's willing to admit."

"He has to want to change and right now, Barbara, I don't think he's capable."

"Don't underestimate him, Natalie. He might surprise you." Barbara glanced at the Cartier watch on her wrist. "Oh my, look at the time, I have to get going for another appointment. Please give Brent my apologies and let him know I'd like for the three of us to have lunch day after tomorrow at the ranch, my treat."

"We would love that," Natalie replied. "Thank you so much."

Once Jonathan's mother had gone, Natalie wondered what her visit was about. Barbara always seemed to be one step ahead of them and knew details about their relationship. They had kept their relationship a secret, staying at each other's respective homes. Then again, Royal was a small town; maybe they slipped up at some point and someone saw them?

Natalie doubted it mattered. What was done was done. It would be foolish of her to get her hopes up and think Jonathan was suddenly about to confess his love just because his mother thought he would realize his mistake. He had plenty of chances to tell her how he felt. Instead, he repeatedly told her didn't want love or marriage. She had to accept his decision and move on with her life. Surely there was another man who could rock her world like Jonathan.

Natalie sighed. She doubted it. Jonathan would always be her vacation crush.

Eighteen

Jonathan thought long and hard about Jayden's advice and analyzed his feelings about Natalie. He'd never met a woman so kind, loving and giving. She opened her heart to him from the start even though he didn't deserve it. She gave herself over and over again and all he did was take and take and never offer her anything in return.

But did she leave him?

No.

Night after night she came to him and showed him with her actions and with her body how much she cared for him. And dare he hope, loved him? He hoped so, because he missed her.

He was in love with Natalie. With her mind. With her spirt. And with her body.

He wanted to shout it from the rooftops, but then he remembered the pain on her beautiful face and the way she'd crumpled when he'd told her he would never commit to her, never love her. He thought he was being cruel to be kind. Instead, he'd hurt the one person in the world who loved him more than his own family. He would never forgive himself for the way he ended things between them. He needed to make amends by telling Natalie what happened between him and Anne. He would tell her how much he loved her and pray that she might someday give him another chance to make things right.

Natalie was feeling uneasy when she and Brent returned to the Lattimore ranch for lunch two days later. She was fearful of running into Jonathan. What would she say? This would be even worse than when they returned from Galveston and were awkward around each other.

"Are you sure you're okay with this?" Brent asked as they drove. "If you want, we can cancel."

She had finally broken down and told Brent everything about her and Jonathan's nearly monthlong affair. He'd been surprised but understood their need for privacy. Brent wasn't, however, happy with Jonathan. He thought that Jonathan's refusal to commit to a relationship with Natalie was a cop-out.

"Cancel lunch with one of our biggest clients?" Natalie asked, glancing out the window. "No way." Their business was at stake, and she wouldn't do anything to jeopardize it, even if it meant her heart was broken at seeing the eldest son.

Thankfully, when they arrived, she didn't see his truck and Natalie found that she, Brent and Barbara could settle in for an easy lunch. Mrs. Lattimore had gone to a lot of trouble and prepared a three-course lunch.

From the mushroom and truffle soufflé with crispy shiitakes to the red snapper with root vegetables, every bite was sinfully delicious.

"You really didn't have to make lunch, Barbara," Natalie said, wiping her mouth with a napkin.

"I want you to know and appreciate the brand you're representing," Barbara responded.

Brent patted his full stomach. "We certainly do."

"When one of my readers picks up that pot or pan with my label to make a dish for their family, I want them to know everything was thought out."

"How did you get into cooking?" Natalie asked. Her grandmother was an excellent cook and she helped Natalie master a few dishes, so she was proficient in the kitchen, but she was by no means a chef.

"When I started cooking for my husband, my mother-in-law wasn't a fan. She thought my husband would go hungry. Much to my chagrin, she took me under her wing. I learned what I could and then added my own touch to each dish. The rest, as they say, is history."

"I love that story. It's authentic and will go well with selling your products," Natalie stated, sipping on the Arnold Palmer that Barbara had remembered she liked.

"It's important to me that I'm one hundred percent myself in everything I represent. The companies we choose to partner with for my products must understand that."

"We'll make sure of it," Brent stated.

"How about some dessert?" Barbara suggested. "I have an heirloom apple tart puff pastry with goat cheese ice cream waiting for you."

Natalie had a weakness for sweet things. "I would love some, thank you."

"Coming right up," Barbara said, "Brent, would you like to join me?"

Brent raised a brow and glanced at Natalie. She didn't know what Jonathan's mother had up her sleeve, but she nodded. Brent and Barbara departed the dining room several minutes later. Natalie was writing a few notes on her notepad when she noticed she wasn't alone in the room.

Jonathan.

She sucked in a breath. What was he doing here? Barbara must have set this up. Natalie rose to her feet. "I can't do this with you, Jonathan. Not now. I'm here on business." And her heart couldn't take another beating and keep ticking.

"Can you spare a few minutes? I really need to talk to you."

Natalie glanced away and then back at Jonathan. His eyes looked tired and his face drawn. It looked like he hadn't slept much, same as her. Each night when she reached for him, she found a cold sheet. "All right." She sat down and rather than sit beside her, Jonathan sat across from her at the table.

"I want to tell you about my marriage to Anne," Jonathan started.

Natalie leaned backward. She wasn't ready for that bombshell. Every time she asked Jonathan to open up about his past, about his marriage, he clammed up. Now in the final hour, he wanted to talk. "You don't have to do that."

"Yes, I do, because that's the only way you're going to understand my perspective."

She sighed. She supposed hearing his reasoning might give Natalie the closure she needed to move on. "Okay. Go ahead."

"Anne and I got married young," Jonathan said. "Neither of our parents supported the marriage, but we were determined to do it anyway and went to a justice of the peace. I was just getting started at the ranch and determined to prove to my father and my grandfather I had the chops to manage the ranch someday. They were doubtful, given my decision-making with such a hasty marriage."

"What happened?"

"Anne got jealous of the time I was spending at work and learning the family business. She got more and more clingy and complained nonstop that I was never there for her and wouldn't be for any kids we planned on. I told her I wasn't ready to start a family for a few years. Then she discovered she was pregnant. She terminated it."

"Ohmigod!" Natalie covered her mouth with her hand. "Had you discussed the termination?"

Jonathan shook his head. "No. I didn't even know she was pregnant, and I don't think she ever planned on telling me, but during one nasty fight she told me what she'd done. I was devastated. I blamed myself. I wasn't there for her. I made her feel like she had to take such a drastic action without speaking to me first. And Anne, well, she blamed me, too. Told me I had never really committed to her and if I couldn't do that, how could I be a father? She said I was more concerned with the ranch than our marriage and she wanted a divorce."

"After such a horrible experience I can see why you never wanted to get married again. You lost trust in your spouse."

"And in myself, Natalie. I've been haunted by the loss of that child, and I got it in my head that I was being punished and I didn't deserve happiness."

"Jonathan, that's not true. Anne made the choice to terminate the pregnancy, not you. You have to stop blaming yourself."

"I don't know how, Natalie. I've carried this load for so long. I never thought I deserved happiness until I found it with you. My brother saw it. Said he'd never seen me as happy as I've been in the last month. And that's all because of you."

Natalie smiled. "I appreciate you saying that." She ached for him and for the pain he was going through, but she'd given him her whole heart. She practically gift-wrapped it and he'd trounced on it. She wasn't sure she could go back down that road again. She needed to accept that Jonathan's heart might be damaged beyond repair.

"But I can't be with someone who clings to past pain or who throws me away when they're hurting. I know I may not seem special, but…"

"Stop that, Natalie!" Jonathan's expression was thunderous, and he slammed his fist on the table. "You *are* special. You're special to me. Please believe that you've made me happier than I've been in a long time, and I don't want to lose that. I want to bask in that happiness."

A tear leaked out from her eyes. "You told me you didn't want to be with me. Could never love me."

"Natalie." He closed his eyes and when he opened them again, she could see tears on his lashes. "I said that because I was afraid. I was pushing you away before you could hurt me because I was afraid to take a risk. But deep down, I knew that you never could. I was dead and cold inside until you came along and brought me back to life. You've reminded me what true love looks like."

"You can't say these things, Jonathan. Because quite honestly, I don't know if I can believe them." She lowered her head and tried to take a deep breath, but her heart was constricting.

"Can you believe that I love you?" Jonathan inquired. "Because I do. I love you, Natalie Hastings. I think I knew it after we were together in Galveston, but I pushed the feelings down. I acted like they didn't exist, but I don't want to do that anymore. I want to embrace life and all that it has to offer *with you* because missing you has made me realize I can't live without you. Please tell me I haven't destroyed the feelings you had for me?"

Natalie swallowed. When she saw him in the doorway her defenses had instantly gone up but hearing Jonathan's declaration of love was more than she could have ever hoped for. It made her want to be honest and more open than she'd ever been.

"My love for you isn't that fragile, Jonathan. It doesn't

come and go like a hot Texas breeze. I was hurt and angered by the words you said, but it doesn't change anything. I love you, too."

"You do?"

"C'mon," Natalie said, smiling across the table at him. "I told the entire town and anyone listening on Facebook Live that you were the most amazing man I'd ever met and that hasn't changed. And now that I've gotten to know you, it's even more true."

"Can you forgive me for being such an insensitive and unfeeling jerk?" Jonathan asked.

Natalie wanted to believe love was enough, but she also knew that one thing could end this reconciliation. Right here and right now. "Of course I can, but what about children? Do you want them?"

Jonathan understood Natalie's reticence. He'd just told her that he was haunted by the loss of a child. A child he'd mourned for over eight years, but he was over grieving a little soul that wasn't meant to be. "I do want children, Natalie. I want them with you."

"Are you sure?"

Jonathan hated that she still had doubts, so he nearly topped his chair as he rushed to her. He squatted and faced her, cupping her cheeks. "Listen to me, I know you may not want to believe me when I tell you this, but I do want children. I can see now that the reason I didn't want kids with Anne was because early on I realized my mistake and that our marriage wasn't going to work out. But I'm done moping about the past. I want a future with you, Natalie. These last several days have proven to me that I can't live without you, and I don't even want to try."

"You can't?"

"There is no one else for me but you, Natalie." A tear slid down Jonathan's cheek. "I've even had visions of starting a family with you. We'd have the most beautiful babies with your round face and your big brown eyes." He grasped both her hands. "Please give me another chance." He kissed her hands. "I know I don't deserve you, but I promise you I will spend the rest of my life winning back your trust as long as you love me."

His heart was bursting open with love and when Natalie's eyes filled with tears, Jonathan thought it might be over, but then she threw herself against him and he hugged her tightly to his chest.

His heart thundered like the beat of a thousand African drums until she said, "I love you, Jonathan, so much. You mean everything to me. And I'm yours, body and soul."

He closed his eyes and cradled Natalie close. "I can't tell you how afraid I was that I'd lost you. I gave you every reason to turn your back on me."

Natalie looked up at him, her eyes overflowing with tears again, and Jonathan knew he'd found the woman he was meant to spend the rest of his days with. "What do you say we get out of here?" He rose to his feet and began leading her toward the door.

"I can't leave," Natalie said. "What about your mother?" She glanced at the door.

"My mother was in on it the entire time. You know she loves matchmaking." Jonathan smiled. "I asked her to invite you here because I didn't think you would see me."

"You mischievous…" She didn't get another word out because Jonathan was covering her lips in a kiss that sent brilliant fireworks exploding through his chest. A kiss that felt right.

When they finally parted, Natalie said, "Take me home."

He tightened her in his embrace. "With pleasure." Lifting her in his arms, he carried her out the door and toward their forever future.

Nineteen

"You look amazing, babe," Jonathan said, taking her hand and walking her into the Texas Cattleman's Club a few days later. Natalie had opted to a wear a draped black halter maxi dress that tied at her neck. It was the perfect figure-flattering maxi for a summer evening. They matched because Jonathan filled out his black suit with a silver tie quite nicely.

Summer was officially over, and the club was embracing the end of season by having a party on the club grounds. They'd both completely forgotten because they'd been wrapped up in each other's arms after days apart. It was Barbara who sent a subtle reminder text to Jonathan's phone that their appearance was required.

As they made their way to the rear terrace, Natalie thought the club would have gone for a good old-fashioned barbecue, but instead a tropical theme was on display complete with string lights, freshly picked colorful flowers, tropical linens and gold-plated cutlery. There was even a champagne bar for guests to choose their favorite juice to go with the beverage. What caught Natalie's attention was the large video screen showing music videos from the summer's biggest hits. Lucky for her, she had no intention of being part of the festivities after the last debacle. She wanted to keep a low profile.

"Look who's finally here." Barbara smiled broadly when they approached. She rushed forward to greet Natalie. "I'm so happy the two of you worked things out."

"Oh, I think we had a little push," Natalie said with a wink. She'd had no idea his mother *and* Brent had been in on the action using H & W Marketing business to get Natalie to the Lattimore ranch, but it worked, and Natalie couldn't be happier. She and Jonathan were talking about their future and what that looked like.

When she confessed her feelings for Jonathan over the jumbotron, she never imagined they would end up like this. Sure, she hoped, but the reality far surpassed her wildest dreams. Jonathan was everything she could ever want, and Natalie couldn't wait for the day when she would become his wife. It was early days yet, but she knew in her heart of hearts that he was the man for her.

Just then, Vic Grandin and Aubrey Collins walked into the crowd. They were holding hands and getting open-mouthed stares and curious glances at their appearance. The couple used to date but had an acrimonious split years ago. It was shocking to see the two of them together.

"Did you know about this?" Jonathan inquired, glancing down at Natalie.

"Not at all." Natalie shook her head. "Chelsea never said a word. After Aubrey fell off the podium at the last Cattleman's Club party and hit her head, I'd heard she had amnesia, but not much else since."

"They used to date back in the day," Jonathan replied.

"Once upon a time they were inseparable. Vic used to bring Aubrey to all our family events."

"Well, from the looks of it, they might be back together."

"I hope so," Jonathan replied. "They were very much in love, kind of like how we are right now." He bent his head to brush his lips softly across hers.

Natalie loved that Jonathan was willing to show PDA, especially because this was their first official outing as a couple. Like Vic and Aubrey, they were getting their share of looks and whispers in the crowd, but Natalie took it all in stride, because this time she had her man. "Then let's hope they found their way back to each other."

He kissed her again and the kiss might have gotten more passionate if Chelsea and Nolan hadn't strolled over and coughed very loudly. They pulled apart quickly and Natalie knew she had to have a guilty look on her face at having been caught making out. She hadn't had the chance to tell Chelsea she and Jonathan were officially a couple because they hadn't been able to get enough of each other the last few days and stayed holed up at his house making up for lost time.

Chelsea smiled knowingly. Her long brown hair flowed in gentle waves down her back, and she wore a strapless maxi dress with palm leaves all over it. Chelsea leaned in for a hug. "Jonathan. I'm so glad to see you came to your senses and didn't let this one—" she inclined her head to Natalie at his side "—get away."

"Yes, I did, and I'm a lucky man," Jonathan responded.

"And don't you forget it." Chelsea pointed her index finger at him. "Natalie is one in a million."

Jonathan looked down at her and said, "Yes, she is. Natalie, will you excuse me for a moment?"

"Of course," Natalie and Chelsea said in unison.

"Nolan, could you assist me for a moment? I need help with something," Jonathan said.

"Sure thing." Nolan gave Chelsea a shrug when she gave him a questioning look. Then the two men quickly disappeared through the crowd.

"I wonder what he's up to?" Chelsea asked, inclining her head in the direction the men had gone.

Natalie shrugged. "Doesn't matter to me." She grinned broadly. She was on cloud nine.

"I love seeing that silly grin on your face," Chelsea said. "Last weekend you were heartbroken, so to see you like this…well, it's exactly what I wished for you. To find the love I've found with Nolan."

"Thank you, Chelsea."

Suddenly, Jonathan's face popped up on the enormous video screen behind Chelsea. "What in the world!" Natalie gasped.

"My name is Jonathan Lattimore and I'm here tonight to tell you all about the love of my life. You might remember her, Natalie Hastings. She announced her feelings for me at the last TCC party and I thought it fitting that I should return the favor and tell you how much I adore her. She's smart and funny, kind and giving, open and honest. She's a good woman. And that's why I'm asking her, here, in front of all of you, if she will do me the honor of making me the happiest man alive."

To Natalie's utter shock, the video caption read "Will You Marry Me?"

"Ohmigod!" Natalie clasped her hand over her mouth. She turned around to look for Jonathan in the crowd, but she didn't have to look far because Chelsea had gone, and Jonathan was right behind her on one knee holding an enormous diamond ring in a velvet box.

"I'll ask you again, Natalie Marie Hastings," Jonathan said. "Will you marry me?"

"Yes, yes, a hundred times, yes."

There was applause and cheers as Natalie flung herself into his arms and Jonathan caught her as she knew he always would. Then he brought his lips to hers in the sweetest, most tender kiss imaginable before slipping the ring on her finger.

Suddenly, all of their friends and family were gathered around them, congratulating them on their engagement. There were hugs and tears of joy from Chelsea and Barbara, who gushed about her matchmaking skills. Heck, even Jonathan's brother, Jayden, welcomed her into the family.

"I always knew you two would seal the deal." Jayden winked and then he was off to chat with one of his many female admirers.

"Natalie Hastings, have you been keeping Jonathan a secret from us?" her grandmother asked, coming toward them with her hands on her hips. Obviously Ben and Barbara had invited them. This made the proposal even more perfect.

It was Jonathan who answered. "I'm sorry, Mr. and Mrs. Hastings, it was all on me. Natalie wanted to tell you, but I kept our relationship hush-hush. Well…until now."

"As long as our daughter is happy," her grandfather said, looking at Natalie's beaming face, "that's all that matters to us."

"I'm very happy," Natalie responded, and leaned over to give them both a hug and a kiss.

"Welcome to the family, Jonathan." Her grandfather shook Jonathan's hand.

Once all the congratulations were over, Natalie and Jonathan wanted to celebrate alone and in private. They were so eager, they couldn't wait to get home and poked their heads into one of the club's pool cabanas. Finding it empty, they locked the doors, sealing them in and everyone else out.

Their eyes met and Jonathan's gaze was hot and dark. Natalie welcomed it. They reached for each other in a hungry, demanding kiss. Their tongues stroked and intertwined together, causing Natalie's entire body to go up in flames. She savagely began yanking at the buttons on Jonathan's shirt and they went flying.

She wanted him. *Now.*

Jonathan must have felt the same way because he relieved Natalie of her dress in two seconds flat. Then he was kissing her again, stroking the curve of her waist before coming to her panties. Gently, he pulled them off until he was kneeling in front of her.

"I want to worship you with my mouth," Jonathan said, and then his tongue was between her legs. He pushed her thighs apart and spread her wide. Natalie clutched at his shoulders to stay upright as he greedily tasted his fill. She cried out when the first rush of her orgasm took over her, and when her legs could no longer support her, they fell to the floor in a mass of limbs.

Jonathan shifted away from her long enough to remove the rest of his clothing and don a condom. Then he was right back where she wanted, angling her hips and pushing all the way to the hilt with one powerful thrust.

"Jonathan," Natalie moaned, wrapping her legs around him and pressing closer. She needed to feel his strength, feel his love. Jonathan gave her exactly what she needed. He grabbed her hips and slowly began pumping in and out in a delicious rhythm. The passion was so intense, the emotion so thick, they were both carried away. It was the most beautiful culmination of their love for each other.

And when their mouths fused once more, they kissed with abandon and totally forgot the world outside the cabana doors because the love inside with each other was all that mattered.

* * * * *

THE MARRIAGE
MANDATE

SHANNON McKENNA

One

"Take heart, girlfriend." Geri, one of Maddie Moss's good friends, lifted her mojito and clicked her glass with Maddie's. "You're in the perfect place. Trix and Terrence's wedding extravaganza is just the place for supercharged man hunting. You'll be matched up in no time."

"I'm not in the mood for man hunting," Maddie Moss said rebelliously as she frowned out at the cocktail gathering, one of the many events that were crowded into her good friend Trix's blow-out wedding weekend. "It's crass and undignified and desperate, and it's not who I am."

"Too bad for you, hon," Geri said, not without sympathy. "You don't have much of a choice, right? And shopping really can be fun. Look around yourself. What about Aston or Gabe or Richie or Herschel or Sam or Bruce?"

Maddie looked at each of the men that her friend had nominated in turn, sipped her margarita and shook her head. "Nope," she said. "They won't do."

Geri rolled her eyes impatiently. "For a woman under

constraint, you're very persnickety. Your grandma said that the rule was, married by your thirtieth birthday, which is in a couple of months. And not just engaged, but full-on married. Am I right? Weddings take time to plan, and you still don't have a groom. Tick tock, tick tock."

"Believe me, I'm hyperaware of my timeline," Maddie muttered. "And of the penalties for missing it."

"Oh, stop complaining. This wedding is a veritable eligible bachelor buffet. And just as a backup, next week you've also got Ava Maddox's wedding to attend. So if you don't get lucky here, you get another shot there. I mean, just look at them, arrayed before you in all their glory, peacock tails spread out. Aston's very smart, and he's going to inherit Hollis Breweries. And Gabe has great abs. Didn't you see them at the beach, earlier today?"

"Couldn't have missed them if I wanted to," Maddie said. "Gabe makes sure that everyone sees his abs."

"Not a single one of them is bad looking," Geri persisted. "And some are pretty handsome. Sam's good-looking, so are Aston and Richie. Bruce is an up-and-coming DA. Herschel just got hired as chief operating officer at some new electronics company. It's not a bad lineup, Maddie. Keep your mind open, okay?"

"I know these guys too well, Geri. Aston is an arrogant asshat. I had dinner with him once, and he yelled into his phone for the entire meal. Sam can't talk about anything but sports. Richie mansplains math theory to me whenever we talk—"

"Oh, God forbid," Geri murmured. "Math theory? To the math goddess herself? Hasn't he been warned?"

"Apparently not," Maddie said. "Herschel is afraid of me, which gets boring really fast. Gabe is like an overexcited Labrador puppy, plus, he can't seem to keep his shirt buttoned over his six-pack."

"That leaves Bruce," Geri encouraged. "He's aggressive, ambitious. A go-getter."

"Yeah, he definitely goes out and gets a whole lot of everything," Maddie said dryly. "Hilary dumped him four months ago because he gave her chlamydia."

Geri sighed and took a sip of her drink. "Well, damn, girl. Nobody's perfect." Her eyes sharpened, focusing over Maddie's shoulder. "Wait. I take that back." Her voice had lowered to an awestruck whisper. "I just saw perfection in human form. One of Terrence's out-of-town groomsmen who couldn't make it to the rehearsal dinner last night. I spotted him when he got out of his cab from the airport. Trix said he was one of Terrence's old friends, some science genius who lives abroad. He has an amazing ass, among his many other magnificent attributes. Lord save us."

Maddie turned to look, her curiosity piqued.

She froze as pure panic made her whole body vibrate like a plucked string. Her mind went blank.

Jack Daly? *He* was one of Terrence's groomsmen? And he was going to be in the wedding party, along with her? Oh, dear God.

It hardly seemed possible, but after nine years, the man was even more gorgeous than she remembered. He looked tougher. He was casually dressed, in loose tan pants and a white linen shirt, open at the throat, showing a sliver of deeply tanned chest. He had a tall, rangy body. Broad shoulders, long legs, huge hands, a square jaw. She'd always loved his hooked nose. Intense, deep-set dark brown eyes under a heavy slash of dark eyebrows. He was more heavily muscled than she remembered, his face harder.

Maddie whipped her head back around as Jack's gaze flicked toward her.

Geri looked puzzled. "You okay? Your face looks

flushed. Is it the hottie? He certainly made my temperature spike. Whew! Be still, my heart."

"I know that guy," she admitted.

"Omigod, really?" Geri's eyes sparkled. "Will you introduce me?"

"No! Absolutely no, Geri. He's bad news. The absolute worst. Total nightmare. Put him out of your mind and lock the door."

Geri's very red lips fell open for a moment. Then she leaned forward across the table, bright-eyed. "Yum. Scandal, eh? Tell me everything!"

"It's not like that, Geri," Maddie said. "It's not fun, hot, juicy scandal. It's sad, awful, stupid scandal. No fun at all."

"Well, I'm still curious," Geri prodded. "Come on. Deliver the goods."

Maddie blew out a frustrated breath, her heart still thumping far too fast. "Fine, if you must know. You know my brother Caleb, of course."

"Of course. Every straight woman with a pulse knows your brother Caleb," Geri said. "We're all devastated that he's been taken off the market. What about him?"

"Caleb and Jack Daly were best friends, back in high school," Maddie said. "They were also roommates at Stanford. After college, they launched a start-up together, called BioSpark. Enzymatic recycling. They grew microbes that produced enzymes that could digest and break down plastic waste at accelerated rates in landfills and the ocean. They'd developed this product, Carbon Clean. Everyone was excited about it. They were just about to go public, and make a real killing."

Geri made an appreciative sound in her throat. "Mmm. So Jack Daly has a brain behind that pretty face, too? It hardly seems fair."

"It's not funny, Geri," Maddie said sharply. "He screwed my brother over. Caleb can't definitively prove that Jack leaked the research to Energen, one of their competitors, but the evidence all points to it. And it's a proven fact that Jack secretly invested seven hundred thousand dollars in Energen stock right before Energen went public, days before BioSpark's IPO. Word got out, and BioSpark's IPO tanked. And Jack went to jail."

"Oh," Geri murmured, crestfallen. "Bummer. What a waste of a delicious man."

"He got out on a technicality six months later, which drove Caleb absolutely crazy," Maddie went on. "But that's who we're dealing with, Geri. A lying, cheating, backstabbing criminal. Leave that guy alone."

"Hmm." Geri studied Jack, eyes bright with speculation. "Strange. Wouldn't he have made more money eventually if he'd just stayed the course with his own company?"

"We all certainly thought so, sure, but who knows how his twisted reasoning went," Maddie said. "Of course, he told everyone he'd been set up, blah-blah-blah, but the evidence against him was overwhelming."

"Strange," Geri murmured again.

Maddie steeled herself not to look. "Please stop staring at him, Ger. You'll draw his attention to us."

"I'm sorry, but I can't. Physiologically, I simply can't. So why would he do it?"

"I doubt we'll ever know. Caleb and Gran figured he must have been jealous."

"Of what? Didn't they open their company together, as equal partners? And equally handsome, too. What stunning foils for each other they must have been. Mmm."

"Jealous of our family background," Maddie explained. "Our upbringing. I mean, I never knew my parents, and Caleb and Marcus just barely remember our mom, but Gran and Grandpa Bertram were always there for us. We had everything we needed in life to do well, and Jack just…didn't. His dad was killed in a work accident when

Jack was just a teenager, and he ended up in foster care. So it was pretty miraculous that he did so well in school. Great grades, great test scores, full ride at Stanford, et cetera, et cetera. But evidently all that trauma left its mark. Some stuff only comes out over time, under pressure."

Geri's eyes went big and soft as she sucked up her drink with her straw, rattling the ice cubes. "Aw," she murmured, "that's so sad."

"Don't you dare feel sorry for him!" Maddie hissed. "He messed up my big brother! It really cut Caleb to the heart. He was never the same afterward."

"I'm sorry for Caleb, too, but damn, how can I help feeling sorry for Jack? It's your own fault, Mads. The way you told the story tugged my heartstrings."

"Well, pull your heartstrings loose because you're not getting anywhere near Jack Daly, if I have anything to say about it."

Geri rolled her eyes. "C'mon, Mads. Agreed, he was a bad boy. Agreed, he did a bad thing. But it was nine years ago, right? He paid his debt to society. And he's a total dreamboat. And he must be scary smart, to go into business with a Moss."

"Sure, he's smart. Genius level. Didn't do him much good, did it?"

Geri rested her chin on her clasped hands, studying her friend with interest. "My, my," she said thoughtfully. "So passionate. It's refreshing, after seeing you mope around for months since this marriage mandate nonsense popped up. You have color in your cheeks. Your eyes are sparkling. Intriguing, Mads."

Her tone got Maddie's back up. Geri just refused to grasp the gravity of Jack Daly's crimes. "Do you blame me for being passionate about this?" she demanded.

"Not at all," Geri soothed. "But you'll be standing up at the altar with this guy at the wedding, if he's Terrence's groomsman. The wedding pictures will have you guys together, plastered all over social media. Awkward."

"Caleb will go ballistic," Maddie said grimly. "He'd rip Jack's head off if he ever saw him. Gran, too. Elegantly, of course, but he'd still end up headless."

"Really." Geri's eyes narrowed thoughtfully. "Honey. I sense an opportunity here."

"How so? I see a big, messy problem."

"Consider this," Geri said. "You need a raw force of nature, powerful enough to push back against your grandma. Could Jack Daly be that force?"

Maddie's body tightened up at Geri's vague, oblique suggestion and its dangerous implications. "What on earth are you talking about?"

"I don't know yet," Geri said. "I'm just feeling my way. But you seem to be stuck, Mads. Maybe, somehow, the powerful emotions elicited by this Jack Daly could be useful to you somehow. I'm just throwing it out there, you know? Chew on it."

"I am bewildered, babe," Maddie told her.

"I get that a lot," Geri said serenely. "In any case, it could be entertaining. I mean, he's gorgeous. Why not bop him around a little?"

"Because he has no conscience? Because he screwed my brother over?"

"I never said you had to marry him, Mads, or even let him near the good silver. You could just use him for your own wicked, selfish purposes. Pretend to get involved with him. Scare your grandma to death with him. God knows, she deserves it, for jerking you around like this."

"Are you actually suggesting that I…holy crap. You're joking."

"Of course I am, honey," Geri said lightly. "But there's a little bit of truth in every joke. And be straight with me. When Caleb brought that stunning Adonis home for

Sunday dinners and spring breaks and summer barbecues—you thought about it." Geri read Maddie's face and nodded sagely. "C'mon. You looked covetously upon his male beauty. Fess up."

"Well, yes," Maddie said defensively. "Of course I crushed on him. But he never even noticed me. I was just the geeky little sister with the braces and the glasses and the bad hair."

Geri gave Maddie an assessing look, and made a low, purring sound of approval in her throat. "Well, not anymore, hmm? You're all grown-up, and smokin' hot. I love that blue halter dress. Does great things for the girls. Not that they need any help."

"Thanks," Maddie said graciously. "The girls thank you, too. And you're looking pretty fine yourself, in that little yellow number. Nice choice."

Geri preened, adjusting her blond curls. "I try," she said demurely. "Just let me know if you decide to make that guy a part of your strategy to wiggle out of your Gran's mandate. Because if he's not otherwise engaged, I just might take him for a whirl this weekend myself."

"Don't!" Maddie burst out. "Promise me you won't, Geri."

Geri blinked innocently. "Wow. The emotional intensity just gives me chills."

"Not at all," Maddie said, her voice grimly controlled. "But that guy is toxic. He would be toxic for you, too. So please. Don't."

"Ah, sweet, sweet poison." Geri leaned her chin on her hand and gazed longingly across the room toward Jack Daly. "Maybe just a little, bitty taste?"

Unable to resist any longer, Maddie dared a quick peek of her own. Jack was at the bar, talking to Terrence, the future bridegroom. He took a pull off his beer, and then glanced out around the room. Their eyes met, and she whipped her gaze away, but not before a shudder of physical awareness had jolted her whole body.

And Geri's sharp blue eyes saw it all. "Well, get out there and mingle," she said. "I'll give you some time to ponder this indecent suggestion, and then, I start making some indecent suggestions of my own. Because life is short—but I am betting that guy is *not*."

Maddie flushed again. "Geri! Did you hear nothing that I said?"

"Wow, honey. If I didn't know better, I'd say you were almost possessive."

"Geri, please stop it," Maddie said through her teeth.

Geri's lips twitched. "Okay, I'll be good," she soothed. "Don't worry about me. Go on. Get out there, Mads. You've got a husband to find. Happy hunting."

Maddie tried to stop it, but her eyes kept being drawn back to Jack Daly.

He was a liar. A thief. A traitor to his friends. She had to repeat that litany of his deadly sins to herself, over and over again.

Until it finally took.

Jack couldn't figure the mystery woman out. She was a jaw-dropping bombshell. Ice-blue halter dress, luscious curves, pale brown skin, a crown of wild black ringlets, fabulous lips. One of the prettiest women he's ever seen. Something about her was familiar, but no way could he forget a face like that. Lips like that, painted with a plum-colored gloss. Just a glance made him break out in a sweat.

She wouldn't look at him. Unlike the sultry blonde at the table with her, who had stared fixedly. Then again, a woman as pretty as the one in the blue dress would have trained herself to avoid eye contact, like a waiter in a busy restaurant. He'd been a waiter, so he knew good and well that the only way through a bustling dining room was to keep eyes strictly forward.

She looked his way for a split second—and then whipped her gaze away as a bolt of horrified recognition zinged through him.

Oh, yeah. He knew that girl. That was Maddie Moss. Caleb Moss's little sister.

She looked completely different than he remembered. Sure, she'd been cute, back in the day, but he and Caleb had been distracted with their big plans, and busy with their high-energy lives, and they had largely ignored her when they came across her. Little Mads, with the metal-mouth and the glasses, all knees and elbows and smart remarks.

Well, goddamn. She was a stunner now.

"Everything okay, man?" Terrence, the bridegroom-to-be, waved his hand in front of Jack's face. "Did you see a ghost?"

"No. The bombshell in the light blue dress," Jack told him.

"Whoo, yeah." Terrence whistled appreciatively. "Good taste. Trix had to really struggle to decide if she wanted to have a bridesmaid that good-looking. The bride doesn't want to get shown up by her bridesmaids, you know? But she liked Maddie so much, she decided it was worth it. She's definitely the hottest in the pack. Want me to pull strings to get her next to you in the procession? And at the reception? I could swing that."

"She's one of Trix's bridesmaids?" Jack's voice cracked with horror.

Terrence's eyes narrowed. "Uh…and this is so terrible why, exactly? I thought you'd be psyched. I mean, look at her. Who can object to that?"

"You remember my troubles nine years ago with Caleb Moss?"

"Sure," Terrence said. "But I also know that you're innocent, and so does everyone else with half a brain. What about it?"

"I appreciate your vote of confidence," Jack said, meaning it with all his heart. "But Maddie Moss is Caleb's sister."

Terrence's eyes widened with shock. "Oh, shit!" He turned to look in Maddie's direction. "But she doesn't look like she could be Caleb's sister. She's biracial, right? Is she, what, adopted, or something?"

"No. Different dads. Their brother Marcus has a different dad, too. Asian. But they're all Mosses. And they all collectively hate my guts."

"Damn, Jack. That totally sucks. I'm really sorry we did this to you. Do you think that she'll make a thing of it? That it'll be a problem?"

"Couldn't tell you," Jack said. "I haven't seen her for nine years, and back then, she was just a kid, so that's a big question mark. She definitely recognized me. She's ignoring me now." Jack stared out into the crowd. "The smart thing would be for me to pull out of the wedding party. Ask someone else to be your fourth groomsman, and I'll revert to being a normal guest, ready to scram if things get complicated."

"Hell, no." Terrence's voice was sharp. "I let Trix have her way about every detail of this wedding, but I'll be damned if you won't stand up with me when I take my vows. You're the only reason I got through college, man. What happened with BioSpark was a disgrace. If the Moss chick gets her back up, she can be the one to scram. Not you."

"Don't get mad at her for something she hasn't done yet," Jack soothed.

Terrence tossed back the last swallow of beer. "Trix is signaling me. Time to mobilize for the bonfire cookout on the beach. You'll be there?"

"I'll be there," Jack assured him. "Sorry I couldn't make the rehearsal dinner last night. Hey, your lady beckons. Don't make her wait."

Terrence headed straight for Trix, a skinny redhead with a toothy smile. She was a nervous wreck, but she was a bubbly, happy nervous wreck, and Terrence doted on her.

Terrence was a great guy. Jack was deeply grateful for that small but precious handful of old friends who had stuck by him after the BioSpark disaster. He'd had an impossible time finding work in his field after that. No one wanted to hire a person who had been accused of passing intellectual property to a competitor, or betting against his own team.

He'd only started to find work in biotechnology a few years ago, thanks to the influence of some friends who had contacts in overseas companies. In the past four years, he'd worked in Asia, Hungary and South Africa. He'd been very glad to leave the long string of random jobs and work in biotechnology again, even at a lower level, with smaller budgets. He'd learned to content himself. To be grateful. Things could be so much worse.

He glanced at the table where Maddie Moss had been sitting with her blonde friend. She had slipped away, avoiding eye contact except for that one electric moment that still reverberated inside him.

It was probably no big deal. She would probably just avoid him. Pretend he didn't exist. That would be the smart thing, and Maddie had the Moss smarts.

So he would do the same. Damn. Terrence had no clue about Maddie, but Trix did, and she should have known better. This weekend was going to be tense and awkward.

Boo-hoo, poor you. It sounded like Dad's gruff voice in his head. *You know what's tense and awkward, boy? A jail cell. Stop feeling sorry for yourself.*

So his life had gotten derailed. At least he had a life, and he was free to live it. He wasn't rotting behind bars.

Therefore, no whining allowed. Even if his efforts to work again in his chosen field fell through, he'd still be fine. He'd live. It was good to be alive.

No more dark thoughts, or else he'd turn into a black hole and suck all the air and the energy out of Trix and Terrence's party.

But it hurt to be reminded that his best friend, as well as that man's entire family, saw him as a ruthless predator. And that he was unable to prove his innocence to them.

That made him so frustrated, he wanted to explode.

Two

Maddie made a big show of having fun at the beach party. There was a gazebo set up, an open-air charcoal fire for barbecuing ribs, steaks, burgers. A table full of salads and sides, cocktails, beer and wine.

But her appetite was canceled out by her intense awareness of Jack Daly.

Not that he got anywhere near her, or even noticed that she was there. Maybe he hadn't recognized her. He was busy laughing and flirting with Oksana, a stunning blonde Russian model. Trix worked at a big modeling agency, so a large number of her female friends were very tall, slim and unnaturally good-looking.

Oksana was putting her perfectly manicured hand on his arm, clutching him to steady herself. As well she should, in those ridiculous shoes. What was she thinking, going to a beach party in spike heels and a skintight sheath dress?

Oksana gulped her champagne spritzer and squealed as her ankles wobbled, grabbing Jack again for support.

Don't count on him, girl. He will let you fall. You'll hit the ground so hard.

Maddie was sick of watching it, so she grabbed an eco-plastic cup of champagne spritzer from the bar, kicked off her sandals and strolled off toward the water to sip it in blessed solitude.

The beach was gorgeous. It was a beautiful night. Chilly, as always, and there was cloud cover, but she'd changed into her sweatshirt and her cut-off jeans for the beach. She dug her feet into the cold wet sand as she walked toward the white foamy water rushing over the sand.

The moon glowed behind the clouds, making an eerie halo. The noise of the party and the crackle of the big bonfire retreated into the distance as the sand got soggier. She gasped with startled delight as the icy water swirled suddenly over her feet.

The deep, pulsing roar of the ocean was so cleansing. *Ahhh.*

"And what are you doing out here, off on your own in the dark?"

She turned to look. Bruce Traynor had followed her. And so it began.

"Hey, Bruce," she said politely, glad it was dark enough so she didn't have to fake a smile. Small mercies.

Bruce jerked back when the icy water washed over his feet. "Shit!"

Maddie stifled a giggle as Bruce scrambled back out of the water.

"Well?" he said. "Aren't you going to join me over here? My shoes are soaked."

Maddie glanced down at Bruce's expensive canvas boat shoes. What kind of guy wore shoes like that to a beach? He should hook up with Oksana. Those two would understand each other.

"I came barefoot on purpose," she told him. "I love to wade in the water."

Bruce hesitated for a moment, and then slogged grimly through the sand toward her. "Fine, if you have to make a thing of it," he grumbled.

"It's not a thing," Maddie murmured. "I'm just enjoying the waves."

Bruce gasped as water rushed over his feet once again. "God, that's cold. So I've been meaning to talk to you, but you're always in a crowd. Bees flocking to honey, and all that. Who can blame them, when it's so sweet."

"I'm not sweet, Bruce." *Not to you, anyway.*

"I beg to differ." Bruce's teeth flashed. "This thing with your grandmother. Is it true, this news going around? That you need to get married by…when, exactly?"

"My thirtieth birthday," she said, with grim resignation. "September."

"So you're a Virgo? My mom's a Virgo, too. You guys would get along."

"Would we?" Maddie had heard gruesome tales of Bruce's control freak mother from Hilary, Bruce's disgruntled ex-fiancée.

"Absolutely. I'm going to get right to the point, since there's no time to waste—"

"Let me stop you right there, Bruce—"

"I have to get this off my chest. I've admired you for years, Maddie. I have to tell you—"

"I don't want to hear it," Maddie said swiftly.

But Bruce wasn't listening. "This may seem out of the blue," he continued, raising his voice over her attempts to speak. "But in our social circles, we have to take a more pragmatic view of things. Dynasties joining, fortunes uniting. The fate of nations, you know?"

"Fate of nations?" She turned her bark of laughter into a stifled cough. "That may be overstating things a little."

"Not at all," Bruce said loftily. "People like us can't afford to be jerked around by romantic fantasies, or unrealistic societal ideals. And if you need a husband to preserve the family fortune? I stand ready. I offer up my services."

"For real, Bruce?" She coughed again. "You want to... service me?"

"Absolutely. I'd be honored. I've thought it through very carefully, looking at every angle, and I've decided that it's really the best thing for both of us."

"Aw," Maddie murmured. "So you've thought it through for me as well as for yourself. Wow, Bruce. That's really generous of you."

"My pleasure." Bruce missed the irony in her tone completely. "I stand ready to help with all your important decisions, as your partner and husband. Think about it, Maddie. It's truly the perfect solution for all your problems. And just in time, too."

"Well, try not to take this personally, but I don't feel that way about you," Maddie said. "I don't want to marry you, Bruce, because I—"

"You don't love me," Bruce finished matter-of-factly. "Of course not. I don't love you, either. It's not necessary, or even relevant. It's much smarter to make choices based on reality. Practicality. Like they did in the olden days."

"In the olden days, women were chattel," Maddie reminded him. "They had no say at all in who they married. So believe me, I am not nostalgic for the olden days."

"You are deliberately missing my point," Bruce snapped. "You have no time to waste, with your grandmother demanding that you get married, and I'm offering you a ready-made solution. I've always thought girls' insistence on romantic love was silly. Love is just lust in a fancy costume, after all. God knows, I'm in lust with you. As far as I'm concerned, mutual respect, honesty, an ironclad prenup and a healthy dose of lust? That's more than good enough for me." He grabbed her hand and jerked her toward him.

Maddie yanked back, trying to pull it free. "That's not the case for me," she said sharply. "Because I'm not in lust with you."

"How would you know?" Bruce jerked her closer, and kissed her.

Maddie lost her balance, the sand shifting beneath her feet as a wave receded. Icy water sucked and dragged at her ankles. Bruce's smothering kiss tasted like wine and onions. His teeth nicked her lip, his tongue probed, slimy and revolting.

Maddie turned her head away, gasping for air. She struggled to free herself, shoving at him. "What the hell do you think you're doing?"

"Giving you a taste." Bruce's voice was an oily ticklish buzz in her ear. "Just relax. Let me show you how good it could be."

Maddie hauled off and landed a stinging slap to his cheek.

Bruce rocked back, his eyes big with shock. "What?" he squawked. "What in the hell is wrong with you? I was offering you marriage!"

"And I was saying 'no,'" she told him crisply. "You weren't listening."

Bruce sputtered helplessly. "But...but do you have any idea what you're turning down? I was willing to overlook your family history—"

"Family history? What family history are you referring to?"

"I was offering you the Traynor family name!" he yelled. "Which is a hell of a lot more than your father offered your mother, from the stories I've heard! And you just throw it right back in my face, like it's nothing?"

"No, I'm throwing *this*." Maddie flung her spritzer into his face.

Bruce stumbled back. His mouth hung open, working helplessly as he wiped his face.

"My mother did exactly as she pleased," Maddie told him. "In that, I take after her. I'm not your girl. Give it up."

"Is everything okay here?"

Maddie spun around at that deep, quiet voice behind her. Jack Daly stood there, his dark eyes alert and attentive. Watching everything.

"We're fine," Bruce snarled, wiping his face. "Move along. Nothing to see here."

"I was asking her, not you," Jack said calmly.

"Get lost, Daly! She doesn't need anything from a thieving jailbird loser like you."

"She doesn't need anything from you, either, from what I could tell. How about you just go, before the situation degenerates any further. You get me?"

Bruce glared at Maddie as he backed away. "You're going to regret this."

"I'll run that risk. Good night, Bruce."

Bruce slogged away through the sand, muttering furiously to himself.

Leaving just her and Jack Daly standing there in the moonlight alone, the ocean waves surging and retreating around them.

"Are you okay?" Jack asked again.

"Fine," she said.

"That guy's a dickhead. Are you sure you're—"

"I'm fine," she repeated. "I didn't need to be rescued, either. Certainly not by you. Bruce isn't dangerous. He's just a jerk."

Understood," Jack said. "What's that thing he said, about your grandmother insisting on marriage?"

"My issues with my family are none of your damn business."

"No, I guess not. I'll just go ask around. I'll get the public gossip version."

Maddie snorted. "Oh, please. All right, to put it briefly, Gran has decided to blackmail all of us into getting married. No carrot, all stick. And the stick is, if we fail to deliver her a legal spouse by the stipulated date, she hands her controlling shares of MossTech over to my pompous, greedy, dumbass uncle Jerome. He'll take MossTech public as fast as he can, and that will be the end of MossTech as we know it."

Jack was silent for a long moment. "That would be a shame."

"Of course, Gran's mandate worked out fine for Caleb," she said. "He got lucky, when Tilda blew back into his life with their kid, Annika. She's just the cutest little girl. Do you remember Tilda?"

"Of course," Jack said. "Tilda had a kid? I didn't know that."

"Neither did we, but she's the best thing that ever happened to us," she said. "Annika is a Moss, through and through. We love her to pieces. But now that Caleb came through with flying colors, Gran got even more fired up, and now she's pressuring me. I turn thirty in less than three months, and that's my cut-off point. Thirty-five for the boys, but thirty for me because I'm female, and my eggs are getting stale, evidently. Word has gotten out, so all the opportunistic slime-bags are coming at me, right and left. The Moss fortune is very motivating, you know? It inspires great passion in many men."

"Maybe it's you they want," he suggested.

"Nope, I have no illusions there," she said glumly. "It's MossTech they want, not me. Which is demoralizing as hell. The worst possible conditions for husband hunting. Who can find the right needle in a haystack of gold-digging assholes? I can't even find someone decent to spend a Saturday night with. Let alone forge a life-time commitment."

It was hard to tell in the moonlight, but Jack seemed to be looking her over, from her bare, sandy toes all the way up to her wind-tossed hair.

"I can't imagine you having that much trouble with it," he said.

She snorted. "Imagine again. The obvious solution is just to not comply. Just let whatever happens happen, and then see what life offers afterward. I could do without MossTech. I could open my own forensic accounting con-sultancy, and get more work than I can handle. I'd be fine. Maybe even happier, in the long run."

"Forensic accounting?" Jack sounded startled. "Re-ally?"

"Yeah. I've always been a number geek. Is it so hard to believe?"

"Yeah, but those words conjure up guys in glasses with paunches and comb-overs, staring at screens until their eyes bug out. I don't picture…well…you know." He ges-tured in her general direction. "You."

"I have the glasses," she assured him. "I love my glasses. And I stare at screens until my eyes look like stoplights. But believe it or not, yeah, that's my jam. Wallowing in numbers. Finding patterns in data. Running statistics. I love it. More than I would love being a C-suite executive at MossTech. But Gran's got this thing, about concentrat-ing all the family talent in MossTech. She wants me to be the chief financial officer."

"Damn," Jack said. "No one could say that's not a bril-liant career move."

She shrugged. "Sure, but if I don't find someone to

marry in the next few weeks, Uncle Jerome takes control and fires us all anyway. So it's all, well. Pointless."

"Ouch," Jack murmured.

"I'd be fine. I wouldn't mind working without my family breathing down my neck. But Jerome would fire Caleb and Marcus, too, and that's a huge shame. And of course, MossTech would go over to the dark side. At least, the way we see it."

"That would suck," he agreed.

"Yes. Gran counts on familial guilt to control us. But that doesn't make husband hunting easier. What am I supposed to do, marry an asshat like Bruce just to be compliant? That would kill me. And Gran herself would get sick of a guy like him in ten minutes flat. She's asking the impossible."

"Absolutely don't marry someone like Bruce," Jack said forcefully.

"Hell, no. I will not flush my life down the toilet to please anybody. But if I can't find anyone I like in time, I blow up MossTech and destroy my brothers' careers, and that makes me miserable. Though eventually they'll be fine. Knowing them."

Knowing them. That reminded her abruptly that Jack did indeed know them. He knew all of them. All too well.

Panic gripped her. What the hell was she thinking? Babbling family problems to this man, of all people? Jack Daly was not her confidant. He was the enemy.

"How about a third option?" Jack asked.

That startled her out of her mini panic. "I don't see any third option."

"Get your grandmother to relent," he said.

"Ha! You've met Gran. Have you ever seen her relent? Or admit she was wrong?"

Jack grunted under his breath. "You have a point. So

strong-arm her into it. Scare her. Bring home someone whose guts she will hate. Fight fire with fire."

Someone whose guts she will hate. A thief, a traitor. A corporate spy. A jailbird.

The excitement flashing through her at that fleeting thought scared her to death.

"I shouldn't talk about my family to you." Her voice had a quaver that she couldn't control. "I shouldn't be talking to you at all."

"Probably not," he said. "But here we are."

Maddie was right. He should back off and leave her be. Right…freaking…*now.*

But she was so pretty in the light of the moon. Her big, gorgeous eyes gleamed in the moonlight. And those lips. God, how could he have never noticed those lips?

Because he'd been dazzled by Gabriella Adriani back then. His ex.

It had been a long time since he'd thought about Gabriella. Nine years ago, he'd thought himself in love with her. Gabriella was beautiful, sexy, smart, full of attitude.

But she'd bailed on him when things went bad with Bio-Spark. He'd nursed hurt feelings for quite some time, but in the end, he didn't blame her. Gabriella had big plans for her life, and a fiancé as compromised as he was would have been a heavy load to drag.

It was odd, but right now, looking at Maddie Moss in those ripped cut-off jeans, he couldn't even remember what Gabriella looked like. The loose, slouchy sweatshirt did not manage to hide the deep sexy curves of Maddie's body. She looked as fine in that casual getup as she had in the stunning halter dress. It made his lower body tighten and thrum.

No, no, no. Not the place, not the time, not the woman. Don't, Daly.

Maddie must have sensed the hungry energy blasting off him, because she backed away. "So, um…bye."

She walked away quickly. Her mass of springy black ringlets bounced sexily with every step. Her footprints were narrow, distinct. Dainty, even.

Though she was hardly dainty. He grinned, remembering how she'd smacked that horse's ass, Bruce Traynor, and tossed a drink in his smirking face.

He wished he'd filmed it for posterity. Maddie Moss, being badass.

He needed to shut this fantasy down, and stay as far away from her as possible. Preferably in a different room. A different state would be even better.

As he walked back to the bonfire, he was hyperaware of Maddie's location in the crowd of partygoers, as if she were lit up by a spotlight that followed her around wherever she went. A crowd of men literally did follow her around. There were at least five of them clustered around her at any given moment: one pouring her champagne, one setting up a folding chair for her to sit down, one bringing her a plate of assorted Italian pastries.

They were totally swarming her, but she managed them easily and graciously. Chatting and laughing politely at their jokes. Pleasant with all of them, favoring none.

There must be scores of men who would go to any desperate lengths just to have a cup of coffee with her, let alone marry her. The idea of getting to see all that elusive, complicated, dangerous, alluring femininity up close…wow.

Look away. You have no margin for error, boy. Dad's voice. once again.

At least, Bruce Traynor wasn't in the swarm. He was on the opposite side of the bonfire, looking damp, sticky and bad-tempered. Traynor glowered at Jack, who grinned back at him, and lifted his beer.

Eat it, bonehead. At least that jackass was out of the running.

Scary, how much satisfaction that fact gave him.

"Hey, dude."

Jack turned to see Gabe Morehead standing there, his denim shirt hanging open to show his deeply bronzed six-pack, and lots of tribal man jewelry on leather cords, featuring shark teeth, bear claws and runic medallions. "Hey, Gabe. What's up?"

"Did I see Maddie Moss talking to you? Was she, what, chewing you out?"

"Just pleasantries," Jack said.

"Pleasantries, my ass. I bet she was biting your head off. I can't believe Trix invited both of you to the wedding. What a gaffe."

"Terrence and I go way back," Jack offered.

"Ah." Gabe sucked on his beer, gazing across the bonfire in Maddie's direction. "Well, at least we don't have to compete with you, on top of everything else. Man, that woman is fine. Look at those legs. Love to have 'em wrapped around my waist while I—"

"Stick a sock in it, Gabe," Jack cut in.

Gabe looked startled. "Oh! So it's like that, huh?"

"Nah. Just not in the mood for your sexual fantasies."

"Okay," Gabe said. "But I wouldn't blame you if you had a crush on her. The woman is a force of nature. Filthy rich, too. And she has brains that just won't quit. Darrell and Frederick had some problems in their accounting department, and they called her in a couple months ago. They told me that she set up a room and worked in there with her computer and a bunch of whiteboards for a few days. Then she came out and told them exactly where the problem was. Who, when, where, how much, down to the penny. They confronted the thief, and he admitted everything. They say she nailed every last detail. They were awestruck."

"Is that so," Jack said.

"Yeah, genius level magic, man. She charged them an arm and a leg, but it was worth it. Shame she hates your guts. If you really were framed in that BioSpark thing, then she'd be the person you'd want to comb through the rubble for you. She's got brains to burn. But you win some, you lose some, right? I'm getting another beer. Want one?"

"No, I'm good," Jack said.

As if she felt his gaze, Maddie turned her head and looked at him. The eye contact made everything inside him light up.

He looked away swiftly. He had to at least try not to be a creeper.

Bad luck and trouble had put Maddie Moss out of his reach forever. But it was hard to swallow. A smart, gorgeous, desirable woman, shrinking away from him because she thought he was a lying scumbag, thief and traitor.

He'd worked hard over the years to get a grip on his emotions. To always keep his cool, deliberately not thinking about certain things, or giving in to certain feelings. Or else the unfairness of it would've driven him over the edge.

But the injustice really got to him sometimes. Hell, if he'd torpedoed his own life out of greed or spite or lust, or something dumb and selfish like that, then fair enough. He'd take his medicine like a man because he would have deserved it.

But he hadn't deserved it.

It was like being under a curse. It was particularly ironic, if Maddie Moss happened to be the one with the secret sauce. The numbers whiz who might actually be able to discern the truth.

But she despised him so much, she would never get close enough to see it.

Three

Maddie was stressed and rattled at the wedding reception. Three days of bridal events had worn her out. The rehearsal dinner, the brunch buffet, the evening cocktails, the beach party. And ever since Jack Daly arrived, all her energy was taken up carefully avoiding him on the one hand, and fending off would-be suitors with the other.

Now, to put the finishing touch on her discomfort, Louis, the groomsman who was supposed to walk down the aisle with her, had pulled a last-minute switcheroo during the ceremony, when she couldn't protest. He'd grabbed the arm of Desiree, another of Trix's bridesmaids, leaving her paired up with…drumroll please… Jack Daly.

So Maddie had walked down the aisle after Trix and Terrence on Jack Daly's arm.

Then, at the reception, she'd found that Louis had switched out Jack's name card at the table next to Desiree with his own, so he could continue his flirtation. Sneaky bastard.

Jack leaned to murmur in her ear. "Don't worry," he said. "This is stupid. I don't want to put you on the spot. I'll find another place to sit. There has to be an empty chair."

"No, don't," she said swiftly. "Terrence will expect his groomsmen to be near him, for the toasts and the roasts. I really don't want to stress them. Let it be. We'll survive."

"But we'll be photographed together," he warned.

"We already have been," she pointed out. "Whatever. The fallout will play out in another time and place, so screw it. Just smile and wave."

He obliged her. That stunning smile made her breath catch in her chest. God. It just wasn't right. He looked so gorgeous in his well-cut suit. But people kept staring, smirking and whispering. People had not forgotten what happened with BioSpark.

After a while, the reception took on a surreal quality. The champagne was cold and fizzy and good. The appetizers were tantalizing, but she was too wound up to eat, not with Jack Daly close enough to her that she could smell his aftershave. Which was sweet and warm, with woodsy, tangy notes and a seductive hint of cloves. She was also close enough to admire the sharp points of his strong jaw. His close shave. The bump on his nose.

"More champagne?" he asked.

She didn't have the presence of mind to refuse. She stuck out her glass, and took another sip of the sparkling wine.

A romantic song began to play, and Terrence and Trix headed out onto the dance floor. It was a song by Moon Cat and the Kinky Ladies, a favorite band of hers.

Trix beckoned imperiously to her bridesmaids. "Come on, girls!" she shouted. "Get out and dance! This is not a suggestion! Everyone in that bridesmaid dress had better get her butt out here and start shaking it, because I wield bridal power tonight!"

"Same goes for the dudes!" Terrence called out. "On your feet!"

Trix wrapped her arms around Terrence's neck and pulled his face down for a blissed out kiss as they melded into a clinch, swaying to the music.

Maddie looked desperately over toward where Louis was seated with Desiree, across the table. "Hey," she called. "Louis? Would you mind…"

Her voice trailed off, as Louis, ignoring her completely, hustled out onto the dance floor, dragging a blushing, giggling Desiree behind him. "I guess not," she concluded.

The others were partnered up, swaying to the music. Two of the groomsmen happened to already be engaged to two of the bridesmaids, so there were no odd men out.

"You don't have to do this, you know," Jack said quietly. "Pretend you sprained your ankle. Or would you rather I sprained mine? It's all the same to me."

"Hell with it. I'm compromised no matter what I do. We might as well dance." She tossed back her champagne. "Come on. Let's do this."

"Wow," he murmured. "Go easy on that stuff."

"I can handle myself. I'm a grown-up."

"I know, but you haven't eaten. You need food to soak up that much champagne."

"I can manage my own self, thanks," she told him. "And it's really creepy that you're paying close enough attention to notice."

"Sorry," he said. "Didn't mean to creep. You should still eat something."

Louis and Desiree swayed by, kissing and nuzzling as they danced.

Maddie sniffed her disapproval. "I'm surprised those two are still vertical."

"Let's not stand in the way of true love," Jack said.

"True love, my butt. Desiree's living with Hector, a

really nice guy who is off in Southeast Asia right now helping set up a new micropropagation lab, and Louis is engaged to Sylvia, an economist whose working at a think tank outside of Cambridge. This is purely extracurricular fun for these two cheating airheads."

"Ah." He spun her around, and her swirling skirt wrapped itself possessively around his knees for a second before it fell free. "While the cat's away, hmm?"

"God forbid I end up married to someone who thinks I'm the cat who has to be away before the fun can start," Maddie said. "It's hard not to judge, in my current mood."

"Most people don't even try," Jack commented. "Not to judge, I mean. Judging is like breathing, for most people."

"I guess you would know." The words flew out before she'd fully vetted them.

She felt a twinge of guilt at the pained look that flashed across his face. No need to turn the knife in the wound.

"Yeah," he said. "I do know."

Do. Not. Apologize. Goddammit. The man deserved to suffer.

They danced on in silence, but the pressure was building up inside her, and the champagne had lowered her inhibitions. "They piss me off, you know?"

"Who?" He swung her into a dip, and she flung her head back with sensual abandon. What the hell. She liked dancing, and Jack was good at it.

"Desiree and Louis," she told him, when he pulled her back up. "And I think I've figured out why. I'm jealous of them. Weirdly enough."

Jack frowned as he swung her around. "Why? What's to be jealous of? There's nothing real between them. They're empty."

"I'm jealous of people who just suit themselves. They just reach out and take what they want, without suffering agonies of guilt. And I can't do that. We had these iron-clad principles drilled into us by Gran and Grandpa Bertram, so we have this outsize sense of duty and responsibility. Then I look around, and see that other people don't have that at all. They do as they like, and to hell with the consequences. No matter who suffers."

Her face reddened. Damn. She'd done it again. Inserted her foot into her mouth as far as she could shove it. "Shit," she muttered. "Sorry."

But Jack didn't look angry. He just shook his head. "No, Maddie," he said, his voice a velvety rumble against her ear. "That's not me."

Oh, please. She'd invited him to say that. So of course, he'd obliged her. Any smooth-talking scoundrel would take an opportunity like that, if it were handed to him. She was babbling like a drunken fool. *Ooh, please, tell me that all these terrible things that I know for a fact about you aren't really true, because I don't want them to be true.*

Lie to me. Make it convincing.

She pulled back as the song ended, breaking his grip. People were swarming out onto the dance floor as the next one started.

Maddie made her way through the tables, grabbing chairs to balance herself. She grabbed a roll from a basket on the table and took a bite. Jack was right about the food. Though she hated to admit it.

"Maddie, darling!"

She turned and saw Joanna Hollis, Aston Hollis's grandmother, bearing down on her. Joanna was the Hollis matriarch, and an old frenemy of Gran's from way back.

"My dear!" she sang out. "You're just precious in that bridesmaid dress! Much prettier than the others. Most girls look hideous in a bridesmaid dress, but not a lovely morsel like you. You look just scrumptious."

Scrumptious? Morsel? She felt like a freshly caught

mouse, dangling from a cat's mouth. "Hello, Mrs. Hollis. Would you excuse me? I have to—"

"Go dance with Jack Daly again?" Joanna clucked her tongue. "I don't recommend that, honey. Not one little bit."

"He's one of Terrence's groomsmen, Mrs. Hollis." She kept her voice even. "I can't avoid him. Not without making an unpleasant scene."

"I saw that dance," Joanna Hollis lectured. "Seemed like you two were having quite the animated private conversation. I can't imagine what you could have to say to such an awful man. Or what your grandmother would think of it."

"I'm sure I'll soon find out," Maddie said.

"So am I!" The older woman pinched her cheek, tittering. "You really should give my darling Aston a chance. He's my favorite grandson, you know? I know we're not supposed to have favorites, but he's such a good, smart, energetic boy."

"Mrs. Hollis, I really have to go. Please excuse—"

"You've only got a couple months left, right? With my help, we could pull off a wedding that blows this one out of the water, in time to fulfill Elaine's demands. And you could not do better than Aston. Think about it. Stay away from Jack Daly. Associating with him will taint you, and I want Aston's bride to be squeaky clean."

"Excuse me, Mrs. Hollis," she repeated, backing away into the azalea bushes.

She climbed onto one of the wooden walkways, which led her over a swampy bit of ferns and wildflowers, and onto a terrace on the other side of the resort's main building.

This terrace had a stunning view of the beach below, and Jack was standing there. Leaning on the railing and looking out at the ocean. All by himself.

Maddie's phone beeped in her evening bag. She pulled it out. Text messages from her family had piled up.

From Caleb: You're paired with Jack Daly in the wedding party? wtf?

From Tilda: call me asap. all hell is breaking loose here.

From Marcus: u have got to be freaking kidding me. have u gone nuts?

From Gran: call me immediately.

As she watched, the phone in her hand began to ring. It was Gran.

Maddie stared at it for a few moments. Then, slowly and deliberately, she declined the call and turned off the phone.

She opened up her pale green evening bag, glittering with Swarovski crystal, and dropped the phone inside. Then she marched back across the terrace toward Jack.

He sensed her approach and turned to her, his eyes wary. "Hey there," he said.

"I want to do a very dangerous thing," she blurted. "It's stupid, and wrongheaded, and probably destructive. But I want to do it anyway. And I need your help."

Jack folded his arms over his chest. "I'm listening."

"I want you to pretend to be engaged to me," she said.

For a moment, there was no expression on Jack's face at all. "Is this some kind of prank?" he finally asked.

"No," she said. "Actually, you suggested it yourself, the other night. Make Gran relent. Find someone whose guts she will hate. Scare her to death. Fight fire with fire."

"So I'm the doomsday weapon."

"Exactly. She'll be horrified, and it will serve her right,

whether or not she relents. I'll still have that small satis-faction, at least."

"But this won't just drive Elaine crazy," he said. "It'll hurt Caleb, too."

Maddie felt a twinge of guilt. "Unavoidable collateral damage. He'll live."

In the silence, she suddenly sensed the depth of the pain behind the stiff mask of Jack's face, and she felt ashamed of herself, as if she'd said something wantonly cruel.

"Never mind," she said swiftly. "Sorry. Crazy idea. Let it go."

"It's no fun being your family's worst nightmare," Jack said quietly. "It's hard to get excited about it."

She took a step back. "Well, okay. I can see that this makes you miserable, so please, forget that I ever sug-gested it."

"I'll do it," he announced.

She was taken aback. "You…you will? But I thought—"

"On one condition."

"Ahh…there's a condition?" she said carefully. "What condition is that?"

"If you fulfill it, I'll go all out. I'll be your most embar-rassing mistake. Your most egregious lapse in judgment. I'll send your family into a state of total meltdown."

"What's the condition?" she demanded again.

"So, you said you were an expert in forensic account-ing, right?"

"Yes. And that is relevant exactly why?"

"I want you to go over all the data from the BioSpark implosion," he said. "I want you to help me figure out who set me up."

Four

From the blank look on Maddie's face, it was clear that she'd been expecting absolutely anything but that.

"What?" he said. "Why the look? I think it's a fair exchange."

"I don't see the point," she said. "I don't have time for bullshit, Jack."

"It's not bullshit. No one knows what really happened nine years ago. Not even me, despite my best efforts. That's why I need your help."

That righteous glow was fading from Maddie's eyes. Now she just looked uncertain. Doubtful. Scared, even. He was losing her. *Damn.*

"I'll make it worth your while," he said hastily. "I'll be so evil. Loathsome and slimy. A heartless seducer seeking only to devour. Elaine Moss's worst nightmare."

She laughed, to his relief. "Don't overdo it, or it won't be believable."

"They'd believe any terrible thing out of me," he said.

Maddie's laughter petered out. Damn. There were so many little buzzkills hidden between them. Emotional land mines, scattered around, blowing up in their faces when they least expected it. It made things so damn complicated.

"Would you take a look?" he asked. "I'm not trying to scam you, and I'm not asking you to come to conclusions that I like. There's no point in that. I just have a big pile of data, and I want you to take a look at it. I just want the truth."

"Jack, I'm absolutely the worst person you could ask," she told him. "The conflict of interest, my personal biases, they would corrupt everything I saw. You need to find someone impartial. Someone with no skin in the game."

"I've hired other people over the years," he told her. "They were useless."

"If they didn't find anything useful, then what makes you think that I will?"

"They're not as smart as you," he said simply. "You're a Moss. You have a very strong grounding in science, and I think that will make the difference."

"I'm sure you could find someone well-grounded in science who isn't—"

"That's my condition. Take it or leave it. You do the math geek thing for me, and I'll do the comic book villain thing for you."

She let out a startled laugh. "You strike a hard bargain, Jack, but you've forgotten a small but important point. If by some wild chance, I should prove you innocent, then you would be instantly neutralized as a weapon to control Gran. It's your wicked scoundrel status that makes you uniquely useful to me. Talk about a conflict of interest."

He whistled under his breath. "Wow, Maddie. That's cold."

"Yes, it is," she agreed. "And I'm not sorry. I am thinking of myself first, for once in my goddamn life. Lucky you, to catch me on that special day."

Jack thought about it for a moment. "So we'll work on both projects simultaneously," he said. "I'll make an effort to scandalize your family while you study my data, but if you discover something to my advantage, I'll keep it a secret until Elaine lets you off the hook. Will you keep working on my project if Elaine stands her ground?"

"Of course. It's only fair. We should sit down somewhere. Talk terms."

"What kind of terms?" he asked.

She shrugged. "Ground rules. Parameters. Time frames. A general plan."

"Okay," he said. "Let's meet at the Seagull's Roost in Carruthers Cove tomorrow morning for breakfast, and hammer it all out. Nine o'clock?"

"Sounds good," she said.

They heard the quaver of an older woman's voice. A younger man's voice answering. Joanna Hollis emerged from the walkway out of the azaleas, clutching Aston's arm. Joanna spotted her, eyes lighting up. She dragged Aston in Maddie's direction.

Approaching from the other side was Gabe Morehead, his abs miraculously covered by a tux, holding a glass of champagne in each hand. Gabe sped up, in a clear effort to get to Maddie before Aston did.

"The vultures are circling," Maddie whispered. "Good Lord, deliver me."

"I could deliver you," he told her. "If you're absolutely sure you want me to."

"What do you mean?" she asked.

"Are you committed to this plan?"

"Of course. It was my idea in the first place. Hey!" She

stiffened, as he pulled her against his chest. "What the hell
are you doing?"

"Chasing away the vultures," he said, as he kissed her.

After the first breathless moment, Maddie found herself in a brand-new state of consciousness. One in which
there existed nothing but the delicious sensation of Jack's
hot mouth against hers, exploring, coaxing, persuading,
seducing. Insisting.

Everything was irrelevant, and forgotten.

His taste was intoxicating. Her knees almost buckled as
he flicked his tongue against hers. Her body reacted with
a rush of helpless longing.

Maddie had imagined kissing Jack as a girl so many
times, fantasizing in her bed, on those occasions that
Caleb had brought him home for days at a time, parad-
ing him around in front of her hungry eyes. Gran and
Grandpa Bertram both liked him so much, they'd been
more than willing to open their home to him. Everyone
loved Jack.

All those dream kisses added together did not begin to
approach the reality.

A vague awareness of their spectators hovered on the
edge of her consciousness. She could hear her rational mind
in the distance, yapping ineffectually, but it couldn't drag her
attention away from his delicious taste and scent, the heat,
the dense, solid reality of him. His strong arms around her
waist, her arms. Her arms, wound around his neck.

The kiss was getting more desperate. Her helpless, in-
voluntary response was telling him dangerous, intimate
secrets about herself, releasing feelings that had been buried under pressure for years. There was only this kiss, this
man, this moment. Only his mouth, pleading, probing,
plundering. His hands wound into her hair as their tongues
stroked and danced and sucked. Her fingers dug in, try-

ing to get a grip on the smooth fabric of his tux jacket. The stiff bulge of his erection against her belly made her want to get closer. To tie herself into knots with him. And pull them tight.

Slowly, she began to hear muffled giggles, slow clapping, amused murmuring.

Reality floated back. Consequences.

Jack lifted his head. His face was flushed, his eyes dazed. "Whoa," he whispered.

Maddie was gasping for breath. "What the hell just happened?"

"It was supposed to be a little bit of theater. It, uh…got away from me."

"We had an audience," she said.

"Wasn't that the point? Probably we were filmed. Somebody definitely whipped out their phone for a show like that. So I hope that you're sure about this."

"Yes, I am," she said, shakily.

They stared at each other, their eyes just inches apart. His parted lips were so sexy. That gorgeous mouth. His full, sexy lower lip. His dark eyes, boring into hers.

Theater. This is theater, Moss. Keep your head on straight.

"Jack," she whispered. "I never meant to imply that we'd…ah. You know."

"Of course not," he said swiftly. "I was just trying to make it convincing."

"Well, damn. You outdid yourself. Method acting. Couldn't be better."

Step back. Now. But her feet would not obey the command. That pull toward him came from deep inside. She couldn't control it.

"I think… I think I need to go to my room." Her voice shook.

"I'll walk you to your cabin," he said. "The whole place

will be buzzing. And your grandma won't sleep tonight."
He paused. "Neither will Caleb."

"He'll be fine," she said. "He has Tilda and Annika to
console him."

"So? Shall I escort you?"

They paced in silence along the branching network of
wooden walkways, lit by strands of fairy lights that glowed
in the bushes and decorated the walkways. They passed
several people, but Maddie avoided eye contact, ignoring
smothered giggles and whispers.

They got to the narrow walkway that led off the main
path, terminating at her own cabin, "The Lupin Lodge."
She pulled her key card out of her evening bag.

"People are still watching," Jack said. "Let me come
inside, just to put the cherry on top of our little fiction. I
promise, I won't touch you in there. You can trust me."

She looked up at him, wishing it were true with an intensity that frightened her.

He looked so damn trustworthy. Sincere and passionate.
She was so hungry for that. To be desired. Craved whole-
heartedly. Desiring and craving in her turn.

She didn't want to resign herself to never finding that.
To be bullied into settling for something less. This stolen
moment with Jack reminded her of everything she stood
to lose with Gran's stupid mandate.

The depth, the wildness, the realness, the magic. She
craved it.

No, she craved him. Specifically. She craved Jack Daly.
God help her.

And damn them all, for putting her back against the
wall.

She beckoned him in. Jack stepped inside. Maddie
closed the door, pulled the hanging blinds on the front
window closed and flipped on the wall lamp by the bed.
It cast a soft, rosy light. There were higher, brighter set-

tings, but a few friendly shadows were just fine with her tonight.

"I hope I didn't offend you, back there on the terrace," he said. "I pulled a Bruce on you. It would've served me right if you'd smacked me. Or thrown a drink in my face."

She shook her head. "No, actually. That was the opposite of a Bruce. That guy's technique needs serious work. But he won't be practicing on me."

"So, you're saying that my technique is acceptable?"

"Yes," she murmured. "You were extremely convincing."

There was a brief, awkward pause.

"I should probably go," he said. "Whoever was watching us go inside has gotten bored by now. I'll see you tomorrow morning. At the restaurant."

"See you there," she echoed.

But their eyes stayed locked, and Jack hesitated by the door. "Sorry," he said. "It's hard to walk away. You look so beautiful in that dress."

"This? My bridesmaid dress?" She laughed out loud. "Oh, please. It's so poofy, and sea-foam green is not my color. But still. Thanks."

"It looks gorgeous on you. You look gorgeous in everything."

Maddie rolled her eyes, but smiled at him. "You're very kind."

Jack swallowed hard, and looked away. "Good night, then."

She didn't even know she intended to move, but suddenly she was at the door, blocking him. Her hand on the handle, holding it closed. "No," she blurted out.

Jack's eyes were wary. "No one's watching us now, Maddie."

Exactly. This was just for her. "Can you promise me something, Jack?" she asked.

"I don't make blind promises," Jack said slowly. "What is it that you want?"

"If I asked you to kiss me again, could you stop with just one kiss?"

His throat worked. "Yeah, I probably could," he said. "It would probably take years off my life, but, ah… I think I could do it."

"I will not have sex with you," she said. "That's a step too far, for me. A lot of steps too far."

"Understood," he said quickly. "Bad idea. The worst."

"But I'm in a selfish, dangerous mood tonight, and I really liked the way that kiss made me feel," she said. "I want to feel that way again."

"You're skating really close to the edge, Maddie," he said.

"I know. Just tell me, yes or no. Can you stop when I ask you to?"

"Ask yourself the same question," Jack said. "Don't put it all on me. I'm not the only one doing the kissing."

She swayed closer to him. "I am in no mood to analyze myself tonight. Are you going to kiss me, or are you going to get the hell out of my room?"

Jack made a rough sound deep in his throat, and seized her.

It was like before, but so much more. Wilder, hotter, deeper, now that they were alone in a locked room. The bed seemed to be exerting a magnetic pull, and they moved across the room toward it, kissing frantically all the way.

When the back of Jack's legs hit the bed, she gave him a little shove. He sat down abruptly at the foot of the bed. He stared up at her, panting.

Maddie kicked off her shoes and straddled him, hoisting up the billowing pale green skirt on either side of his legs, and settled herself against him, seeking the perfect angle where that bulge in the front of his pants was right where she needed it. Where she could rock against him, arms twined around his neck. Abandoning herself to that slow, sensual tongue-kissing that only he could do.

The straps of her dress had fallen down, showing the scalloped lace of her bra. Jack was cupping her breasts, peeling down the lacy fabric.

She leaned back, arching her back. Letting him look. His eyes on her body felt hot, deliberate, exciting. As palpable as a physical touch. She shivered at the sweet rush electrifying her skin, as his lips moved over her breast, and he drew her nipple into his hot mouth.

"God, Maddie," he muttered. "You're so beautiful."

Her voice was gone. Her fingers wound into his hair, her ragged breath catching with wordless whimpers at the tender swirl of his tongue...the deep, suckling pull...

This is Jack Daly. Pull this back. Before you hurt yourself.

But the answer that surged up from inside her was simple, and powerful.

No.

She felt lit up, from the inside. Shining like the moon, as he slid his hand under her skirt and between her legs. She moved against him helplessly, as he caressed her sensitive nub, then his hand slid deeper into her panties, exploring her fuzz of hair, the tender folds inside, the slick heat between them. He kept getting it just...exactly...right. Oh, God...

The pleasure that pulsed through her was so huge and startling, she almost fainted.

She collapsed, her head draped over his shoulder. Amazed, and abashed.

Jack nuzzled her throat, his hand still under her skirt, gently caressing her.

"Your skin is so soft," he whispered. "I love how you feel around my fingers when you come, squeezing me. You're so perfect."

She let out a jerky, helpless laugh. "Hardly."

Jack made a choked sound as she shifted against his erection. "Maddie," he said. "This is the end of my rope. I can't keep that promise any longer. If you don't want to have sex with me, then throw me out."

Oh, it was hard. But she lifted herself up and off him, reluctantly. Her face was very hot as she tucked her breasts back into her bra cups, and pulled up the straps of her dress. Her legs felt liquid in the aftermath of that orgasm. Her knees and ankles wobbled.

"I'm sorry if you feel used," she said.

"Oh, I don't," he said. "Don't worry about me. That was a peak life experience. I'll never be the same again." He backed slowly toward the door. "We still on for breakfast?"

"Why wouldn't we be?"

He pushed the door open. "Just wondering if this experience might have scared you off. But it looks like you're made of tougher stuff than that."

"I'm on a mission to emancipate myself, preferably without ruining my brothers' lives," she said. "A little sexual tension won't hold me back."

He stopped outside the door, and gave her a ghost of a smile. "A little?"

She laughed. "Okay, a lot of sexual tension."

"God help me. Good night, Maddie." The door swung shut.

Maddie sank down onto the floor, scared to death.

She'd couldn't believe herself. She'd done a dumb, dumb

thing. She'd unleashed something that was too big and wild for her to wrangle. And she had no intention of walking it back. No intention at all.

Like she didn't have enough problems.

Five

Jack stared out the window of his cabin, at the little slice of ocean visible through the madrone trees. In the clear light of dawn, last night's pact with Maddie seemed even more rash and self-destructive than it had the night before.

He hadn't slept, partly from jetlag after flying from Johannesburg, but mostly from unsatisfied lust. Whether his eyes were open or closed, all he could see was Maddie Moss, straddling him, kissing him while he slid his fingers into her hot, slick, secret flesh.

Pleasuring her until she shattered in his arms.

Ah, great. There he went again, with the erection that just would not die, even when given a hand, quite literally. In the shower last night, and once again this morning, but he may as well have not bothered, for all the good it did.

The front desk had called him a taxi to take him down to the restaurant he'd suggested at Carruthers Cove. He got there in good time. The Seagull's Roost was busy at this hour, but he snagged a window booth with a sea view.

He'd wanted a few minutes alone before she arrived, to get some practice in keeping his face composed.

He was in way over his head. No idea how to manage these feelings. He hadn't had this problem with Gabriella, or girlfriends before her. This was a brand-new problem. Frustration, grief, impotent rage…those were familiar. Routine, even.

But wild, frantic sexual desire…that was a whole other thing.

It was a long time since he'd felt frantic. To survive the BioSpark fallout, he'd buried his emotions very deep. It was the only way he could cope.

And all of his careful work had just gone straight to hell.

"Good morning."

Jack's heart bumped as he turned toward the source of the velvety feminine voice.

Maddie looked fresh and sporty, in a battered, silvery gray sweatshirt with a big colorful dragon stenciled on the chest and a pair of raggedy blue jeans that molded sexily to her gorgeous curves. Her hair was twisted up off her neck in a high messy bun, held in place by hair sticks that could double as lethal weapons if the need arose.

Her smile was brilliant, but she didn't sit down.

"Good morning to you," he replied. "Do I sense cold feet?"

"I just wondered if you might have them."

"Not me," he said. "You're the one with something to lose. I have no family left to alienate or scandalize, and no reputation left to trash. So why not?"

"I see your reasoning." She slid into the booth opposite him.

"But if you wanted to walk this back, I'd completely understand," he offered. "You'd have a hard time explaining that kiss on the terrace last night, but hey, you could always just blame it on me. I'll be your bad guy. I'm used to it."

Maddie folded her hands primly. "That's gallant of you, but I can take responsibility for my own indiscretions, thank you very much."

"Coffee, miss?" A white-haired waitress hovered near the table with the pot.

"Yes, please," Maddie said.

The woman filled her cup, topped up Jack's and left them with menus. They studied each other surreptitiously over the tops as they surveyed the day's specials.

"So how do we start?" he asked. "And where? Do you live in Seattle these days?"

"Yes, but I don't want to go home right now," she told him. "My family would get all up in my face. It would be impossible to concentrate."

"But don't you need to get back to work? Aren't you working at MossTech?"

"Not yet. Caleb wanted to make me official CFO, but with this marriage mandate nonsense, I figured it made no sense to take the job now. If I'm not married in two and a half months, Jerome fires us anyway, so why even start?"

"I see your point," he said. "So what are you doing in the meantime?"

"Not loafing," she said. "I took the opportunity to do some more consulting jobs in forensic accounting. I really enjoyed it."

"Gabe told me what you did for Darrell and Frederick's company."

Her eyebrows shot up. "Really? I'm surprised Gabe could even grasp what I did at Darrell and Frederick's."

"Ouch," he commented. "You are hard on your suitors."

"Only when they're clowning, half-dressed idiots," Maddie said. "Gabe Morehead is impossible to take seriously, even when his shirt is buttoned. What about you? What are you doing right now?"

"I'm working with a team in Johannesburg that's developing a new line of enzymatic recycling products," he said. "I've got meetings set up, the week after next. To discuss partnership possibilities for larger scale manufacturing."

Her eyes widened. "Oh. Wow."

"You look surprised," he said.

"I just didn't think—"

"That I would ever find work again in my field? It did seem that way for a while."

The waitress appeared to take their order, to his relief, breaking off this thorny line of inquiry just in time. Jack got a seafood omelet with home fries, and Maddie ordered French toast with a side of bacon.

"Back to us, and our strategy," Maddie said briskly, when the waitress had left. "As I said, I don't have an actual job right now, and I have nothing on my calendar that I can't postpone between now and Ava Maddox's wedding next weekend, so this week would be a great time to get started on both projects."

"Ava Maddox is getting married?" he said. "Wow. Her fiancé is a lucky guy."

"Yes, Ava's the best," Maddie agreed. "She's getting married to the Maddox Hill chief security officer, Zack Austin. They're madly in love. And my invitation has a plus-one. Would you go to the wedding as my fiancé? That'll drive Gran bananas."

The prospect made him uneasy. "Will Caleb and Marcus be there?"

"No," she assured him. "Marcus is in Southeast Asia, and Caleb is in Spain with Tilda, on the honeymoon that just won't quit. They're not supposed to be back for another ten days. Gran was invited, but I doubt that she'll go, since those things exhaust her. Besides, Annika is staying with her right now while her parents are traveling. It's a girls-gone-wild slumber party over there."

"I'll think about the wedding," he told her. "If you don't

want to go back to Seattle yet, then why don't you come up to the Olympic Peninsula with me? I rented a house in the rainforest, right near Cleland. It's on the edge of a canyon, with rapids and waterfalls. You could get started there, if you don't want to be bothered by your family in town. Give me the time to rent myself a car, and you can just follow me right up to Cleland."

"Oh, I'll just drive you there," she told him. "Rent a car when you're up there. We just need to stop at a big stationery store to get some supplies, my whiteboards and markers that I'll need to live up to my end of the bargain. On the way up, we can start to chronicle a swoonworthy, torrid online romance. Maybe I'll get a big shiny ring, and we can make a great big deal about it on all of the socials—"

"I should be the one to get you the ring, right?"

"Wrong," she said sternly. "This is a theatrical production, and I'm the producer, so I fund the props. Duh."

"Okay, fine. Of course. Whatever."

"When it comes to lodging, though, I'm not sure if your mysterious secluded house hidden in the rainforest is quite the right choice for me," she said.

"No problem," he said swiftly. "There's a nice bed-and-breakfast in town just a couple miles away, run by the same woman who rents me the house. The last thing I want is to make you uncomfortable."

Her eyes slid away. "Um, yeah. About that. We have to address this…this thing between us."

"Our sexual attraction, you mean?"

"Well, yes. For lack of a better term."

"There is no better term," Jack said baldly. "That's literally what it is."

"Fine, fine. Call it what you will," she said, waving a dismissive hand. "So for all those many reasons we don't need to list right now, I'm stating, for the record, that giving in to that attraction would be a disaster. Isn't going to happen. Ever. Agreed?"

"Agreed," Jack said.

"We'll keep on exactly as we are right now," Maddie said. "I mean, look at us. We're just sitting here, like normal people, having breakfast. If we can do it here, we can keep on doing it. Right?"

"I won't come on to you," he assured her. "Except for those moments when we need to put on the show as an engaged couple. Like last night."

"Right." She bit her sexy lower lip. "Right. That's going to be…interesting."

"For lack of a better term," he said.

They both snickered under their breath.

Maddie savored a bite of her French toast. "I think it's doable," she said, as if trying to convince herself. "We just have to be really clear about the rules. For instance, can I call on you to keep this fiction going until it becomes irrelevant? Which is to say, my thirtieth birthday, or when Gran has a change of heart, whatever comes first."

"Of course. And for this entire period, you will keep an open mind and keep studying my data, until you feel like you've exhausted all possible avenues of inquiry."

"I can't guarantee that I'll find anything revelatory," she warned him. "In fact, I highly doubt that I will. But I do promise that I'll put my back into it."

"Thanks. That's all I want."

"But it's a very long shot," Maddie reminded him.

"So is your project," he said. "Knowing Elaine."

"Yeah, two lost causes. God knows why we bother."

"God knows," he echoed. "But let's have at it."

"Damn right," Maddie agreed. "So. The rules are, no kissing."

Jack laughed out loud. "That's out of character for us,"

he pointed out. "Aren't we supposed to be engaged? Isn't it supposed to be scandalous and juicy?"

"Fine, then. Kisses only when I say," she amended.

"Ah. Yeah. You mean, like last night in your room?"

Her face went rosy red. "Um, no. There will be no more of that nonsense," she said primly. "Chaste, controlled kisses. No crazy tongue action, or roving hands."

He couldn't stop grinning. "Okay, fine," he said. "Dry kissing on command. Frigid little pecks with tightly puckered lips."

"Don't you dare make fun of me. We have to keep a lid on this. When we get started, it's really hard to stop. So the only place to stop it is at the get-go."

"Of course," he assured her. "I'll be good."

The laughter had broken the tension. As they polished off their food and paid the tab, he realized that he was enjoying himself. Dangerous in itself.

Afterward, they strolled through the touristy town of Carruthers Cove, Washington, heading toward the parking lot where Maddie had left her car.

"Are you ready to take off for Cleland now?" she asked.

"My bags are still at the resort," he told her. "I checked out of the room, but I left my stuff in the luggage storage room and got a taxi down to Carruthers Cove this morning."

"Then I'll just drive you back up there to get your bags, and we'll take off."

Maddie dropped him off in front of the resort entrance. Bruce, Gabe and Aston were in the front lobby, and saw him getting out of Maddie's Mini Cooper.

They stared at him, open-mouthed, as he walked in and retrieved his bags.

"So it's true?" Bruce said slowly.

"Not sure what you're referring to," Jack said.

"I know girls like to go slumming, but I wouldn't have

thought she'd stoop that low," Bruce said. "So, Maddie Moss is kinkier than I thought. That bad, bad girl."

Jack instantly weighed the pros and cons of putting his fist through Bruce's teeth, and just as quickly concluded that such a move would not help him achieve his goals.

Ice...cold...control. "Get out of my face, Bruce," he said.

"Hey there, fellas!" Maddie's voice was bright and cheerful. "Gorgeous morning, isn't it? I thought I'd come in and see if you needed any help with your bags, Jack."

"No, thanks. I'm good," he said, without breaking eye contact with Bruce.

Bruce's gaze dropped. Aston and Gabe exchanged knowing glances as he stomped away, muttering.

Maddie scooped up Jack's garment bag. "Shall we?" she asked briskly.

As they walked away, Maddie shot him a sidelong glance. "It looks like the hairy eyeball has begun," she murmured. "Our work here is done. Shall we hit the road?"

"Great idea." Jack tossed his stuff into Maddie's Mini Cooper, and got in.

As she pulled out onto the highway, he couldn't help feeling like he was escaping from some dark, cramped place and into freedom and possibility. Here he was, on a beautiful, coastal highway, in the company of a gorgeous woman who made his body tingle with sexual awareness. The windows were down, the air smelled sweet like rain and the sea. The side of the road was thick with brilliant golden poppies in the vivid green grass. Rainbows appeared in the mottled clouds without warning.

Maddie turned on the radio. A song played, about breaking down your walls.

Dad's voice in his head was kind, but stern. *Feet on the ground, Daly. You're cruising for a bruising, boy. Watch yourself.*

Maybe so, but screw it. He couldn't get any more bruised than he already was, and he knew how to take it on the chin.

Hell, he'd gotten plenty of practice.

Six

After about twenty minutes on the coastal highway, Maddie saw the sign for Carruthers Bluff Road. She flipped on her turn signal.

"Where are we going?" Jack asked.

"We're taking a brief detour," she said. "There's something I want to see. When Caleb and Tilda got married, Gran confessed to buying us all a beach house out here, as a future wedding present. Can you believe it? Three beautiful beach houses, all in a row. Tilda and Caleb spent a few days here after their wedding, and loved it. But what with one thing and another, Marcus and I haven't even seen our future houses. Or rather, Gran's houses. They are hers, and hers they will probably remain, the way my life is going. But this might be a fun place to do some Instagram and Facebook stories that will make Gran froth at the mouth. I don't have the keys, but we can run around on the grounds."

"I'd rather not risk running into Caleb. Not until I have proof of my innocence."

They crested the top of the bluff, and a breathtaking view of the Washington beaches was visible in both directions. "Caleb isn't here," she reminded him. "He and Tilda are in Spain."

The sun was breaking through the clouds, a bolt of it hitting Paradise Point in the distance, the resort where they had spent the weekend. The sunlight lit up the green of the grass, the smudges of bright gold mixed into the green from the yellow poppies.

They came upon a row of mailboxes. "The first one is Caleb's," she said. "The next one is supposed to be mine. Shall we go and take a look?"

The driveway wound through green, flowering fields and trees. They passed Caleb's house, which she recognized from Tilda's photos and videos, and finally pulled up into a beautiful garden, exploding with multicolored flowers, outside a lovely old cottage.

It was sheltered by wind-twisted trees. Gray-shingled, time-weathered, exquisitely well-kept. Two stories, with a deep porch all the way around.

"Sweet," Jack said. "Elaine must have a really good gardener on call."

Maddie got out of the car, speechless. She walked over to the front porch, which was wide and beautiful, with plenty of room for porch furniture. There was a big swing facing the sea. She walked up the steps, peering through the windows into the rooms inside. They were lit up with sunshine, which showed all the gleaming hardwood planks, the paneling, the ancient beams in the ceiling. There were hanging baskets of blooming petunias and bleeding hearts at intervals on the porch.

Emotions she wasn't prepared for overflowed, and to

her embarrassment, she found herself with tears running down her face.

"Wow," Jack said, startled. "What is it? Maddie? Are you okay?"

"Nothing, nothing. I'm so sorry." Maddie waved him away, digging in her pocket for a tissue. "It's this house. It just…pushes all of my buttons."

"Why? Don't you like it?"

"I love it," she said. "Of course, I love it. That's the problem. It's gorgeous. Everything about it is perfect. It's exactly what I like, and she knows it, because she knows me so well. And she's jerking me around with that, because she can. Like I'm a thing that belongs to her. She should trust me to live my life, not treat me like a baby."

Maddie lost it for a few minutes. When she lifted the tissue from her goopy face, Jack was standing a few feet away, looking uncertain.

"I'm sorry," he said. "I want to hug you. But that rule. It inhibits me. Are hugs permitted?"

She laughed, fishing for a fresh tissue. "Best not, I think." She blew her nose again. "You know what? I used to hate my mom for running away. But now, I totally get her. She might have been frivolous and selfish and shallow, but she was fighting for her life." She gave Jack a sideways look. "I expect you know the story of my mom, right?"

"Yeah. Caleb told me that she sent all of you kids off to your grandparents."

"She hadn't gotten around to sending me yet, but she would have soon enough," Maddie said. "She just wanted to party. She died when I was less than a year old. I used to be so angry at her for blowing us off like that, but she was just trying to breathe."

"What about your dad?" he asked. "Why didn't you go live with him?"

She shook her head. "Not an option," she said. "I don't even know who he is. No one did."

Jack looked pained. "Oh. I see. Not to judge, but maybe she could have found a way to breathe without abandoning her kids."

"Maybe," Maddie conceded. "Right now, I'm appreciating the advantages of extreme selfishness. She wasn't mired in guilt and responsibility, like me. And by all accounts, she certainly did enjoy herself."

"There has to be a balance," he said. "Between holding on to your principles, and maintaining your personal boundaries. Maybe that'll be the point of this whole experience for you. Learning where that sweet spot lies."

She laughed at him. "Jack Daly, life coach."

He shrugged. "Shitty things happen. What else can you do with that but try to find the lessons in them?"

"A wise observation," Maddie said. "Are you up for a little more theater?"

"Meaning what?"

"Meaning, I fix my mascara and lipstick, and you and I do a video shoot. I'm thinking, a romantic montage at the beach house of us exploring our future vacation home. We can go down to the private beach, and shoot some video of us frolicking in the surf, me jumping playfully up onto your back. Us walking away from the camera holding hands. Too bad I don't have a ring, but we can do another one later. I'll hashtag the crap out of it. #SheSaidYes, #HeProposed, #BeachFantasy, #WeAreEngaged, #HePoppedTheQuestion, #TyingTheKnot, #SurpriseEngagement, whatever else comes to me. Let's get this publicity machine humming."

"Sure, I'll do whatever. Pose me where you want me."

Maddie pictured Jack, stretched out on the bed, like last night. But this time, naked.

She turned away as heat rushed into her face. "I appreciate the helpful attitude," she said lightly. "So? Let's get started."

They wandered around the property, taking pictures, filming videos of each other, or of the two of them together. Blowing kisses at the camera, her laughing at him from under the hanging petunia baskets, making a heart shape with her hands. The two of them on the tire swing, each suspended upswing showing a stunning glimpse of the bluff, the ocean. The longer they went at it, the more silly, playful, romantic ideas came to them.

The time just slipped away, and finally Maddie looked down at her phone and was startled to realize that two and a half hours had gone by.

"We don't want to drive in the dark," she told him. "Let's wrap this up. A romantic kiss, with a beach view backdrop, and we'll call it good."

Jack's expression didn't change, but she felt the surge of heat in the air. Tension.

"On a scale of one to ten, how convincing do you want this kiss to be?" he asked.

She studied him, eyes narrowed. "Is that a trick question?"

"It's the opposite of a trick question. I'm trying not to step over the line."

"The kiss has to be hot," Maddie said. "Make it convincing. Make it a ten. If you can handle holding up the phone and kissing me at the same time."

He grinned at her. "I can walk and chew gum at the same time, Maddie."

"Yeah?" She handed him her phone. "Prove it."

Jack held it up. "Ready?"

"As I'll ever be."

Jack tapped the screen delicately with his fingertip, and leaned down.

Their lips touched, in a delicate, searching kiss. Then

it softened, deepened into something that was suddenly bigger, and there they went again. Melting together, like always. The world fell away. She forgot everything she ever knew and just kissed him back, hungrily, with all the longing in her heart. She twined closer, heart thudding.

When Jack finally pulled away, they were silent. Sobered. Her phone lay forgotten in the grass, recording the empty sky.

Jack picked it up. "Damn," he muttered. "Sorry. I screwed that one up. Shall we try again? I'll prop it up on the porch railing this time."

"No," she said quickly. "No, we've got plenty to work with. Let's get going."

They got back onto the road. Maddie drove in self-conscious silence as Jack busied himself examining all the videos that they had shot.

"There's great stuff here," he told her. "I'm actually pretty good at editing videos. Want me to put together your romantic montages?"

"Sure, thanks. That would be great."

Pull it together, Moss. She had to dial this down. It was unmanageable. The tire swing, the heart hands, the kiss.

Already, she was wishing it was real.

Seven

The only way to survive was by keeping busy.

Jack had learned this life-saving trick even before Bio-Spark. He'd learned it after Dad died, living in that string of foster homes. If he kept his mind fully occupied, he could keep moving forward somehow, like riding a bike. That was one of the reasons he'd hit the books so hard at school. Savage focus on studying had been his only refuge.

So to that end, he opened up the back of the car when they stopped for lunch on the road, and pulled his laptop out of its carrying case.

Jack downloaded the video clips they had shot, once they had ordered lunch, and got to work with all the focus of a guy expertly sublimating his sexual energy into another activity. His fingers chattered on the keys as he manipulated the tiny videos, trimming them, timing them. In not too long, he'd come up with three short video montages.

Maddie watched, fascinated, as she sipped her iced tea

through a straw. "You're so smooth with that program," she said. "Where did you learn to do that?"

Jack didn't even break stride. "After I got out of jail, I was flat-ass broke," he said. "I used up all my money for my legal defense. Some friends believed in me, but I didn't want to lean on them. And I couldn't get work in my field, for years. So I did a bunch of random jobs. I worked on a fishing boat in Alaska for a while. Stank of fish for months afterward. I worked construction jobs, I tended bar, I worked for a PR company, creating content for social media accounts. I got pretty fast at this kind of stuff."

"Did you ever find work that you liked more than what you did before?"

He gave her a level look. "No."

Maddie winced. "Sorry. I shouldn't have asked that."

"It's okay. Hey, if you want these videos to pop, we need a few clips of music. I'm thinking, blues, rock, steel guitar. Something gritty and rebellious, with a heavy beat."

Maddie's golden eyes widened, and she smiled. "Oh yeah. I know just the song." She lifted up her phone and selected it from her playlist, offering him her earbuds.

He put them into his ears, and listened to the first few bars. "Wait, isn't this the group that did that song that played for Trix and Terrence's first dance?"

"Yes, it is," she replied. "Moon Cat and the Kinky Ladies. It's my little niece's favorite band. This is their latest single. Listen to the words. A single verse should be about the right length, and there are three verses, one for each video."

Jack raised the volume and listened to the girl singer's wispy, and yet somehow compelling voice.

You say my skirt's too short,
My lips as red as fire,
Now you're calling all my shots,

But you're making me a liar,
I know you want to say,
It's just my restless heart to blame,
But I just can't wear,
Oh, I just can't wear,
No, I just can't wear,
Your golden chains.

"That's perfect," Jack said. "And exactly fifty seconds, too." Jack deftly applied the three clips of the song to accompany the videos, and then spun the laptop around so she could see the result.

Just as the first video ended, the waitress brought their sandwiches. Grilled cheese on sourdough for her, corned beef on rye for him, tomato basil soup for both of them.

Maddie set the second video to play again as she took a bite of her sandwich.

"They're perfect," she told him, after she'd watched them all twice. "Like those advertisements for high-end luxury products, for cars, jewelry, perfume. Where you can't quite figure out exactly what they're advertising, but you still want some."

"That's the vibe I was going for," he told her.

"Can I go ahead and post them?"

"Sure, be my guest. Let me just send you the final files."

In a few moments, Maddie had uploaded the first video, and was holding her finger over the post button. "Here goes," she said. "Fully braced for family disapproval."

"I'm glad you have a family to disapprove," he said.

Her smile faded "Oh. I'm sorry I—"

"No, no. I didn't mean to lay guilt on you. I mean it literally. I lost my dad when I was fourteen, but he would've liked you. He would've been sorry this wasn't real."

Just like me. He pushed the thought back down into the depths. Not now.

Maddie posted the video, and snapped her laptop closed. "I'm sorry you lost him."

"Me, too, but that was the one thing I was grateful for, when everything went to hell," Jack said. "Dad never had to see me in handcuffs or shackles. A prison jumpsuit."

"I'm so sorry," Maddie said again.

"It's one of the reasons I need to clear my name," he went on. "It's for him, even though he's gone."

Jack saw her smile fade, and stopped talking. She didn't believe him, and after the fun and laughter all afternoon, that realization was jarring.

She might never believe him. He just had to swallow that down and behave like a gentleman, because that's just what you did. Dad would've wanted it.

There's no excuse not to be classy, son. Not in any situation.

Maddie's phone began to ring as Jack paid the tab. She looked at the display, and glanced at him, eyes sparkling. "Word is spreading," she said, holding her smartphone up. The display read "Gran." "Our work has been seen and evaluated."

The phone kept buzzing. "Are you going to answer her?" he asked.

Maddie shook her head. "Too soon. First, I let her sweat." She declined the call and typed in a text message, holding it up for him to read.

I'm fine. Don't worry. Just trying to do my duty to family and MossTech. I'll contact you when I get back into town.

"What do you think?" she asked. "Too snarky?"

He whistled as he read it. "Oh, man. That's gonna sting."

"Yep, that's the whole point," she said with grim satisfaction, tapping the screen. "There, it's sent, and the phone is off. I am officially incommunicado."

"You just can't wear those golden chains."

"Exactly," Maddie said.

When they were in the parking lot, she pointed toward the strip mall they had driven through. "I saw a big stationery store a mile or so back," she said. "Let's stop there and pick up my whiteboards and markers."

"Whatever you need," he said. "I wasn't expecting you to hop right to it."

"You came through for my project, so it's only fair. And the videos are a great beginning. I feel better now that I'm doing something proactive, other than just scrambling for eligible bachelors, feeling all sweaty and desperate and uptight. It's so not me, you know? It feels good to just be my own wacky self."

"I'm happy to help your wacky self," he informed her. "I'm also glad that my trashed reputation is actually good for something, for once."

After a quick stop at the stationery store, they packed the supplies into the car and got back on the road, Jack driving.

The afternoon on the bluff, the video and lunch had drained away the tension between them. They still had to steer around the danger zones, but they were getting used to them, and there was still plenty left to talk about. With a little judicial prodding, he got her to tell him all about the twists and turns of her career path. How she discovered the thrills of forensic accounting entirely by accident, while getting her MBA. She'd been interning at a hedge fund in New York, and one of the senior partners had been cooking the books.

She had been the one to find the breadcrumbs, and trace them back to the source. To piece it all together.

"And that's what you'd prefer? More than being CFO for MossTech?" he asked.

She nodded. "Yeah, I'm not really the type to be an

executive. Caleb's better at that kind of thing than me. I like getting into the weeds, really going deep, and I don't think executives ever have a chance to do that. They're too busy dealing with the big picture. I've studied forensic accounting in all different kinds of industries, and I've even developed some of the latest technological tools for it myself. Although nothing will ever replace my precious whiteboards. But I use it all, simultaneously."

"You actually make it sound interesting," he said. "I can hardly believe it."

That made her laugh, which felt like a conquest. He loved the curve of her luscious lips, the way her dewy brown skin glowed. Her bold cheekbones. Her bone structure was elegant, striking. Regal, even. Every now and then, he caught a glimpse that made him think of Caleb, but not much. She must take after her father. And the guy must've been damn good-looking, to generate a gorgeous creature like her.

"What?" she demanded. "Watch the road, Daly."

"You don't look much like Caleb, or Marcus," Jack said. "I've seen pictures of your mother, and Caleb looks a lot like her. But you don't. Do you have any pictures of your dad?"

"I've got nothing," she said. "Not a name, not even a nationality. My mother never got around to discussing my parentage with anyone. The only thing the housekeeper was pretty sure about was that my father was not her current boyfriend, the guy with the yacht. Yacht guy was a redhead. Definitely not my progenitor."

"No, I would say not," he agreed.

"We did a genetic test once, a few years ago, out of curiosity," she told him. "The Moss side is English and Irish. Caleb has Spanish and Portuguese ancestry, Marcus has Japanese and some Korean, and mine is mainly Ethiopian and Egyptian, and some other countries in Africa. We're a global grab bag. My mother had wide-ranging tastes."

"The results were pretty damn optimal. You're all extremely good-looking."

"Thanks. The housekeeper thought that my father might have been a musician who was in town on tour, but she didn't know his name, or even what instrument he played," Maddie said. "My mother never wore any golden chains. She just left me with the housekeeper and partied like a maniac. Up to the very end."

"I'm sorry about the accident, but I'm glad you weren't on that yacht," Jack said.

"Me, too. I'm grateful for my grandparents and my brothers, however much I bitch. I know I've been blessed. I try not to complain, but lately, it's got the better of me."

"You have a right to feel how you feel," he assured her. "It's better to just unload it. You breathe easier when you aren't trying to be perfect."

There was a silence, and they both broke into smothered, startled laughter.

"I promise I won't try too hard," she told him. "What about your mom? I knew about you losing your dad when you were fourteen, but I never heard about your mom."

"Cancer," he said. "She died when I was six."

Maddie winced. "Ouch. Jack. I'm so sorry."

"Thanks," he said. "It was a long time ago, but it was harrowing. I remember her, but just barely. Like a warm glow through a curtain. I wish I could remember specifics, but Dad's gone, too, so there's no one who can help me with the details. Time just grinds them all away."

"You're still lucky," Maddie said. "I can't remember my mother at all. Not even a glow. You must have pictures, right? Do you look like her? Or your dad?"

"My complexion is hers, dark hair and eyes, but everything else is my dad."

"Did you get those long eyelashes from her?"

He laughed. "Must have. Hard to say."

The miles sped by. Their conversation wound on, long and meandering. They talked about anything and everything, and by twilight, he was making his way through Cleland, the town nearest to his vacation house.

"My suggestion is, we check you into your B and B, and then go to the Broderick Tavern for dinner, since it's right nearby," he said. "I'll show you the house, and we'll put up your whiteboards in a spare bedroom. Then you can head off to your B and B whenever you're ready."

"Sounds great," she said. "It's so beautiful here."

"Yeah, I always stay up here, since I discovered this town, and this house. The forest relaxes me. I could take you on some of my favorite hikes, if you're into that kind of thing. I love big mysterious forests. They put my problems into perspective."

"I'd love it," she said. "I adore hiking. And forests. I want my problems put into perspective, too. It sounds very therapeutic."

Jack pulled over in front of the large, brightly painted Victorian house that belonged to Delilah, the woman who rented him the vacation house. Delilah came out to greet him, rattling a bunch of keys. She had a cloud of curly silver hair and was dressed in a brilliant tie-dyed T-shirt. "Jackie!" she sang out. "Glad you're back, handsome. The house is all ready for you. I even picked up some of those cinnamon rolls you like from the bakery and left them on the counter."

"Thanks, Delilah. Hey, could you rent my friend a room in your B and B?"

Delilah looked distressed. "Oh, honey, I'm so sorry to disappoint you, but we have a fiftieth wedding anniversary in town, and they all checked in today. I'm full to the gills. If you'd asked me two days ago you could've had any room you liked."

"Yikes." He shot Maddie a worried glance. "I figured, since it was a Monday evening…"

"That's almost always true, just not today," Delilah said regretfully. "I'd send her to the Eagles Nest, but Kris is full up, with two weddings. Your best bet is the Marriott in Beckinsdale."

"It's a half-hour drive back the way we came," Jack said.

"I know, hon. So sorry. If all else fails, there are plenty of extra full-size sheets for the other bedrooms. I just made up the bed in the master bedroom."

"Okay. Thanks." Jack turned to Maddie. "I'm so sorry."

"It's fine," she assured him. "It's a straight shot back to Beckinsdale. I think I saw the Marriott near the south freeway entrance, right?"

"Yes, that's exactly right." Delilah's curious blue eyes darted between her and Jack. "Shall I call and make a reservation for you?"

Maddie smiled. "Thanks, but I'll handle it."

Jack waited outside while Maddie found the Beckinsdale Marriott on her phone, and booked herself a room. When she hung up, she strolled alongside him toward the Broderick Tavern while scanning her text messages.

"Gran texted eight times," she said. "Caleb, four times. Tilda, three. Marcus, three. Even Annika called me. They're out of their freaking minds."

"Are you going to read the messages?"

"Maybe later. Right now, I'm channeling Susanna Moss and thinking of only myself. Let's see how our video montage is doing out in the world." She clicked it, and looked up, eyes sparkling. "It's been viewed nine hundred times so far."

"That's wild. But good, for your purposes. Right?"

"Right," she said. "Very good."

"Any regrets?" he asked.

Her eyes flashed at the challenge. "Hell, no."

"Ahh." Jack held open the door to the Broderick Tavern. "That's my girl."

Eight

Maddie savored a bite of her grilled marinated halibut, and pulled out her notebook. The food was great, the ambience was relaxing, there was even live music playing in the back of the room, and it wasn't half bad. She was having way too much fun.

It was unfortunate, that the B and B had no rooms, but whatever. It just meant that she had to drive, and therefore couldn't drink with dinner. Just as well, considering. With Jack, she certainly didn't need any help lowering her inhibitions.

She pulled out her black-rimmed geek-girl glasses and put them on. "Okay, Jack. Behold me in work mode. Let's get started."

"They look great," he said. "The $E=mc^2$ vibe is very hot. Works for me."

"So glad you like it," she said. "So. What I want from you now is an overview of what I have to analyze. I also want to know who looked at the records before, and why you felt that their efforts fell short. And if you have their documentation, great."

"I have it all in my files," he said. "I'll show it to you back at the house. But it's been a long day. Wouldn't you rather get started tomorrow?"

"Gran always says, why put off till tomorrow what you can do today? Gimme the goods."

"I see why you Mosses are freakish overachievers," Jack said ruefully.

"Yeah, we're twisted that way. So? What can you tell me?"

Jack got a look on his face that she'd noticed before. Like he was bracing himself.

"You know about the products we were developing at BioSpark, right?"

"I have a rough idea, but it was a long time ago," she said. "Also, I was off in college at the time, and Caleb doesn't talk about it. So refresh my memory."

"We called them the Carbon Clean line. The base was a cocktail of selected bacteria and fungi that produced super-enzymes that could digest plastic. We had a range of products. Some for landfills, others for water. Time release capsules for oceans, lakes and rivers."

"That much I do remember," she said. "There was lots of buzz. I remember the adulation. Magazine covers, interviews, screaming fangirls, like you two were rock stars. It went straight to Caleb's head. He thought he was God's gift back then, though he had his hands full with Tilda. How about you? Were you involved with anyone?"

Maddie knew the answer to that question perfectly well, having consumed every last scrap of news ever published about Jack Daly. But he never needed to know that.

"I was with Gabriella Adriani back then," Jack told her. "Our head of marketing."

"Oh, yeah. I remember her. Super thin, platinum blonde, very black eyebrows?"

"That's her. Caleb and I were too busy to be distracted by screaming fangirls."

"Right. So, BioSpark made the Carbon Clean line, and everyone was really excited about it. Who dreamed that up, anyhow? Caleb never told me."

"I guess it was me, at the beginning," Jack said. "One of my summer jobs when I was at Stanford was at a dump and recycling center. I spent hot summer days in a festering trash heap. Man, was it ripe."

"I just bet it was," she said.

"I noticed that in some places, the plastic was degrading faster than in others. So I took samples from the slime, and cultured them. My coworkers at the dump thought that I had psychological problems, rooting around in the stinking trash. They called me the Garbage Guy."

"Inspired," Maddie said.

"Anyhow, Caleb and I selected the microbiomes that were the hungriest, looking for the super-enzymes. When we found them, we modified the genes to supercharge the process. It took years of iterations to find a balance of microbes that would make degrading plastic economically viable."

"Hence, your preoccupation with balance."

"Maybe. Anyhow, that was the first version of Carbon Clean. We recruited a dream team of our favorite researchers, microbiologists, organic chemists and geneticists. We fine-tuned it into something that worked. And I mean, really worked. We were about to go public. And the sky fell."

Jack looked away, his throat moving.

Maddie helped him out. "Energen Corp came out with almost the same product."

"So you do remember," he said.

"The broad strokes, yes. The news was full of it. Caleb was…well, never mind."

"I know how he felt." Jack's voice was bleak. "Someone set me up."

And there they were again, at the heart of her dilemma. How could she proceed in good faith if she didn't believe his story? Maddie tapped her pencil against her notebook.

"So tell me, Jack," she persisted. "How am I supposed to help you?"

"Whoever did this plotted for a long time," Jack said. "It wasn't an impulse. And Energen could never have come up with a product like ours out of nowhere. It took us years, with top-notch researchers and a sizable budget. And we were busting our asses, working like maniacs, never sleeping. As far as the Energen team goes…well, Joel LeBlanc, their lead guy? He was no heavyweight, and that's putting it kindly. He was a mediocre biochemist no one had ever heard of, and no one on his small team had ever stuck out in the crowd, either. And yet, with a fraction of the time, resources and personnel, they pulled a product very similar to ours out of their asses. Ta-da. Energen Vortex was presented to the world."

"And Caleb knew this about them?"

"At that point, Caleb was no longer listening to me," Jack said. "Someone planted all that evidence on me. He couldn't get past that, and I don't blame him. It looked bad."

"Refresh my memory," Maddie said. "What was the evidence?"

He let out a slow breath. "A couple days before the Energen public offering, a broker filled an order to buy seven hundred thousand dollars of Energen stock," he said. "But the broker came forward afterward, and said that the request came from my IP address. My desktop computer at home. As if I would be stupid enough not to mask my IP, if it were me who placed the order."

"You couldn't have been hacked, or spoofed?"

He reluctantly shook his head. "Not with the kind of encryption we had in place. It was made to order, exclusive, specific to us. The order was placed a little after two in the morning. They also found bank accounts in Panama that I had ostensibly set up, and a plane ticket to Rio that I never bought. The whole scene was meticulously organized."

"You were in the apartment alone when this order was placed?"

"I was asleep," he said flatly. "I'd drunk a glass of wine with Gabriella, and crashed."

"How much was the Energen stock worth, after the company went public?"

"About forty-six million dollars," he said. "Confiscated, of course. Not that I would have kept it in any case."

Maddie was relieved that the details he cited matched up with her own version of events...so far. "That's quite a chunk of money," she mused. "But it's very small change for Energen, particularly now. Energen's Vortex product must've earned billions by now."

"It has." Jack's voice was bitter. "And their product is weaker than ours. It's slower, less reliable, it has problems in salt water, it has problems at both lower and higher temperature ranges, it's useless on polystyrene and polyvinyl chloride...they're hacks. They stole a perfectly functional thing, and covered their tracks by fucking it up."

Maddie studied his face. He was so believable. Then again, Caleb had been taken, too, and Caleb was no fool. "Tell me something, Jack," she said.

"Anything," he said.

"If you're so sure that Energen stole BioSpark's research, why not accuse them and nail them to the wall?"

Jack hesitated. "I'm not supposed to have some of this information, about Energen's research and development timeline."

"Meaning what? You have it or you don't."

"Not exactly," Jack said. "I have a friend who shared inside info with me. But she still works there, and if they knew she told me, she'd be shredded by their legal department. Her career would be over, if she didn't end up in jail. So I can't show this stuff to the police. Besides, it's inconclusive. It paints a picture, it suggests things, it points. But there's no smoking gun in the mix."

"So you have information that's useless," Maddie said ruthlessly. "You can't use it without exposing your friend. So why should I take it seriously? Why should anyone? And what's the point, if you can't clear your name?"

"I just want to prove to my best friend that I never sold him out," Jack said forcefully. "I squeezed my source because I hoped the data would at least point me in the direction of the person who wanted to destroy me. So that I can tear him to pieces."

Maddie's spine stiffened. "I want no part of any violence."

"No, no," Jack assured her. "Metaphorically speaking."

Maddie tapped her pen frantically against the notebook, pondering that. "Who's your source?" she asked. "Can you even tell me?"

"Will you promise to keep it to yourself?"

Maddie gave him a narrow look. "You're asking for a big leap of faith."

"Please, Maddie. I need your word. I don't want to hurt my friend."

She hesitated for just a moment. "Okay, you have my word. But I don't see the point, if you can't use the data. It's not like you can get that money back."

"It was never about money," Jack said. "Money was just

a byproduct of what we were doing. It's useful, for moving forward, but it doesn't drive me. It never has."

Maddie nodded. "Fine. I get it. Tell me about your secret source."

"Her name is Amelia Howard, and she works in the R & D department of Energen. She's an administrator, not a researcher."

"And I'll be looking at her data tomorrow?"

"Among other things," Jack said. "Gabriella introduced us. Amelia rented a condo in our complex. I had an apartment down in San Francisco, but I came up to Seattle so often, I decided to keep an apartment here, too, and Amelia and I became friends. She's a sweet person. She was breaking up with a real turd of a guy who treated her like dirt, and I was trying to be supportive of her. Then my world fell apart. We were both a mess."

"I need to talk to Amelia," she said. "I agree to not expose her role in sharing data with you, but I still want to look her in the eye and ask her all my questions."

Jack nodded, and pulled out his phone, selecting a number. "I'll see if she'll talk to you," he said, as it rang. "Hey, Amelia?… Yeah, it's Jack. I'm back in town… Yeah, staying up in Cleland again. Yeah, I'd love to. Let's set something up. Hey, I've got a favor to ask of you. I've asked a friend of mine to analyze my BioSpark archives… Yeah, I know… Uh-huh. She was hoping to talk in person… No, she's given me her word… Hold on and I'll ask." He looked at Maddie. "When could you meet her? This week, next week?"

"How about after Ava's wedding next weekend?" Maddie said. "I could meet her on Sunday, if she prefers not to do it on a weekday. We could grab lunch. Someplace discreet, where no one will see me with her."

Jack relayed all of this, and then closed the call, slipping the phone in his pocket. "Twelve-thirty on Sunday," he confirmed. "She sent me the address of a bistro near her place where you two can get lunch. I forwarded it to you."

"Great. I look forward to talking to her. So? Anything else?"

"That's my backdrop," Jack said. "The broker told everyone about the order I was supposed to have made, but didn't. BioSpark's public offering tanked. I was arrested, for fraud, malfeasance, insider trading. And I went to prison."

"But you got out after six months," Maddie said. "How did you manage that?"

"Random luck," he said grimly. "The crime scene was poorly handled. There were mistakes made by the criminologists, so some of the key evidence was inadmissible. So it was enough to convince everyone that I was guilty, but not enough to convict me, at least not for very long. All I want now is to be able to convince Caleb that it wasn't me."

Jack sounded so sincere. She was almost tempted to entertain the possibility that he really was innocent. But that was dangerous. She liked that story. Liked it way too much.

The waitress came back. "Dessert? Another drink? Coffee?" she asked them.

"I'm fine," Maddie said. "We should call it a night, after I get you home."

"I hate to have you drive all the way back to Beckinsdale," Jack said.

"Oh, I'll be fine. I'll drop you at your house and head on out. I want to get started bright and early tomorrow."

The winding road through the forest was eerie in the headlights of her car. Even in the dark, she was charmed by the house when they arrived. It was a bold modern design, interlocking steel-and-glass cubes that let all light and the colors of the forest in. It was perched on the edge of a narrow canyon. One of the terraces cantilevered out over the canyon, right over the rushing rapids and water-falls. The scent and sound of the place was a sensory embrace, a great chittering and humming, chirping of birds and insects, the rustle of wind in the branches, the sweet, cool smell, the constant rush of water.

The inside of the glass house was understated and comfortable. Soft couches in warm earthy colors were grouped around the stone fireplace. There was a big, welcoming kitchen, and a long wooden table, big enough to seat twelve.

"Hey," he said. "I just thought of something. Why don't you stay here, and I'll just drive to Beckinsdale? The bed's made up, the bathroom's ready. Just settle in and relax."

"No way," she said. "This is your place."

"But I don't want you to—"

"You know what?" she said, on impulse. "I won't go to Beckinsdale. I'll crash here. I just decided. It's silly for me to drive all that way when you have plenty of room." She paused. "Unless you're uncomfortable with that, of course," she added.

"Of course not." Jack looked pleased. "That would be great. I'll go and find those sheets and fix up your bed right away."

"Let's get those whiteboards set up tonight, so I can start at first light."

"Will do," Jack called from one of the bedrooms.

Maddie turned on the phone to call the hotel to cancel the reservation, and saw messages piling up. Missed calls from everyone in her family, and some of her friends. Geri alone had called three times. There were dozens of text messages. Word was out.

The phone began to buzz. This time it was Caleb. *Not tonight, bro. Not a chance.*

She declined that call, and went into the family group chat.

For God's sake, people, relax. I'm fine. I'll get in touch when it suits me. Give Annika a kiss for me. Later, people.

Take that, Gran. Attitude to the utmost.

Nine

Jack woke up from a restless doze, and smelled coffee and toast. It was barely light. He looked around, disoriented, until the events of the last few days suddenly hit his conscious mind, knocking him right back down onto his back. Freshly astonished.

He stared up at the ceiling in disbelief. Maddie Moss, in all her seductive gorgeous glory, was in the other room, studying his BioSpark archives. Miracles did exist.

Of course, she was biased against him, but hey, she was here, and that was huge. He had to keep his cool. Stay the hell out of her way. Try not to stare, if at all possible.

He washed his face, brushed his teeth, threw on some sweatpants and a T-shirt, then grabbed a cup of coffee from the kitchen, noticing toast crumbs on a butter knife in the sink. The rooms were all on one side of the corridor, and a wall of glass was on the other, showing the forest in the misty dawn.

He pushed open the spare bedroom door they had prepared last night. Maddie stood with her back to him, staring at one of her whiteboards, a black marker in one hand and a piece of toast in the other. The table behind her held her laptop, markers, piles of Post-it notes. Her notebooks.

"Good morning," he said.

"Morning." Her voice was faraway. "Can't talk. Gimme a sec."

"Sure, sure. Carry on," he said.

A few minutes later, she joined him in the kitchen and refilled her coffee cup. "I didn't mean to be rude, but I was chasing a thought," she said.

"Sorry to interrupt you," he said. "Did you catch it?"

"I hope so. Time will tell."

She wore the same baggy sweatshirt she'd had on at the beach bonfire party, but today she wore soft striped athletic leggings instead of cutoff blue jeans. It was a mystery how slouchy athletic wear could be so sexy on her. Her hair was tied up off her face with a scarf, with an explosive twist of ringlets showing on top. She wasn't wearing makeup. Her unpainted lips were a deep blush rose. The skin on her face was so exquisitely supple and soft. He'd memorized every detail from that last kiss. His fingers ached to feel it again.

"You know, Jack, I've been looking through stuff, and this thing really is not my area of expertise," she admitted. "I'm a hard numbers kind of woman. This involves comparing BioSpark's research to Energen's, right down the line. A whole other thing."

He was crestfallen. "So you don't want to continue?"

"I never said that. Truthfully? I'm hooked. I really want to see more. It's just that it makes me less confident of being absolutely sure of my results."

Something inside him relaxed. "That's fine," he said. "I'm just happy to have a smart person with fresh eyes looking at the whole mess again. That's all I need. I don't need guarantees or certainties. I already know that I can't have them."

"But it will take a while," she warned him. "I like to lay out everything where I can see it, and then organize it, and reorganize it. For a while, it's like waiting for popcorn to start popping. Right when you start to wonder if the kernels are all duds, it starts to happen all at once. Ideas and patterns start bubbling up."

"Should I stay out of your way?"

"For the most part. I tend to be kind of rude when I'm concentrating. But I'd like to have you within shouting distance, in case I need elucidations about microbiomes, or super-enzymes, or bioremediation, or breaking polymer links, or what all."

"Fine. I just need to run in to town to grab some groceries. Can I use your car?"

"Of course. Feel free." Her eyes were already far away, and she was tapping her pen against that little notebook. "The keys are in my purse."

He forced himself to drag his eyes away from the spectacular back view of Maddie Moss, which he could gaze at worshipfully forever. So hot, working at her whiteboards, standing on her tiptoes, reaching above her head, which lifted up the sweatshirt and showed off the shape of her butt, and the pink, narrow bottoms of her highly arched feet.

He drove to the farmers' market, the grocery store, the bakery. When he got back and hauled in all the bags, Maddie had moved on to another whiteboard.

Some of the info she was noting down was familiar, but the way she organized her information was not comprehensible to him. It looked almost sloppy, but clearly, it wasn't, judging from the laser focus in her eyes, and the way she utterly ignored him. If he weren't so invested in her conclusions, he might even get his feelings hurt. As it was, no.

You go, girl. Do your thing. Don't ever stop.

He came in a couple of hours later, and found her seated at the computer, tapping away. Yet another whiteboard was full of scribbling, which he studied, fascinated. "Could you tell me what you're doing?"

"No," she said, without looking at him.

"Ah. Okay. I'll make us some lunch. Gotta fuel the magic machine."

Maddie didn't even change expression. "Huh?"

He left her to it with a snort, and went to fire up the grill. Then he wrapped a salmon fillet in foil, loaded it with butter, lemon and dill. When the meal was organized on the terrace, along with some fire roasted summer vegetables and some fluffy rice pilaf, he opened the door. "Hey, I've got food," he told her. "Out on the terrace."

She turned to him, her eyes blank. He could almost hear the gears grinding loudly in her head as she dragged her mind back to a plane where such things as food existed.

"Thanks," she said, distractedly. "Uh…yeah. Be right there."

"We'll eat outside," he said. "Come whenever you're ready."

She looked down at her hands, which were blackened with ink from the markers. "I'll just go and wash up."

Maddie was quiet as they were eating, but he didn't take it personally. He remembered that zone, from college, from grad school, from BioSpark. She'd forgotten how to talk, and it took a while to remember. The deeper you went, the harder it was to come back.

"By the way, when I was shopping in town, I saw a jewelry store," he said. "If you want, we can go there, and make another video that's all about the ring."

"Oh, yeah. I'm glad you reminded me," she said. "I'd forgotten all about that. It's important to feed the beast."

"Have you checked in with your folks?"

"You mean, have I glanced at their hysterical text messages? Not since last night. Let's see the heights of madness they've risen to now."

Maddie pulled out her phone and turned it on, and it immediately began to ring.

"It's Tilda," Maddie said, studying the display. "I love her like a sister, but not now. Their timing is insane. Every time I turn on my phone, it rings instantly. I can't face it."

"What time did you wake up?"

"I was already working at 4 a.m.," she said. "I didn't sleep well."

"No? Was the bed okay?"

"The bed was fabulous. I love those trees, and the sound of the water. But I was restless, so I got up and went to work." She clicked through messages, and gasped in dismay. "Oh, God."

"What is it? Is everyone okay?"

She clapped her hand over her eyes. "Caleb is cutting his and Tilda's Spain trip short. They're flying home from Barcelona today. To deal with me."

"Yikes," he said. "That's awful."

"Yes, it really is."

"At least your gran is okay," he said. "You scared me for a second."

"You thought I'd given her a stroke or a heart attack? No way. She's a tough old bird."

Jack just shrugged and looked away.

Maddie leaned over the table and tapped his arm. "Hey. What's wrong? Are you upset about something?"

"I just wish that we were messing with people I dislike," he said. "Like Bruce Traynor, for instance. Jerking him around would be a blast. But it's no fun doing it to people that I care about and respect, like Caleb and Elaine."

Maddie stared down at her food. "Dammit, Jack. Stop.

You're making me feel guilty, and that's exactly what I'm trying to avoid right now."

"Sorry," he said sheepishly. "I'll shut up and get you some pie."

"Great. Then we go ring shopping, and I can compound my cruelty to my family even more. Ruthless, monstrous hag that I am."

Jack cut her a slice of blackberry pie with shortbread crust, and scooped up a sphere of honey vanilla ice cream. "As you command, Oh Dreadful One," he said. "Your evil truly knows no bounds."

"I'm sure that's exactly what Caleb is saying about me to Tilda right now in the airport at Barcelona," Maddie said. She took a bite of pie and gasped with pleasure. "Oh, my God, Jack. This is freaking divine."

Yes. So far, so good. He was keeping it classy.

After lunch, they went to the jewelry store. The town was a tourist haven for wealthy Seattle residents, so there was a large selection of beautiful, unique designs. Jack paid close attention and noticed how one of the rings made her eyes sparkle. It was a square cut sapphire flanked by cabochon rubies, set in a thick band of white gold. It looked both modern and somehow ancient.

"Pretty." Maddie admired it on her hand. "I feel like a Sumerian queen."

Jack glanced at the price, and was suitably impressed. "Shall we take pictures of that one?"

The shop was deserted, and the saleswoman was obliging, so they shot a bunch of pictures and videos, some with her arms around his neck, eyes closed in bliss, the ring on display, some of their hands clasped, some of them kissing with her hand extended, showing the ring off. Jack wanted to buy it for her on the spot, it looked so damn perfect on her hand.

"We'll be back later," Maddie told the saleswoman.

When they returned to the house, Maddie went back to work, and Jack got busy editing the video, glad to have something to keep him busy. He killed another couple of hours looking over material for his business meetings next week, and then it was time to start dinner.

It was twilight when Maddie came out of her cave, drawn by the scent of tangy marinated chicken skewers on the grill outside, accompanied by a tomato and cucumber salad, some fresh, crusty bread from the bakery, and a summer vegetable stew, flavored with marjoram and basil.

When they had finished eating, he spun the laptop around for her.

"I picked the song this time, but I could switch it out for something else if you want," he said. "I used 'Bring the Bling,' It's a new single by Jackhammer, and it's got that gritty, rebellious vibe that you like."

The video opened to a shot of Maddie's slender brown hands, still smeared with ink, and that gorgeous ring, glowing on her finger. Her hands wound around Jack's neck, the ring on full display. Holding him with that hungry grasp, her fingers clutching the nape of his neck, to the wail of the steel guitar, and the singer's rough, resonant baritone voice.

It was earthy, sexy. Anyone watching would envy them. Want to be them.

Damn. He wanted to be them, himself. How twisted in knots was that.

"It's perfect," Maddie said. "Brilliant. Can I post it everywhere?"

"Of course," he said.

She smiled at him. "I think you missed your calling, Jack."

"No," he said flatly. "I found my perfect calling. Someone stole it from me."

That wiped the smile right off her face, to his dismay. *Not classy, Daly.*

"I'm sorry," she said.

"No, I'm the one who should be sorry," he said. "I promised myself not to burden you with my crap, but sometimes it sneaks up on me."

Maddie stood up, looking uncertain. "Well, then. I guess I'll try to get some sleep, so I can get an early start tomorrow. I've still got a lot of work to do. Dinner was delicious. You're a fabulous cook. I'll do the dishes."

"Don't worry, I've got it," he assured her. "I'd rather you spend your time at the whiteboard, doing your magic thing, or else sleeping. Good night."

Jack finished cleaning up the kitchen, and attempted to relax with a shower. But being naked and wet, knowing that she was right through the wall just wound him up more.

He kept seeing that beautiful, long-fingered, ink-stained hand, with the pale gold ring, bright as moonlight against her golden brown skin. It made his chest hurt.

This cycle of emotions was becoming routine. He started to enjoy their playacting just a little too much, and then boom, he crashed and burned, because it wasn't real. And it could never be real.

He had to learn to keep his tender goddamn feelings to himself.

Ten

Maddie spent the next two days studying the BioSpark archives, teasing out every bit of information she could, and plugging it into her own mental matrix.

And after three days, the magic started to happen. Her mind started bubbling up what felt like new information, but which was actually a reworked version of the old.

This was the fun part. The piercing flashes, the aha moments. The excitement.

Problem was, this was the first time that her restless body was getting in the way of the truth by clamoring for its own reward, its own satisfaction, its own agenda.

She was walking a tightrope, because she really, really wanted Jack Daly to be innocent. Not only because of her crush, but just because she simply liked the man. He was funny, smart, his sense of humor matched with hers.

And he was so sexy, it was just outrageous. It shouldn't be allowed.

The overall sense growing inside her was that she didn't

believe that Jack would have devalued his own creation enough to sell it out for a flat fee, while also screwing over his best friend and burning his own professional reputation. True, his Energen stock had zoomed up to forty-six million dollars, but that was nothing compared to the billions that BioSpark would have generated for him as the company grew and diversified.

The story of the scam just didn't hold up against their original story of two scrappy young entrepreneurs, putting their hearts and minds into a product that could save the oceans and earn untold billions. The kind of story that inspired Hollywood movies. Compare that to running off to Rio all alone with his ill-gotten gains, having lost all his professional credibility, having betrayed his friends and having sold his life's work to the highest bidder. A traitor, despised by all.

Why would he do that? A man with his talents?

The more she got to know Jack, the more she thought that it wasn't the right question to ask, simply because he hadn't done it. That was the work of a smaller, craftier, more self-serving person. One who cared only for himself.

But dammit, she couldn't expect reality to align with her own personal preferences. That was childish and dangerous. She was afraid to trust her gut on this one.

Jack walked in. "Hey there. Dinner's ready. You hungry?"

"Yeah," she said. "I'm done for tonight."

He walked closer, gazing at her whiteboards covered with a dense scrawl of notes, her fluttering mass of colored sticky notes. "Have you come to any conclusions? Throw me a bone, Maddie."

She hesitated before answering. "Well. If Amelia's data is accurate—"

"It is," Jack said.

"If it's reliable, then I have no doubt that BioSpark's research was stolen by Energen," she said. "I've researched the people whose names are on the Energen Vortex project, and I agree with your assessment of their limitations. There's no way those people could have generated that body of work in that time frame, compared to BioSpark's team and timeline. Plus, in the past year and a half before the IPOs, the big breaks in research for both of the companies start to follow the same arcs, but with a pretty consistent time lag. As if the Energen team were getting regular infusions of information, and then scrambling to incorporate them."

"Yes," Jack said. "Yes, my thoughts exactly."

"So, keeping that in mind, I've been trying to figure out if you were the one to pass them the BioSpark research," Maddie said.

"I see." Jack looked pained. "What did you decide?"

"I'm on shaky ground, here," she admitted. "Because I don't trust my own perceptions when it comes to you. But honestly, Jack? I just don't see you trading what you had with BioSpark for this bullshit." She waved at the whiteboard. "Even if it had worked, and you'd gotten away clean with forty-six million bucks, what's that, compared to BioSpark's potential? You guys would've been billionaires many times over. Famous. Celebrated. Venerated for saving the oceans. People would name libraries and elementary schools after you. You wouldn't trade a lifetime of service to become one of the idle rich, sipping umbrella drinks on a beach. That would bore you to death."

"Not just that," Jack added, his voice rough. "Caleb was family. Your grandmother Elaine was, too. All of you were. And the people at BioSpark. They were the only family I had, and I wouldn't have traded that for forty-six million, or forty-six billion. I hope you believe me."

Maddie gazed directly into his eyes, and nodded. "I do believe you, Jack," she said. "God help me, but I do."

Jack closed his eyes, and turned away for a moment.

"Thanks." His voice was thick and unsteady. "You can't imagine what that means to me."

Maddie's world was readjusting, recalibrating to this new reality, one in which Jack was innocent. She was still holding both realities suspended in her head: the old one, where Jack was a conniving thief and liar, and the new one, where Jack was just… Jack.

The real, true Jack. The shining truth of him, blazing out of his eyes as he turned to her, wiping away tears that he was too embarrassed to show.

She wiped away her own tears, sniffing aggressively. "Do not make a fool of me, Jack Daly," she warned him. "Or I will tear you limb from limb."

"I have never been anything but honest with you," Jack said. "I swear to God."

"My one doubt is how badly I want this to be true," she told him. "It makes my judgment suspect."

He took a step toward her. "No," he said. "Your judgment is spot-on."

"I'm still in a bind, though. Unless we can prove your innocence. Because what I've got is subjective. Not solid proof. We need more."

"I know." He touched her cheek with his fingertip, then took her hand, pressing a soft, hot kiss to her palm.

His lips were so warm. She felt the contact throughout her body. Her breath caught, and her thighs clenched around the sweet melting ache of longing.

He felt it. "Oh, man," he said. "We better cool it."

She laughed. "Good luck. Got an ice-cold stream to jump into?"

"Actually, I do," he replied. "Throw on some shoes and a jacket. There's just enough light left tonight to show you one of the waterfalls. The closest one."

Maddie backed away, smiling like a fool, and retreated

SHANNON McKENNA 99

to her room. She pulled on her sweatshirt and her kicks, and tossed her phone on her bed. She wouldn't need it.

She was leaving it all behind. The rest of the world could wait.

She followed him out of the house, and into the forest. Her senses opened up inside her as he led her deeper into the vast cathedral of towering trees, fuzzed with vivid green moss and lichen. The delicate leaves of the foliage at their roots seemed to float in midair. The place hummed and twittered and rustled, fragrant and sweet. It vibrated with life.

And so did she, like never before. Everything she saw and heard and smelled was poignant, charged with brightness. Every tender tree leaf, every crystalline warble of birdsong. Incredible, that this forest had always been exactly this beautiful, exactly this magical—but she hadn't seen it. Hadn't felt it.

Because of Jack, new eyes inside her mind had opened up, and were staring around the world as if she'd never seen it before. Dazzled.

He was so beautiful. Outside, inside. She'd known it all along, since she first met him, but she'd been holding her hands over her eyes, not letting herself see who he really was, because she didn't trust him. Or herself.

Now her doubt was crumbling, her fear lifting. Without it, she felt as light as air. She floated through the hush of the primeval forest with him, awestruck and amazed.

Jack led her to the rocky edge of a canyon. Ice-clear water sluiced through a gleaming chute of water-smoothed granite, and sprayed out onto a rocky downhill slope, creating ethereal bouncing waterfalls all the way down, like a flounced skirt.

"Oh, my God," she said. "All that time, I was in there, guzzling coffee and crunching numbers, while this was outside. This wonderland."

He looked pleased. "You like it? It's one of my favorite places in the world."

"I've never seen anything so beautiful in my life," she told him.

"Me neither," he said quietly. "Until I saw you."

Their hands hung at their sides, but somehow, the outside of her little finger brushed the outside of his, and a sweet thrill of awareness went through her.

Suddenly, their hands were joined, clasped, fingers twined. Her face was so hot, it had to be cherry red. Her heartbeat thrummed, fast and frantic. "Same," she whispered.

He turned to her and took her other hand. "This role-playing we're doing for Elaine," he said. "I want so badly for it to be real."

She gazed up into his eyes. "Me, too."

Then the distance between them closed, and they were kissing.

There was a pleading desperation in the kiss, as if they could be ripped apart at any moment. As if they were gasping for air.

She could have torn off her clothes and had sex with him right there. On the wet stones, bent over a mossy log, pinned against a tree, her bare skin cooled by the misty spray in the waterfall. She felt feverishly hot, straining against that hard bulge against her belly. Melting with readiness.

Jack pulled away. "Back to the house?"

She nodded, and their hands joined again as they walked, though the narrow suggestion of a path really wasn't wide enough for two. Their fingers couldn't let go. They were made to be together, and she'd hungered for that contact, ever since that first kiss at the resort, when the curtain was first torn back on this hunger.

It felt so good, so exquisitely right, to finally give in to it.

The dusk had deepened almost to darkness. There was barely enough light to follow the path, but Jack knew just where he was going, leading her through the gnarled roots of the towering trees, up slopes and back down again. The house came into view, the glass of the long windows glowing in the trees like a dark crystal.

She followed him inside, and they stood there facing each other for a moment in the dimness, locked in a state of wordless, heightened awareness, and anticipation.

There was just enough light to see the somber expression in his eyes. "Maddie," he said. "I want this more than anything I've ever wanted in my life. But once we do this, we can't walk it back. I certainly can't."

"Why would we want to? I want to go forward. With you."

"I just think…" His voice trailed off for a moment, his throat working as he swallowed. "I think that you should think it through. One last time."

She shook her head. "I'm not thinking right now, and I don't miss it one bit. I'm feeling, which I don't usually let myself do. But with you, I can't seem to help it. And I love it, Jack. I love the way this makes me feel. It's…it's just incredible."

"Yes. And this was hard enough when it was just make-believe. But I know how it feels to be exiled from my people. I don't have family left, but BioSpark was my chosen family. To have them turn against me for something bad they thought I'd done—it was terrible, Maddie. Being banished punches a huge hole in your life. You'll always feel it. No matter who you're with, no matter what you're doing, that hole is always there."

She bit her lip to keep it from shaking. "I can make this decision for myself."

"Yes, but you're making the decision blind. You won't

know how it feels until you get there." His voice was bleak. "But I do know, Maddie. And I have to tell you."

The pain radiating off him hurt her heart. She stepped forward, putting her hand on his chest. "You're a really good guy, Jack," she whispered.

"You'll be the only one who thinks so," he told her. "My life was totaled, Maddie. I don't want to trash yours, too. You might not feel it now, but you need your people."

She swayed closer to him, placing both hands on his chest, craving his heat and electricity. "Jack," she said simply. "I need you."

"I feel the same way. But unless my name is cleared, your family will never accept a relationship between us. You know how they feel about it. Caleb, Elaine, Marcus."

"If they love me, they'll reach out. They'll try to understand. They have to." She seized a fistful of his shirt, and jerked him closer.

"Whoa!" He laughed under his breath, covering her hands with his. "I'm trying to do the right thing."

"And I appreciate your gallantry, but you brought me here, to this magical love nest in the enchanted woods, and paraded around in front of me, being sexy and gorgeous, and when I give in to the temptation, that's when you pull back? You big tease."

"No, it's not like that. I just want you to remember—"

"No." She stretched up onto her tiptoes, wrapping her arms around his neck. "I don't want to remember whatever it is. Shut up and kiss me."

Jack let out a low, rasping groan, his arms around her waist, cupping the back of her head, his fingers winding into her hair.

She melted. Her eyes, her throat, her heart, between her legs. She went hot and soft and liquid, surrendering to it completely. All the doubts and fears and second-guessing were swept away entirely, and all that was left was a desperate need to get closer.

She ached to explore every inch of his skin, the hot taste of his mouth moving on hers, the rasp of his beard scruff against her cheek. To pet the short scrub brush of his hair that was shaved down to nothing at the nape of his neck. To breathe in his scent, spicy and salty and complex. She pawed at the buttons on his shirt before she even knew she was doing it, and he helped her unbutton them.

She laughed when she saw his naked torso, and ran her hands down his chest to his belly with a low, appreciative purring sound.

"What?" he asked. "Do I amuse you?"

"I was thinking about Gabe at the beach the other day," she said. "Running around with his shirt flapping open to show off his abs. He's got nothing on you."

He laughed. "I never thought I'd be competing with Gabe Morehead."

"You aren't. Or rather, he's certainly not competing with you." She stroked her hands down over the silky dark hair on his chest that arrowed down to his belt. She grabbed the buckle, yanking on it. "Get this off."

"Wait. Hold on. Let me catch up," Jack protested.

He lifted up her sweatshirt and tossed it off over her head, and breathed out a sigh of awe as she undid the front snaps of her sports bra, and shrugged it off.

"Oh, Maddie," he said softly. "You're so beautiful. I can hardly breathe."

"I'm very glad you think so, but you should definitely breathe," she told him, popping the buttons of her jeans. "What I have in mind requires lots of oxygen." She stepped out of them and wiggled to get the thong panties down her legs. "Take yours off, too."

Between the two of them, they got rid of his clothes very quickly. The rest of his naked body was as ridiculously gorgeous as his powerful torso. She loved his thickly muscled thighs, his taut ass. The air was goose bumps cool, making his dark nipples taut over his chest muscles, and his body was so hard. So solid and hot against her hand.

And that erection. Ooh la la. World-class. Long and thick and flushed, and so very eager looking. It was hot and hard, pulsing in her grip as she petted him, stroked him.

She felt lit up from the inside, in that breathless confusion of gripping hands, twining legs. Stroking and clutching, madly kissing. His hair was too short to get a grip, but she kept running her hands through it anyway. His long fingers wound into her thick curls, his lips dragging across her skin, his deep voice murmuring something incoherent and desperate between kisses, as his mouth moved to her throat, her shoulder, her breasts.

The sensation was exquisite. He licked and suckled and stroked, drawing out pure pleasure and delight until she felt as if the sun was shining right out of her chest. Her heart burst with it, as the first orgasm rocked her. She threw her head back, clutching the thick, clenched muscles of his back for dear life.

His growl of satisfaction vibrated against her chest, which expanded to make space for everything, everywhere. Endless space. Infinite bliss.

Jack held her until gravity reasserted itself, but when her eyes opened, he sank down to his knees, gripping her hips and kissing her belly. Stroking the small swatch of hair on her mound with his fingertips as he looked up at her.

"Let me taste you," he said roughly.

Speech wasn't an option, so she just gave him a nod, her breath quick and jerky between her trembling lips. She had no idea if she could even handle this voltage.

He pressed his face against her, kissing her, parting her. Sliding his tongue over and around her most sensitive flesh. She clutched his head, pressing herself eagerly against his skillful caresses. It was so perfect, every flick or lick or swirl or slow, tender suckling pull of his tongue… slowly…slowly…over and over…until that vast, obliterating pleasure throbbed through her body once again, and she was lost in sweet oblivion.

This time, she came to her senses in his arms, being carried down the corridor. He pushed the bedroom door open with his foot, and laid her down on the bed.

He climbed on top of her, shielding her from the cold. The cool sheets were a sensual contrast to the intense heat of his big body.

She strained toward him, reaching. Every part of her trying to pull him closer.

Jack reached over her and felt around in a drawer in the bed stand, pulling out a string of condoms. He ripped one off, opened it and rolled it on, then grabbed her hand as he shifted into position between her legs, wrapping her fingers around his broad shaft.

"You put me inside," he said. "At your pace. I won't move until you say."

She wanted to respond, but couldn't. She was in a shivering state of extremity. Sheer, naked need. She wiggled closer, stroking his thick rod against herself. Arching and squirming until she had him right where she craved him. Lodged inside.

She dug her nails into his butt, and pressed him to her. "Now," she begged. "All."

He thrust slowly, deeply inside her, and they both gasped with the intensity of it.

She'd never imagined how wild and out of control she could feel. The limits kept moving, the map kept shifting, the rules changing, and she sobbed with wild eagerness, egging him on with her gasping cries.

His heavy thrusts were exactly what she craved. She wound her legs around him, arching herself to get that perfect sweet sliding pressure, right where she needed it, deep inside, so bright, so slick, so exquisitely good. A honeyed lick of fresh delight inside at every stroke. They strained toward something impossible, inevitable, and it exploded in pure sensation, blasting through them.

And she just knew it. She felt the shining truth of him, and knew that he had never lied to anyone. Which meant that the world was very different than she'd thought.

It was bigger, deeper, wilder, more magical. Infinitely more dangerous.

The stakes had just shot up through the roof—and lost themselves in the stars.

Eleven

Jack buried his nose in her curls, stroking the impossibly smooth skin of her back. Maddie sighed, shifting in his arms and snuggling closer. She dropped a little kiss against his collarbone, and his body stirred. He was stone hard, all over again. Prodding her thigh.

Maddie chuckled lazily when she felt it. "Look at you. Tireless."

"You should talk," he said.

"You inspire me," she told him. "I've never been like this before."

"Like what?"

Maddie's laugh sounded self-conscious. "You know. Jumping you, ripping off your clothes, being a naughty hellcat with voracious sexual needs. You bring it out of me."

That pleased him. It also stimulated him, judging from the stiff, aching state of his hard-on. Maddie shifted with a murmur and reached down, idly stroking him. Squeezing.

"Like titanium," she murmured. "Ready for more?"

"I don't want to overdo it for you," he said.

"I'm just fine, thank you very much." There was laughter in her voice.

She moved over him, stretching across his body to the bedside table and groping until she found the condoms, ripping one of the foil packets open. "I see you were prepared for anything, hmm?"

"I actually didn't stock that drawer," he told her. "That was my landlady, Delilah. It's her sexy little joke. She thinks I should get more action, so she always loads up the drawer with condoms when I come here, and then teases me about it."

"Ah," she murmured. "That's cute. Weird and inappropriate, but cute."

"Yeah, she's a salty dog. A whole lot of fun. I've been coming here for years, and we're old friends... Oh. Whoa." His words cut off in a gasp as Maddie rolled the condom over him, with a long, tight, possessive squeezing stroke. "Oh, God, Maddie."

"Too hard?" she asked, with another slow, expert twist of her hand...and again.

"Slow down, or I'll lose it," he said, his voice strangled.

"Oh, we can't have that. First you must attend to my insatiable appetites."

"Can I turn on the light?" he asked her. "You're so beautiful. I want to see it all."

She hesitated, for just a moment, and then nodded. Jack flicked on the bedside light to its lowest setting. A gentle glow, like candlelight. They smiled at each other.

"Happy now?" she asked.

"Ecstatic," he assured her. "Fulfillment of insatiable appetites, coming right up."

She laughed. "It certainly has come right up," she said appreciatively, swinging her shapely thigh over him. Swaying and undulating as she stroked his stiff phallus, then lifting herself up to nudge him slowly inside.

He gasped as she sank down, taking him so deep. Hot, tight, plush. Clinging.

She grabbed one of his hands, putting it against her mound. "Touch me again, like you did in my room at the resort," she said, her voice breathless. "I loved that."

Oh, yeah. Caressing the taut, sensitive nub between her tender folds while she rode him, rising and falling, breasts bouncing…that was his idea of earthly paradise.

Her face was dewy and flushed, eyes dazzled with pleasure. So beautiful. Her first orgasm came quickly. He was glad the light was on. He loved how she looked, gasping for breath, head thrown back. Those sexy sounds she made.

He kept at it, making her come yet again…and again. After that, she leaned over him, wordlessly demanding with her body that this time, he follow her. All the way to the explosive end.

God, yes. He held her, pumping up into her body. The deep, surging rhythm intensified…and they were swept away, lost in the surging waves of sensation…and tossed up on some distant shore afterward, dazed and exhausted.

A while later, she lifted her head. "The last thing I want to do now is move a single muscle. But you'd better do something about that condom."

"Yeah, that would be smart." He held it as she lifted herself off, and went to the bathroom to dispose of it. He splashed his face, irrationally afraid that she would vanish if he took his eyes off her. Something this good just didn't belong in his raggedy, cobbled-together life. And knowing what Caleb and Marcus and Elaine thought of him, it almost felt as if he were stealing for real. Something far more precious than money or IP.

When he came out of the bathroom, he just stood there

for a while, dazed by her smile. Her intelligent, beautiful golden eyes, so full of light.

Then something occurred to him: his duty as a host. "Hey," he said. "You know what? I cooked dinner for you, and we forgot all about it."

Her eyes widened. "Oh, dear. I hope it didn't burn."

"No, it's just waiting for us in there on the table. Are you hungry?"

"At this hour?"

He glanced at the clock. "A midnight feast. Seems appropriate."

"Give me a couple of minutes in the bathroom, and I'll be right in," she said. "My appetite just woke up. That appetite, anyway. Others have been raging ever since…well."

"Since when?" he asked, intrigued.

"Truthfully?" She let out a soft laugh. "Do you remember that time you came to the lake with Caleb, the summer after you graduated from high school?"

His mouth dropped open. "No way! You were just a little kid!"

"Not really. Almost fourteen. Old enough to notice a gorgeous guy in swim trunks, dripping wet, full of muscle. Old enough to pine for him."

"Um…wow," he said, bemused. "And I had no clue."

There was an awkward pause, and Maddie waved it away. "Sorry. I didn't mean to put you on the spot or make you feel weird. Perved on by the youthful, teenage me."

"Oh, no," he said. "I just can't believe that I never noticed."

"Thank God," she said. "I would've died of embarrassment."

"Well, you're not embarrassed now, are you?"

"Nope." She gave him that smoldering stare, and his body reacted predictably.

Maddie laughed, scooping up his jeans and flinging them at him. "Feed me before you raise the flag again, buddy."

"Oh, yeah. Of course. I'll be in the kitchen. See you there."

She disappeared into the bathroom, throwing a seductive smile over her shoulder, while a dazed, flustered Jack stumbled into the kitchen, pulling his wits together.

The necessary sequence of events was simple. Wrap up the barbecued ribs in foil. Stick them into the oven to warm. Heat up the spiced potatoes, peppers and sweet red onions in the big cast-iron skillet. Throw a handful of shredded pepper jack cheese on top to melt. Toss the salad greens with vinaigrette. Pull out a couple of local beers.

"You live dangerously," said Maddie's teasing voice from behind him. "Cooking, naked to the waist? Shouldn't you at least wear an apron? I bet that would look kinky and fetishistic on you, with all those tight, cut muscles you've got."

"I'm not frying bacon." He gave her a grin. "Besides, you've jacked up my temperature permanently by a couple of degrees. I'm not cold at all."

"Me neither." She walked into the kitchen, wearing one of his T-shirts. It had slid off her golden brown shoulder. "I swiped one of your shirts," she said. "Hope it's okay."

"It looks awesome on you," he told her.

She gave him a smile that made him forget his own name. He fought to get his mind back on track. "Uh... I have beer, if you want," he said, holding out the bottle to her. "A very good local brew. Or else there's wine. White or red. Whatever you prefer."

"Beer's fine." She took the bottle.

He'd set the table hours ago, in preparation for the dinner they had forgotten to eat, so all that was left was to open the foil on the steaming, tender meat and slide the packet onto a serving plate. He placed the sizzling potato, pepper and onion concoction onto the table, put down the salad bowl, and pried open the tops of their beers. "To us," he said.

They clicked bottles, and drank.

"Oh, that's good," she said with a sigh. "The food smells divine. I've been enjoying your cooking. I'm not a bad cook myself, but oh, do I love being cooked for."

"It's my pleasure," he assured her.

They devoured dinner. He didn't remember having an appetite this keen since he was a teenager. When they slowed down, they exchanged almost guilty looks.

"I don't think I've ever pigged out like this in my entire life," Maddie said.

"We worked up an appetite."

"I can't believe how much fun I'm having," she said. "I've been so wound up for such a long time now. And suddenly, kaboom. Here's you, unraveling me."

"You're having the same effect on me, too," he admitted. "I can breathe, for the first time in forever. This is the best thing that has ever happened to me."

"Same." Maddie lifted her beer bottle. "To the truth," she said.

"To the truth," he echoed.

They clinked bottles and drank as an odd thought formed in his mind. "This is the first time I've ever seen any sense in my misfortune," he said. "A larger design."

"What kind of design?" she asked.

Jack had to think carefully before he could put it into words. "If all that bad stuff hadn't happened nine years ago, I'd be in a different place right now," he said. "I'd be a tech mogul, running BioSpark with Caleb, which would have grown tenfold. I'd probably be married to Gabriella. I'd already given her a ring, back before it all happened."

"A ring? Did she send it back to you when she dumped you?"

Jack shook his head, lips twitching. "Not a freaking chance," he said. "Not her."

"That's grasping," Maddie said. "She gives women a bad name."

"Anyhow, my point is, I would've been married for seven or eight years, so probably we would have had a couple of kids by now. My life would have gone down that path, and I'd be a million miles from here. I would not be in this kitchen, eating a midnight feast with Maddie Moss, who's dressed in my T-shirt."

"And absolutely nothing else," she added.

That made his groin tighten. "Really?"

"Absolutely," Maddie said, rucking up the bottom of the shirt with a teasing finger to give him a brief glimpse of the shadowy glories beneath. "But by all means, finish your thought. We'll get back to that little detail later."

"Ah…yeah," he said. "Anyhow. I was just thinking that if all that crap was the only path toward this moment, then it was worth it. Just this, right now, with you. The way you make me feel." He shrugged. "It's worth it, to me. Worth any price."

"Oh, Jack," she said. "That's such a sweet thought, but I would never want you to pay so high a price for anything."

"It doesn't matter," he said philosophically. "We don't get to choose."

Maddie gazed at him, chewing her lip, a thoughtful little frown between her brows.

"I don't see it that way," she said. "We're always making choices, going through this door rather than that door. Every choice has its gifts, and its price, too. If you'd married Gabriella and had kids with her, and even if for some reason it hadn't worked out with her, still you'd love those kids with all your heart and soul. You wouldn't be able to imagine the world without them. For that reason, it would've been worth it, and you'd be committed to it. Anything you might have gone through would've been worth it because your kids would have been the gift of that particular timeline."

"Maybe you're right," he said. "But in this timeline?

I am so incredibly glad that I did not marry Gabriella Adriani."

Maddie's long lashes fell, veiling her eyes. "Me, too."

"I like the idea of having kids, and loving them with all my heart and soul," he went on. "But Gabriella is not the woman that I want to have them with."

She slanted him a stern look. "Jack. We're getting ahead of ourselves."

"Probably," he admitted. "Sorry. You have that effect on me."

Maddie waved that away. "I used to think, for instance, suppose my mother had decided not to get on that yacht, on that particular day. Would my life have been different, ultimately? She still would have sent me to Gran, once she got bored with having a toddler around. I'd just have a different set of psychological complexes, brought on by a lifetime of trying to get the attention of a woman whose only interest was in herself. Instead, I got Gran, who is intensely interested in me and my potential. It's maddening, either way."

"You don't think certain things are destined to be?" he asked. "Children, lovers, the hour of your death? All that big stuff?"

She shook her head. "No. It's chance, it's choice. An unpredictable blend of the two."

As he thought about chance and choice and destiny, he couldn't help imagining kids that were a blend of him and Maddie. What they might look like, and be like.

Dial it down, boy. You're a long way from the finish line. Dad's gruff voice.

Maddie stood up, walking slowly around the table toward him. "Jack."

"Yeah?"

"I have a contraceptive implant," she said. "And on my

last checkup, I had no diseases of any kind. What about you? What's your status?"

His heart practically stuttered with excitement at the implications of her remark. "No diseases at all," he said. "But I can't believe you'd trust me that much."

She gave him a sweet, open smile. "Well, believe it. You've convinced me."

"I… I don't know what to say."

She took his hand, sliding it under the front of the T-shirt. Such fine skin. Flower-petal soft. "I didn't ask you to say anything," she whispered. "Just touch me."

He caressed her, expertly, fingers sliding with such unerring skill around her hidden folds, circling and stroking and driving her mad. It wasn't long before they were stumbling back to the bedroom, kissing wildly.

He let go of her just long enough to drop his sweatpants, peel off her T-shirt and tumble back onto the bed with her. Both of them ravenous for that feeling, that magic fusion. He was addicted to it. The sense of new beginnings, infinite possibilities.

They wrapped around each other's bodies, giving in to a surging rhythm. Melting into each other as extreme pleasure welled up through them, pulsing up so deep, it wiped out all thought. Wordless, timeless. Perfect.

When he came back to waking consciousness, his eyes were wet. Already, he felt cold reality encroaching on this miraculous thing. Threatening it from every side.

Maddie stirred next to him, lifting her head with a frown. "Jack? You okay?"

"Fine," he said.

"So why do you look so sad?"

He shook his head, not wanting to invite the dangers any closer by naming them, but Maddie patted his chest insistently. "Tell me," she said.

He let out a sigh. "There's a good chance that we'll

never find an iron-clad way to prove to Caleb and your grandmother that I'm innocent," he admitted.

"We'll cross that bridge when we come to it," Maddie said.

"No, actually. You should think about that bridge before."

"Just keep a positive outlook," she urged. "We'll find a way somehow. Together."

Jack winced. "A positive outlook means nothing," he said. "When you lose something precious, it's gone. A parent or a grandparent, a company, a lover, your reputation, your career, whatever it is, it's gone. You grieve it, you learn to live without it, but your life is smaller afterward. There are consequences to everything. You just can't see them yet. Elaine is old. You don't want to be estranged from her."

"Gran is not helpless," Maddie said sharply. "She could meet me halfway if she cared more about me than being right. She's no frail, helpless victim. She's a powerful person who can make her own choices." Maddie jerked up onto her elbow and glared at him. "And I do not think that being with you will make my life smaller."

"I really hope that's true," he said.

Maddie waved her arm, sharply. "So, what are you telling me? That we made a mistake, that you've changed your mind? That you're sorry we did this?"

"God, no," he said. "I said it's worth any price to me, and I mean it. I just don't want you to pay the price, too. I wish I could spare you that."

"I appreciate the thought, but I can take responsibility for my own choices," she said. "We'll find a way to fix this, Jack. I want to rewrite the script."

He laughed under his breath. "Easy for you to say," he said. "You're a Moss. You're accustomed to being the master of all that you survey. Caleb was like that, too."

"You think?" she said. "Being Susanna Moss's daughter has been no bed of roses, Jack. I don't even know my father's name, let alone bear it. Remember how Bruce threw that in my face? A defect he was willing to overlook. How magnanimous of him."

"Dickhead," he muttered.

"Pretty much, but the point is, I've been driven to excel at all costs, and that twists you up inside," she said. "Gran feels guilty about driving us and stressing us to achieve in our careers at the expense of our personal lives, which is why now she's trying to overcompensate for that with this stupid marriage mandate. I've had her controlling me and breathing down my neck and lecturing me my whole life. I love the woman, but my God. She definitely screwed us all up, each in our own special way."

"You seem perfect to me," he said. "Kissed by fate. You have beauty, brains, heart. Loads of charisma. A sense of humor. Courage. Compassion. Glamour. Luck."

"That's so sweet," she told him. "But you have all those things, too."

"Maybe not the luck," he said wryly.

"Oh, no?" Maddie climbed on top of him again. "Really, Jack?" She reached down, caressing his stiff, aching penis with a snug, expert swirl of her hand. "Look me in the eye and tell me you don't feel lucky right now."

He was about to reply, but then Maddie sank down and pulled him in her hot, teasing mouth…and he could no longer speak at all.

Twelve

Maddie felt the faint light of dawn pressing against her eyes. She was floating on air. Soft, pliant. Weightless. When she opened her eyes, there was Jack, next to her.

So it wasn't a dream.

He was so beautiful, it hurt to look at him. She studied his beard stubble, the sweeping line of his dark eyebrows. The ridiculous thickness of his black eyelashes. His mouth was relaxed, sensual, like she remembered him as a boy. It was so tight and sealed when he was awake. Always braced for whatever the world might throw at him.

His eyes opened, just a slit, and he grinned. "Is this real?" His voice was a sleepy rasp. "Or am I still dreaming?"

"I'll seem real enough when I start getting way up in your face," she teased. "I'm no fantasy woman. I have my fatal flaws. Give me time. You'll see."

"Take all the time you want," he said. "Forever."

Maddie blinked at him, eyes wide. "Um...."

"Oh, crap," he muttered, rolling onto his back and clapping his hand over his eyes. "I'm overdoing it again, right? Getting ahead of myself?"

"Little bit," she admitted. "But I'm handling it. You're just...very intense."

"I know," he said wryly. "It's just really hard for me to keep it light. After last night, it's going to be even harder."

"I know." She leaned over to look at his clock. "It's late," she said. "Lolling in bed with you is my new favorite thing in the world to do, but it's Saturday. Ava's wedding is at the Triple Falls Lodge at five this evening, and it's way up in the mountains. I have a room already reserved, but if we want to get there in time to check in and freshen up, we have to get moving."

"Do you need to stop at your place in Seattle first?"

"Not if I recycle a dress from last weekend."

Jack's eyes lit up. "The blue halter dress?"

Maddie smiled. "Oh, you like that one? Good. It's a favorite of mine."

"I love that one," he said. "You look like a goddess from Mount Olympus."

"Okay, then. I think that dress is still in wearable shape, so there's no need to stop at my house in Seattle," she said briskly. "Excellent. We should still get going, though."

"You shower while I make some coffee," he suggested. "Breakfast?"

"Let's grab it on the road."

In less than an hour, they were showered, dressed, bags by the door, sipping coffee. Maddie looked around at the mess from last night's feast, completely forgotten in the throes of passion. "Shall we take a moment to get the kitchen in order before we go?"

"No, I've texted Delilah, and told her to send the cleaning service," he said. "They'll take care of it. Let's get on the road."

Jack insisted on taking the first turn at driving, and paying for gas. But when these details were dealt with and they were sailing down the highway, he fell silent.

There had been many types of silence between them. This one wasn't at all like yesterday's silence, in the woods, when they'd walked together in perfect shining communion, their minds so linked there was simply no need to speak.

This silence was a wall. She tried to make conversation, several times, but all her attempts fell flat.

Finally, Maddie gathered her nerve. "Jack, what the hell?" she demanded.

"What?" He looked over at her, bewildered. "What's wrong?"

"Why the grim silence? Did I piss you off somehow?"

Jack looked horrified. "No! I had the best night of my life last night. You're amazing."

"Then what the hell is the problem?"

Jack looked hunted. "That *is* the problem, Maddie. How perfect it was."

Maddie gave him a narrow look. "Dude. You've lost me. Orient me, in your maze of a brain."

"Hell, I don't know." Jack shook his head. "This time with you…it's like a magic bubble, and now it's about to pop. We're going back into the real world, so I'm getting defensive and uptight. That's all this is. Please don't take it personally."

Maddie reached over and placed her hand on his knee. "That magic bubble hasn't broken with me," she told him. "I believe in you, Jack."

Jack laid his hand on hers. "Thanks. But it's weird, because I'm not sure what part I'm supposed to play today. The unscrupulous bad boy who's cruelly toying with you in order to drive your family to the brink, or…"

"Or what?" she demanded.

He let out a sigh. "Or the guy who's head over ass in love with you for real. Engaged to you for real. Making love to you, all night, every night, for the rest of our lives for real. How do I sort that out? It's tying me in knots."

Maggie stared at his stark profile for a long moment. She was digging her nails into his thigh, hard enough to leave marks, but he didn't seem to notice.

Jack was right. They were at a crossroads. Her heart was dragging her like a team of wild horses, right toward what must look like a cliff, from the outside. Doom, in plain sight. Very hard to explain to people who couldn't possibly understand.

But the alternative was to close her heart down. Turn away from him. Stay in the suffocating gray zone, where she was frustrated, stifled, bored to death.

"It only matters to the two of us, ultimately," Jack mused. "Our behavior in either scenario is the same. But after what happened between us last night, I can't pretend to fake something that's so incredibly real to me. I just want to live this. Fully and honestly, like a normal person with normal feelings. Do you see my dilemma?"

"Yes," she said, and in a split second, her decision just made itself. "I think we should go for it. Feel what we feel, and act accordingly."

Jack gave her a wry look. "That's too cryptic for me," he said. "Be clearer."

"Clear how? What should we do, then? Make a formal declaration to each other?"

"I'm game," Jack said swiftly. "If you think it would help."

"Well, okay," she said, uncertainly. "Clarity is always good, right?"

Without saying another word, Jack flipped on the turn signal, and directed the car onto the next off-ramp. They got off the highway, cruising along until they found themselves on a side road through some alfalfa fields, bordered by a swampy little creek.

Jack pulled over. Thick green grass swished the car's undercarriage. "Let's go."

"What in the world are we doing here?" Maddie asked.

He gave her a blinding grin. "Seeking clarity."

Once outside the car, he took her hand and led her out into a field, near a stock pond where a weeping willow tree stood. The ground was boggy, thick with weeds and cat-tails. Cows gazed over the fence at them with mild curiosity.

"Jack, what the hell?" she asked, baffled.

"We're here for the tree," he said, gesturing at the wil-low. "I was looking for an appropriate setting for this dec-laration. On such short notice, this is the best I can do. It's definitely not something a man can do while driving on the interstate."

"Oh," she murmured. "Ah…this is a little more than I bargained for."

But Jack was undeterred. "Madelyn Moss, I don't look great on paper right now, but my heart is yours completely. I see what you are, and I love it." He sank down into the wet grass onto one knee. "I wish I had a ring, but this is my formal declaration of intent. Let me love you for the rest of our lives. Please. Marry me."

Maddie's eyes filled. Her free hand had floated up to hide her shaking mouth. Her heart galloped. "I thought, um…that couples got to this place gradually," she faltered.

"Sure, in the normal world. But our lives aren't normal. And sometimes, you just have to take your shot." Jack kissed her hand. "You don't dare let it slip away."

She looked down at his warm hand enveloping hers. His beautiful eyes, blazing at her. Expectant. Hopeful. It was like looking into the sun.

"Jack, you are a piece of work," she whispered.

"You're pretty damn memorable yourself, babe. And

you know? Even apart from the fireworks, and outrageously good sex, I think we make a pretty good team."

She kept trying to reply, but the words wouldn't come out.

Then Jack gave her a smile so sweet, it made her breath catch. "I get it," he said gently. "You don't have to answer now. I'm rushing you. You're just so amazing, I lost my head. We can save this for later. My feelings won't go away."

He kissed her hand again, and got up, brushing at the muddy splotch on the knee of his jeans. "I guess we should get back on the road, if the wedding is at—"

"Yes," she burst out.

Jack's eyes narrowed, uncertain. "You mean, yes, let's get back on the road?"

"No, I mean, yes to the fireworks, and the outrageously good sex, and to being a team. Yes, to taking our shot. Yes, to all that. Yes, yes, yes."

Jack's eyes lit up, and they came together, kissing again like the fate of the world depended on it. The long, swaying willow fronds were a magical bower—

Beep. Beeeeep.

They jerked around, startled. An old green Ford pickup was lumbering along the raggedy asphalt road. An old man with a visored cap was driving, and his wife sat beside him, tight-lipped, helmet-haired, wearing schoolmarmish glasses. The old couple stared at them with obvious disapproval, slowing almost to a stop. *Beeeeep*, one last time, and then the woman said something sharp to the man, and the pickup accelerated away.

"Maybe it's his stock pond," Jack said. "I guess that's our cue. Shall we pick this up again in the hotel room at the Triple Falls Lodge? Exactly where we left off?"

"I'm counting on it," she said.

"This is real, right?" he asked her. "I'm not dreaming, or hallucinating?"

"I said yes," she told him. "I said it emphatically. I made

a formal declaration. We can both be crystal clear when we put our minds to it."

They squelched through the mud and the boggy grass, hands clasped, smiling helplessly at each other. They got into the car, and he looked over at her.

"I'm floating," he said. "Three feet in the air."

"Sounds distracting. Want me to drive?"

He laughed at her as he started up the engine. "Nah, I'm still functional. It's just been so long since I felt this way, you know? Hell, maybe I've never felt this good. This is sky opening up, blaze-of-glory-type happiness."

"Me, too," she said softly.

They got back onto the highway, and Maddie found a radio station. She stopped when she heard the opening guitar riff for the Jackhammer song, "Bring the Bling."

"That reminds me," Jack said. "The ring. We're going to Ava Maddox's wedding, formally engaged, and you've got no ring."

Maddie shrugged. "So we're getting it sized, or something."

"I believe one of your hashtags was #ItFitsPerfectly."

She shrugged. "Who cares? We're no longer putting on an act, so we no longer need to worry about looking authentic. We're real. People can think what they want."

"God knows, they will anyway," he said.

The song lyrics suddenly came to the foreground when they fell silent. The singer's deep, scratchy baritone voice punched the words out to the heavy beat.

I don't care what the haters think,
I just do my thing.
Let them cut and spit and stab,
But I still bring the bling,
Yeah I always bring the bling.

She felt the shift in Jack's mood, as if the sun had gone behind a cloud. He took his hand away to switch on the turn signal, passed the truck, and then left his hand on the steering wheel afterward. He didn't put it back on hers.

Her own hand felt lonely. Longing for his touch.

They were barreling into the thick of it now. The real world, people they both knew, with their strong opinions and their prejudices. Haters gotta hate, and they just had to keep doing their thing, no matter what.

But Jack was dreading it. And she didn't blame him.

Thirteen

"Stunning," Jack said, from where he lay still lounging on the bed, naked and relaxed.

Maddie slowly turned in front of the full-length mirror on the wall, showing him every angle of the pale blue backless halter dress as she studied herself critically.

They had gotten to Triple Falls Lodge and checked into Maddie's room without seeing anyone they knew, and he was grateful. He'd have to face all of them eventually, but he just wasn't ready to give up this euphoric feeling yet.

It felt so good, but it could be crushed with a curt word, an ugly laugh. And there he'd be again, fending off shame for a thing he had not done. Rage, for the unfairness.

Stop. He couldn't let his toxic shame-and-rage crap anywhere near Maddie. She didn't deserve it. She was a miracle.

"You should grab a shower," she told him. "We don't have much time left."

"I still can't move," he drawled. "You drained all my

strength. I'm spent. And besides, you're so damn beautiful when you're getting dressed. How can I look away from that?"

"Aww." Maddie gave him a sultry smile as she fastened a pair of glittering drop earrings, and then positioned a square cut aquamarine on a ribbon around her throat. The stones caught the light, glowing against her gorgeous golden brown skin. Then she twisted up her curls into a high French roll, fastening it with an aquamarine clip.

She looked like a Greek goddess. The long, finely pleated skirt skimmed her perfect curves, the crisscrossed bodice cradled her full, gorgeous breasts. The dress was braless, backless, but she tossed a stole over her shoulders. It was the same pale blue on the inside, and a deeper, stormy blue on the outside.

"If you're not ready in five minutes, I'm going down alone," she warned.

He slid reluctantly out of bed, enjoying her appreciative eyes on his naked body. "I'll be quick," he assured her.

"Hey," she said. "You don't have to do this, understand? It's not required."

"But I promised. We had a deal."

"That was before, when it was all theater, to shock Gran," she pointed out. "We're past that now. So if you don't want to deal with all of them today, don't come down. I'll join you afterward. It's fine. Really."

Jack was tempted for a moment, but he shook his head. "I can't start our life together as a couple cowering in a hotel room."

Her dazzling smile was his reward. "Well, hurry, then."

Jack showered and shaved, donned the shirt and suit that he'd gotten cleaned and pressed last week in Cleland, slid on his dress shoes, all in record time, then smiled and offered her his arm. He had a lump of sick dread in his belly, but he wasn't going to burden her with it. He'd just brazen it out, and act like any other insanely lucky man who found himself engaged to a brilliant, sexy bombshell of a woman.

His good luck far outweighed the bad.

Downstairs in the big, turn-of-the-century mansion, there were signs pointing to the flower-decked hall where the wedding would take place. They took the seats close to the back, so they weren't immediately noticed. Which made him hope that he might slide through this entire event unobserved. That it might not be as bad as he'd feared.

The enormous wood-paneled room glowed with light from tall, arched windows, and was filling with people, all dressed to the nines. The groom, Zack Austin, was a tall, tux-clad guy with short dark hair whom Jack remembered seeing at parties long ago. He waited at the flowery, beribboned arbor at the front, flanked by two men Jack also knew. One was Drew Maddox, Ava's older brother, an architect, and the other was Vann Acosta. Both of them worked at Maddox Hill, the famous architecture firm founded by Drew's uncle. Drew was the CEO and Vann was the CFO. He'd met them through Ava, back when she'd done some PR work for BioSpark.

A string quintet swelled, playing the wedding march, and they twisted around to see the grizzled, white-haired Malcolm Maddox, Drew and Ava's uncle, walking slowly up the aisle, one hand clutching his cane, and the other clutching Ava's arm. He frowned fiercely, but his eyes were suspiciously shiny, and he kept dabbing his nose with a tissue.

Ava looked as stunning as ever. Her face shone with happiness, and her hair was a loose mass of honey-blond curls. Her long white dress was deceptively simple and low-cut, showing off her stunning body. Her eyes were also wet. She carried a big sheaf of bright sunflowers.

She was followed up the aisle by two extremely good-looking women. Jack vaguely remembered the cute, curly redhead, who was visibly pregnant. Jenna was her name. Ava's best buddy. Some sort of engineer. He'd heard that she'd gotten married to Drew.

The other woman was a tall, beautiful brunette he'd never seen before.

So Drew was going to be a father. Jack was assailed with a sudden image of Maddie pregnant, and got zapped by a feeling so powerful, he had to shut it down.

Now was not the time to be vulnerable and naked. He needed full battle armor.

Maddie leaned over to whisper to him. "The brunette is Sophie, Malcolm's long-lost daughter, and Ava and Drew's cousin. She and Vann Acosta fell in love last year. It's a crazy story. Remind me to tell it to you sometime."

"Sure. Can't wait." Right now, he was a fan of crazy, romantic stories. The more improbable they were, the better. He needed all the hope he could get.

The ceremony went smoothly, and was charged with emotion. There were readings, and a sermon, of which he didn't understand a word. The bridesmaids and the groomsmen all read carefully chosen poetry about love and trust and commitment. And in the middle of the brunette's reading from the Song of Solomon, Drew spotted him.

His smile faded. His face froze, and he nudged the guy next to him. Vann followed his friend's gaze, and his eyes locked with Jack's. Vann's face hardened, too.

Jack realized that with one slick move, he could create a big, unpleasant scene and mar Ava's wedding. He'd been so focused on himself. Ava was one of the nicest people he knew. She did not deserve to have her big day upstaged by his toxic crap.

Then Malcolm Maddox noticed him, too. Jack had met Malcolm at parties, galas. The old man glared at him, but the ceremony went on, the bride and groom oblivious in their incandescent happiness. They were pronounced man and wife, and they came together in a passionate kiss, arms wound around each other. The room erupted in wild applause.

Ava and her guy were so happy to be kissing each other, they had clearly forgotten the existence of hundreds of hooting, cheering people around them. Which was exactly how Maddie made him feel. Ava and this Zack guy…they had no idea how lucky they were. The whole damn world approved of their love. Applauded it.

Stop feeling sorry for yourself, boy. You're luckier than most men ever dream of.

It was Dad's gruff tone in his head again, always keeping him honest. Jacking up the armor he'd developed long ago, first in the foster homes where he'd landed after Dad's sudden death. He'd perfected it during his trial, and his hellish stint in prison.

Shoulders back, head up, back straight. He was Maddie Moss's fiancé. He had nothing to be ashamed of. His force field was up, buzzing hot, full strength.

But it wasn't enough for him to face the receiving line. Maddie could run that gauntlet on her own.

Jack retreated to a library at the end of the hall, steeling his nerves for the clashes that would come next. The view from the library was beautiful. The sun was setting, and snowcapped Mount Rainier reared up, glowing golden against the fading sky. The trees were thick and dark on the steep, shadowed slopes. He gazed at the mountain, letting it steady him.

"Jack?"

He turned at Maddie's voice. Her graceful figure was silhouetted against the light from the glittering Belle Epoque chandelier in the hall outside. "What are you doing in here?" she asked.

"Recharging," he told her. "This situation burns up a lot of juice."

She walked in. "I noticed Drew and Vann and Malcolm were looking at you."

"I noticed, too," he said.

"Jack, like I said, you don't have to—"

"Maddie? Are you in here?"

They spun around to see a tall, gorgeous redheaded woman in a dark green sheath dress at the door.

"Ronnie?" Maddie said. "Yes, I'm here."

"Did I really see you sitting with—" Veronica Moss's voice trailed off, as her eyes adjusted, and she saw Jack. "Oh. So it's true."

"You know my cousin Veronica, right, Jack?" Maddie kept her voice cheerful and normal, as if Ronnie's eyes weren't full of confusion and dread at the sight of him.

"Yes, I believe we've met," Jack said. "You're the one who hosts that show, *The Secret Life of Plants*, right? Very smart, beautiful show. My compliments."

Ronnie folded her arms over her chest, her green eyes narrowed. "Thanks," she said coolly. "Could you give Maddie and me a moment alone, please?"

"Sure," he said, but Maddie grabbed his arm.

"No," Maddie said. "Anything you have to say can be said in front of my fiancé."

"Oh, God," Ronnie said. "So you're doing this, for real? Gran was supposed to come to this wedding, did you know that? But she didn't. She's too stressed and exhausted. And my dad keeps calling her to gloat, the bastard. Which doesn't help."

"I was under the impression that she didn't intend to come to this event," Maddie said stiffly. "And I'm very sorry that she's finding the consequences of her own actions to be so unpleasant. I'm just living my life, Ron."

"We know why you're doing it, Mads, but you've gone

too far with this charade." Ronnie's voice was low and impassioned. "You're hurting Gran and Caleb for real, and that's not like you. I understand that you want to shock her. I get where you're coming from. But waving the nuclear option, at your own grandmother?"

"Nuclear option, huh?" Jack murmured. "Harsh."

"I asked for privacy," Ronnie retorted. "You wouldn't give it to me. I didn't ask for your input, so please shut up."

"It's not a charade, Ron," Maddie said.

Ronnie's eyes were big and shocked. Her mouth dropped open. "Not a charade?" She faltered. "Then…what the hell is it? What the hell are you doing?"

"Exactly what it looks like we're doing," Maddie said. "Jack and I are together. We're engaged. He's innocent, Ronnie. He didn't do what he was accused of doing. And I'm going to help him prove it."

Ronnie clapped her hand over her mouth. "Oh, no," she whispered. "You can't let him get to you like that. He's scamming you."

"I didn't 'get to' anyone," Jack said, though he knew it was futile.

"Don't speak of him in that way," Maddie said sternly. "He's my future husband, and I won't let anyone badmouth him."

"This is so much worse than we thought," Ronnie said. "You're not just punishing Gran. You're genuinely in love. With Jack-freaking-Daly. God, Mads!"

"Ron, you know me," Maddie coaxed. "Trust me. I'm not stupid, or gullible. I studied the data. If you had studied it, you would've come to the same conclusion. Please, just give us the benefit of the doubt, until I can find some hard proof. I swear to you, the BioSpark thing didn't happen the way they said. Let me explain how the—"

"No." Ronnie backed away. "I'm not joining you in fantasy land."

"But it's not true!" Maddie wailed. "None of it is true! He was set up!"

"I can't. I'm sorry." Ronnie ran out of the room.

Maddie flinched as the library door banged shut. Jack put his hand on the hot, smooth skin of her shoulder, and she jerked back at his touch. He lifted his hand away.

"Shall we take a break?" he asked her gently. "Go up to the room for a while?"

She nodded. Jack put his arm around her and led her out of the library, calculating the closest stairwell with the lowest probability of encountering other wedding guests.

No such luck. Just a few feet from the stairwell, Drew Maddox and Vann Acosta emerged from the ballroom, their faces grim with resolve.

They blocked their path to the stairwell. Maddie clutched his arm.

He repeated the mantra in his head. *Shoulders back. Head up. No shame.*

"I don't know what the hell you think you're doing here," Drew said, his voice low and furious. "But my little sister's wedding is not the place to do it."

"Drew, he's my plus-one," Maddie explained. "Jack's my new fiancé, and I—"

"And you!" Drew turned his thunderous gaze on her. "I thought you were Ava's friend. And mine."

"I am your friend," Maddie protested.

"Really? So you bring your family's big ugly drama to play out at Ava's wedding? That's selfish, Maddie. And sloppy."

She rocked back, startled. "Drew, I never meant to—"

"Fine. You didn't mean to. Good to know. I'll give you the benefit of the doubt, if he leaves right now, before Ava notices you two together. The Moss family's weird dynamics are not what she should be thinking about today. Understand?"

"Perfectly," Jack said quietly. "Just step out of our way, and I'm gone."

Drew gave him a curt nod, and stepped to the side.

Jack took Maddie's arm, and tugged on it. She drifted alongside him, looking lost.

The stairwell was mercifully close, and once inside the door, he resisted the urge to hug her right there. She needed the privacy of a locked room.

They climbed the stairs to the third floor, and made their way to the room. Once inside, he led her over to the bed and sat down next to her, twining his fingers through hers. They sat in silence for several minutes.

A big shudder racked her. She finally spoke. "God, Jack. That was awful."

He nodded, squeezing her hand. "Welcome to my world."

She looked at him, her eyes wide and wet, and pulled a tissue from her bag, wiping the teary smears of mascara with it. "Really?" she whispered. "It's like that?"

"Yes," he said. "With anyone who knew me from that time. And that's a lot of people. Caleb and I were pretty notorious, back in the day."

"Yes, I remember all the magazine covers," Maddie said. "*GQ. Wired. Rolling Stone.* Gran had them framed and on the wall in the library, until it happened. Then she took them down."

"I just bet she did," Jack said.

"I'm so sorry I put you through that," Maddie said. "I didn't know how bad it would be. I was just thinking about myself. Not what it would cost you."

"Do you understand now what I was trying to tell you last night?" he asked gently. "The price is real, Maddie."

"I don't accept it," she said, her voice rebellious.

Jack sighed. "Reality doesn't give a damn if you accept it or not."

"We'll clear your name," she said. "We'll prove it to everyone."

"What if we don't?" He stroked a springy, corkscrewing lock of her hair back off her forehead. "Or what if we prove it, but people still doubt us? I might be dragging this thing behind me my whole life. Just admit that the problem is a real one. That's all I ask."

She grabbed his hand. "Yes, it's real, but have faith. I want you to believe that we can find a life that's good. Even if we have to go away. Europe, Asia, Australia."

"And what about your grandmother? She's old, Maddie."

"Please," she said. "One thing at a time. Just promise me you'll fight like hell."

He considered it for a moment, gazing at her amber-colored eyes, blazing with fierce intensity. Maddie was a golden child, like Caleb, capable of bending the world to her will. She thought she could do the same on his behalf. Just use her powers to make it all okay.

Who knew. Maybe she actually could. But it wouldn't happen unless he was all in.

Jack nodded slowly. "Okay," he said, "I'll fight like a demon from hell. For you."

"For us," she corrected.

He smiled at her, and lifted her hand to his lips. "For us," he agreed.

Fourteen

Maddie called downstairs to get them checked out. They changed into their normal clothes and melted away without engaging with anyone else from the wedding. Neither one of them felt like being social after those two disturbing encounters.

They were very quiet in the car as Jack drove them down the mountain highway.

"Hey," Jack said, after a long silence. "Thanks for sticking up for me, when Ronnie found us in the library."

She reached out, and squeezed his thigh. "They're all going to feel terrible when they find out how badly they misjudged you," she said. "And I, for one, will enjoy it."

Jack let out a dry laugh. "Nice little fantasy, but I outgrew it years ago."

"Try it on again," Maddie told him. "Things are about to change."

"Things already have changed," Jack said. "Just having you on my side changes everything. Everything feels different." They passed an exit sign, and he turned to her. "Do you want me to take you home? You'll have to give me some directions."

"No, not home. Marcus and Gran would show up for sure, and I just can't face it. Tomorrow I have that lunch date at the bistro, with Amelia Howard. You?"

"I have to do a bunch of prep work for Monday's meetings. I'm meeting with some potential manufacturing partners for the enzymatic recycling products we're developing. Shall we stop at a hotel, then?"

"Let's go to the Crown Royale. It's centrally located, and I know the general manager. MossTech keeps a suite there, so we're in and out of there all the time."

Jack glanced over at her, looking alarmed. "You aren't proposing staying in the MossTech suite, are you?"

"By no means," she assured him. "We'll have our own suite. Never fear."

She called the hotel, and set it all up. Penthouse suite. Panoramic terrace. Hot tub. King-size bed. By the time she'd finished, they were almost there, and Jack was laughing under his breath, shaking his head.

They left their car to be parked by the attendant and their luggage to be brought up to the room, and went in to the front desk to collect their keys.

He studied her intently in the elevator going up. At the door of the suite, Maddie held up the key to the sensor, and turned to him as soon as they were inside, the door closed behind them. "What's that look all about?" she demanded. "What have I done now?"

"I was just impressed," he said. "The magic phone calls that shift the axis of reality and re-stitch the fabric of space and time. One phone call from Maddie Moss, and the sun would rise in the west, if she so desired. It's your secret superpower."

"Superpower, ha," she scoffed. "I just happen to be in

and out of this place a lot, so they know me. And I know the general manager. We dated for a while."

Jack's eyes sharpened. "Really? So what happened?"

"It didn't work out."

"No? Why not?"

She frowned at him. "It's not really your business, you know."

"Yes, I do know that," he admitted. "But I'm still curious."

She rolled her eyes. "I don't really like to say it because it sounds kind of mean," she told him. "But I got bored. There was no heat. We're just good friends. Still are."

"Ah." He thought about that for a moment. "So I don't bore you?"

She shook her head slowly back and forth. "Nope," she whispered. "You sure don't, Jack Daly."

That earned her one of those devastating grins. The delicious, crackling heat roared up between them.

In that moment, the porter came to the door with the luggage.

When he was tipped and gone, she watched Jack wander around the huge, luxurious room. He looked out at the big terrace, the skyline view, the bucket of ice with the bottle of Veuve Clicquot, the vase of floating, ethereal orchids.

He stroked an orchid petal with his fingertip. "Very nice," he said softly. "Orchids. Only the best for the Mosses."

His tone gave her pause. "I hope you don't resent me for that."

"Not at all," he said. "I might have been conflicted about it when I was younger. In high school. It seemed to me then as if Caleb and the rest of you lived like royalty."

"Caleb thought that the BioSpark thing happened because you were jealous," she said.

Jack looked horrified. "God, no. He was my best friend.

And your family was so good to me. I was dazzled by the luxury, yes, but not jealous. And even less so, now."

"Less so?" That made her curious. "Why is that?"

Jack gazed intently at the orchid blossom. "We were living pretty large back then," he said slowly. "When things started picking up for BioSpark. There was a lot of money coming in, and more on the horizon. Sweet cars, sharp clothes, hot girlfriends. Apartments in two cities. I had my penthouse in San Francisco, and Gabriella found me a condo in Seattle, too. Caleb and I had plans for swanky corporate headquarters with a view of the Bay. Even a corporate jet. Then, one day, boom. It was all gone, and I was back down to zero. Below zero, actually. I would say that prison definitely puts you below."

Maddie reached out, putting her hand on his arm. "I'm so sorry, Jack."

"Don't be," he said. "I wasn't looking for pity. It was a long time ago, and I'm fine now. Even financially. It took a while, and it's not Moss levels, but I do okay."

"I didn't mean to open a can of worms," she said.

"You didn't," he assured her. "I'm trying to explain myself. When you get money and then you lose it, you start to understand deep in your bones that it's just a game. Smoke and mirrors. Ones and zeros on a screen. Whose dick is bigger. Now that I've seen through it, I can never take it seriously, ever again. It's lost its grip on me."

Maddie considered his words. "I think that may just be your secret superpower, Jack. Or one of them, at least."

He laughed out loud. "Oh, yeah? Really? How do you figure?"

"You might not see it that way, but most people are battling to the death in that stupid game. Not you. You're already free. You don't have to wait until your third divorce or your deathbed to figure it out, all full of regrets. You're there right now. Lucky you."

He laughed. "I never saw it quite that way, but a win is a win, I guess. And that said…" He gestured at the champagne chilling in the bucket. "Can I pour us a glass?"

"Yes, please. That would be great. I'm just going to change. Be right back."

In the bedroom, Maddie rummaged through her suitcase. She'd hit rock bottom when it came to fresh clothing, but her silk nightgown was clean. She tossed it over her head, and let the champagne-pink fabric settle around her, whispery soft. It had delicate spaghetti straps, lace insets, and it skimmed her curves, the skirt swaying above her ankles. She fluffed up her hair, brushed her teeth, slicked on lip gloss.

When she went back out, Jack was gazing out the window, silhouetted against the skyline. He turned to look at her, and his eyes went hot. "Oh, wow. Maddie."

Her face was very warm, but she brazened it out, smiling and twirling for him. "Do you like my sweet silky nothings? We skipped the sexy nightie part of the evening's festivities last night, so I thought we could make up for lost time tonight."

He shook his head. "I'm just…my God. I forget how to talk when I look at you."

"It appears to be just a momentary lapse," she observed. "In my experience, you recover quickly, and then you're capable of talking for hours."

"True enough." He turned toward the ice bucket. "Want that champagne now?"

"Lay it on me," she said. "God, what a day."

Jack expertly popped the cork, and poured out two flutes of the ice-cold, fizzy champagne, passing one to her. "To momentary lapses," he said.

She lifted her glass. "To secret superpowers."

They clinked glasses, laughing. The champagne was a sensual explosion. The burn of the fizz, the icy cold, the bright flavor. They savored it silently, and then Maddie moved closer to him, and linked her arm through his, lifting her glass.

"To trust," she said.

The look in his eyes shook her inside. They were suspended in an odd, timeless silence. Jack finally let out a slow breath, and lifted his own glass.

"To trust," he said, his voice uneven. "Thank you."

They drank, arms linked. The moment felt almost ceremonial.

Jack slid his arm around the small of her back. "I love that you trust me," he said, in a low, wondering voice. "I still can't quite believe it."

Maddie set down her champagne flute on the table, then took his and set it down, too. "I feel you, Jack." She patted her heart. "Inside. This part of me I never felt or knew before just knows you're for real. There's no way to fake that. It's in there, or it's not."

"I feel it, too," he said. "It scares me to death."

"Why? You're safe with me. Trust makes us safe."

Jack's gaze was stark. "Nothing makes us safe."

She put her hand against his cheek. "Nothing? Ever?"

He shook his head. "I've taught myself to let go of a lot of things. I take it all lightly now. Money, fame, ambition, my reputation, whatever. I've lightened my grip on all these things by sheer necessity. But I just can't do that with you."

Maddie reached up, looping her arms around his neck. "Then don't," she said. "Hang on tight. Never let me go."

"God, no," he whispered, as their lips met.

Fifteen

Slow down. Cool it. Breathe, Daly.

He was teetering on the edge of reason, and the final blow was that sheer, silky nightgown that showed every detail of her body. He couldn't lift his hands away. Couldn't lighten up the desperate kisses. The jut of her dark nipples against his chest, his hands cupping, stroking the warm curves of her hips, it was driving him wild. He was a heartbeat away from screwing this up. Being too emotional. Out of control.

His hands were constantly amazed by the exquisite softness of her. The smooth, supple texture of her skin. The springy, luscious swell of her breasts. Every ticklish stroke a lick of fiery awareness. The fine fabric of her nightgown snagged on the rough parts of his hands. He gripped the curve of her waist, pulling her against the hot, aching bulge in his pants.

Maddie pressed closer, gasping with eagerness. Jack reached down, tugging up the nightgown, and slid his hand reverently up the silken heat of her thighs. So smooth. All the way up to the luscious curve of her...*oh...yes.*

No panties. Not one stitch. Just soft skin, silky fuzz and her slick, hot, secret woman flesh, wet and welcoming, yielding to his probing hand.

"Maddie," he moaned against her ear. "You're just... perfect. So hot."

"Touch me there, while you kiss me," she directed. "I love the way you do it."

He couldn't even speak, but she felt his passionate assent.

He was swept into an altered state of consciousness by her luscious mouth, by the sinuous moving of her lithe, vibrant body against his hand. He sought out her tongue with his own, delving in as he probed that hot well of slick moisture, caressing that tight nub of exquisite sensation between her legs, coaxing her right toward where she needed to go, following her shivers, her breathless moans.

She arched back, rigid, crying out as her climax pulsed through her body.

When her eyes fluttered open, their gazes locked, and it was time.

There was a brief, confusing tussle of wrenching the bedcovers off, then his shoes, his belt buckle, his buttons, his socks. They worked together to strip it all off like the fate of the world depended on it. At last, he was naked, and Maddie was stretched out on the rumpled sheets, her arms lifted up to him. The silk nightie pooled up around her waist, showing everything, the thin shoulder straps fallen down so that her nipples peeked over the scalloped lace of her neckline.

He was helpless. He would do anything to satisfy her. He'd resolved, in the last rational part of his mind that was still active, to keep it slow, make sure he made her come again, but there was no way to slow this down now, not with her dragging him down on top of her, her strong legs twining around his waist, her nails digging into him. Egging him on.

He eased himself inside her hot depths. So tight, hugging him, but so slick and welcoming. Her perfect body clung, caressing him with each deep stroke.

There was a lot of noise, and he was making some of it himself. The big, heavy bed vibrated against the floor, and pleasure kept swelling, bigger every time until it encompassed everything, and they came together, explosively.

They lay there for a sweet forever. First panting and sweat-dampened. Then floating and dreamy. Finally, Maddie stirred, yawning, and gave him a smile that set off fresh fireworks, deep in his body. She was so pretty. He just couldn't get used to it.

"Wow," she whispered. "That was amazing. Like it always is."

"Yeah." Jack coughed, clearing his throat. Raspy from the gasping, the shouting. "Every time, it gets more intense. I don't understand the math of that. How it can just keep getting better. I mean, where can it possibly go from here?"

She propped herself up onto her elbow, giving him a very direct look. "Home," she said. "It goes home. To your friends, to your job, to your rightful place in the world."

Jack wound his fingers through her curls. "It's not your job to solve my life, much as I love you for wanting to," he reminded her. "We can only do that for ourselves."

"I know that," she said. "But I still want to help."

"You already have," he told her. "What you've done is a miracle. Your trust, your understanding. Yourself. I'm so lucky. Even if this was all I got, I'd feel lucky."

"Well, it's not all," she said. "So don't think that."

He pulled her closer. "I'm just trying to be grateful. To stay in the moment."

"The moment is great," Maddie said sternly. "Tomorrow will be great, too."

"I don't trust tomorrow. But I do trust you."

Maddie smacked his chest. "Oh, stop it. You're going all Zen-dude on me. Come back down to earth."

"Oh, I'm with you." He seized her hand and slid it down, to feel the stiff heat of his erection, stubbornly high and hard against his belly. "And feeling pretty damn earthy."

At that moment, his stomach rumbled, and Maddie's beautiful lips curved in amusement. "Speaking of earthy. Let's order up some food before we get involved again. They have an excellent chef here. The room service menu is legendary."

"Sounds great to me," he said.

Maddie sat up, and grabbed the phone by the bed. "Yes, this is Maddie Moss, in the east penthouse suite," she said. "I'd like to order dinner to be sent up… Yes. We'll have the Chef's Choice for two… No, we want to be surprised… Oh, yes, definitely include a couple of desserts… Red wine, yes, unless it's mostly fish… Sure, whatever Gianfranco recommends. Thanks." She hung up. "It's a mystery meal, but rest assured, it'll be good."

"Whatever Gianfranco recommends? Whoo-hoo. Look out, Maddie. You're showing your secret superpower again."

"Nah. You've mistaken it for my credit card."

That led to a playful, giggling tussle on the bed that ended with Maddie straddling him and moving over him in a way that drove him mad. Looking down on him with those hot, sultry, heavy-lidded eyes that just made him throb with need.

But she shook her head in answer to the silent question in his eyes. "They'll be here with the food pretty soon," she said breathlessly. "We'll get back to this after. Definitely. Let me get you some more champagne. And I'm grabbing a quick shower."

Jack threw on the terry cloth robe the hotel had provided, and refilled their champagne flutes while she was in the shower. Jack felt euphoric. Flying higher than he'd ever been in his life. Buzzed on champagne, and Maddie.

The knock sounded on the door. "Room service," a voice called.

"I've got the door," he called to Maddie, who had just emerged, fragrant and damp and perfumed, wrapped in her own robe.

The waiter pushed in a rolling tray crowded with covered dishes, and went away grinning hugely. True love and wild sex had made Jack an extremely generous tipper.

The food was amazing. It consisted of multiple plates of finger food. Fried eggplant wrapped around aged caciocavallo cheese, bubbling in tomato sauce. Mint-scented zucchini fritters. Calabrese friselle, loaded with oil, basil, creamy stracciatella cheese and glowing golden datterino tomatoes. Meltingly tender oven-roasted pork rollups, crackling in an earthenware terrine. Fresh tagliatelle pasta with cream and black truffle. Tender crepes filled with sheep's milk ricotta and wild mushrooms. A cheese plate, a fruit platter. A lemon cream cake, a plate of fudgy brownies and chocolate-dipped shortbreads for dessert.

Every bite was amazing, but nothing had ever tasted so good as Maddie's kiss.

They feasted, laughing and talking. Then, at one point, all the words just drained away, and were replaced by that buzzing heat that he'd begun to crave.

Maddie stood up, took his hand and tugged. He let her lead him back to the bedroom, then pushed her down until she sat on the bed, and knelt in front of her, stroking her bare knees as the terry cloth robe fell open over her thighs, then over her belly. Then her breasts. He pulled the sash free, and stroked down her knees in silent pleading, until her legs fell open, and he leaned forward, pressing his face to her sweet, tender folds. Taking his time. Caressing them worshipfully with his lips, his tongue. Lapping up her essence.

She stiffened, gasping, pressing herself to his face as pleasure rippled through her.

After the sweet tremors finally subsided, she rolled over and got up onto her knees, turning her back to him. Parted her thighs as she leaned forward on all fours. Lifted herself. "Like this," she invited him, her voice throaty. "Come here. Behind me."

"Oh, yeah."

Once again, he was too far out on the ledge to control the timing. Not with her on her knees, back arched, clutching the pillow. He gripped her hips, each heavy thrust jolting a shocked whimper from her throat. He saw them reflected in the picture window: her eyes were closed, gleaming lips parted, breasts swaying. Wailing in helpless pleasure as they pounded toward the explosive finish. He let go, losing himself inside her.

Such a perfect place to be lost. He never wanted to be found.

Sixteen

Maddie took a detour and drove past the lavish, space-age Energen facility on her way to the lunch meeting with Amelia.

It was impressive, completed only a few years ago by a prominent New York architecture firm. It was showy, a bold, innovative modern design, and it looked more like a docked spaceship than anything else. Lots of gleaming steel struts and unexpected angles, every part filled with glass, flooded with light.

She couldn't help but reflect, as she circled the enormous complex, that the outrageous price tag of this building had been paid with profits that had been stolen from Caleb and Jack.

But it was only money, and it was in the past now. Caleb and Jack were tough and smart, and there was more where that came from. When it came to ideas and innovation, those men would never need to steal from anyone.

If only she could just prove that, for Jack. Beyond the shadow of a doubt.

She drove to the bistro, left her car in a nearby garage and walked in. The place was buzzing with activity. The Sunday brunch crowd.

Amelia was already waiting for her, and stood up to shake her hand. She seemed sweet, but rather wispy and ethereal. She was a tall, pretty, dark-haired girl, with big, dreamy eyes, and she was clearly nervous.

They ordered a couple of chicken Caesar salads, and Maddie got right to work. She carefully and methodically asked Amelia about the most salient pieces of data that Jack had shown her, listening carefully for discrepancies. Most specifically, she concentrated on the research and development timelines of the Energen Vortex project.

Amelia's voice was hushed and tremulous, but she was very forthcoming, and she said nothing that was incongruent with what Jack had told her. After an hour or so of patient grilling, Maddie was convinced that Amelia knew her stuff, and was telling her the simple truth. She also couldn't help but sense that this truth made the other woman feel sad, conflicted and guilty.

After she finished all of the questions that she'd prepared in her notes, she hesitated for a moment. "Amelia, may I ask you a personal question?"

"Um, okay," Amelia said, blinking rapidly.

"This whole thing seems to have made you extremely miserable," Maddie said.

"Oh, God, yes. It did, it really did. Jack didn't deserve any of that. He's the nicest guy. A true friend to me. And he was innocent of everything they said he did. Completely innocent."

"And yet, you didn't come out with this at the time."

Amelia's eyes slid away. "No," she murmured. "I didn't."

"Admittedly, you would've paid a very high price for doing so. But forgive me if I say that it looks to me like you're paying a pretty high price for it anyway."

"The truth is, when it all exploded, I'd just been checked into a private clinic," Amelia confessed. "I had a nervous breakdown, you see. And I was in there for a long time, heavily medicated. When I came out, Jack was in jail, and had been for months. I wanted to say something then, but when I visited Jack in prison, he urged me not to. He was afraid I'd have another breakdown. He wanted to protect me. That's...that's just the kind of guy he is."

"Were you two together?" she asked.

"Oh, no," Amelia said swiftly. "Much as I would have loved to be. But he was with Gabriella at the time. No one would ever even dare to try and steal Gabriella's boyfriend. Gabriella's the type that would gladly wreck your life just for spite. Besides, I was involved with someone else back then. Which was why I had the nervous breakdown."

Maddie's curiosity was piqued, but Amelia grabbed her napkin and dabbed at her lips, her panicked gaze rising to whoever stood behind Maddie's chair.

"Hello, Amelia." It was a female voice, with a clear ring of accusation.

Amelia looked trapped. Maddie looked around.

A man and a woman stood there. The man was huge, with icy eyes and a lantern jaw, and his big, wide body looked like it had been shoehorned into a business suit. The woman was a thin blonde with a taut, sharp jawline, dressed in a tight red minidress and red stiletto heels. Her lips were very red, and her eyebrows so dark, it was clear that the glossy blond ringlets had gotten chemical help.

"Hi, Gabriella," Amelia said, in a subdued voice. "What are you doing here?"

"Bill and I just happened to see you here," the woman said crisply. "So we came over to say hi. Who's your friend?"

"This is, ah… Maddie Moss," Amelia admitted, after a reluctant pause.

"Oh, really?" Gabriella's red lips twisted. "And what brings you here, Maddie?"

"I was in the neighborhood, so I took the opportunity to grab lunch with Amelia," Maddie said coolly.

"Really. I had no idea you two knew each other."

"How on earth would you?" Maddie asked. "I don't believe we've ever met. And your name is…?"

Amelia pulled herself together, with visible effort. "Maddie, this is Gabriella, our new senior VP of marketing, as of this Wednesday." She gestured behind her at the beefy guy without looking at him. "And that's Bill Greer, Energen's chief security officer."

Maddie offered her hand to each of them. "How do you do."

Bill Greer's hand was huge, sweaty and hot. It closed over hers in a strangling grip that stopped just short of pain. Gabriella's felt tense, as if her cold, thin hand were made out of twisted piano wire in a clammy glove. After the handshakes, they fixed Maddie with a cold stare, as if waiting for more information. To which they felt completely entitled.

When she offered none, Gabriella's eyes narrowed to slits. "Humph. Well, fine, then. Enjoy your lunch. Amelia, come see me tomorrow, when you get in to work. First thing. We definitely need to talk."

Gabriella gave them a fluttery finger wave and stalked away, heels clicking. Greer followed, shooting a cold, suspicious glare at her over his enormous shoulder.

When they were a safe distance, Maddie whistled. "Wow," she murmured. "That was weird."

"Yes, it was," Amelia said miserably. "Looks like I'm in for it. I wonder if they've been following me. Surveilling me."

Maddie was horrified. "Good God, Amelia. Do you really think they would?"

Amelia shrugged. "Since Gabriella got hired a few days ago, yes, I do," she said. "She's been very cold to me since she got here. I think my days at Energen are numbered."

"I am so sorry if I made problems for you," Maddie said. "I guess we should have been even more discreet."

"It's okay," Amelia said quietly. "Maybe it's time to grit my teeth and face up to this, no matter what happens."

Maddie crossed her fingers, silently wishing the woman luck. "Tell me about those two," she asked.

"The nightmare pair," Amelia muttered. "Gabriella just showed up last week, like I said. She's clearly our CEO's new pet. And I can't believe she actually came to work here, after what happened with Jack."

Maddie gasped at the sudden realization. "Oh, my God! You mean, she's *that* Gabriella? Jack's ex? And she's working here now, at Energen? That is really strange."

"Agreed," Amelia said grimly. "And Greer? He's the guy I was going out with at the time. I hate him so hard. That snake. Ice in his chest instead of a heart."

"How did you meet him?" Maddie asked.

"At the condo complex. He was head of security there, at the time. That's where I met Gabriella. Then she finagled a condo one unit down and one unit over for Jack. I was 518, and he was 416. Jack and Gabriella were together back then. Engaged, I think."

"And you were with Greer," Maddie prompted.

"Yeah, Bill and I had this on again, off again affair. Sometimes he acted so sweet, and then suddenly he'd be ice-cold and bored with me. But I never knew how it would be. It made me frantic. I figured maybe it was because of his military background, you know? He was a Special Forces vet, and he saw a lot of combat, and that changes a guy. That's what I told myself, anyway."

"Then what happened? If you don't mind me asking," Maddie said cautiously. The woman seemed so brittle. The slightest breeze, and she'd shatter like fine crystal.

"It was that awful last night, in my apartment," Amelia said. "Bill had been acting strange again. He'd brought a bottle of wine, and he was all lovey-dovey during dinner, and then I got really faint. I must have passed out, because I woke up in the morning with the worst headache of my life, and Bill was gone. So I took some aspirin and went to work. And that morning, he came to my office. He told me loudly he was dumping me because I was a sloppy drunk, and it disgusted him. I tried to explain that I'd been sick, not drunk, but he didn't listen. He just left. And I… I crumbled. Jack was the one to come and get me. He gave me a ride home. And the next morning, I checked into the clinic."

Maddie put her hand out, and squeezed Amelia's hand. It was clammy and cold.

"What a cruel, horrible thing to do to you," she said fiercely. "And at your workplace, too. You mean, you have to see this asshole, every single working day?"

"I avoid him as much as possible," Amelia said. "But it looks like he and Gabriella are…together now. They deserve each other."

It was clearly painful for Amelia to dredge up her past heartbreaks to a stranger, so Maddie wrapped up the conversation, hoping against hope that she hadn't put Amelia in a bad spot with her employers. They said their goodbyes, and Amelia hurried away, clearly relieved that the conversation was over.

Maddie had a lot to think about as she made her way back to the parking garage. She had just pulled out her phone and was about to call Jack and tell him what she'd experienced as she turned the corner to where she'd left her car.

She let out a cry, jerking back.

Gabriella Adriani and Bill Greer stood in front of her car. Staring at her like ghouls.

She blew out a sharp breath. "Good God! You guys startled me!"

"Sorry," Gabriella said, sounding anything but.

Maddie waited for them to move out of her way, but they just stood there, examining her as if she were an unexplained growth in a petri dish.

"Excuse me, but can I help you folks with something?" Maddie asked.

"I doubt it," Gabriella said. "But maybe we can help you."

"I didn't ask for help," Maddie said.

"I heard rumors that you were engaged to Jack Daly," Gabriella said.

"So?" Maddie said. "It's hardly your business."

"You might want to rethink that." Bill Greer's voice was oddly nasal and thin for such a big man, as if his sinuses were pinched closed.

"I didn't ask for your advice," Maddie said.

"We're not your enemy, Ms. Moss." Gabriella's voice was sweetly patronizing. "I understand the trap you've fallen into better than most. I got out just in time. Don't marry him. He can seem like the most honest guy you ever met, but he is a born predator."

Maddie clenched her arms around her purse, resisting the urge to back away. She had to stand her ground. Besides, that was her car behind them. "Thank you for sharing," she said. "Now get out of my way."

"What has he told you?" Greer took a step closer to her.

Maddie stepped back. "None of your business. Move, please."

"Come get a drink with us," Gabrielle coaxed. "We just want to talk to you."

"Not interested," Maddie said.

"We have information that you need," Gabriella pressed her. "You'll be glad you did."

Like hell. "Move," she repeated, icily.

"At least, take this." Greer held out a small object. A flash drive, she realized.

Maddie shrank away from it. "What the hell is that?"

"The truth about Jack Daly," Greer said. "I was head of security at his condominium complex. This is video of the night he invested seven hundred thousand dollars in Energen stock, the day before their public offering. I have video of his door, the lobby and two shots of the outside building. The only person going in and out is him and Gabriella, and she left the apartment an hour and a half before the order was placed. She was out of the building altogether. But don't take it from me. Watch the tape. It speaks for itself. The only person who could have possibly placed that order was Daly himself."

Gabriella let out a martyred sigh. "I was such an idiot, believing in him."

"You were there that night?" Maddie asked.

"I was the last one out of the apartment," Gabriella said. "He was drunk, and he was getting ugly, so I went home at 12:22. As you will see on the tape, if you have the guts to look at it. That was the night he bought the Energen stock. He'd lost faith in his own product. He knew that Carbon Clean was fatally flawed, and he wanted to cash out as much as possible before anyone found out. The Energen product was a better design, and he knew it. And when word got out, sure enough, BioSpark's IPO tanked. But the message was traced back to Jack's IP address. His desktop computer, in his apartment. He got sloppy and didn't mask it. Probably because he was drunk. Not thinking clearly. I remember it well. I was so upset that night, I went out to meet some girlfriends for a drink afterwards."

"Bullshit," Maddie said.

"Honey, face it." Gabriella's voice was pitying. "Jack Daly is guilty as sin, and if he tells you otherwise, he's lying." Her lips twisted, the lipstick garish against her skin.

"Stop harassing me, or I'm calling the cops," Maddie said.

Gabriella and Greer glanced at each other. Greer leaned over, and dropped the flash drive into the outside pocket of Maddie's purse. "Look at the video," he said again. "It speaks for itself."

"They all say you're supposed to be so smart," Gabriella said. "Show it."

Maddie pushed past them, and got into her car. They stepped out of her way as she revved the engine, and in the rearview mirror, she saw them staring after her as she turned the corner.

Her phone began to ring. She was too rattled to answer it. She pawed at her purse, glanced at the phone. It was Jack's name on the display.

Oh, God. Not now.

That encounter had completely unnerved her. She was shaking. Her purse lay open on the seat, and the flash drive had fallen out. Just a simple plastic rectangle, but it looked malevolent. As if it were radioactive.

Maddie drove aimlessly, trying to make her mind stop racing. She'd gone to Energen to fish for some more info, and instead, she'd been blasted with more than she could swallow. Jack called again, twice more, but she didn't pull over to answer.

Eventually she found herself in her own neighborhood. She pulled off on a side street, still not ready to put weight on her shaky legs. She fished out her laptop, and hesitated for only a moment before plugging in the drive.

After all, Gabriella and Greer were in no position to make accusations, given that they were both working for Energen now. Amelia had said that Gabriella was the CEO's pet. She and Greer were lovers. They'd all lived on top of each other at the condo complex where Greer did security. It stank. Whatever she found on that flash drive, she'd take with a whole handful of salt, not just a grain.

She opened the video, and set the four displays to play simultaneously, two indoor, and the two outdoor, of Building 6 of the Sylvan Luxury Condominiums. The time frame covered eight hours, starting at 8:00 p.m.

Even fast-forwarding, Maddie had never stared so intently at something so boring for so long. She sat there for what felt like forever, watching numbers flash on the bar showing the passage of time, while absolutely nothing happened on the screen. She slowed down, checking every flash of movement on the screen, when someone walked in or out.

At the eight o'clock mark, she slowed down a flash of movement, and spotted Jack walking in the front door of the building and heading toward the elevator. Moments later, she saw him exit the elevator on the fourth floor, unlock his door, and go inside.

At 9:23, Gabriella came to the door, knocked and walked in, and another long, dull bout of nothing-to-see-here began. Gabriella walked back out of the apartment at 12:22 a.m., looking agitated. She slammed the door and stalked toward the elevator, anger radiating from her thin, narrow shoulders. Fifteen minutes later, she emerged from the elevator in the lobby, and left the building.

Then, once again, nothing. She slowed down the film and watched the critical period between 1:30 a.m. and 2:30 a.m. in real time, when the fateful order to the stockbroker had been sent.

Only Jack was in that apartment. Only Jack could have used that computer, with that IP address. His encryption had made hacking and spoofing an impossibility. He'd said so himself.

Outside the building, she saw nothing. He had two balconies leading to the bedroom and the living area. Both of them had closed doors and showed no movement, though lights were on inside. The only movement was the wind moving the leaves of the big tree outside the building. The sway of the branches.

She ran the video back, over and over. Baffled. No one had gone in. No one had gone out. She could see that from every angle, every entrance.

The truth is staring you right in the face.

Caleb had gone through this agonizing process, too. He'd been unable to believe that Jack was capable of doing this…but the evidence was overwhelming. The encryption on the desktop computer. The order to buy the stock, from that IP address. The plane ticket. The offshore bank account. The money deposited in it.

Still, Jack had no motive to do what they had accused him of doing. Unless, of course, he was different than she had perceived him. She wouldn't be the first to misjudge a man she'd fallen in love with.

She just couldn't make this square with her powers of reason. If it were true, then Jack was broken inside. A liar who was drawing her into a trap. Using her to hurt Caleb. Making a fool of her.

No. It wasn't possible. She couldn't believe it—but she couldn't un-see the blatant evidence against him, either. It was squeezing her mind like a vise.

She could hardly breathe from the pressure.

She snapped the laptop shut, and drove home. She pulled her suitcase out of the car, with the vague intention of dumping out dirty clothes, and loading up with fresh ones.

Her home seemed strangely unfamiliar when she walked

inside. The Maddie Moss who had lived here a week ago was a different woman, inhabiting a different world.

She'd been trained, as a scientist and as a person, to follow truth the way a sailor followed the North Star, but truth had never flat out betrayed her like this before.

She pulled out some clothes, at random. Some work stuff, some casual stuff. She was usually meticulous about planning outfits when traveling. Mixing and matching so that every piece could serve double or triple duty. Tonight, she couldn't focus at all.

She changed out of the suit she wore, and threw on some soft ripped jeans, and a long, slate-blue sweater made of loose-knit raw silk. She splashed her face in the sink. Swabbed off her raccoon smudges. Mascara and emotional turmoil did not mix.

She looked around, wondering what she was forgetting, but whatever. She could always come back later. She tossed on a leather jacket, and opened the front door.

Her entire family was arrayed on the lawn, right in front of her porch.

Oh, God. There was Caleb, back early from Spain, looking like she'd just stabbed him right through the heart. Tilda, his beautiful blonde bride, was next to him. Those two lovebirds were blissfully happy together, and were usually laughing and whispering into each other's ears, but they weren't smiling now.

Her second brother, Marcus, was back from one of his many trips to Asia. Like Caleb, Marcus looked nothing like her, taking after his mystery father. His genetic test had revealed Japanese and Korean ancestry, but the only sure thing about the guy was that he must have been tall and good-looking, because Marcus was starkly handsome. His thick black hair had gotten very long, and he had sharp cheekbones, a chiseled jaw, keen dark eyes.

Gran was in the middle, standing bolt upright, as perfectly dressed as ever, her snow-white spiky pixie cut perfectly styled. But she looked stricken. And scared.

Seeing Gran look scared was unnerving in the extreme.

The suitcase fell from Maddie's hand, thudding on the porch by her feet.

"Hey," she said. "What's this about? Is my house under surveillance?"

No one replied, for a long moment, and then Gran spoke up. "Not exactly, love. Can we come in? I'd prefer not to have this conversation with your neighbors watching."

"Just tell me," Maddie asked. "Did you guys stake out my place? Because I am not okay with that. It's creepy and controlling, and I won't stand for it."

"We'll discuss that issue inside as well," Gran said.

The regal authority in Gran's tone worked its usual magic, and Maddie stepped aside, letting them all file past into her house. She hoped when she was in her eighties that she would possess that handy superpower. One could only hope.

"Make us coffee, sweetheart," Gran admonished. "Did you forget your manners?"

"I'm not the one who's spying and sneaking and bursting in uninvited. I don't think anyone here has the right to lecture me about manners," Maddie said.

"Even so. Coffee, please."

Oh, what the hell. She got to work in her kitchen, setting up the coffee maker and scooping in grounds.

Tilda joined her in the kitchen, pulling down coffee mugs from the cupboard, and setting them on the table. She leaned close, and kissed Maddie's cheek. "Don't be upset," she whispered. "We all love you. You know that. Nobody is going to attack you."

Maddie gave Tilda a sidewise look. "Thanks, sweetie. Maybe you won't, but you'd better not speak for them."

When all the coffee had hissed and gurgled down into

the pot, she set it out on the table near the mugs and the fixings, and briskly brushed off her hands.

"There. My sacred hostess duty is now done," she said. "Please, help yourself to coffee. Now, maybe you could just tell me. To what do I owe the honor of this visit?"

Caleb and Marcus exchanged grim glances.

"Don't play dumb, Maddie," Caleb said.

"At first, we were all furious," Gran broke in, pouring out coffee for everyone. "Then Ronnie told us about Ava's wedding. What you said to her there. And we realized that the problem was much bigger than we'd ever dreamed."

"Spare me the dramatic language, please," Maddie muttered.

Gran reached out and put her hand on Maddie's. "Tell me the truth, sweetheart. Are you in love with him? Ronnie was convinced that you were. I hope it isn't true."

Maddie opened and closed her mouth. Her emotions were too tender and raw to throw out in front of her family when they were in this mood. Or ever, really.

"My feelings are my own private business, Gran," she said stiffly. "What's relevant here is that I have reason to believe that Jack is innocent."

Marcus put his coffee down so sharply, coffee slopped out onto the table. "Damn. Here we go. Strap in for the roller coaster ride of objective reality, Mads."

"Marcus, do not start," Maddie said.

"We have to." Caleb's voice was hard. "Because we love you."

"I have very compelling evidence," Maddie said. "All I ask is for you to look at the big picture one last time. To have an open mind."

"I'm not opening a damn thing to that bastard. He stabbed me in the back. He waited until the perfect moment to do the greatest possible damage to BioSpark, and to me personally. Now, years later, he sees you, and sees a fresh and entertaining way to hurt me again, by hurting you. I can't let him do it, Mads."

"But it's not like that, Caleb," Maddie pleaded. "He was set up."

"He was not." Caleb slammed a huge manila accordion file down on the table. "I'm not supposed to have this, and Detective Stedman would be furious, but I called in some favors at the police department and had Jack's file copied. I went through it myself, and flagged the important parts for you. Things that would be impossible to fake."

"There's no sign of intrusion at his apartment, Mads," Marcus said. "And the trade in Energen stock came from there. No fingerprints but his, Gabriella's and the people from the cleaning service. The ticket to Rio has his fingerprints all over the envelope. And the email to that broker was from his IP address."

"Either he sold our research data to Energen, or he decided that theirs was better than ours, and threw us under the bus," Caleb said. "I'm not sure which is worse. But the police file has multiple clips of him visiting Energen in the months previously, from Energen's security footage. Unexplained visits."

"He was good friends with a woman who worked there," Maddie argued. "Amelia Howard was her name. He visited her sometimes. And speaking of Energen, you guys don't think it's strange that Gabriella is suddenly working there now, after everything that happened?"

Caleb shrugged. "I never liked the woman, but she wasn't in that apartment when that order was placed, Maddie. It wasn't her. Maybe Energen is the best she can do now. Poor her."

Maddie shook her head. "You don't have the guts to give Jack an instant's chance, even in your own head. You won't consider that he might have been set up. That's unfair."

"Very," Caleb said. "I'm sure that was the problem all

along, from back when we were in high school together, and college. I had no problems paying for school, or taking internships, or having a nice apartment. I'm sure he thought that was very unfair."

"He's not like that! Just give him a break!"

"Baby, we can't," Gran said gently. "That door is closed. It has to be."

"I'm sorry that you're in love with him, Maddie," Caleb said. "But switch on your brain and grow up, for God's sake."

Gran squeezed Maddie's fingers. "My poor love," she said gently. "I hate that this ugliness had to touch you. I would have done anything to spare you. I'm so sorry."

"Me, too." Tilda squeezed her shoulder. Her big green eyes were wet. "Annika is still at Gran's place, and she would love to see you. Would you come back with us? So we can all be together?"

"No." Maddie's voice was choked. "Please, all of you. Just go away. I know you mean well, but I need to be alone."

Gran got up, drawing herself up to her full height, and Maddie braced herself, knowing the look on her grandmother's face all too well.

"Whatever you meant to accomplish by this idiocy, the mandate still stands," Gran announced. "Remember this, sweetheart. I will always love you. To the moon and back. Never forget it. But if you choose that man, don't come to my home. Don't call me. Don't write me. If you choose him, you must cut off all contact with me. It breaks my heart, but those are the consequences of your actions."

Maddie swallowed over the rock-hard lump in her throat. She looked at her brothers. "How about you guys? Am I dead to you, too?"

Caleb looked miserable. "I don't want that man around my wife and kid, any more than I want him around my sister."

"Please, Mads," Marcus said tightly. "Don't do this to us."

Tilda put her hand on Maddie's arm. "Honey—"

"I get it," she said, flinching away. "I understand. If I do this, I'm on my own. Forevermore. Just leave, please. So I can contemplate that in peace."

Her family filed out the door, and Maddie shut the door behind them. She peeked through the blinds until they were in their cars and had driven away. Tilda with Caleb, Gran with Marcus.

Gone. All of them. For good, maybe. If she threw in her lot with Jack. Oh, God.

She stumbled back into her kitchen and sank heavily down on a chair, staring down at the jumbled cups, the coffee rings, the spilled sugar.

And that huge, forbidding file. Challenging her faith with its weight and size.

She put out a reluctant hand and pulled it toward herself. She slid out the heavy, jumbled sheaf of paper, and began to read.

Seventeen

Jack pulled the sedan he'd just rented into the parking garage of the Crowne Suites, and got out his phone. For the umpteenth time. He reminded himself to breathe.

Earlier that afternoon, after her lunch with Amelia, Maddie had gone suddenly incommunicado. No more calls, no more text messages. It didn't seem in character for her, but of course, today was the first day since Paradise Point that they'd been apart. Maybe she liked her privacy and resented being constantly badgered. Some hyperconcentrated types were like that. Hell, he'd been like that himself, back in the day, when working on a project that consumed him. He could forget the rest of the world existed. Maybe he was just being needy.

Yeah. Keep telling yourself that, Daly. A woman in love didn't act that way.

He tried calling her again, but it went straight to voice mail. He didn't bother leaving another message. He'd left more than one already.

Damn. It wasn't as if he could call her family to make sure she was okay.

His own day had gone fine, until Maddie cut off communication. He'd gotten everything organized for tomorrow's meetings with the potential manufacturing partners for the enzymatic recycling products he'd helped develop, and then he'd gone out to rent himself a car. It looked like his efforts to rehabilitate his life and win back some semblance of his chosen career were bearing fruit.

That called for another bottle of champagne and another fabulous Chef's Choice meal with Maddie. Maybe even a long soak in a hot tub out on the terrace, looking over the glittering skyline. Naked in steaming hot bubbling water, with the most beautiful woman in the world.

A woman who wouldn't return his calls.

When he walked into the penthouse suite, it was dark and empty. Not that he'd been expecting her, but his heart still somehow managed to thud down a few more stories.

He stared out the window at the sparkling skyline. He remembered how he'd perceived the city lights as a very young man, clueless and innocent, everything still ahead of him. Those lights were possibilities, mysteries to solve. The city had been his to conquer. Then things had gone bad, and the lights had seemed like a million glittering, accusing eyes.

Then he'd gone to prison. No bright lights in that place. Just darkness.

Maddie's suitcase was gone. No sign of her at all. Last night had been so full of hope and possibility. Now, in the silence, all he felt was a sinking sense of dread.

Jack stripped off the suit and tie, threw on some jeans and a sweatshirt, and headed down to the bar with his phone in his hand, just in case Maddie called. He proceeded to prowl through the huge lobby, conference rooms, coffee shops, both of the cafés, the restaurant, looking for her. Then the gym, the spa. Back to the bar.

And there she was. She must have come in while he was cruising the rest of the place. She sat at the end of the bar, her face reflected in the mirror between shelves of liquor. She wore jeans and a loose blue sweater, her hair a wild cloud of ringlets.

Her eyes were down. She had a drink in front of her. A tumbler of whiskey.

When he approached, she saw him, and lifted her glass to him, unsmiling. "Hey."

Jack stopped a few steps away, chilled. "You turned off your phone."

"I really needed to concentrate today," she told him.

That made him irrationally angry. "Really? For nine hours?"

"Yes." She offered no further explanation.

Jack looked down at her drink. "What's with that? I've never seen you drink whiskey. I thought you liked mojitos, cosmopolitans, Moscow mules, margaritas."

"They seemed too frivolous tonight." Her tone seemed distant. "Not right for my mood. I needed something serious. This is what Gran drinks when she's upset with us. Fine, single malt Oban Scotch, aged for fourteen years. A grown-up's drink."

Ah. So there would be no celebrating tonight. Jack caught the eye of the bartender and pointed at Maddie's drink. "I'll have what she's having," he said.

The woman glanced at his face, and sloshed a very generous shot into the tumbler. Taking pity on him. He could see his own face reflected in the mirrored wall, and he knew that grim look. Braced for pain.

Jack sat down next to Maddie and took a sip. The whiskey went down with a deep, earthy burn. It tasted like fire and smoke.

Time to get this over with. "So tell me about your day," he said.

Maddie rubbed her eyes. She wore no makeup, and her face looked soft and vulnerable. "Well, I had a very interesting conversation with Amelia," she began. "She struck me as a sad and fragile person who badly needs to find a new job. That place is toxic for her. But she corroborated everything you showed me, very authoritatively. Much good it does you, if she doesn't have the guts to stand up for you."

"She was already checked into the clinic when the hammer fell on me," he said. "She was sick. And when she finally got out of that place, I was already in prison. Then, when I got out, I figured, why destroy her life, too? They could have really hurt her."

Maddie grunted under her breath. "Then Gabriella Adriani and Bill Greer ran into us at the bistro. What are the odds? She's their new senior VP, evidently. Just hired."

"Gabriella's working at Energen?" Jack was genuinely startled by this news.

"Yes. And Bill Greer, too, as chief security officer. According to Amelia, Bill and Gabriella are lovers."

Jack made a face. "That must really suck for Amelia. Are you sure that it's the same woman?"

"As sure as sure can be," Maddie said.

"So?" Jack prompted. "Then what happened?"

Maddie shrugged. "Not much, at first. They did a little intimidation routine with Amelia, and made her miserable, but I got the sense that's nothing unusual. But then Gabriella and Greer followed me into the parking garage, and cornered me."

Chills raced up Jack's spine. He put the whiskey glass down. "They did *what*?"

"You heard me. Greer gave me a flash drive with the

security footage from that night at the Sylvan Luxury Condos, when the email was sent to the broker."

"I see," he said. "Did you watch it?"

"I did," she admitted.

Jack looked down into his whiskey glass. "I cannot account for that tape," he said, his voice bleak. "I just cannot understand it."

"I know," Maddie whispered. "I know."

They stared straight ahead for a moment as they sipped their whiskey.

"Was that why you turned off your phone?" Jack finally asked.

"Partly," Maddie said. "After that, I went home to fill my suitcase with fresh clothes, and Gran and Caleb and Marcus and Tilda all descended on me. Evidently, they had staked out my house. It's just that kind of day."

Jack gestured to the bartender for another shot. "So you're saying that they got to you?"

"Not exactly. Caleb brought a photocopy of Detective Stedman's file. He left it for me to look through."

"I see," Jack said, his voice colorless.

"It's not that they got to me," Maddie said. "It's just a lot to take in. It's a huge file. It looks bad."

True. That file had blown his mind, too. Everything in it was both completely fabricated, and somehow, completely airtight. As if he'd been placed under some evil spell. That goddamn IP address on his desktop, damning him to hell.

"You're right about that," he admitted. "I know it looks bad."

"It's just so crazy," she said. "The email to the broker from your IP address, the security tapes that show no one went inside after Gabriella left, her taking off for the nightclub, the plane ticket with your fingerprints on the envelope, the fake IDs, the investments in Panama—"

"Maddie," he repeated, though he knew it was useless.

"I told you about this stuff before. I told you that it wasn't me. Even though it looks like it was."

She turned her beautiful, intense, golden eyes on his face, studying him like she was trying to see right into his soul. "Jack, I…" Her voice trailed off. She waved her hands expressively. "It's not that I don't believe you. And it's not that I don't love you. I'm just…so confused. It's tearing me apart. You want me to keep the faith and trust you, against all the evidence, but the evidence is over-whelming. My family is hounding me and strong-arming me. And there's no hard proof that I can cling to. Just a story I made up about who I think you are. And I want it to be true so damn badly, I'm afraid to trust myself. I don't know where else to turn. What else to look at."

"I always trusted you," he said.

"Don't torture me. It's not fair." Her voice was sharp. "There's nothing I'd rather do than just jump off that cliff with you, trusting that we'll figure out how to fly before we hit the ground. But I can't seem to let myself jump. I… I can't let go."

Jack tossed back the rest of his second glass of Scotch, pulled out some money and placed it on the bar, under the tumbler. "I understand." He tried to keep his voice steady. "I should never have put you in this position in the first place."

"It's not that I don't believe you," she said again. "I feel the truth, shining out of you. But I feel like I'm stuck in a tar pit."

He stood up. "I know the feeling. It's the lies, dragging you down. They can drown you, if you let them."

She winced. "Jack, please don't."

"I'll get my stuff, and check out right away."

"I'm so sorry."

The pain in her golden eyes made it worse. He backed

away. "Good luck with everything, Maddie," he said. "Forever."

He headed for the elevator, trying not to run into any walls.

He'd thought that he'd suffered nine years ago, when his life fell apart. He thought he'd been through the worst. But no. His punishment wasn't over yet.

They'd saved the worst for last.

Eighteen

Ten days later

The latest Moon Cat and the Kinky Ladies tune, "Aloof Angel," was playing in Maddie's earbuds as she jogged down the street. She checked the odometer on her phone: 6.3 miles, and she still needed to go back the way she came.

She'd been out running every day, ever since that night in the bar. Trying to outrun her own misery, but misery kept pace with her like a patient shadow.

She was hiding out from the other Mosses. Her brothers had tried to console her, but the harder they tried, the worse she felt. Tilda, Ronnie, Marcus, Caleb, her friends, all of them tried. Even little Annika had brought a batch of lemon cupcakes with pink glaze and silver sprinkles to Maddie's house, just to cheer her up.

Which was absolutely adorable, and it broke her heart. Of course, she couldn't be bad-tempered with sweet little Annika. She'd become a doting aunt to Annika as soon as Caleb had discovered that he was a father, and the connection she'd forged with the little girl had got her dreaming about motherhood. And lately, about starting a family with Jack.

She kept imagining their sweet little faces. Gifts from that timeline when she'd still thought herself able to prove that Jack was innocent. To everyone, even herself. She'd failed, and that timeline had faded into the mist, its gifts lost beyond recall.

She'd be mourning that vanished alternate life forever.

One thing was for sure. She wasn't marrying anybody else before her thirtieth birthday. Or at all, ever. Moss-Tech was going to the dogs, and Uncle Jerome was welcome to it.

After all, Caleb, Marcus and Tilda would survive. They were talented, they had grit. They'd find other work. Found other companies.

Last week she'd written them all a formal letter and had it couriered to their private addresses. One for Gran, one for Caleb, one for Marcus. She had informed them of her final decision not to comply with the conditions of Gran's mandate. Told them she regretted more than she could express that the consequences of that decision touched them all, not just her alone. She finished by telling them that she loved them, and was taking some time alone to think. Before they had a chance to respond, she'd shut up her house and moved into a friend's apartment. Turning off the phone. Withdrawing from social media.

It wasn't like anyone was gloating, or saying *I told you so*. Her family was too kind and decent for that. But the hushed whispers, the pitying looks, the pep talks, the endless advice…for God's sake. Enough. She was too raw to tolerate it. If she spent time with her family, she'd end up lashing out. Saying something unforgivable.

Conveniently enough, her friend Wende had left to

spend six weeks in London, and had given Maddie the keys to her apartment before she left. Perfect timing. Once Wende returned, Maddie's current plan was to go to Hawaii to visit Lorena, an old college friend. Lorena had called her to conduct an audit of her accounting department. The timing was perfect, and the ticket was booked. Her trip was in two days, and she couldn't wait to climb on that plane. Though she was afraid that this sickening ache would travel with her wherever she went.

She reached the end of the park, and was sprinting down the street when she noticed the six-story office park towering on one side, the logo on the side of the building.

Ballard ChemZyne. A chemical manufacturer that had partnered with MossTech in the past. She had met Steve and Jodi Ballard. They were down-to-earth, funny, devoted to each other. Lucky them, to be able to run their professional life as a couple.

Oops, wrong train of thought. She put on a burst of speed, as Moon Cat crooned the refrain of the song into her ears.

If Aloof Angel dares to seek the bitter truths of love,
She'll find those truths are only seen from very high above,
Oh, so very high above.

At that moment, the sign outside the condo complex came into focus. Sylvan Luxury Condominiums. Oh, crap. Seriously? She was sprinting for miles through town to unload her feelings, and she ran straight to Jack's old apartment building?

Fate was jerking her around, playing dumb, malicious pranks on her.

She ran around the corner, and skidded to a halt, blocked by massive scaffolding. Restoration work was being done on the facade of the building, and the only way forward was to cross the street and go around the whole thing. Panting, she stared up at the workers as they lowered a big bucket on a rope from a third-story window, filled with chunks of broken concrete. The refrain swelled in her ears.

She'll find those truths are only seen from very high above,
Oh, so very high above.

Maddie straightened up, wiping the sweat from her forehead as her eyes followed the bucket being dragged back up. She turned around, and went around the corner, staring up at the Ballard ChemZyne building. Four stories higher than anything else around here.

A black sports car was waiting for the Sylvan Condos gate to open. Maddie started running again, timing it so that she'd run right through the gate after it.

She followed the signs to Building Six, Jack, Amelia and Gabriella's building, and walked around it, gazing up from every angle while doing glute and hamstring stretches. She thought about Amelia's apartment. One floor up. One apartment over.

That huge tree had a long, thick branch that extended in front of Jack's apartment. She thought of how the leaves had trembled and the boughs had swayed in the wind.

The tree was taller now, after nine years. Of course. She wondered if the other trees in the video had been shaking in the wind, too. She hadn't thought to check. She'd been too focused on Jack's balcony. Watching it fixedly for signs of an intruder.

Outside cameras watched the entire side of that building, but because of the tree, apartment 416 was uniquely positioned to have a small blind spot behind that tree branch, right over what must be a smaller window, since all the other apartments had a window in that position. Probably a bathroom.

In unit 416, that window could not be seen behind the thick foliage.

She looked up at Ballard ChemZyne, estimating the angles, the sight lines. There could be cameras on that building that would be able to see into that blind spot.

Damn. Now she was attracting attention. A woman who had walked out the front entrance was giving her the fish-eye. Time to stroll away and break into a jog, before anyone accused her of loitering or, God forbid, called the cops on her. She winced to think of what Caleb or Gran would say when they came to bail her out. If they came at all.

She headed toward the gate, pulling her phone out of her armband strap, and found Jodi Ballard's number.

"Hello, Jodi Ballard's office! This is Samantha speaking," chirped a young woman's voice.

"Hi. Could I speak to Jodi, please?"

"May I ask who's calling?"

"Certainly. This is Maddie Moss, from MossTech."

"Oh! Okay. One moment, please."

Maddie thought of Jack's teasing about how she navigated through the world so smoothly with her magical phone calls. But it was really just that oh so magical word, MossTech. She couldn't take personal credit for that. Only Grandpa Bertram could. For Maddie, it was just an accident of her birth. But it would be stupid not to take advantage of it.

"Hello, Maddie!" Jodi Ballard's warm, friendly voice came on the line. "Great to hear from you!"

They exchanged pleasantries. Maddie got to the point as soon as politeness would allow. "This is a strange request, Jodi. But could you tell me if your security camera at the Blake Street ChemZyne offices surveils the outside of the building across from it, facing east? The Sylvan Condos complex?"

Jodi thought about it. "I assume so," she said. "I believe we have an outdoor shot of the building on every side. Why do you ask?"

"Would you still have archived security video from nine years ago?"

"Good God, I have no idea. Why do you ask?"

"This is a very long shot," Maddie said. "But do you remember what happened with BioSpark, my brother Caleb's company, and Jack Daly?"

"I certainly do," Jodi said. "Terrible business. I was so sorry about all that."

"Jack Daly lived at Sylvan Condos at the time," Maddie explained. "An email was sent from his desktop computer there that he swears he didn't send. An order to buy stock in Energen. He says he was set up, but there is no record of anyone entering his apartment that night. At least, not any that appears on the Sylvan Condos security footage. The email in question was sent at 2:10 a.m. I looked over the video from the Sylvan Condos security, and I noticed that there's a blind spot. But it wouldn't be blind from the top two floors of the Ballard ChemZyne building. And I'm wondering if there's a camera up there that might have Jack's former apartment building in its sight line."

Jodi was quiet for a moment. "What an odd request," she said. "After nine years."

"I know, I know," Maddie said. "Very strange. If it's not possible, I understand."

"Oh, I didn't mean that. I'm just thinking, well…if you had your own personal reasons for wanting to find Jack Daly innocent, let's just say, don't get your hopes up."

"Oh, I'm really not," Maddie said hastily. "No hopes. I'm just being thorough. Out of an abundance of caution. And fairness. There's certainly no reason not to look, right?"

"You're absolutely right. I'll call my security people right away," Jodi said.

"I'll leave my email with Samantha," Maddie said. "Thank you, Jodi. I appreciate you being so kind and understanding."

"I'll get back to you soon," Jodi promised. "Just the time it takes to ask them if we can help you out."

Maddie had wings on her feet for the run back to Wende's apartment. She went straight up and sat down at the table in front of her laptop, checking emails without even taking a shower first.

There was a page full of unread messages, mostly from her family, but at the top were two new ones. She clicked on the one from Jodi Ballard.

Hi, Maddie. As discussed, our security team dug up the archived video for you. Hope it helps! Keep me posted, and good luck with everything.

There was another email, from someone on Jodi's security team.

Dear Ms. Moss:
As per your request, attached is the video covering the hours of 6:00 PM to the hours of 6:00 AM on the referenced date. Please let me know if you have any trouble with the format.

She set it to play, and fast-forwarded the video to midnight, before Gabriella had left. She could widen the timeframe later if she needed to.

The first thing she noticed was that there was no wind in those trees. They were absolutely still, as the seconds on the counter ticked by. The camera showed an outdoor terrace café on the top floor, and Jack's building in the background was blurry, but still visible. The camera looked down on it from above.

Then she saw it. A dark flash, disappearing into the trees. But it wasn't Jack's balcony. It was from a floor above, and one over. Amelia's balcony.

She watched it again, slowing it down. A dark figure clambered over the railing of Amelia's balcony, and swiftly lowered himself down on a rope. He disappeared into the branches of the tree below. The branches trembled and swayed. He must be creeping along the big branch. Nothing was visible from Jack's balcony. The intruder had climbed into the bathroom window, hidden by foliage.

Which must have been left open for him by Jack's lying, traitorous fiancée.

Maddie was startled to realize that she was pressing her hands to her mouth and rocking, tears streaming down her face.

Oh, Jack. He'd been exiled from his whole world. He'd gone to prison. She herself had left him twisting in the wind, alone. And he had deserved none of it. None.

She felt ashamed of herself, but she kept watching in helpless fascination.

Sixteen minutes later in the video, the tree bough started to shake. Shortly afterward, the dark figure swiftly and athletically climbed the rope back up to Amelia's balcony. He pulled the rope up after himself, and disappeared inside.

The whole thing had been invisible from below.

They had framed Jack. Smoothly, expertly. Who would do that to a decent, hardworking man? What the hell was in their heads? She would never understand.

Her phone buzzed. It was Jodi Ballard. She hit Talk. "Hi, Jodi."

"Did you just see what I just saw?" Jody sounded awe-struck.

"You watched the video?" Maddie said.

"Yeah, Steve and I are home right now, watching it to-gether. Oh, my God, Maddie. This changes everything, doesn't it?"

"Yes." Her voice broke. "Yes, it absolutely does."

"Oh, honey," Jodi said. "Do you need someone with you? I could come over."

"I'll be fine," Maddie whispered. "Thanks, Jodi."

"Will you share this info with the police, or should we?"

"I'll make sure that it gets to the detective who handled the case," Maddie assured her. "That'll be my next phone call. I'll let you know when it's done."

"Great. But we'll be more than happy to help, if they contact us directly. Oh, Maddie, this is just huge. I want to tell everyone. Oh, wait a minute. We can tell people about this, can't we?"

"Why not?" Maddie said. "You guys shot that video. You own it. Tell anyone you want. Tell everyone, Jodi. The more people who know, the better it is for Jack."

"Music to my ears," Jodi said jubilantly. "It's the juici-est gossip I ever got to spread, and it's positive, so my conscience can be clear. I never really thought Jack Daly was a crook, you know? It just felt wrong to me. Just off somehow."

"That's great, Jodi," Maddie said. "Spread it abroad. To everyone you can."

"Thank you for bringing this to our attention," Jodi said. "A great injustice has been done, and it's high time that it was put right. I'm so glad to help with that."

"I couldn't agree more," Maddie said.

She got off the phone, still feeling dazed. The rehabilitation of Jack Daly's reputation had already begun. Jodi knew everyone in the tech business world, and she loved to talk. It couldn't be better.

Maddie sat there, staring into space. Then she shook herself into movement, and composed an email to her brother, attaching the video footage from Ballard ChemZyne.

Caleb, you were wrong about Jack. Attached is security video of the night the Energen order was placed, shot from the top of Ballard ChemZyne. Fast forward to 2:05 a.m. The intruder climbed down from Amelia Howard's apartment, and into Jack's bathroom window. Once you've watched, please contact Detective Stedman, and send the video to him immediately.
Maddie.

She sent the email, shaking with emotion.

After about twenty minutes, her phone rang. The display showed Caleb's name.

She picked up. "Did you see the video?" she demanded.

"Maddie… I don't know what to say." Caleb sounded as dazed as she felt.

"I can think of a few things you can say. To Jack, anyway. Did you tell Gran?"

"Yes. She can hardly believe—"

"Show her the video. She has to believe it if it's right in her face."

"Maddie, this doesn't necessarily answer all of the questions—"

"It answers enough of them," she said. "Amelia lived in that apartment above Jack's. Greer was sleeping with Amelia, in order to have access to her apartment. He drugged her that night. She lost consciousness after drinking wine he'd brought. Gabriella must have drugged Jack, too, and while he was unconscious, she entered his password into his computer and opened that bathroom window for Greer. Then she left, and went to the nightclub to establish her own alibi while Greer did her dirty work. They made Jack their scapegoat. And everyone fell for it. Even his best friend." She swallowed. "Even me," she finished, in a whisper.

"Don't scold me. I'm blown away by this, too."

"Yeah, right. Did you call Stedman?"

"Of course. I sent him the video. He's reviewing it now."

"Call Jack," she said forcefully.

"Maddie, I—"

"Call him. Now. I just sent you his contact info. You owe him that, Caleb. Tell him you know the truth. It'll mean the world to him."

"Why not tell him yourself? I'm sure he'd rather hear this from you."

"No, he wouldn't." Maddie's voice caught. "He won't want to talk to me. I left him high and dry, after you guys worked me over. I displayed absolutely no backbone at all. He's never going to want to see me again. And I don't blame him. Not one little bit."

"Maddie, that's ridiculous," Caleb said brusquely. "Would you just tell us where the hell you are, so that we can talk about this like adults?"

"I don't feel particularly adult right now. Goodbye, Caleb."

She ended the call, and pulled up the number for the car service. "Hello?" she said, when they picked up. "This is Maddie Moss. I want a car to take me to the airport in one hour." She rattled off the address, and hung up.

She wasn't waiting for her flight to Hawaii in two days. Her work here was done, and she was riding off into the sunset right now. Starting the next phase in her life, however bleak. She'd missed out on earthly paradise— out of cowardice. She'd burned all her bridges. The ones that led to the only place on earth that she wanted to be.

In Jack Daly's arms.

Nineteen

The coffee had gone stone-cold.

This had been happening way too often. He'd get himself a fresh cup, sit down to stare at raindrops sliding down the slanted skylights of the Cleland forest house, or dripping slowly off the ferns outside. After an hour or two, he'd look down at the cup. Cold, again.

He'd turned off the phone ringer a while ago. It was too much. All the noise and furor, people talking too loudly. Everyone he'd ever known, trying to hunt him down to assure him that they'd always been sure he was innocent.

Had they, now. He wished he could believe it. He wished even more that he could enjoy it. Everything he'd dreamed of all these years, finally happening. But it gave him no satisfaction. Because the one phone call or message that he craved never arrived, and he couldn't seem to stop waiting for it. Hoping for it.

Maddie had cleared his name, rehabilitated his reputation with one brilliant stroke of her usual genius, let the whole world know about his changed status, and vanished.

Jack poured the coffee down the sink, and briefly considered trying again, but why bother? Sometimes, a man just needed to learn when to quit.

He activated the computer screen, and scrolled numbly through pages of unread email messages. Some from Detective Stedman. Most from former business associates who had shunned him after the BioSpark disaster, and were now all excited to be his friend again. Very touching. Useful, too. It would help in building back his career. He guessed.

But he just wasn't ready to make nice yet.

Elaine Moss had sent him a stiffly worded but sincere handwritten letter of apology on embossed MossTech letterhead, and he'd appreciated that communication more than all of the "I never doubted you" emails. Elaine was no bullshitter. She had the guts to admit when she'd been wrong, and she wanted to make amends. He respected that.

His heart revved when he heard a car engine outside, and he lunged for the window. Not Maddie's Mini Cooper. This was a black Porsche, one he did not recognize.

It pulled to a stop. Caleb Moss got out.

Jack observed himself as if he were outside of his own body as a complicated rush of emotions boiled up inside him. Disappointment. Anger. Hurt. Confusion.

And hope.

Caleb stood by his car and waited, not approaching the house. He'd seen Jack watching him through the window.

Jack took a deep breath, and went to the front door. Opened it.

They stared at each other. Rain was pelting down, and the air was heavy and sweet from the damp, fragrant earth.

Caleb made no move to shield himself from the rain. He just stood there, silently waiting for Jack's invitation.

Aw, screw it. Jack beckoned wearily. "Come on in. You're getting soaked."

Caleb followed him in. "Great place," he said. "I love the canyon and the creek."

"It's just a vacation rental, but I really like it," Jack said. "I keep coming back here. It's worth the long drive to the city."

"Yeah." They stood staring at each other. Jack forced himself to break the spell, waving him toward a chair. "Sit down," he said. "I'll make us some fresh coffee."

Caleb sat down at the table while he got to work. This time around, Jack was in no danger of zoning out as he scooped the coffee. The air sang with nail-biting tension.

"You wouldn't answer my calls," Caleb said. "Or my emails."

Jack set it to brew and sat down at the table. "Lots to process," he said. "It's been a weird week."

"I bet it has," Caleb said. "So it's all out in the open, now that Bill Greer and Gabriella Adriana confessed. The papers are full of it, you know? There's a long article in *Time*, in *Wired*. One in *The Economist*, too. Did you read them?"

"No," Jack said.

"They say that LeBlanc has admitted to stealing our research. The whole industry is in an uproar. It's a legal nightmare."

"I'm sure it'll all shake out eventually."

"Crazy, how long they planned this thing. And Greer? What an asshole. Getting involved with that woman just to drug her and use her apartment. Gabriella, too. What a piece of work. So calculated."

"And the whole time, she was sleeping in my bed." Jack's voice was dull. "We were talking marriage, while she plotted to destroy me. So much for my powers of perception. I don't have much judgment when it comes to women."

"Oh, I don't know," Caleb said, his voice carefully neutral. "Maddie was a prize."

Jack shrugged. "Well, she's not here, is she?"

"No, but it's complicated. And I didn't help with that—"

"You most certainly did not help with that," Jack broke in. "But I don't blame you. At least, not for that part of it. If she'd been my sister, I would've done the same."

"I appreciate your understanding," Caleb said. "Have you gotten in touch with her?"

Jack did a double take. "Why would I? She walked away. She never called back. What could I possibly say to her?"

"Oh, *thank you*, maybe?" Caleb's voice rang out. "For not giving up? For flogging away until she found the truth? That's more than anyone else did. Even you."

Jack couldn't seem to stop shaking his head. "Of course I want to follow her. But I can't force myself on her. I don't want to be that pathetic bad news boyfriend that hangs on like a tick even when things are over."

"You aren't," Caleb told him. "Maddie thinks it's you who doesn't want her."

Jack jolted upright. "What? She said that?"

"She said, 'I left him high and dry, after you guys worked me over. He'll never want to see me again.' Her exact words."

Jack's mouth worked. "But I…but she…"

"You already let Gabriella and her merry band of thieves knock a hole in your life," Caleb said. "Don't miss out on Maddie, too, just because you're chickenshit."

The coffee gurgled. Jack was too dazed by Caleb's revelation to take offense. He got up, pouring fresh coffee into their mugs. "Wait. Are you sure she said that? Those exact words? You're not jerking me around?"

"I'm sure," Caleb said. "You got Gran's letter, I take it?"

"Yes," Jack said. "And I appreciated it. I intend to send a reply as soon as I get my brain back online."

"It's simpler if you come in person. Come to dinner. We all want to see you."

"All?" He looked up, staring directly into Caleb's eyes.

"I can only speak for me, Gran, Tilda, Marcus and Ronnie," Caleb admitted. "Maddie's gone AWOL. We have no idea where she is."

"Gone?" That gave him a nasty jolt. "What do you mean, gone? Like, missing?"

"No, not missing," Caleb assured him. "She just doesn't want to be bothered with us. She's done this before, when she gets sick of family drama. She takes off and sends us snarky little messages, letting us know she's fine, telling us to get over ourselves and leave her the hell alone. Like she did during that week she spent with you."

"So you have absolutely no idea where she is," Jack said.

Caleb shook his head. "Actually, I was hoping she'd said something to you."

Jack set his coffee down with a thud. "No," he said. "She hasn't gotten in touch."

Caleb's phone buzzed. He pulled it out. "It's Ronnie. Give me just a second." He accepted the video call. "Hey Ron. What's up?"

"Caleb! I'm glad you picked up!" Ronnie sounded excited. "I have news!"

"Great," Caleb said. "I'm up here in Cleland, talking to Jack."

"Yeah? Wow. Give him my best. Better yet, put the phone where I can see him."

Caleb held up the phone between them before Jack had a chance to shrink out of sight, and he was waving at Veronica Moss, who was outdoors someplace sunny, the wind whipping her long red hair around her head. "Hey, Ronnie," he said.

"Jack," she said. "I'm really glad about what happened."

"Thanks," he said.

"And I'm sorry for what I said to you, at Ava's wedding."

"It's all right," Jack said. "To be honest, in all the excitement, I barely noticed it."

"Okay. I really mean it, though. Pass me back to Caleb. I have news for him."

Caleb turned the phone around toward himself. "What news?" he asked.

"I got a video call from Maddie," Ronnie announced.

Jack's ears pricked up.

"Did she say where she was?" Caleb asked.

"No, but I recognized the place!" Ronnie's voice vibrated with excitement. "She was on the beach when she called, and when she turned around, I recognized the hotel behind her. It was the Royal Embassy Suites, in Honolulu. I stayed there with Jareth last winter."

"That makes sense," Caleb said. "She mentioned that her friend Lorena wanted her to do a consulting job in Hawaii. Good detective work, Ron."

"You bet. Shall we go look for her together? You, me and Marcus?"

"No," Jack broke in. "Stay here. I'll go to Hawaii. The rest of you guys can stay the hell out of my way for once. You owe me that."

Caleb and Ronnie were both startled into silence. Nervous seconds ticked by.

"Uh, right," Caleb said carefully. "Ron, call you later, okay?"

"You better believe you will," she replied.

Caleb ended the call and slid his phone into his pocket.

"So?" Jack said. "I don't want to trip over you guys. I need space for this."

"Will you take off right now?" Caleb asked.

"As soon as you leave," Jack said.

Caleb let out a bark of laughter. "So in other words, don't let the door hit your ass on the way out."

"My life in recent years hasn't polished up my manners," he said, unrepentant.

"Fine, fine. Go to Hawaii. We all wish you luck. Just promise me that you'll message me the second that you find her, so we can all breathe easier, especially Gran."

"I can do that," Jack promised. "I'll see you out."

Caleb cast a bemused look over his shoulder as Jack herded him out the door.

"What's next for you, Jack?" he asked.

"That depends on Maddie," Jack said.

"I mean professionally," Caleb specified.

"That also depends on Maddie," Jack told him. "If it's a no, I'll probably leave the country. Go trek in the Himalayas. Eat lentils and grow my beard down to my waist. Join the French Foreign Legion. Who cares. I certainly won't."

"I know you're anxious to go, but just so it's out there. I've heard about your new super-enzyme project," Caleb said. "Word's gotten around. And MossTech is interested."

"No kidding." Jack was startled.

"You might not want to partner with MossTech, since as you know, the company is in flux. And since Maddie has officially blown up Gran's plot to marry us all off, I'll soon be out of a job myself. Uncle Jerome will fire Marcus and Tilda and me. I just want you to know that I'm interested in partnering with you again."

Jack stopped on the stone walkway outside. "Really? After everything that went down between us, you want to reboot BioSpark?"

Caleb turned around, and nodded. "I've never worked with anyone with a mind like yours," he said. "Except for Tilda. She's in your league. With the two of you, we could go for world domination. Plus, I just miss my best friend." His jaw was tight, a muscle pulsing in his cheek. "I get that you're pissed," he said, his voice halting. "I know that actions have consequences. If you want me to leave you the hell alone, I'll understand. But that's what I would want. In my perfect, ideal world. Think about it."

Jack was barely aware of the rain plastering his hair to his forehead. "I am still pissed," he admitted. "But I missed you, too. I missed our brain-meld."

"Me, too," Caleb said.

"But if Maddie cuts me loose, I'm out of here," Jack told him. "As far across the world as I can go without coming back the other way."

"Understood." Caleb pulled open the door and got into his car. "But you'll be going with my friendship, and my apology. If you'll accept it. Good luck."

"Thanks," Jack replied.

The window hummed up, and Caleb's car started up and drove away.

Jack went inside, still dazed, and sat down at the computer to check flights to Honolulu. There was one that took off in about four hours, that he might make if he was lucky, and hit no traffic.

He threw some stuff haphazardly into a bag, grabbed his passport and hit the road. There was no time to waste, but even so, on his way through Cleland, he hit the brakes so hard in front of the jewelry store, the car fishtailed on the rain-slicked asphalt.

He burst into the shop. "Hey. A couple of weeks ago, I was looking at engagement rings with my girlfriend," he told the saleswoman, already fishing out his credit card. "There was a sapphire and ruby ring in a thick white gold band. Is it still available?"

"I do believe that it is!" the woman said, with a big smile. "I'll go check."

Jack stared at the seconds ticking by as he waited for

her. He was desperate to get on that plane, but by God, he would be completely equipped for this encounter first.

As equipped as a man head-over-ass in love could possibly be.

Twenty

Maddie walked through the churning foam, letting the rush of the surf soothe her ears. It was the only thing that helped her breathe. Otherwise, the air stuck somewhere around her breastbone in a lump, burning and cramping.

She'd worked nonstop on Lorena's project, keeping too busy to think or feel. But today, she'd wrapped it up and presented her friend with a complete analysis, so the rest of the day stretched out, long and dull and empty. Sort of like her whole life.

She'd put on a light, gauzy dress that floated at knee length, and headed off for a walk along the beach. She had to keep moving, or she'd drown in these feelings.

She'd followed the story in the press. Bit by bit, the sordid tale of how Gabriella, Greer and LeBlanc had set Jack up emerged. Some articles had pictures of Jack, but they were old, from before the BioSpark scandal. In all accounts, Jack Daly was "unavailable for comment."

He wasn't in the mood to indulge anybody's curiosity. She could relate.

Now that Lorena's job was done, she had to come up with a plan. She had plenty of job offers. Maybe she could just keep bouncing from job to job forever. It was as good a plan as any, and had the advantage of keeping her a step ahead of her inquisitive family.

But the work didn't satisfy her anymore. The fun factor was gone.

Maybe fun and thrills were too much to ask of an adult working life. Maybe they always had been, and she'd been childish and unrealistic all along. Time to face reality.

So freaking much reality. It made her tired. Day after day of it. Dull and flat.

"Maddie."

The sound of Jack's voice behind her made her freeze, heart galloping. She didn't look around. She must be imagining this.

She turned slowly, and air whooshed out of her lungs, leaving her light-headed.

Jack stood there, barefoot in the surf. His soul in his eyes.

"Jack?" Her voice shook. "What are you doing here? How did you find me?"

"Ronnie recognized the hotel behind you in the video call."

"Oh," Maddie said. "So you're in cahoots with my family? That's weird."

"No, just using any resource available to me," he said. "I needed to see you."

"For what?" she asked.

"To thank you," he said. "For clearing my name."

Maddie bit her lip. The look on his face was making her confused. Almost as if—but no. She didn't dare to hope. She wouldn't survive being disappointed again.

"You're welcome," she said stiffly. "It seemed like the least that I could do."

"The least that you can do is a whole lot better than everybody else's best," he said. He stepped toward her, his eyes pleading. "Please, Maddie."

"Please, what?" Water swirled, tugging at the bottom of her skirt. "I fulfilled our bargain. Your name is cleared, your enemies are brought low, you have your friends back, career possibilities open to you. What are you complaining about?"

"I don't have you," he said. "Without you, the rest is worth nothing."

Her eyes filled, to her dismay. "I didn't think you wanted that." Her voice quavered. "Not after that night. I let Gabriella and Greer and my folks shake my faith in you. I knew you felt betrayed. And I was so sorry. But I can't take it back."

"Don't be sorry," he said. "I was framed by experts. They fooled the police, too. How could you not be shaken? You're trained to look at facts and draw conclusions, not to make wild leaps of faith and hope it'll turn out okay. I don't blame you for being confused. Particularly not after you saved my ass by hunting down that video."

She still stood there, shaking. Eyes full. Speechless.

Jack took her hand. "Babe," he said gently. "The tide's coming in. You're going to get soaked. Or knocked over."

"You're not angry?" she whispered.

"Are you kidding?" He tugged her hand. "You put me to shame, Maddie. I flounced off to sulk in the dark, and you went off to nail those dirty bastards for me all by yourself. Why did you even bother helping me, after I behaved like that?"

She looked at her hand, cradled in his. "It was the right thing to do," she said. "You have important work to do. The world needs it. I wasn't going to let a greedy, snotty hag like Gabriella stomp all over that with her spike heels. Much less that muscle-headed goon who does her dirty work. I hope they both enjoy prison."

"Me, too," Jack said. "So you just helped me on principle?"

"No." Maddie's voice felt unsteady. "I just wanted you to have a shot at being happy. I thought, if I could give you that, it would be some small satisfaction."

"Why stop at small satisfactions?" he asked. "Let's go for the big ones. All of the amazing things that life could offer us. I want them with you, Maddie. Only with you."

"Oh, Jack." Her throat was quivering. She felt out of control.

"I love you," Jack said roughly. "You are an astonishing woman. Fascinating, brilliant, mysterious. I want to spend my life giving you satisfaction. Every day. Every night." He reached into his pocket, pulled out a ring box and opened it.

It was the ring she'd fallen in love with back at the jewelers in Cleland. So much had happened since then. "Oh, my God, Jack," she breathed. "It's my ring."

His face lit up. "That sounds promising. Yes, it is your ring, and I hope you'll wear it. Maddie Moss, will you be my wife? Will you let me love you forever?"

She dug for a tissue, and mopped her nose. "Yes," she said brokenly. "Yes."

Jack was so beautiful when he grinned, with those sexy lines around his eyes all crinkled up. His face shone with joy as he slid the ring onto her finger and kissed her knuckles. They melted into each other's arms.

Sometime later, he lifted his head. "Hey. It occurs to me that if we get married now, we'll be playing into your gran's hands. Do you want to encourage her like this?"

Maddie's laughter felt free and happy. "Shall we pass this hot potato to Marcus, and watch him squirm?" she mused. "I bet he was so relieved to be off the hook, even if it meant that he was also out of a job. It could be very entertaining. Let's think about it."

"All I can think about is you," Jack said. "This timeline, the one where you and I get our crap figured out just in time, and latch on to each other for all eternity."

"Yes." She hugged him again, burying her face against his chest. "Isn't it funny? It all started for us at the beach, with our feet in the surf. And here we are again."

The surf swirled and churned wildly around their feet as they kissed. But they stood together, as solid and steady as a rock.

* * * * *

COMING SOON!

We really hope you enjoyed reading this book.
If you're looking for more romance, be sure to
head to the shops when new books are
available on

Thursday 1st September

MILLS & BOON

THE HEART OF ROMANCE

A ROMANCE FOR EVERY READER

MODERN

Prepare to be swept off your feet by sophisticated, sexy and seductive heroes, in some of the world's most glamourous and romantic locations, where power and passion collide.

HISTORICAL

Escape with historical heroes from time gone by. Whether your passion is for wicked Regency Rakes, muscled Vikings or rugged Highlanders, awaken the romance of the past.

MEDICAL

Set your pulse racing with dedicated, delectable doctors in the high-pressure world of medicine, where emotions run high and passion, comfort and love are the best medicine.

True Love

Celebrate true love with tender stories of heartfelt romance, from the rush of falling in love to the joy a new baby can bring, and a focus on the emotional heart of a relationship.

Desire

Indulge in secrets and scandal, intense drama and plenty of sizzling hot action with powerful and passionate heroes who have it all: wealth, status, good looks…everything but the right woman.

HEROES

Experience all the excitement of a gripping thriller, with an intense romance at its heart. Resourceful, true-to-life women and strong, fearless men face danger and desire - a killer combination!

To see which titles are coming soon, please visit

millsandboon.co.uk/nextmonth